Return of the
The Spider and the Flame King
and Blood Bond

THREE CLASSIC ADVENTURES OF

THE SPIDER ™

by Norvell W. Page
writing as Grant Stockbridge

plus a new historical essay
by Will Murray

SANCTUM BOOKS

International Standard Book Number: 978-1-60877-135-6

First printing: March 2014

Series editor/publisher: Anthony Tollin
anthonytollin@shadowsanctum.com

Consulting editor: Will Murray

Copy editor: Joseph Wrzos

Proofreader: Carl Gafford

Editorial assistant: Rebecca Searson

OCR text reconstruction: Rich Harvey

Cover restoration: Michael Piper

The editors gratefully acknowledge the contributions of Chris Kalb (www.spiderreturns.com) and David Saunders (www.pulpartists.com).

Published by Sanctum Books
P.O. Box 761474, San Antonio, TX 78245-1474

THE SPIDER

MASTER OF MEN!

Volume 3

Thrilling Tales and Features

Cover art by Raphael de Soto

**Interior illustrations by J.T. Fleming-Gould
and Joseph A. Farren**

ABOVE THE LAW ... SWORN ENEMY OF THE UNDERWORLD ... HATED BY BOTH ...

Return of the Racket Kings

By Grant Stockbridge

106th Book-Length Novel, Based on the Case Note Books of the *Spider*

While the nation's law enforcement bodies, great and small, engage in all-out action against elements seeking to undermine America's stupendous war effort, a long-dormant menace blooms into dreadful flower! The racket kings rise once again with all the murder-trimmings of the bloody, corpse-strewn alky days of the Twenties! Can Richard Wentworth, alias the Spider, combat such overlords of crime as The Snake and the Weasel, even as the F.B.I. and Commissioner Kirkpatrick combine forces to crush the Spider?

CHAPTER ONE
A Murder in Time

RONALD JACKSON didn't look like a man walking into a murder trap. He was just a citizen walking with military precision down Washburn Street. His eyes glanced neither left nor right. The tension that pulled at his muscles did not show. But Jackson knew he was in grave danger.

Somebody was trailing him.

Jackson hadn't spotted the shadow. With dusk in the streets, and the lights not yet on, he couldn't be sure of his man. Nobody had dodged into a doorway, or anything as amateurish as that. But he *knew.* He couldn't have worked with the *Spider* for years without learning a simple thing like that.

Jackson's wife had warned him to keep his eyes open... and to carry a gun. And Marianne wasn't the worrying kind. She wouldn't worry, even though he was late now—it was almost eight o'clock. All spring, steel and warm ivory, that girl. The grim smile that moved Jackson's wide mouth had its hint of tenderness. It did not touch the keenness of his eyes. He had thought Marianne was wrong; and he didn't have a gun.

But, hell, a guy who had fought beside the *Spider* didn't become panicky because he had tossed a chiseler out of his gas station. Not even when the mug made threats. No racketeer was going to put the squeeze on Ronald Jackson!

Behind him, Jackson heard an auto horn blat three times. It might be some man signaling his girlfriend. It *might.* But if the mob was planning to do something, it would have to be quick. He was only two blocks from home and his gasoline station. Jackson's eyes tightened at the corners; his stubborn chin tucked in toward his chest... and then he swore, harshly.

Ahead of him, the street was empty except for a girl who had just turned the corner of Second Avenue and was hurrying toward him. She wore a pert military cap with a red feather that he would know anywhere.

It was Marianne!

Jackson turned abruptly in against the wall of the building, and made an elaborate business of drawing out cigarettes and lighting one. His eyes swept the street behind him, jerked back toward the girl. Except for the two of them, the street seemed deserted. Yet this spot was getting hot. He didn't want his wife in range when the shooting started. There was much danger!

The anger was churning up slowly, powerfully inside of him, but he held it down. That was another of the lessons he had learned from Major Wentworth—Jackson thought of Richard Wentworth that way, rather than as the *Spider*. You had to keep your head clear when you went into action. Use your anger as a springboard of strength, but keep cool. Even if they had lured Marianne into the trap, too!

His every impulse was to hurry toward the girl, but that was one thing he must not do. As long as they kept apart, it would be hard for the mob to strike. He turned his back and sauntered the other way... and still the street was apparently empty. The street lights went on suddenly, but only deepened the shadows. There were blank windows in the apartment fronts, and dark doorways. Up near the corner, where the girl would soon pass, there was the red and yellow illumination of a barroom's neon sign.

He quickened his pace, hurrying away from Marianne. The new sound struck him like a bullet: a woman's scream!

Jackson whipped about. Two men had the girl, one on each side. They jammed her through the doors of the barroom, and were gone. The street was entirely empty now, except for Jackson... except that on the sidewalk, where the flickering glare of the barroom sign washed, there was a small hat with a pert red feather.

Jackson's lips drew back flat against his teeth. His shoulders arched, rolled with tensing muscles. Somewhere near, a heavy-toned bell began to boom out the hour of eight o'clock. It seemed to repeat one word, over and over. *"Trap!* Trap! *Tra-ap!"* Nothing military about Jackson's walk now. He was a man going into battle, for his mate.

The big bell struck its final syllable and the vibration quivered in the air: *"Tra-a-a-p!"*

RICHARD WENTWORTH'S living quarters were a penthouse atop a Fifth Avenue apartment building. Its accoutrements were expensive as became a wealthy sportsman and clubman, a dilettante of the arts and sciences. Through a doorway, there was a glimpse of shelves filled with rich bindings, and the books overflowed into the drawing room So did the evidences of travels in a score of foreign lands: a Persian prayer rug on the wall; on a casual shelf, an African *ju-ju,* or idol, flanked by a Cretan goddess of ivory and a serene Buddha of priceless jewel-jade; through another doorway, a glimpse of weapon-hung walls where Medieval battle-axes jostled *samurai* swords.

Against that background, Richard Wentworth just now seemed a little incongruous. It was the background of an idler, and a playboy adventurer. Wentworth himself, tanned and lean, looked the man of action even in repose. At his side was a small portable radio whose humming was broken now and again by the curt voices of police broadcasters. Beneath half-lowered lids, his blue-gray eyes had the glint of deep ice.

A broad and turbaned Sikh stepped silently in through the doorway from the foyer. His dark eyes were fierce above an unshorn beard, but they rested almost with idolatry upon the rapier-figure of Wentworth.

"Yes, Ram Singh?" Wentworth had not looked toward the man.

"Jackson *memsahib* is coming up." The Sikh salaamed stiffly.

Wentworth's eyes flicked toward him now. There was an undertone to the East Indian's voice, a hint of excitement. He, too, had been trained in the *Spider*'s school. He knew that Marianne's visit, unaccompanied by Jackson, was unusual. In their lives, the unusual was always suspect. For the *Spider* was outside the law of man, hunted as a criminal by the police and hated by the Underworld. He obeyed a higher law: justice and the service of humanity!

"Phone the *missie sahib* and ask her to come at once," Wentworth said crisply. "It's only eight and she was coming at nine." Nita van Sloan and he had appointed this last evening together before he left for the West, to whose police calls he was listening now. For a month, there had been a slow increase of crime out there. Redoubled police activity seemed to have only stimulated the growth. It was critical now, and spread throughout a score of Middlewestern cities. It was a tocsin for the *Spider.*

Ram Singh salaamed and left without sound, his lithe hillsman's stride at strange variance with the luxury of a New York penthouse. A moment later, Marianne Jackson hurried in, and Wentworth rose to meet her.

"What's Jackson up to now?" Wentworth asked. His tone was faintly humorous, but there was an undertone of gravity. He felt the girl's tension.

Marianne pulled off her small dark military cap with its pert red feather and tossed it to the davenport. Once more, Wentworth was struck with her appearance of extreme fragility, like porcelain, her graceful throat too slender for the weight of honey-colored hair upon it. The appearance was deceiving.

Wentworth reached behind him and switched on a light, for dusk was creeping into the room. Below, in the city streets, the lights had not yet bloomed. He gestured to a seat, but Marianne stood before him, small white fists clenched at her sides.

"Ronald went out without a gun," Marianne said, her low voice taut. "He wouldn't listen to me. Courage isn't a shield against bullets."

"Why a gun?" Wentworth asked quietly.

Marianne gestured abruptly. "I'm sorry to be so vague. I'll explain. This afternoon, Ronald threw a gangster out of the station. He was trying to force

From behind the grilled radiator, two high-calibre machine guns belched twin hails of deadly fire!

Ronald to handle bootleg tires; talked about protection. He sounded like something out of the past, the old racketeering days: 'You handle these tires, or *else...* The big shot ain't *asking* you, he's *telling* you.'" A smile trembled on her soft mouth. "Ronald gave him the bum's rush and tossed him into the gutter. It was what he deserved."

Wentworth nodded crisply. Without ostentation, he changed the wave band on the radio so that New York police calls would come in.

"The man made more threats?"

Marianne shook her head. "He didn't. He just looked at Ronald and smiled. It was... nasty."

To both of them, her words brought a sudden increase of tension. Threats could be empty. The man's behavior spoke of reserve power, of assurance... of danger.

"Jackson can take care of himself," Wentworth said quietly. "I'll talk to him."

MARIANNE twisted her hands and didn't answer at once. She took a short turn up and down before the divan. "Ronald is... reckless. He carried no gun, and he was on foot—" She bit it off. Her knowledge that Wentworth was the *Spider* was a tacit thing, never admitted between them. Only one other woman in the world, the woman he loved, knew the truth about Wentworth. Marianne had guessed, inevitably, and proved her trustworthiness in battle and peril.

"Is Jackson at home now?" Wentworth asked carelessly.

"No!" Marianne burst out. "And he's late! Oh, I know he was probably detained at headquarters. It must be that. But he is late: It's eight o'clock or after."

Wentworth crossed to the windows, making his swift calculations. Below, all the streets bloomed suddenly with lights. All over the city, the street corners were illumined at the same moment. Blackouts were still only sporadic here.

From the radio, there was a shrill call-signal and the police announcer's voice:

"Car two-o-five, Car two-hundred-and-five. Go to Washburn and Second Avenue. Signal Thirty. Signal three-o. Silent. Eight-o-two p.m. That is all."

Marianne stared at the radio. "That's only two blocks from our place," she said; her voice sounded strangled:. "What's *signal thirty?"*

"Just an accident," Wentworth said carelessly. "Jackson is probably at home now. I'll take a run down and talk to him. Why not wait here, with Nita? I'll bring Jackson back."

Marianne relaxed suddenly. "You make everything sound so easy," she said. "I think I'll take your advice."

Wentworth's stride toward the exit was casual. As he entered the foyer, he began to run! He clapped his palms together twice, saw Ram Singh spring to the telephone to have his car brought to the door. Wentworth caught his hat from a closet, plucked a gun from a wall-compartment.

He had lied to Marianne. *Signal thirty,* in police radio code, meant *"violence... shooting... probable homicide!"*

CHAPTER TWO
"Or Else—"

RONALD JACKSON stormed through the barroom doors. He checked just inside and his eyes swept over the long and narrow saloon. At one side, the heavy-jowled barkeep leaned on his mahogany counter. In a booth against the opposite wall, two men sat behind half-emptied schooners of beer. In the corner near the phone booth, a third man had his chair tipped back, eyes closed, mouth open, asleep against the wall.

There was a door at the end of the bar. It was closed.

Jackson went the length of the bar in three leaping strides.

"Hey!" the barkeep said, his tone surprised.

Jackson had his fist in the left hand pocket of his jacket. He jerked it into line with the barkeep. "Hands flat on the counter, you!" he ordered.

The man's water-reddened hands flattened hard on the mahogany. The pressure made a white rim to his nails.

Jackson jerked open the door and sprang through—into darkness. The door crashed shut behind him. His shoulder hit a plaster wall in a narrow hall. The plaster cracked. He could smell the dust. He jerked his head about. Street light filtered in through the dusty glass of a door up front. There was a stairway that led upward. To the rear was darkness.

Silence, thick as the shadows, pressed in upon him. Jackson blew out a shallow breath, strained all his senses. A woman's voice made a faint protesting wail. It was back along the hallway. Jackson's posture was pantherish. He took long strides and they were soundless.

There was a faint slit of light ahead, pinching out beneath a poorly fitted door. There was something here that puzzled Jackson. He had a knife-cut frown between his eyes. He couldn't spot what it was. A trap, of course, but what puzzled him was something else. He shook it out of his mind. He was beside the door.

A man's voice made a low mutter inside, two rasped words. They were curses. Jackson waited. They didn't want Marianne, except to trap him. Did they expect him so soon? Yes, of course. His eyes swept the hallway again. It was lifeless. It felt empty. He sucked in a sudden slow breath. On the floor, half under the door, was a woman's handkerchief.

Jackson's lips dented at the corners, and his chin tucked in. He struck a match and gazed at it with concentration, accustoming his eyes to light. Then he drew back against the opposite wall and drove a foot hard against the lock of the door! The flare of light did not blind him. He went charging into the room.

A blow glanced off his hunched shoulders and he heard the hard exhalation of a man's breath. There was another man across the room. It was the chiseler he had thrown out of his gas station. He had a blackjack in his fist, and a hard, eager grin on his mouth. Those two men were all. Marianne was not in the room, but there was another door.

Jackson laughed, a sharp bark of exaltation and anger. As he leaped forward, he caught up a wooden table and carried it before him. He rammed it hard against the second man, drove him back to the wall. The man's head flung back. His mouth wrenched open in a curse of pain. Jackson dodged aside, whirled. He was in front of the second door, the one through which Marianne must have been thrust.

The other man was leaping across the room with a poised blackjack. He checked so suddenly that he heaved up on his toes, off balance. Jackson struck like a dive bomber. His lancing left smacked solidly into the man's face, and his right almost tore his jaw loose. The man wheeled, went down on his face.

The table crashed to the floor and Jackson pounced like a cat upon the reeling thug. He pinned him against the wall, and crossed the right again. The jar shook down plaster. The man's body went limp and Jackson let it fall. His anger was happy inside of him. There was a spreading pain in his shoulder. Blood was on his knuckles. He ripped open the second door of the room. It was a closet. It was empty.

JACKSON stood staring into the shallowness of the closet. A single limp overcoat hung on a rack and he whipped it aside, futilely. Bewilderment was like a blow on the head. He had been so sure.

His daze made him slow in his reaction to the sound behind him. The man creeping toward him was small and agile. He pounced and swung a heavily weighted sock. He swung it sideways and it caught Jackson just above and behind the ear.

Jackson was spinning and he almost completed the movement, his head driven far over on his shoulder by the blow. His feet tangled. He landed on his shoulders, and the back of his head struck the closet door. He didn't move.

The small man laughed and the sound of it was shrill, like a giggle. "It's all right, boss. Like I always say, the Weasel never misses!"

The man he called boss did not come entirely into the room. The shadow which the high light slanted down from the lintel struck across his chest. His hands were white, well-tended, and the fingers were flexible. Between the knuckles were pads of hair that was black and wiry and curled slightly. He held out his right hand, and there was a gun in it, wrapped in a handkerchief.

"This gun came from the fool's gas station," he said. "You know what to do. Collect the blackjacks first."

The Weasel had narrow teeth and the canines were long and yellow. He giggled as he took the blackjacks, giggled again as he took the gun, carefully held in the handkerchief. He stepped toward the thug who lay on his face.

"Not too close," the boss said quietly, "and you be sure the angle is just exactly right."

The gun blasted, and a little pat of dust lifted from the back of the unconscious thug's coat. His body jerked. His head pulled up from the floor, and then flopped back. His feet stirred, and then the heels fell outward again.

"Between the eyes?" the Weasel whispered as he knelt by the other thug. "Leave me put it between Butch's eyes?"

"Make this fast," the boss said. "The cops are already on the way."

The Weasel crouched so that the angle would be right and sighted along the barrel. He squeezed the trigger and the bullet went pretty straight. Not between the eyes. Through the right one. The Weasel still held the gun in a handkerchief. He tucked it into Jackson's right hand, then darted to the door. The boss had already vanished. Their feet made no sound.

Other feet made a loud noise a moment later. They came pounding down the hallway with authority. A policeman checked in the doorway, a short-barreled revolver in his fist.

"God!" he said.

Another policeman checked just behind him and they peered into the room from the threshold. "Three of them," he whispered. *"Three* of them!"

Jackson rolled his head, and his arms twitched. The cop in the lead reached him in a bound and knocked the gun from under his right hand.

"This one ain't dead," he said. "I'll watch them. Call homicide. Send that barkeep down here. Sew the place up."

The barkeep came heavily and reluctantly down the hall. His eyes bulged. "Holy heaven!" he gasped.

"What happened?" the cop snapped at him.

The barkeep swallowed. "I don't know," he said hoarsely. "I don't know a thing."

The cop said, "Nuts! They came in through your place. Talk!"

THE barkeep swallowed again, lifted his reddened hands. "Look," he said, "all I know is those two guys came in here with a dame. I seen her with them before, see. So they come back here and say they don't want nothing to drink right now. So I wait for them to buzz me. Then this guy comes barging in. He looks pretty wild and he points a gun at me and tells me to keep my hands in sight—"

"This gun?" the cop toed the revolver on the floor.

"Jeez, I guess so." The barkeep shook his head. "There's a lot of banging back here, and I decide to call the cops. I'm on my way to the phone booth when I hear the gun go off. Then before I can do anything about calling youse guys, you're here."

"You didn't call us?" a cop asked.

"I didn't have time, honest I didn't."

The cop growled, "Okay, okay. So it was a row over a dame, hunh, and this fellow charges in and shoots up the bunch. I don't see any other guns. Where's the dame?"

The barkeep spread his hands, lifted his shoulders heavily. "Skipped, I guess. I seen her come in, but there's other doors. No, I don't know her name. They calls her Babe."

Jackson's eyes opened sluggishly, blankly. He looked up at the cop, started to get to his feet.

"You stay there, buddy!" the cop snarled. "Just stay right there! I'm taking no chances on a killer that bumps off two unarmed guys over a dame!"

Intelligence came sharply back into Jackson's eyes. He rolled his head and squinted to see through the pain. He saw the man propped against the wall, and what had happened to his head. He shook his head and the pain blinded him, but when he could see again, it was the same picture. What in the name of heaven had happened? Had he got hold of a gun, and— He started to shake his head, didn't. His eye fell on the gun on the floor.

"No you don't," the cop snapped.

He caught up the gun and a painful frown was between Jackson's eyes. It looked like his gun, but it couldn't be, of course. Still, if this was a frame-up... He swore under his breath. It didn't make sense. Why should somebody bump off two guys just to frame him? He heard the thick sound of a heavy siren and, a while later, more police came trooping down the hall: detectives and cameramen from headquarters. The homicide squad took charge, three more men in the small room. Jackson didn't know any of them.

The man in charge was a thin, stooped guy with a tired voice. He looked at the bodies as if they were waxworks in a museum. He heard the radio cop's report with exaggerated patience.

"Okay, you can go," he drawled. "Write it up when you go off duty."

The cop saluted, "Okay, Lieutenant."

He went down the hall and the detective lieutenant looked down at Jackson, still in his enforced position on the floor.

"Like the floor, do you, mister?" he said, "or do you want to take this lying down?"

Jackson pushed heavily to his feet and, from the doorway, a voice said, "Okay, Lieutenant."

It sounded like the cop speaking, and the lieutenant turned with his slow affected boredom. He stiffened like that, half turned around, and the other two cops in the room caught his movement and looked, up too. They looked up casually, too casually.

It wasn't the cop who stood in the door. It was the *Spider!*

The *Spider* spoke with a biting whisper that was like zero-wind to men's blood. "Just stay as you are, gentlemen," he said, in a cold monotone. "I won't detain you long. My business is with the gentleman who seems to have been doing all the shooting!"

His eyes flashed bitterly to those of Jackson, and Jackson felt their force like an electric shock. He stared at the hunched figure in the long black cape, the ruthless face beneath the broad brim of the slouch hat. The *Spider...* condemning him?

Jackson shook his head jerkily. "I didn't," he whispered. "I tell you—I didn't!"

The *Spider* said harshly, "You coward! *You tombe-toi! You dog! You Va-chezma!"*

Jackson heard the French words without any clear understanding of them at the moment. He knew the *Spider* wasn't calling him names. He knew the names people could be called in French. He had fought in France. Those French words... Jackson glimpsed their meaning.

"Gentlemen!" the *Spider* was saying to the police. "I am going to save you the trouble of executing this *tombe-toi!"*

His heavy automatic lifted, blasted! Jackson gasped. He pivoted on his right foot and then fell, face forward, into the closet!

The *Spider* laughed in cold menace. He turned and vanished into the darkness of the hallway!

CHAPTER THREE
The Net Tightens

THE police stood, for a stunned instant, motionless in the murder room. Then the bored-looking lieutenant made a tremendous leap through the doorway. His gun blasted. Glass crashed at the corridor's end. Then his feet beat a hard, fast tattoo forward. After an instant's hesitation, the two remaining police officers followed him. One was sent charging up the steps, another into the barroom, the third plunged out onto the street.

A moment after they raced past, the shadows beneath the stairway moved and swelled... and the *Spider,* black cape belling behind him, swept back into the murder room.

"On your feet, Jackson," he whispered.

He reached into the closet, fumbled... and the back of the closet swung outward, a door. Jackson stumbled through it, and was in a duplicate room, but this one had a window that stood open on the night. The *Spider* motioned him sharply toward it.

"But Marianne is here," Jackson said.

"She's at my place," Wentworth snapped. "You've been decoyed. Fortunate you picked up the French, and the police didn't. I kept it simple."

Jackson said, numbly, "Fall. Go to my home.' And Marianne is there?"

"Out the window," the *Spider* commanded, and Jackson, still moving like a man in a dream, climbed over the sill. The back of the closet was shut again now. It was not concealed very carefully. The *Spider,* scouting the building, had spotted it at once. They were racing now across a shadow-darkened yard, scaling a fence. Jackson's head reeled dizzily with pain, but he followed. They ducked into a basement, emerged into a narrow alley between two buildings.

"There's the car," Wentworth said quietly. "Get into it and drive."

"But you, Major!"

The *Spider*'s voice was crisp with authority,

"Orders, Jackson!"

Jackson's hand snapped up to salute. He stumbled across the pavement and into the waiting coupé. After a moment, the engine started and he tooled it away. The *Spider* watched him go with gentleness in his eyes. Jackson was more badly hurt than the man realized. He thought that he could make home all right. If not, he at least would be out of danger here. As for the *Spider*... he whirled about, and his eyes were pale and cold in the darkness. The *Spider*'s work was not finished!

Moments later, he was back beside that secret door again. No sound in the murder room. The *Spider* slid into it. Throughout the building, there were shouts and running feet as the police hunted for him. He had lost precious minutes convoying Jackson to safety, but it had been necessary. Now he bent swiftly over the bodies of the slain men, seeking some clue to their identities, to their connections.

There was nothing that would afford a clue. It was true that one of the men wore a snake ring on his left hand, a twist of gold representing a serpent with its tail in its mouth, with two bits of red jewel for eyes. Once it had been a common enough type of ring. A little incongruous on this younger man, but still nothing to remark on.

THERE was no warning sound in the hallway, but suddenly the lieutenant spoke there. *"Don't move, Spider, or I'll have to blow your spine in half!"* He tried to keep it drawling, but his voice was taut.

Wentworth made no visible move, but his gun was in his hand. He fired it straight upward, and blasted light out of the room. At the same moment, he wheeled and dived. The crash of the lieutenant's gun sent a flicker of hot light across the room, spotted his quick movement. The gun flamed again. Through the deafening concussions came the excited yelps of racing police. Wentworth felt both bullets. They had not struck him, but they plucked at his figure-distorting cape. In the darkness, that garment made him enormous. It was better than a steel shield, because it did not hamper movement... and it had tricked many an expert marksman!

Wentworth whirled it high now... and went in, low. He caught the lieutenant's feet and yanked

them out from under him. The man yelled hoarsely, lost his gun as he flung out his hands to catch himself. Wentworth smacked his fist to the point of the man's jaw and, an instant later, had carried him to the hidden door. His presence there would delay the police for a moment. As he shut the door, the lieutenant's weight pressed against it from the opposite side.

Minutes later, his disguise a neatly wrapped bundle under his arm, a cap upon his head, the *Spider* entered the Lexington Avenue subway and was whirled northward. When he swung the corner in front of his apartment, a smile touched his lips. His car was parked nearby. Jackson had made it!

IT WAS Nita van Sloan who met him at the door... and Wentworth saw an automatic held, low against her right side. She smiled at his glance, and lifted her lips to his kiss.

"It looks as if the gangs had come east to save you the trouble of going after them," she said, with a pretense at lightness.

"You've figured part of it right," he said and, arm about her waist, moved swiftly to the drawing room. "This is undoubtedly a move to hold me here. It won't succeed."

In the drawing room, Jackson stood stubbornly in front of the fireplace. His eyes were bloodshot, and his face drawn. Marianne was looking at him with exasperation.

"It's the only sensible thing to do, Ronnie," she said. "Go straight to Commissioner Kirkpatrick with the whole thing. With Mr. Wentworth."

"It's not as simple as that," Wentworth said quietly from the door. "Jackson has been neatly framed. I don't know why the mob should have killed two of their own men to frame him, but that's what happened. The witnesses were not gangsters, but seem to have been men from the barroom."

Jackson said harshly, "One of them was the man who tried to shake me down and got tossed out on his ear. The other was his driver. Maybe the gang thought I'd gone to the police and didn't want any leads left behind."

"Maybe," Wentworth agreed. There was a reservation in his tone that Nita's quick ear detected. "I

RICHARD WENTWORTH

don't know exactly how you're set now, Jackson. I had to get you out of it the way I did because no man can afford to be rescued from the police by the *Spider*. It's damning. Can they identify you, or have they?"

"Not that I know of, unless..." He bit it off. "Never mind."

Wentworth understood that he didn't want Marianne to worry and did not press him. "You're in a jam, Jackson," he said shortly. "I'd like to take you west with me, but now that you've signed up with the Army—again, you're not a free agent.

"I'll be working with the police whenever possible—and useful—and they'd probably pick you up quickly."

Jackson said, "That's right, Major. I'd only impede your progress. I'll get out of this some way." His voice sounded a bit dubious. "When do you have to leave?"

Wentworth frowned. He said, "I cannot delay. The situation in the middlewest grows worse every day. This may be a clever move to block me. I don't say that it is. I don't see how any connection could possibly be established between you and me. From the way things are happening out west, I should say that there are at least a score of big shot racketeers and gangsters operating... under one central head. It may be that the agents of the big leader stepped into this picture tonight, over the heads of the local gang. It may be—"

There was an imperative summons at the door. Ram Singh was in the foyer entrance, silent as a shadow. "Kirkpatrick *sahib,*" he rumbled. "He has police *wallahs* with him."

Jackson was suddenly tense. His face was uncertain between anger and chagrin. With a quick gesture, Wentworth sent him into the music room. There was a hiding place there which Jackson knew.

"Well, Ram Singh," Wentworth said easily. "What are you waiting for? Let Commissioner Kirkpatrick in."

The Sikh showed his white teeth in a flash through his beard. "On my head be it, *sahib!*" he salaamed.

He opened the door and Stanley Kirkpatrick strode well into the room before he halted. He had left his men at the door, and Wentworth saw that the man in charge of them was the drawling lieutenant he had knocked out in the barroom! Wentworth walked to meet Kirkpatrick, his hand held out.

"Welcome, Kirk," he said. "Nice of you to drop in—"

"This is business," Kirkpatrick said shortly. His clear blue eyes were withdrawn, his face sternly set. These two men were warm friends, but nothing could stand between Kirkpatrick and his sworn duty. He stood uncompromisingly at the threshold, a dapper man with military bearing, firm mouth shadowed by a military mustache. There was gray at his temples, but everything about the man was young.

Wentworth smiled at him. "I still say, 'Welcome,'" he said. "What can I do for you?"

Kirkpatrick rapped out, "You can explain why your coupé, now parked in front of this building, was within the half hour parked near the scene of a double murder in which the *Spider* took a hand!"

Wentworth lifted his brows in slight mockery. "Still riding that old trail, Kirk?" he asked, sardonically.

"You haven't answered my question, Wentworth!"

WENTWORTH shrugged and took out his cigarette case, his lighter and made a slow business of getting a smoke going. His lips were faintly amused. Kirkpatrick had often suspected that Wentworth and the *Spider* were one; had never been able to prove it. So Wentworth and Kirkpatrick remained warm friends; while the *Spider* and the Commissioner were dauntless enemies! But the thing that Kirkpatrick now mentioned was no real evidence of a connection between him and the *Spider*. Suspicious, yes. But Kirkpatrick was always suspicious. Wentworth knew that Kirkpatrick was concealing the real purpose of his visit.

"I could refuse to answer, Kirk," he said easily. "Or I could say that, to the best of my knowledge and belief, the coupé has never been away from in front of this building for hours... of course that would lay me open to a parking violation."

Kirkpatrick took an impatient stride forward. "Two men have been killed! The *Spider* killed a third and carried off his body!"

"In my car?" Wentworth laughed. "Did you search it for traces of blood?"

A slight flush was in Kirkpatrick's cheeks. He glanced toward Nita, who smiled at him prettily; at Marianne Jackson who was leaning, a cigarette between her fingers, on the mantel. His eyes went from her to the divan where the hat with its pert red feather rested. He said nothing about it.

"May I inquire how long Mrs. Jackson has been here?" he asked sharply.

Wentworth's voice lifted, "You may ask what you please, Kirk, but we will use our own discretion about answering. Are you trying now to involve Marianne? Or are you asking, in a round-about way, for my alibi?"

"I am arresting Mrs. Jackson as a material witness," Kirkpatrick said, curtly. "I am also arresting you, on suspicion, until you can explain about your car's presence in the neighborhood of those murders. *Lieutenant Hampshire, place these people under arrest!* Put cuffs on both of them. Mrs. Jackson is not as fragile as she looks!"

Wentworth turned his head toward Nita and his face showed a whimsical smile, but against his trouser leg his fingers were tapping out a message in Morse which he knew she saw.

"Kirk after Jackson," he signaled. *"This is bluff to force Jackson to come out. Signal Ram Singh."*

Marianne said, indignantly, "This is completely uncalled for. I have been in this house since around eight o'clock, or a little before. I heard a radio signal just after I came in. The signature was eight-o-two. Whatever it is you're trying to prove—"

"All right, Commissioner," Jackson spoke quietly from the doorway of the music room. "I'm here and I'll surrender. The reason the coupé downstairs was where it was is simple. I borrowed it. Marianne was urging me to come to you and explain things."

"That would have been better," Kirkpatrick said dryly. "The bracelets, Hampshire, before the *Spider* comes and kills him again."

Wentworth was quiet, too. "Would you mind telling me, Kirkpatrick, just what this is all about?"

The Commissioner was a little more relaxed now that his subterfuge had worked. "Certainly. Jackson should have used something else to kill those two men. A gun, registered in one's own name, can always be traced so easily."

CHAPTER FOUR
Captive City

THE transcontinental plane carrying Wentworth dropped down through the light pattering of rain toward the blurred lights of the airport at Wissouri City. In the East the sky was graying with the uprush of the sun. Wentworth had left New York City on schedule.

Wentworth's face had a grim cast as he waited for his luggage in the plane terminal. It had not been easy to leave Jackson locked tightly in a murder frame. He could hardly expect Marianne to understand, but to the *Spider* it seemed definitely clear that the leader of the middlewestern gangs had tried to stop him in the East. The entire thing was too pat to have been coincidental. Yet only a few, a very few—and all those deeply trusted—had known of his plans. Every inclination, save one, urged that he remain to free Jackson of the murder charges against him, and to fight the racketeers who had arisen. But that one inclination outweighed all others. It was the call of duty.

Wentworth climbed into a taxi. "Monterrey Hotel," he ordered quietly, and settled back against the cushions. He shifted his shoulders a little. He was wearing the two heavy automatics, his invariable armament, under his arms. They were making good speed along the glistening, deserted road. The headlamps were pale with the increasing day.

Wissouri City rushed to meet him, a huddled black outline of buildings, untouched as yet by the sun. Wentworth had chosen this point of attack because it seemed the central hub of the crime area. Across the Mississippi River, in Illinois, gang crimes were rife. It spread north and south on both sides the great stream, and pushed west until it reached almost to the Rockies. It covered industrial and farming areas; the heart of America.

Wissouri City, at the crossroads, seemed the logical place for gang headquarters.

They were burrowing through the outlying warehouses and factories now. The windows were livid with mercury lights, under which men were working twenty-four hours a day on war orders. A poor residential section followed, and they were speeding into the outskirts of the business district when Wentworth saw the attack. Three men had hammered another to the sidewalk and were beating him with blackjacks. The scene was clear against a background of dawn sky and gray light.

"Stop!" Wentworth snapped at the driver.

Instead, the man bore down on the gas! "Not me, buddy!" he yelled. "Not when those gorillas are around!"

Wentworth's hand flashed to his pocket and he held out a cupped palm in which metal glinted. "Stop the cab!" he ordered again, harshly.

The man glanced at his hand, slammed on brakes... but the moment Wentworth leaped out, the gears ground, the taxi leaped onward! Wentworth swore softly and sprinted toward the corner past which they had swept. His coat was unbuttoned, his gun-butts free. He was aware that he might be running into some new trap. If the gangs had been able to plan so cleverly in New York, they could easily do this in their capital!

He whipped around the corner... and the street was empty, save for the limp body of the man on the sidewalk. In three long bounds, Wentworth reached the man's side. But he crouched cautiously above him, his back to a wall, his eyes questing sharply over the street. His hand found the man's pulse. It was feebler but growing faster even while he counted. That meant internal hemorrhage. The man's head rolled.

"Who did this?" Wentworth bent toward him.

The man mumbled a sound that might have been a word. Wentworth bent closer and this time, he caught a sound *"... snake..."* It was at that moment that guns blasted in the street!

A PART of Wentworth's brain had been expecting that. His eye corners even caught the first glint of gun-steel from a doorway across the street. His own automatic thudded against his palm, kicked with blasting death in the same moment. The man he had spotted wheeled out into sight with his hands clawing at the bricks. He fell. But there were other guns!

Wentworth was already in motion. He made a quick feint toward the corner, whirled and nailed a shoulder hard against a steel lamppost. Bullets were clawing the bricks in the path he had feinted. He got another target and his gun blasted even as his eyes focused. His bullet plucked at the head of a man who crouched in a stairwell beside a building. The man's whole body showed as it jerked him upright, then he went down out of sight again.

There was that much pause, and then there was the heavy hammer of a racing automobile engine, the scream of burning tires. A heavy black car slewed around the corner! It straightened out, and bore straight down on the pole behind which Wentworth crouched! it was a suicidal move—if carried through. Even that car's great weight couldn't break the steel pipe, and—

With a harsh cry, Wentworth hurled himself prone upon the pavement. From behind the grill-work of the radiator, two machine guns spat out a stream of its deadly fire in hot steel! Wentworth heard the furious, broken ringing as the powerful bullets tore through the hollow steel pole which he had used for protection!

But Wentworth did not lose his head. Death was an old familiar, whom he could shake by the hand. He knew, as many would not have, that those machine guns must be fixed and could not be aimed except with the whole car. He rolled, brought up on his belly with an automatic in either fist. He flung one bullet experimentally against the windshield, and nodded. Bulletproof. He poked another slug into a tire... and nothing happened.

Then there was another tearing scream of tortured rubber, and the big car slithered about within yards of the pole. From ports in the side of the car, two machine guns took up the deadly hail. And these guns were maneuverable!

Smoothly as a tiger, Wentworth was on his feet and behind the pole again. These were lighter guns, whose bullets could not penetrate steel. His automatics flamed twice and he knew that one of his bullets had reached through a gun-port to mark a killer! Then, as the murder car roared up the street, something was whipped free from its back end, something that was shaped like an over-sized egg and wobbled erratically as the momentum of the car sent it rolling toward Wentworth! A grenade!

Wentworth flung himself toward the corner of the building, hit rolling on the cold wet pavement. In that split-second, the grenade exploded!

Windows crashed along the street. Bits of broken metal whined angrily through the air. The concussion jarred Wentworth to the spine. A foot above his head, a jagged lump of steel tore the bricks. Wentworth picked himself up dizzily, but the car had disappeared. One thing alone had saved him; the grenade had been close to the curbstone when it let go, and that six-inch block of stone, so close to it, had sheltered the area in which Wentworth lay.

Wentworth reloaded his automatics with steady hands, while grimness made his face stern. "Dive bombers!" he said softly. "You can't run a car like that through the streets without police collusion! Built-in machine guns, bulletproof tires and glass, and a bomb port in the stern! The gangs have come back with a vengeance!"

HE CROSSED back to the prostrate man on the pavement. His body had stopped a half dozen slugs, and fragments of the grenade. But he had been dead even before that, Wentworth could see. A siren wailed in the near distance. No use waiting for the police. It could serve no useful purpose. Wentworth doubled around the corner and after fifteen minute's fast walk reached the Monterrey Hotel. As he had half expected, his luggage was there. The hotel had paid the taxi driver.

Wentworth registered and was shown to a two-room suite that faced an inner court. "Quieter, don't you think?" he remarked to the bellhop.

It was also easier to leave without being seen!

In a swift search of the suite, Wentworth located a hiding place. He detached a long plaque of tile which sealed in the tub in the private bath, tucked into the opening beneath the tub itself his guns and his *Spider's* robes. He sealed the tile back with toothpaste. He was in the midst of preparations for a shower when the expected knock came at the door.

Wentworth put irritation into his voice as he answered, donned his robe and turned the key. The door was flung wide and two men barged into the room. They had guns in their fists... and badges in their cupped palms.

"I don't remember inviting you in," Wentworth snapped. "Get out!"

The two men were solid in the shoulders, hard-eyed, tough-looking. One of them laughed through lips that opened only a slit.

"Tough, eh?" he winked at his companion who had moved to cover Wentworth from another angle. "A big city tough guy."

Wentworth permitted a slow smile to stir his lips. "Is this just your usual reception committee for distinguished visitors?" he asked dryly. "Or is this a special favor? In either case, you'd better be seated, gentlemen. The drinks appear to be on me." He gestured with his left hand, and on the first finger a ring caught a gleam of light. It was a snake-ring, a twist of gold that comprised a serpent biting its tail. There were two red stones for its eyes. "I have," he said, "some of what is known as—snake-bite."

The detective's faces underwent a subtle change. Wentworth turned his back on them, went to his suitcase and took out a pint of whiskey. When he turned around, he was apparently just opening it. "I'm afraid I haven't any glasses," he said. "If you're particular, we can ring for some."

"The bottle's okay," the first detective said. The hostility had oozed out of him.

Wentworth let him take the pint and his eyes rested merrily upon the fellow's face. "Your city isn't very well patrolled, sergeant," he said. "I was coming into town by taxi and saw three men beating up another one. There wasn't a patrolman in sight. It was pitiful."

The first detective strangled over his drink. He laughed. "Haw! That's pretty good!" he gasped.

His face was red. He handed the drink to his companion, wiped his mouth with the back of his hand appreciatively.

"Good whiskey," he said heavily.

Wentworth smiled at him. "Naturally, I went to help the poor fellow," Wentworth continued. "He was almost dead when I got there. Before I left, he was quite dead. The three thugs had left him still able to talk. Careless of them, wasn't it?"

"Damned careless!" the first detective agreed, and laughed again.

Wentworth nodded at him. "Have a seat," he suggested. "There are a few more details to my complaint against the police here."

The detectives sat down, side by side, on the davenport to which Wentworth motioned them. He stood before them, held up the bottle to the light. He whistled softly. "You don't leave much!" He tipped the bottle, and then crossed to a waste basket, his back to them and dropped it in. "Another dead soldier!" he said.

He stood looking at the two representatives of the police. They looked uncomfortable, their faces slightly flushed. "My other complaint has to do with the type of cars you allow to roll around the streets," Wentworth said gently. "Really, most unusual. Regular dive bombers." As he went on talking, his voice was a monotone, insistent with authority. It was low. "It's rather warm in the room," he said. "A little close. It tends to make you feel sleepy. Most people feel sleepy in a warm room when there isn't much fresh air. Whisky makes you sleepy, too."

The second detective's eyes closed, his head sagged. He lifted it with a jerk; His companion was already asleep. He started to gather his feet under him but Wentworth put a hand on his shoulder.

"Why not sleep where you are ?" he asked. "You will sleep where you are. You will sleep until I tell you to awake."

The man's head drooped forward and stayed that way. Wentworth straightened and used a handkerchief on his palms, on his temples. He looked down at the snake-ring on his finger and his lips grew bitter and grim. He forced them to relax, to smile.

"We will see," he murmured to himself, "if these gentlemen of the police can tell the truth—even under the influence of the truth drug!"

CHAPTER FIVE
Men of the Snake

WENTWORTH'S tone was light, but his mien was serious as he bent over to test the heart action of both men. The truth drug was a dangerous and unreliable medicament, and the tolerance of various individuals varied greatly. What one man would throw off, would kill another. And Wentworth was working in the dark, not knowing the physical conditions of the two detectives.

A faint gleam of relief shone in his eyes as he straightened, and he set deliberately to work upon the man who had been mostly silent throughout the interview. As a subordinate, the man would be less willful... and more pliable. It was necessary to work swiftly. He had only a limited time before the men sank into deep coma in which questioning would be impossible. Meanwhile, questioning under the truth drug was a great deal like getting answers out of a man who talks in his sleep. Irrelevancies would creep in, and not all of the answers would make sense. There would be, moreover, a good deal of mumbling and slurring of sounds.

Wentworth addressed the man in the crisp authoritative tones that an operator uses with a subject under hypnosis.

"What is your name, officer?"

The man's head jerked, his lips moved, but there was no definite sound. Wentworth repeated twice before the man got out the slurred syllables: "Names... John Gibbons."

"What department?"

"Homicide."

Wentworth flung his questions fast, keeping the man moving.

"Your pay!"

"Fifty..."

"How much on the side?"

The man's head shook heavily. "Nothing," he mumbled. "Not one damned cent."

"There is graft!"

"Sure. Oh, sure."

"But you don't get any?"

"Not one damned cent!" His lips sneered. "Chief gets it all. Damn him."

Wentworth's eyes narrowed as he considered that bit of knowledge even while he flung his next question.

"Who pays off the Chief?" he demanded.

The man's head was sagging. Wentworth shook him erect, repeated the question. "Who pays off the Chief?"

"Big... shot." It was a mumble.

"Who's the big shot?"

"Everybody knows... big shot."

"What's his name?"

"Max... Ma..." A shake jerked him up. "Max Vellie."

"The snake!" Wentworth snapped. "Why are you afraid of the snake?"

The man's face twisted in anger. "Damned snake!"

"Why are you afraid of it?"

The detective swore, slumped forward, was jerked back. "Snake..." he mumbled. "Gotta watch out or you'll get shipped to the sticks."

That made sense. The detectives obeyed orders and watched their step around men who wore the snake emblem because they had that mysterious something that is the bane of law enforcement officers everywhere: influence. Step on the wrong toes, and you got shipped to the sticks, shifted to a minor spot, pocketed, dead-ended. If you got too tough, you were suspended and that meant loss of pay. It was shattering to morale. A cop could make an arrest... and instead of being patted on the back; he got kicked into a corner and forgotten. One or two such occurrences and the whole force began to walk softly, hit in two tender spots: the pocketbook and morale. A man worked hard at a job only when it demanded the best in him. Here, the best a man could do got him in trouble.

"Max Vellie is the Snake?" Wentworth demanded harshly.

Gibbons mumbled what sounded like, "Don't know."

Wentworth shook him again, tried another question or two, but there was no answer. The man had slipped into coma, but his heart action was still satisfactory. The other detective was in the same condition.

Wentworth's mouth was grim. He had some information on which he could work, and it was not to his liking. He knew Max Vellie by reputation. He had been one of the big racketeers of the Middle-West, too smart to be caught by income tax prosecution. When the F.B.I. began to turn the heat on others, Max Vellie stepped out of the rackets and let other men take the rap. Ruthless, murderous and shrewd, the man was dangerous in the extreme. Further, it was plain that the graft situation was of the worst kind. You could weed out crooked cops, but when the corruption was at the top, the whole structure was rotten.

While these thoughts coursed through his brain, Wentworth was in swift action. He removed the tile plaque under the tub and drew out the garments of the *Spider,* swung on the shoulder holsters. He had mapped the hotel in his mind. He knew how to slip out without being spotted. The garments of the *Spider* looked like a bundle of laundry...

HE RENTED a car and half an hour later—the office-bound traffic was just beginning to thicken— he was parked near one of the government financed housing projects where families of low income could live in pleasant surroundings. The play yards were crowded with children; in the apartments vacuum cleaners sang; the men were off to work. Wentworth rapidly altered the appearance of his face, changed his manner of walking. The apartment to which he went was silent. As he approached the door, a woman opened it and came out. She had a stunned and sympathetic expression. She glanced at Wentworth and hurried to another door in the hall. She was apparently a neighbor. Wentworth rang the bell.

After a slow while, the door was opened by a boy with a red and angry face. There were tears ready in his eyes and that was what made him angry. He was about twelve years old.

"What do you want?" he asked, sharply.

Wentworth smiled. His heart went out to this boy. "I'm an insurance representative. Your father had a policy with us. We always pay off promptly. If your mother can answer a few questions, she can have the money right now."

The boy turned his head to look back into the apartment, then hesitantly opened the door. "I guess it's all right," he said. "Ma ain't feeling so good. And don't you torment her none, see?"

Wentworth nodded. He put his hand on the boy's shoulder, not saying anything. The boy started to pull his shoulder away, and didn't. They walked that way for a moment, and then Wentworth dropped his hand. The boy looked up at him uncertainly. This guy wasn't being kind or sympathetic or anything, just friendly. You could stand a guy like that. But all these women, crying and carrying on. They made Ma feel worse.

There were toys in the hallway so that it was necessary to step aside around them, the toys of a smaller girl and boy. The children weren't in evidence; neighbors had taken them in charge. The boy went ahead of Wentworth and into a darkened room.

"Ma," he said, "there's an insurance man here. He's got some money..."

Wentworth bowed on the threshhold. The curtains were drawn. Two women sat bolt upright in chairs, rocking, rocking. The tears slid silently down the cheeks of the younger.

"If I could have some light," Wentworth said quietly. "I have some papers to read." He raised the shade, and the sunlight had broken through the clouds. It laid a yellow shaft across the floor. The women shifted uneasily and Wentworth took out a packet of paper in a blue stiff wrapper.

"I'll have to ask some questions," he said easily, "but I don't think there'll be any trouble. Your husband has a thousand dollar equity.... There will be some identification. Your husband's full name?"

The younger woman buried her face in her hands and it was the older one who answered: "James Riley, and he never harmed a soul in his life. Things like this ought not to happen."

Wentworth's lips tightened. "No," he agreed, quietly. But they did happen... and so the *Spider* had his work. "His occupation?"

"Motor mechanic," the older woman said. "A good one, too. People came to him from all over when they couldn't get their boat engines to work. Just this week, he overhauled four big ones, all just alike. Outboards they were; had to have a truck to deliver them—"

"Mother!" the widow's voice was strangled, frightened.

The older woman's face changed, too. There was fright there, suddenly.

WENTWORTH waited and no more was said. He nodded, reached into an inner pocket and drew out a wallet. He counted out a thousand dollars in small bills.

"I hope they get the men who... did this thing to Jim," he said. "Any idea who they were?"

The two women looked at him with dumb eyes and their fright increased. There were not even tears.

"It's the duty of every citizen," Wentworth said quietly, "to help the police..."

"Those crooks!" It was the boy who cried it out, harshly.

"James!" his mother said, fiercely.

The boy swallowed what he had been about to say. His mother stood up and picked up the money. She twisted it in her hands. "I don't know anything about insurance," she said. "You'll want a receipt?"

Wentworth gave her a small printed form, already filled out, and she signed it. He said, curtly, "I wouldn't mention that money to the police."

She shook her head and Wentworth turned and strode out of the room. The boy walked sharply at his heels. Wentworth's thoughts were grim. There was no question as to why the women were terrified. Gangsters had already paid them a call! It was the old story of intimidation that had worked so well in the years of the rackets. The crimes were committed openly. Everyone, including the police, knew the guilty men, but witnesses were afraid to testify. And the processes of law being what they were, by necessity, it didn't do even honest police any good to know the guilty man.

The law would not restrain the *Spider!*

As he reached the door, there was a sharp jab at the bell, then a heavy and authoritative knocking on the panel. Wentworth narrowed his eyes. It sounded like the police! He opened the door himself, and confronted two obvious detectives.

"Police," one of them said. "We gotta talk to Jim Riley's widow."

"What do you want to know?" Wentworth demanded. "She's not in condition to talk to anyone."

The cop was belligerent, "Who in the hell are you?"

"A friend," Wentworth told him. "I'm going to talk to you. Without asking Mrs. Riley one question, you know who murdered her husband! If you're honest, arrest them. But don't go in and bother his widow just so that you can make a routine report at headquarters. It isn't worth it."

The cop flushed, "Listen, brother—"

Wentworth cut him short. "I'm holding you personally, and the department as a whole, responsible for seeing that justice is done. You're going to ask who I am. Here's my card."

He strode past them and, in his wake, there was a stunned silence. It was followed by a frantic yelp, and the two policemen sprang toward the stairs... and they were empty. They raced along the hall... and found nothing.

James Riley bent over and picked up the card they had dropped. On its face there glowed a symbol in scarlet—*the seal of the Spider!*

CHAPTER SIX
The *Spider* Strikes

THE door of a closet across the hallway opened quietly and Wentworth stepped out. He smiled at the boy. "Anything you would like to tell me, Jim?" he asked.

The boy gulped. "Sure. Sure! Golly, I'd tell *you* anything."

Wentworth knew that he was placing this family in peril, but if they did not talk to the police—and he knew they would not—they would be comparatively safe. His visit could make no difference.

"Take a ride with me, then, Jim," Wentworth said. "Come along."

They went down the stairs. "But those cops!" Jim said.

Wentworth smiled and made no answer. Presently, the feet of the police began to beat their way upward through the building again. Wentworth stepped to an apartment door and rang the bell. The door opened.

"Mrs. Riley sent Jim down to borrow a cupful of flour," he said, "and I'd like to talk to you a moment."

The woman ushered them in, and Wentworth gave his message. "I've advised Mrs. Riley to leave town as soon as possible. You know what the situation is. I'd like you to urge the same thing. She would listen to a woman more than to a man. She can't do any good by staying."

The woman said, flustered, "Why, I'd be glad to."

They left, and the police were above them. Wentworth led the way casually down the stairs. "There will probably be a policeman on guard at the door," he said. "Let me have the flour. Now, you run out the door in a hurry."

The boy slammed outdoors and, as the policeman looked after him, Wentworth stepped up beside the man.

"Hold this flour for me, officer," he said pleasantly.

The man started, turned and looked down into the cup full of flour, opened his mouth to swear. Wentworth hit the bottom of the cup sharply. The flour hit the cop's mouth and eyes in a solid lump, and then spread. Wentworth plucked the officer's revolver from its holster and walked with lithe strides, that seemed unhurried, to his car. He was underway by the time the cop's flour-muffled shouts began to make sense.

"We'll have to make this fast," Wentworth told the boy. "Tell me about your father."

The boy's eyes were big and there was an incredulous grin on his mouth. "You make it seem so easy!" he said, admiringly.

Wentworth looked at him sharply. "Don't get wrong ideas," he said curtly. "We both had an excellent chance of being shot. These police are crooked, and therefore unsure of themselves—inefficient. But there is only grief and disaster for those who live outside the law."

"You do it!" the boy said, fiercely.

"Yes," said Wentworth softly. "I said—outside the law, there is only grief and destruction. My end is as certain as the revolution of the Earth. Did you ever stop to wonder whether the *Spider* was... happy?"

Jim Riley continued to look at him. A shadow crossed his eyes. "Gee," he said. "Gee, I guess you don't have much *fun*. Then why in heck do you do it, *Spider?*"

"Each of us," Wentworth said quietly, "is born to do some work. Our souls know what it is. We don't. Only someday, everyone of us finds some-

thing that he feels he has to do. Something good. When you find that, Jim, you do it at all costs. Then you'll be happy. That's man-talk, Jim, but you're the man of the house now."

Jim's face was grave. He had the quiet, listening quality that all people have when they hear their own particular truth spoken to them. He said, quietly, "Okay, *Spider.* Okay."

"Now, tell me, Jim."

James Riley's hands became fists on his knees. His eyes were angry against the tears. "I don't know much," he said. "But after Pop took those last four motors, all just alike, back where they belonged, he began to look worried. Finally, he told Ma he'd have to go to the police about something. Ma tried to keep him from it, but Pop said something like what you just said, *Spider.* He said there were some things a man had to do; or he couldn't look his conscience in the face. He went this morning, and—and—"

"You don't know whose motors those were, or where your father took them?"

Jim shook his head, not trusting his voice. Wentworth dropped his hand on his shoulder. "Look, Jim," he said. "Your father did what he had to do, and *he's* not unhappy about it. Probably, he didn't want to leave your ma and you, but he knows you're almost a man, and he's not going to worry. So don't you be unhappy, either. Here we are, back at the place. Don't go in just yet. Play with the other boys for a while."

Wentworth whipped the car around and sent it racing back toward the city.

He had learned a little, not much. But he knew enough to realize that the police had to be shaken up, and quickly! The *Spider* thought he could stimulate some activity there! His face parted in a grim smile. From the seat beside him, he began to use makeup materials. He didn't need to look in the mirror. He had put on too often the disguise of the *Spider.*

THE lax discipline, typical of the entire police department, had worked into the radio room also. The manner of the telephone officer, who received calls, was desultory and there was a lapse of precious seconds in every step of the transmission of vital messages although the general purpose of the bureau was speed. The radio man had a bottle of beer at his elbow and stopped to swig and joke with the message runner before he put the call on the air. There was no incisiveness in his voice; no authority in his instructions. Ultimately, it would be communicated to the men in the cars.

One call did jar them temporarily into activity: An alarm that the *Spider* was busy in Wissouri Gardens. But as is always the case with men who make a habit of inefficiency, the attempt at effective action was badly fuddled. The radio man communicated excitement rather than stimulation to the men in patrol cars. Afterward, he went and stood at the phone board instead of staying at his post.

The sergeant stood at the door of his office in a corner and jeered at them. "You better all be good little copsies now," he said. "The big bad *Spider* has come to town." He guffawed. "Max Vellie's boys will eat him alive!"

He slammed the door of his office and frowned at the sudden realization that he had left it closed. He took a step forward, and checked as whispering laugher of mockery pierced his ears.

"Be a good little copsie," a voice bade him coldly. *"Keep your mouth shut, and your hands down."*

The sergeant swallowed a sound like a squeak, and twisted his head about. Against the wall, there was the crouched and ominous figure of the *Spider!* A tremor like a chill rippled over the sergeant's fat body. His effort to remain motionless increased the trembling.

"Go to your phone, Sergeant," the *Spider* ordered coldly, "and have the radio man plug you straight into the mike. You and I are going to make a little broadcast to all the boys. You may rehearse your speech first, to make sure you have your voice under control to my satisfaction!"

The sergeant moved like an automaton and the *Spider* glided along the wall. His gun was less than a foot from the sergeant's ear. The man cleared his throat three times, and then spoke with a faint squeaky self-consciousness:

"Plug me into the radio circuit. I got something to say to all the cars."

The *Spider*'s lips parted in a thin smile. "Do better than that when you use the phone," he suggested. "If they come in here because they suspect something—it will prove unfortunate for you."

The sergeant tried again, and there was excitement in his voice and tension, but that was all right. The *Spider* nodded at him and he picked up the phone and gave his order. In the radio room, the operator lifted a startled head and peered through the glass door of the office. He saw the sergeant with the phone to his mouth. That was all he could see. He plugged the phone into the circuit.

In the office, the *Spider* took the phone. His eyes, glittering with challenge and cold merriment, pinned the sergeant to the chair. The sergeant's face would be all he needed to see. Danger to him could come from only one direction... that glass-paneled door. The sergeant faced it.

Wentworth spoke into the phone, and it was as if the sergeant himself were talking!

"Calling all cars," he said, harshly. "Calling all cars! General alarm!"

Abruptly, he broke off the imitation of the sergeant

and the *Spider*'s cold and mocking laugher went out over the air! It was the *Spider*'s metal-edged whisper that vibrated harshly over the waves!

"This is the *Spider* speaking!" he said. "I have come to Wissouri City because criminals and racketeers have taken it over! I fight criminals. I kill criminals."

THE sergeant was sweating. His hands shook on top the desk. His eyes strained wide through the glass panel of the door, but there was no hope in them.

"As a rule," the *Spider* went on, *"honest* policemen enjoy immunity from the death that waits in my guns. But only honest police! Crooked police are worse than criminals. They are traitors. The whole city knows that the police here take their orders from Max Vellie! The *Spider* knows it. His guns know it!"

The sergeant whispered, *"God!"* He closed his eyes.

The *Spider* flung a fleeting glance toward the glass door. There was no one in sight, as yet.

"The *Spider* permits you to run one last errand for Max Vellie! Tell him that tonight... he will receive a visit from the *Spider!* Tell him his days of rule over Wissouri City are finished. Tell him that even his police force cannot protect him now!"

The sergeant's eyes popped open. "Not me, *Spider,"* he whispered. "I never took a penny off him. It's the Chief... the Chief—"

The sergeant's eyes were suddenly sly. So, the men in the outer room had taken alarm. They were coming toward the door, perhaps with guns in their fists. The *Spider* moved behind the sergeant and pressed the muzzle of his automatic into his right ear. The men outside stopped suddenly. They were stone-still, looking at the sergeant, with the *Spider*'s gun whispering of death in his ear.

"After that, gentlemen of the police," his voice was harsh with menace now, "after that—if you are wise you will begin to fulfill your sworn duty! You will crack down on gangs and racketeers! You will enforce the law!

"If the police fail to do this, hereafter you may count the *Spider* your sworn enemy! Run when you see him, traitors, and run faster than his bullets... or you will pay the full traitor's penalty for your treacheries!"

The *Spider* thrust the phone in front of the sergeant. "You may sign off, Sergeant," he said.

The sergeant's voice was a whisper of terror. "That is all," he stammered.

The phone dropped to the desk.

"Stand up, Sergeant!" the *Spider* ordered.

The sergeant lurched to his feet with shaky effort.

"Now, march to that door, Sergeant," came the

command. "No need to open it. Just march to it and stand there. I want the boys to be able to see your face when..." The *Spider* broke off with a flat and bitter laugh.

The sergeant stumbled. His voice began a feeble, quavering protest. His legs still carried him forward. When he hit the door, he stood there numbly. He seemed unaware of the door, and of the men in the outer room. He pleaded, faintly.

"I never done a thing, *Spider,*" he said. "Swear I didn't. Maybe I ain't been all that I should be. I ain't kept the boys on their toes, but that's all. It's the Chief... the Chief—"

There was no answer from behind him, not even laughter. The sergeant's shoulder muscles twitched.

"Don't shoot!" he screamed. "I swear it's the Chief!"

In desperation, he twisted about. The spot where the *Spider* had stood was empty. The whole office was empty. The *Spider* had vanished!

The sergeant's eyes rolled up. A whimpering moan came from his lips. Then he pitched forward on the floor.

It was only a faint.

CHAPTER SEVEN
A Matter of Seconds

CHIEF DRINKER, of the Wissouri City police, was enjoying himself. He leaned back in his office chair, clasped both hands behind his head. His eyes rested appreciatively on the girl who was perched on a corner of the desk.

"Look, baby," he said pompously, "you could do worse. Lots worse."

The girl took a cigarette from her mouth. She pouted her red lips to thread out the smoke, but her eyes slid sideways toward Chief Drinker and there was laughter in them.

"You reckon so?" she drawled.

Chief Drinker came forward in his chair, and reached out a pink and white hand. His voice was ponderously playful. "I got orders what to do with little girls like you," he said. "Suppose I forget those orders. Suppose, besides that—"

The girl rested the coal of her cigarette on his hand, laughed caressingly at his oath. "Maybe you don't get it, fatso," she said. *"I come from headquarters!* If I feel playful, I may play. But I'm bringing orders right now, and—"

The whirring of the phone bell interrupted her, and Chief Drinker caught it up and swore luridly.

"What?" he gasped. "What? The *Spider!* On the air! On the *police radio!* By God, I'll kill him!"

He was glaring straight ahead over the phone. He didn't see the girl's eyes grow wide, nor see her fist press hard against her red mouth. He didn't see

a hand glide past his body and press a button under the edge of the desk. It was standard equipment in police offices. It meant, *"Trace this phone call!"*

Chief Drinker was stammering into the phone, making excuses. "But, hell, Max... damn it, how could I... All right. All right. Sure, Max... I'll—"

The girl slid down off the desk. She turned and ran on tottering feet across the floor. A silken rope sailed through the air and noosed about her arms, just above the elbow. She bent forward against the strain of it and began to scream.

In Chief Drinker's ear, a voice spoke coldly: "You may pass this word to your boss, Chief. Tonight, the *Spider* will pay him a visit!"

There was a sharp knocking at the door, but it was locked. That would be routine for Chief Drinker, entertaining a gang girl.

"I would tell them," the *Spider* said softly, "that everything is all right."

Drinker tried twice to speak, but the muzzle of that automatic against his ear made it hard to think. He finally managed a weak shout, "Get the hell away from that door!"

The girl was on her knees now, still straining against the silken rope, the Web of the *Spider* which he had thrown as a lariat. She had stopped screaming. She was sobbing with terror.

Behind Chief Drinker, the *Spider*'s black crouching figure was ominous, like a shadow of death. He reached out and scooped up the phone, but it was dead. Presently, another button whirred and the *Spider* picked up the instrument.

"That call you wanted traced—"

"Yeah!" It was as if Drinker spoke.

"Well, it came from the Horse's Club." The man's voice sounded scared. "Jeez, Chief—"

Wentworth slammed up the phone. His voice rasped in Chief Drinker's ear. "I have a prejudice against killing policemen," he said. "It is a prejudice I am able to overcome on occasion. Do you think this is one of them? I have arrived in time to hear you receive orders from a gangster. Do you think that is enough reason to... overcome my prejudice?"

Drinker said, hoarsely, "You'd never get out of the building alive!"

The *Spider* laughed. "You forget, my dear Chief. You have been at work for months destroying the morale of the department. They will run when Max Vellie's men are on the prowl."

The Chief was a big man, but he seemed shrunken now. There was laxness about his mouth.

"Get to your feet!" the *Spider* rasped.

THE CHIEF staggered up, and together they walked toward the girl.

The *Spider* flipped his Web clear of her, thrust it into his cape. The girl reeled back toward the door.

"Take her arm!" the *Spider* commanded. "Now listen to me very carefully. You know something about my shooting ability, no doubt. And that of my men. My men are all about the place. You cannot move without being under the guns of one of them. They have their orders. You will walk out of this building, get into your car and drive north along Grand Avenue. You will take the girl with you. If you do anything else than this, if you say anything to your men except—'Get the hell out of my way' —you will be shot dead, and the girl, too. Am I quite clear, Chief Drinker?"

Drinker was completely unmanned. He nodded his head in a wobbly way and fumbled at the key in the door. He had the girl gripped firmly by the right arm. She shivered.

Wentworth laughed, harshly, "The first bullet will strike here!" He pressed the gun muzzle into the center of Chief Drinker's spine.

The Chief opened the door. He said, "Get the hell out of my way!"

The door closed behind him. The key turned silently in the lock. Wentworth darted to Drinker's desk and caught up a phone. There was a precinct map under the glass. He located the Horse's Club.

"Precinct Seven," he rasped into the phone. "Captain Small! Small, Chief Drinker. I want you to raid the Horse's Club with full reserves. Clean it out. Bring the men into headquarters. Max Vellie is there, and I want him. I want him, *dead or alive!*"

Small said, incredulously, "Do you mean it, Chief?"

Wentworth swore. "Listen, the squeeze is on," he said. "The Governor has given us just two weeks to clean up, or else! It's our scalps if we don't. Go in there, and do it right!"

Small's voice was excited, happy. "Boy, will I! I've been waiting for this chance!"

Wentworth slapped up the phone, glanced to the window. Inside the sill trailed the end of a length of the silken Web by which he had entered the radio room, by which he had dropped to the Chief's office. He moved toward the window. A gun crashed, and the bullet whined past his ear. The *Spider* smiled. Apparently, the Chief had overcome his terror, or else Max Vellie had sent gunmen for the job.

Wentworth took off the *Spider* cape and hat. He made swift alterations in his facial appearance. There was a small suitcase in the Chief's closet, and he appropriated it for his own use, walked to the door and unlocked it. He stepped outside... and three policemen jerked guns into line.

Wentworth glared at them. In the Chief's best manner, he snapped. "What the hell's the matter with you?"

Their jaws sagged, "Jeez, Chief—but you went downstairs, and—and you said—"

"You fools!" Wentworth howled at them. *"I said. I said—"* He fell silent. "God! That must have been the *Spider!"* he gasped. "He was up in the radio room! Get after him, damn it! *Go after him!"*

The bewildered police stumbled about as Wentworth thrust at them violently with his open hands. His back was to the light. As long as he could hold that position, they would not detect his disguise. He sent them pounding toward the stairs with hoarse yells in the police chief's tones. As soon as they were out of sight, he slipped down the back steps of the headquarters building and went to a side door.

A guard there jumped up off a stool to salute. Wentworth grunted at him in the Chief's best manner and went outside. Two minutes later, he heard gun shots crash out behind him, but there was no pursuit. He wondered grimly if the Chief had been able to reconvince his men of their error!

CHIEF DRINKER was apoplectic with rage when finally he got the courage to return to police headquarters. The girl had fled at the first opportunity and Drinker did not even try to detain her. The *Spider* had played hell. Everywhere, the police were edgy, nervous; their faces pale. They were on their toes as Drinker had never seen them before. They would be hard to control, for a while.

Back in his office, he was harassed by a constant and furious whirring of many phones. He cut them out... except for one. He dared not cut out the phone on which Max Vellie would call! That phone was whirring, too. He picked up the instrument, and the strident, furious voice of the gang leader bellowed in his ear.

"No, damn it, I didn't!" Drinker howled. "I didn't order the raid. The *Spider* sneaked up behind me and I chased him out of my office. He disappeared. I mean, he just vanished. Maybe he doubled back and gave the order, but I didn't. Put Captain Small on the phone. *I'll* talk to him. Yes, Max. Yes, Max, I will right away. Yes, Max. Yes."

He caught up another phone. "Send a raiding party to the Monterrey Hotel. Man there named Wentworth. Richard Wentworth. Suspected of being the *Spider.* He's got a wad of money so you'll have to go a little slow, maybe—if we're mistaken, but sew up the room and look for evidence!"

The raiding party raced across Wissouri City in two cars. They picked up the house detective at the Monterrey and went in a compact wedge along the corridor toward Wentworth's room, where the two drugged policemen had been left. The key turned soundlessly in the lock, and they pushed open the door.

Detective John Gibbons was on his feet with a pint bottle of whiskey in his hand. His partner slept, his head thrown back, on the divan. He was out cold. In a chair nearby sat Richard Wentworth. His eyes were bleary and red and he lifted a maudlin hand to the officers.

"Come on in," he cried. "The more the merrier. John, see if there isn't another bottle you can open for your pals."

The lieutenant in charge stalked up to Gibbons. "What the hell goes on here?" he demanded.

John Gibbons enunciated very carefully, "Mr. Wentworth here is buying drinks. Very good drinks."

"How long you been here?"

Gibbons frowned and then smiled happily. "All day," he said. "We been here all day. It's some party, man, a pip!"

Behind deliberately reddened eyes, Wentworth hid a cold smile. Let them try and break down that alibi!

The hotel radio squawked with an indignant voice and now that the greetings were over, the words became distinct. Chief Drinker was making a speech over the city radio.

"The *Spider* has dared to challenge the police of Wissouri City," he cried, and his voice trembled with very genuine rage. "We will teach this big city crook that the police of Wissouri City cannot be trifled with! We warn the *Spider!* Leave town, or you are a dead man!"

Wentworth nodded somberly, lifted a half emptied pint bottle. "Here's to Chief Drinker," he said. "May the best man win!"

The lieutenant scowled, "What the hell do you mean by that?"

Wentworth looked at him owlishly. "Can't a man drink to Drinker?" he asked. He laughed. "Come on, boys, drink a little drink to Drinker!"

The lieutenant swore. "All right, get out of here," he ordered his men. "We haven't got time to fool around with a drunken playboy. We got to get this *Spider.*"

The men filed out slowly, and the door closed behind them, loudly. Wentworth's lips parted in a slow smile. It was a cold smile, and full of menace. He had stopped the police, but Max Vellie would not be fooled. He had just time for a nap before the *Spider* kept his appointment with the criminal boss of Wissouri City!

CHAPTER EIGHT
Taken for a Ride!

FOUR MEN sauntered together into the lobby of the Monterrey Hotel. They walked close together and without glancing aside. People got out of their purposeful way. The house detective spotted them, swore, and started forward. One of the four men peeled off and walked straight toward him.

He stopped in front of the house detective. His hands were in his coat pockets and his eyes were just visible under the brim of his hat.

"You ain't interested," he told the house man flatly. "Let's take a walk."

The house detective kept his hands flat against his thighs. He turned round stiffly and walked, a little ahead and to the right of the man. They turned a corner into a dim corridor. They went into a washroom. In response to a curt order, the detective opened the door to one of the booths.

He must have caught a half-glimpse of the blow aimed at his head. He ducked and the blackjack caught him full on the temple. He gasped, twisted sideways, crumpled against the wall. The crook walked out and threw the lock on the booth. Steel letters on the catch now read *"Engaged."*

The thug laughed, silently. He went back to the lobby and stood teetering on heels and toes. He had a toothpick between his lips. He sucked at it and kept an eye on the elevator doors. His three companions had disappeared upward.

In the third-floor corridor, the three men walked in the same purposeful, compact formation. They stopped before a door, and one of the men used a key. It made no sound at all, and they slid through into darkness. Inside, they waited through long seconds while their eyes became accustomed to darkness. From the second room of the suite, there came the sound of heavy breathing. The place smelled of whiskey.

Two of the men went toward the other room, while the third stood guard at the entrance. They went through and stood over the bed. Wentworth was sprawled loosely across it. He seemed to be sleeping heavily. The two drew guns.

"Why not do it right here?" one breathed.

"Orders!" the other said.

He leaned over, caught Wentworth by the foot and suddenly hauled him off the bed. He hit the floor heavily, cried out, sat up in a dazed way. Flashlights blazed into his eyes.

"Come on, punk," the leader said flatly. "We're going to take a little ride. You made a date with Vellie, and he likes to keep his dates."

They hauled Wentworth unceremoniously to his feet, and fanned him. He carried no guns. They thrust him into the outer room and one of the gangsters clipped him behind the ear with his gun muzzle. Wentworth went to his knees. They threw his coat and hat at him, waited until he put them on. Then the three of them left the suite.

Wentworth muttered, "Yon can't get away with this."

A gun clipped him again, in the same place. It hurt. He reeled and they jostled him with hard shoulders. After that, he did not speak. His eyes were veiled under lowered lids. There was no anger in them, only a calm waiting. This was something out of the past, as brutal as Nazi occupation. Wentworth wondered briefly, as he had before, if the *Heil Hitler* boys had learned their technique from underworld mobs. It was a fleeting thought deliberately pursued. Wentworth was having a little trouble to keep his temper. He was not afraid.

It was no surprise to him that the elevator boy kept his eyes turned rigidly away. Things like this used to occur in gang-ridden cities, but they had been cleaned up thoroughly by the F.B.I. Now, the federal men were busy with the defense of the country against spies and saboteurs. The rats were playing because the cat was busy elsewhere... and what they were doing was as vicious as any sabotage; as any Fifth Column. They and their criminal allies, were suborning treachery in government and undermining the people's trust in their elected officials.

THERE were few persons in the lobby. Wentworth spotted the fourth guard at once. The man kept his post while they moved across toward the doors. And then Wentworth felt tension race through him! A girl had just come in through the door of the hotel; a lovely girl, quietly but modishly dressed, with calmly determined eyes beneath a smooth white brow. It was Nita van Sloan!

Her eyes flicked toward Wentworth and widened slightly. Wentworth clenched a fist against his thigh, moved it slightly away. Nita turned aside from their path and did not look again. They were too familiar with situations which required lack of recognition between them for her to be startled after that first glance. But Wentworth felt anguish mount within him. It had been the one bright spot in this so far losing fight that Nita van Sloan was in a region of safety. Now, she had deliberately walked into trouble! He had been expecting his comrade, Ram Singh, to drive the car out for his use. But Nita—

He was across the walk, being thrust into a car. The gun caught him again on the skull.

"Get behind the wheel, punk, and drive carefully," the leader ordered. "And I mean carefully. This gun has a hair trigger, and if you went over a bump too fast, it might go off!"

The gun was cocked. Its muzzle pointed into Wentworth's body just above the waist. The other two men climbed into the back.

"Get going, punk!"

They weren't going to wait for the fourth man, and Nita was in the lobby of the hotel. If she had betrayed herself that first, startled moment—

The gun ground into his side. Wentworth punched the starter button, tooled the car out from the curb.

"Turn right," the leader ordered.

There were other directions and Wentworth found

that they were leaving the river behind, boring out toward the fiat country that surrounded the town.

"You mentioned Vellie," he said, and managed to put an accent of fear into his voice. "Are we going to see him?"

"The big shot don't bother with punks," the man sneered.

"I'd like to see Vellie," Wentworth said mildly.

The man laughed, "He'd like to see Vellie!" he repeated, and the men in the back seat laughed, too, sneeringly.

Talking to them, Wentworth gradually increased the speed of the car. Suddenly, he jammed on the gas. The machine leaped forward in a wild surge. The leader yelped, thrust his gun forward. Wentworth didn't look at him.

"I'm going to see Vellie," he said. "If you want to shoot, just remember what will happen at this speed. We are now doing sixty."

"Slow down!" the leader ordered, harshly.

Wentworth whipped the wheel over and took a corner on two skidding tires; he did that again. He had reversed their direction. The gunman lifted his gun to crack Wentworth on the skull with it, and Wentworth swerved twice in swift succession. The man braced himself in his corner and swore.

"All right, punk," he said. "All right. You gotta slow down sometime."

Wentworth's tone was mild. "Certainly, or I couldn't see Vellie."

The man beside him was furious with anger. Wentworth could feel the killing readiness of the others like a cold weight against his neck. Death was very near; as near as the first moment he should slow down by the slightest fraction. Wentworth was not careless of that threat, but he had considered it before he had acted. He was deathly cool, but he could not prevent that feeling of tension across his shoulders, the tautness of his scalp.

The car howled at mounting speed along the outskirts of the city. A policeman leaped out and skirled his whistle. Wentworth missed him by a yard, heard the whistle start again... and stop.

"He recognized your car," Wentworth said, quietly.

The killer beside him kept his eyes on Wentworth and, alternately, on the speedometer. His revolver was ready in his fist.

"Cops can't save you," he said, flatly.

WENTWORTH conned his mental map of the city. He had a definite goal. Max Vellie had escaped danger in the raid on the Horse's Club, as was to be expected. That had been only a device to shake police and gang morale, and to anger Vellie to the point of taking overt action with his own men.

"Vellie is on his houseboat, of course," Wentworth said quietly, "or didn't you know he had a houseboat on the river?"

The killer said, "Go on talking. You gotta slow down sometime."

"You don't mind?" Wentworth said casually. "Thank you. Yes, Vellie has a houseboat on the river. It is obviously a very large one because it requires four heavy outboard motors to propel it. Vellie should have been more careful in his choice of men to murder, when he tried to trap me on my arrival in town. It was easy to find out what Jim Riley's last job was. You don't use speedboats in your gang work, therefore it has to be a houseboat. A very large one. There aren't enough of the larger ones around to make it hard to locate Vellie's."

"Wise guy, hunh?"

"Oh, yes!" Wentworth whipped over the wheel, made a brake-and-throttle whirl around a corner. He was racing along the waterfront now. A steamer, brightly lighted, was speeding downriver with the current. Close in shore, there was a small houseboat tied up. It was gay with lights and a snatch of music flicked to their ears as the car sped past.

The car surged over a bridge that spanned a river branch, and lifted at the crest. It swept down the far rise and the needle wavered above seventy. Wentworth held it there. Ahead now, he could see the houseboat which his inquiries had located. It was a small palace afloat... a literal house on the water. Even those four powerful motors would serve to give it no more than a few miles an hour of speed.

Beside him, the killer's tension increased. He had his gun poised, his finger already tight on the trigger.

"Get ready!" the leader snapped.

"When he slows down, we all let him have it together."

Wentworth made no answer to that. He jockeyed the car up to eighty. The houseboat swept past and, a half mile beyond it, there was a dark wharf that thrust out into the river for a hundred yards. Wentworth's lips were grimly set, and the muscles bulged faintly along his jaw. His hands were alert on the wheel, but he gave no warning of his intention.

Suddenly, as the wharf whirled abreast, he whipped over the wheel and jammed on the brakes hard! The car heeled about in a screaming skid, and Wentworth stomped on the throttle again! The car rocked violently, wove and careened as he hurled it straight at the dead end wharf!

There were screams from the men in the car. The killer beside him took one startled look at what was happening. In that instant, Wentworth acted. He seized the man's gun-wrist with both hands and threw himself sideways toward the floor. The weapon blasted, but its bullets whanged harmlessly through the floor boards.

The careening car swerved wildly. Its front wheel glanced off the stringpiece that edged the wharf. It skidded about, broadside to its previous course. The rear wheel caught a steel capstan and the machine leaped, whirling, into the air. Falling, it struck the wharf end with the two right-hand tires. They exploded. The car bounced, still spinning. It made two complete turns in the air and hit the black water of the river right side up, throwing a great splash.

The tremendous momentum still carried it along. The car skated across the water, churning it to a froth. It settled more deeply. The drag of the river had it suddenly and it flopped over on its left side and went out of sight beneath the flood.

CHAPTER NINE
Vellie's Reception

MAX VELLIE'S guests made considerable noise in the big salon which took up most of the houseboat's main deck. Too much noise for them to pay any attention to the crashing of the sedan Wentworth had driven. The fireplace at one end of the salon, glowing with a coalgrate, shed no peace. A radio as large and crashing as a juke box filled the place with furious music.

In a corner, two women drank and screamed at each other above the racket. In another corner, Max Vellie played stubborn solitaire. He was seated with his back in a solid wall corner, the table before him. Now and again he lifted eyes that were angry and vicious.

He looked at the windows of the salon in rotation and watched his hired guards go past. If one were a half-breath late, a tension began to grow through him. His hand crawled toward a gun nested under his arm. He wasn't afraid; not exactly. But he was as dangerous as a shedding snake. It was the first time in many months of increasing dominion over Wissouri City that anything had threatened his absolute power. And one man had done it!

Max Vellie smiled with a harsh twist of his lips. That made his job easier; rub out the one man and things fell back into their pattern. It would take a little pushing and shoving. He might have to bump Chief Drinker.

His eyes narrowed a little as he considered Drinker. It was all right to have a dumb punk for a front. Drinker was as harmless as two percent beer.

But if guys like the *Spider* were coming around, then Max had a right to expect protection from Drinker. What the hell were the police for, if they couldn't wipe out meddlers like the *Spider*?

Max Vellie sat with his thick palms pressed down on the scattered cards and let the anger and the resentment grow within him. By God, he'd have protection from Chief Drinker, or he'd get another police chief in his place! He was boss here. He... he winced inwardly and glanced toward the dark door which, at his right, opened into the only other cabin on the main deck. A flickering slow red light came out of the room. Max Vellie tongued his upper lip.

A guard stepped in front of one of the windows and made a fist with his right hand, brought it down once on the sill. Max Vellie nodded, and his eyes brightened. One of the boys he had sent after the *Spider* was coming to report. But why only one?

Max lifted his voice in a shout: "Cut off that damned radio!"

The silence that fell was heavy and sudden. Through it, the hollow sound of slapping waves came, and there was the hoot of a steamer's whistle. The boat shifted a little at its heavy quadruple anchors.

There was a waiting while in which the splash and creak of oars became more and more clear, then the thud of a boat bumping against the hull. Presently a door opened and a man came in. He had a truculent roll to his shoulders, and his head was pulled down so that his eyes showed only as a glitter under his hat brim. He walked up to the table where Max Vellie sat and put his knuckles down on it.

Vellie said, "Well?"

"He's gone," the gunman said.

"What do you mean?" Vellie's voice rose harshly. "Spit it out, Craik."

Craik said, "We took him all right. I knocked out the house dick, and the other three went up and took him. They got him in the car and I followed along, like you said, as a safety man."

"Are you telling me he got away?"

Craik said, "Jeez, Boss, leave me tell you. I don't think he got away. He was driving and he started going like all hell. I guess the others was afraid to shoot while they was going fast. Well, he came down here to the river and drove right off the wharf, about a half mile up the river. Nobody got out, so far's I could see. He just drove the whole damned car into the river at about eighty miles an hour, sank it with himself and all three of them still in it. I drove right onto the wharf, with the tommy gun, ready in case anybody should come up. But nobody did, far as I could see."

MAX VELLIE began to swear in a cold hard monotone. He pushed to his feet. Craik fell back a step. "Jeez, Chief, what could I do?" he asked. "My job was to hang around with the tommy in case he made a break for it. I did, and he never showed. He was in that car when it went over into the river. He's sure as hell dead."

Somebody laughed on the deck and Max Vellie yelled furiously, "Stop that damned racket!"

It didn't sound like the *Spider* laughing. He didn't think it did.

"You get up on top," Vellie ordered harshly. "You get that searchlight going and take your tommy with you. If any boat comes near us, blast it. You damned fool, the *Spider*'s got more lives than a cat. "

Craik said, "Jeez, chief—

Vellie hit him with a looping overhand right. It smacked him high on the cheekbone and twisted him half around. He stumbled toward the door, jerked it open and went outside. Vellie stood with his fists clenched and his breath making hoarse noises in his nose. His lips were clamped so tightly, there was white about them—and a trace of scarlet.

One of the girls teetered toward him. It was the same one who had been in Drinker's office. "Hell, Maxie, we aren't afraid of that guy. One man!"

"Who said I was afraid?" he asked harshly. "What you don't know about these rackets would fill a library. Or a morgue."

The girl smiled at him across the table. "Let's have fun then," she said "How about some more drinks?"

Max Vellie looked her over slowly and contemptuously. "Look, Frankie," he said. "I'm the one who says what we do and when. Get it? Keep your trap buttoned or I'll toss you into the drink. You bungled that job at headquarters today. One more slip like that, and you go out the way they all go out."

The girl blanched. "Sure, Maxie," she said. "Sure. I had Drinker going when the *Spider* barged in. You don't need to worry about Drinker double-crossing you. He ain't got sense enough." She sidled around the table and Max let her get close before he slapped her.

He strode toward the fireplace and felt a little better. He had reestablished his opinion of himself by slapping around two underlings. The girl's terrified face made him feel happy inside. He'd put a little hell-fear into Drinker and get things back in shape. He'd feel better if he could bump Drinker off. He looked again uneasily toward the dark room where the red light flickered. From where he stood now, he could see the altar. There was that damned seven-headed snake with the red flame burning on

---

(Facing page) The car went out of sight in the black water.

each side of it. All right to scare the gang with, but it didn't scare *him,* Max Vellie.

A guard stopped at a window again and showed his fist, hit with it twice, and showed his fist again. Vellie shouted at him, "Who is it?"

The man lifted a hand to his mouth like a bottle and tipped back his head. Vellie grinned wolfishly. He laughed, harshly.

"All right," he yelled, "All right."

Drinker was at least following orders. Only Max had wanted the *Spider*'s body here to chuck at Drinker's feet. It would make things a whole lot easier if he were sure the *Spider* was out of the way.

Max Veilie stepped through the door into the darkened room. He whispered, "You there?"

The voice that answered was not identifiable as either man or woman. It was a whisper, "Who you going to kill?"

"Craik," Vellie said. "He's getting careless and I want to give Drinker a lesson. You all set?"

There was a giggle in the darkness and that was the only answer. Vellie came out of there and found himself sponging at his forehead with his handkerchief. It was good stuff, but damn it, he didn't like it!

WHEN Drinker came in, Vellie was standing in front of the fireplace, glaring. "You sure as hell messed things up today!" he said, angrily. "Nobody will go near the Horse's Club after that raid. Now we gotta start a new lay. The rich boys aren't going to gamble where there's a chance of a raid."

Drinker said, soothingly, "I know, I know, Max. That damned *Spider* pulled a fast one. He won't do that again. I got triple guards on police headquarters."

Vellie laughed, and it was a sneer. "You get paid to put triple guards on headquarters!" he said. "You do your job, or I'll get me somebody that will! Maybe you don't know what happens to guys who get careless in this racket?"

Drinker waved his hands excitedly.

"I'm not careless: How in hell could anybody guess the *Spider* would come in like that?"

Vellie said, coldly, "It's your job to guess. I pay for protection and I want it." He raised his voice. "Send Craik down here and put another man in his place! I'm going to show you, Drinker, what happens to guys who get careless in this racket."

Drinker said, "Now, Max—"

"Shut up!"

Craik came in stiffly. His cheek had a dark red mark on it, and his eye was swollen. It was going to be black, if he lived long enough. He looked at Drinker with hostile eyes, focused on Vellie. The gang leader waited. His glare was cold.

He jerked his head toward the dark room of the shrine. "Go in there," he said. "You got some questions to answer, and you better make it good."

Craik turned gray. "Hell, Max," he whined. "I did just like you told me, and—"

Vellie lifted his shoulders. "What have I got to do with that?" he said. "You know I'm only the boss of Wissouri City. Go in there and talk to the big boss."

Craik said, "Hell, Max—"

Two guards stepped through the door at Vellie's gesture. They took Craik and tossed him bodily through the door into the dark room of the shrine.

"This is going to be good," Vellie whispered to Chief Drinker. "Only it's not so good if you're the guy inside. Look out you don't get tossed in, too!"

Craik was a stiff, terrified figure against the red dim light of the shrine. The flames began to push upward and throw out more illumination. The red eyes of the seven-headed snake glittered. Craik twisted his head around on his shoulder and the two gunmen stood at the door, weapons ready.

He cried, "Max. Listen, Max—"

A voice boomed hollowly, trumpeting out of the darkness. *"On your knees!"*

Craik shivered. The stiffness went out of him and he slumped down on his knees.

Drinker said, nervously, "What's all this mumbo-jumbo for?"

Vellie looked at him. "Want to go in and talk to the snake?" he asked smoothly.

Drinker shivered. Craik was on his knees, moaning. The trumpet voice belled at him again:

"Have you dishonored the Snake?"

Craik said, "No, no! I did what I was told. I swear I did what I was told!"

"Did you succeed for the honor of the Snake?"

Drinker moved a little closer to Max Vellie. The women were huddled in a corner, together. Their eyes were wide, glassy.

Craik stammered, "I did my job. It was the others that failed."

There was no answer to that. Craik lifted his head and his voice rose, too. "I did my job! It was the others that failed! I swear it! Look, I'll explain what I had to do—"

The trumpet voice broke in upon him. *"For failure, there is only one reward!"*

CRAIK screamed. He tried to get to his feet and he got as far as one knee. His head wrenched back and he couldn't scream anymore. Nothing was touching him; nothing showed in the room except the high dancing light of the shrine flames, but Craik was strangling!

He plucked at his throat with his hands. He fought against something that no one could see, but which was, nevertheless, choking him to death! His eyes bulged. His tongue was bitten between champing teeth. He fell forward on the floor, writhed for a while, and was still.

The flames danced higher and higher until hell's own glare shone out of the shrine room. The snakes seemed alive in the dancing shadows. On the floor, Craik ceased to struggle and was still. For a while the dance of the flames continued, and then it subsided. The light slowly flickered back to normal.

"Throw the carcass overboard," Vellie ordered coldly, and turned back to Drinker. "Would you like to explain to the Snake how come you failed today?" he asked, flatly.

Drinker pulled at his collar as if it strangled him. "Look, Max," his voice was pleading. "Look—I'll have the *Spider* behind bars inside of a day, or else dead. You don't need to worry about him anymore. I promise you, inside of a day."

The door was open and there was a splash as the body was thrown overboard. There was that splash and then there was some laughter. It was just a whisper of sound, flat and metallic, mocking; sinister as night.

Max Vellie whirled toward the open door... and the lights went out!

Max Vellie shouted hoarsely. The two women screamed, and Chief Drinker began to run blindly. He crashed into a wall and recoiled. He fell over a table and carried it to the floor. There was still light in the room, from the flame-flicker in the shrine, from the fireplace. It was pale red light and across it again and again, leaping shadows moved in odd design.

Drinker struck the wall again and crouched down beside it. He covered his face with his hands against the leaping shadows that crossed and recrossed the fire lane. The women were still screaming, but he couldn't hear Max Vellie's shouts. He couldn't hear Max Vellie at all.

The lights flared on as suddenly as they had gone off. There was the sound of running feet along the decks. The guards lunged into the room, stood in all the doors. Guns were in their fists, and they looked about.

"Where's Max?" one of them asked hoarsely. He lifted his voice in a shout, *"Hey, Max!"*

There was silence then, while they waited for an answer. The answer came, but it was not Max who made it. There was again that thin and mocking laughter in the night, and then something flicked into the middle of the room. No one saw it until it settled in the middle of the floor, a white oblong like a visiting card.

They left it lying there, for a moment, and then one of the guards walked toward it cautiously. He picked it up and then gasped an oath and dropped it. As it fell this time, it turned face up and there was the gleaming, brilliant red... of the *Seal of the Spider!*

"God," Drinker whispered, "God... *he said he would pay Vellie a visit!"*

CHAPTER TEN
Trail's End

THE terror which the *Spider* had spread among criminals served him well once more. While the men within the houseboat were paralyzed with dread, while they moved fearfully toward the doors to make their search, the *Spider* ran lightly to the rowboat which had brought him down river. The unconscious gang leader, Max Vellie, already had been deposited in its bottom. Wentworth shoved off and was immediately swallowed up in the shadows. The gangsters would overcome their fear in a few moments, but they would find no boats in which to reach shore! By the time they overcame that obstacle, Wentworth must be far away!

Wentworth's wet clothing made him cold, despite the softness of the night wind. He sculled silently toward the pier head a hundred yards away, and the exercise warmed him slowly. But he was less than halfway to the protection of the wharf when the searchlight atop the houseboat licked out over the water! The *Spider* whipped out a revolver he had captured from one of the overpowered guards. The shot would reveal his whereabouts, but he could not afford to have that light thrown on him! He wore no disguise!

Before he could shoot, there was a gunshot from the pier itself! The bullet sped true... and the searchlight was smashed! A grim smile straightened Wentworth's lips. He ignored the houseboat after that though they sent a deluge of bullets toward the pier itself. That shot could mean only one thing: Nita van Sloan had caught his signal in

DRINKER

THE WEASEL

The Snake

the lobby of the hotel. And she had been wise enough to spot Craik and follow him, rather than trail the death car itself!

Minutes later, Nita helped him haul Vellie up to the pier and they sped away in one of the powerful but dilapidated-looking coupés which the *Spider* used.

"They've already called for help... from the police," Nita told him curtly. "They have a shortwave radio aboard. I picked it up on ours in the car."

She twisted swiftly away from the waterfront with a skill that showed she, too, had learned well the map of the city. Siren wails sounded from three directions. Nita kept the radio turned on, drove steadily at moderate speed. Vellie was in the trunk.

She flashed a smile at Wentworth. "You gave me a bad moment when you crashed that car off the pier," she said.

Wentworth said, drily, "I gave myself a bad moment, too. We were almost on the river bottom before I could wriggle out of the window. It's pretty deep at that point."

A police car, running silently, slashed out of a side street. A flashlight blazed squarely in their faces, and Nita swerved deliberately, put on brakes.

"What are you trying to do?" she called fiercely out of the window. "Trying to wreck me?"

"A dame!" she heard a policeman mutter. "Nuts, let's get going."

The car raced on and Nita resumed her steady progress toward the city proper. "The police aren't on their toes here," she said, without excitement. "We wouldn't have got away with that in New York. Things are pretty bad there, Dick. Kirkpatrick spends almost twenty-four hours a day at headquarters. I've never known such an outbreak of lawlessness."

"Nationwide," Wentworth said, shortly. "But Kirk can't accomplish anything by tackling the crimes themselves. You can't cure pneumonia by treating the headache. The hotel is useless now, Nita. Wentworth is washed up here, as Wentworth."

Nita said, quietly, "I've rented an apartment. It has a private entrance."

Wentworth laughed softly. "I've needed you here, Nita. You've anticipated my every requirement."

Nita smiled and threw him a quick glance. "I had a most excellent teacher." The police sirens were behind them now.

In the apartment, Wentworth subjected Vellie to the truth drug in an effort to learn the identity of the overlord of the gangs. Even under drugs, though, Vellie was too terrified to talk; or else he did not know. The fear of the overlord had seeped deeply into his subconscious. Wentworth learned only the whereabouts of the secret headquarters of Vellie's own gang.

"Your books are there?" Wentworth asked harshly. "Yes."

"Where?"

Vellie mumbled, and his face twisted with fear. *"Where?"* Wentworth insisted.

Vellie fought a moveless struggle within himself and, at the end, his head sagged forward. He was in coma.

Wentworth smiled grimly toward Nita. "Not much, but enough!" he said. "Those books will wreck Vellie's gang, once they're in the hands of the F.B.I., and perhaps give us a clue to the overlord himself!"

THERE were three guards in the headquarters of the Vellie mob. It was an old house on the edge of the business district. Once it had been a lavish home, but now a gasoline station had bitten off a corner of its once extensive lawn and a row of brick store and tenement structures jostled the pealing paint of its side. A Board and Rooms sign perched in the window, but no one ever succeeded in renting a room there.

The three guards were jumpy tonight. The grapevine had brought them word of the happenings of the evening. The Snake had bumped Craik for failure, and three good guys had been killed by the *Spider.* They didn't know that Vellie had been kidnapped, but they sensed panic in the voice that gave them their orders. They prowled restlessly around the building and longed for their relief.

One of them was peering out the front door when a darting shadow of a man ducked into the gate. He jerked out his gun, crouched back from the door... and then swore in cold hatred. The man came in through the door and stood looking at the guard with small wicked eyes. He grinned and his teeth were narrow, the canines pointed.

"I do not know why," he said, in a squeaky voice, "but you mugs don't seem to like me."

"Some day, Weasel," the guard snarled, "I'm going to plug you and let on it was a mistake."

The Weasel laughed, and the sound was shrill, a giggle. "It would be a mistake, for you, Legs. A bad mistake. Get the guys together. I got a message."

The guards came sullenly and hatred glittered in their eyes as they regarded the small man with his weazened, animal face. "The Boss says the *Spider* is coming here, probably tonight," the Weazel said. "Let him get in. Take posts at the phones. Bullets can't reach you in the booths. There'll be some more punks here, too. You'll get your orders over the phones."

The three men looked at the Weasel and now their hatred was complicated by fear. Legs dragged the back of his hand across his forehead. "We gotta let him get *in!"* he said.

The Weasel giggled at him. "Do *you* want to stop him, Legs?"

Legs snarled at him, then the men went to the posts they had been assigned. Soon another six men came into the house and were placed in position. Two of them carried a huge crate. They set it down in a closet and wrung their hands.

"God that thing is cold!" one said.

"Take your posts!" the Weasel ordered. "The *Spider* will be here any minute. When he goes out again, he'll be stiff. Stiff and cold!"

The Weasel giggled again.

FROM the roof of the nearest tenement, the *Spider* surveyed the house that was gang headquarters. There was movement within the building and a few dim lights; more of both than he had expected. The *Spider* smiled grimly and, by means of his Web, slid down to the steep roof of the gang house beside a dormer window. He took no extra precautions; did not need to. The *Spider* always assumed the possibility of a trap.

His exploration of the dormer window located an alarm contact. He cut a small section out of the glass and fixed the alarm so it could not ring. Afterward, he climbed in. At the scuttle which gave ingress to the top floor hallway, the *Spider* stopped for a full five minutes. At the end of that time, he had spotted the whereabouts of five men in the house. They were patrolling.

The *Spider* shook his head as he dropped soundlessly into the house proper and prospected about. Five men was too large a guard for ordinary purposes; too small if they were laying a trap for the *Spider*. There must be others here whom he had not located. Wentworth found what he wanted. This house had been built in the era when the utmost in luxury was a laundry chute that went from top floor to basement. He found the chute and, moments later, was gliding silently down it with the able assistance of his Web!

At the first floor level, he checked his descent and looped the silken rope about his foot. Rapidly then, he drew out a listening device and attached its suction disc to the door. Its thin panel made an excellent diaphragm. He could hear the sound of roughened breathing, close by. A faint smile stirred the *Spider*'s lips. He flipped open the door and struck, in one swift movement. His gun muzzle caught the crouched guard on the nape of the neck. Without a sound, he slumped to the floor. An earphone, clamped over his head, swung loose.

Wentworth rapidly gagged and bound the man, looped his Web under the man's arms and allowed him to dangle in the laundry chute. It was rudimentary concealment, but at least no prowler would stumble over the body. He caught up the earphone then, and held it to his ear. The wire was alive, but silent. He frowned at the device. Was this a listening post? Were there dictographs hidden over the house to pick up any sound?

The *Spider* let the instrument down carefully, so that it made no sound. He slipped out through the door. His movements were always silent. The watch-system scarcely constituted an obstacle to him. He had left behind the butler's pantry and was in what once had been a dining room. His robes blended with the shadows. He was nearly invisible. To most men, the search of a guarded house would have seemed an impossible task, but Wentworth was not going about it blindly. He wanted the books of the gang, and he had very definite ideas about their probable hiding place. Max Vellie would have wanted to guard them, also, against treachery within the gang; therefore would have chosen a place

to which his men were unlikely to go in his absence.

Somewhere here, there should be a shrine of the Snake, where Wentworth expected to find the books hidden!

For when Vellie's men failed, they were sent to the shrine... *to die!*

The *Spider* was quite sure that death would be waiting for him there, too! He had to take that chance!

HE GLIDED across the dining room and, from the shadows beside the entrance, sent his gaze questing along the corridor, across into the old drawing room. From it came a red flicker of lights! That, then, was his goal. But there would be watchers in the hallway, though he had not spotted any one of them.

Deftly, Wentworth swept off cape and black hat. He tucked them in a small bundle under his left arm. Then, a gun hanging carelessly in his right hand, he stepped openly across the hallway. He did not hurry, but took the time to glance guardedly about. The lights were dim. The watchers might well mistake him for one of the patrol. Certainly, he did not look like the *Spider!*

The flicker of lights came from a deep alcove in the back wall of the room; what would have been the library. Wentworth moved toward it, cape and hat once more on. He was looking at the shrine of the seven-headed Snake!

Quietly, his ears acutely alert, he surveyed the small room. There was an altar, covered in a black cloth. On each side of it, censers sent up small twisting spires of flame. That was all, except for the upreared heads of the brass Snake, their red eyes glittering. The wall was covered with a black cloth behind it.

With a quick stride, Wentworth whipped up the altar cloth. The barren legs of a table showed, nothing else, except for two fine wires which went through the floor. There was only one other possible place... the wall behind the altar. Wentworth pulled aside the cloth. In a corner was a door that apparently led into the hall. The wall itself was paneled in squares of old wood. With a satisfied nod, Wentworth studied those squares of wood. One of them undoubtedly opened to reveal a safe in which the books would be stored. But it would take time to locate the right one.

Wentworth pivoted about as a sound of movement caught his ear. Nothing showed in the entrance to the drawing room. The *Spider* crouched behind the altar, waiting. But his mind was busy with the problem of locating the safe. Those fine wires leading down from the altar might mean something. If they connected with the snake in some way... the *Spider*'s eyes narrowed, as he inspected the snake more closely. Curious that the necks of two of the heads should show more tarnish than the other five! Wentworth laughed silently, gripped those two necks with his hands.

Behind the wall cloth, there was a click... then a bulge in the hanging. The secret door had been opened!

But even as Wentworth turned, he saw a steel panel slide into place over the entrance of the alcove! All light was cut out save that from the torches and suddenly they, too, were extinguished! At the same moment, Wentworth caught a faint hissing sound... like the blowing of an angry snake!

Wentworth flicked light from a pocket flash, and his breath sucked in sharply. His ears had not tricked him. There were snakes in the room, seven of them! They were *kraiks,* as his keen eyes told him instantly. Their fangs brought death within seven seconds!

But the hissing went on, and it did not come from the snakes. The hissing went on... and there was a stronger scent of incense! At the same instant, Wentworth felt a sharp constriction of his throat. He knew then what had killed the gunman, Craik, in the Snake shrine on the houseboat.

It was poison gas!

CHAPTER ELEVEN
The Trap Develops

INSTANTLY, Wentworth whipped out a silken scarf and saturated it with fluid from two phials carried in the leather girdle about his waist. He bound the scarf over his nose and mouth, tightly. He wasted no time on the snakes; no time hunting for the gas inlet. He ducked behind the arras and, flashlight propped on the floor, studied the safe.

Relief flooded him as he inspected it. Apparently, Vellie had not bothered to install a new safe, but was still using the one left in the house by the previous owner. The *Spider* attached his listening disc to the face of the safe and set swiftly to work on the dial. His concentration was absolute now. He knew that he had a space of minutes before the gas would penetrate behind the arras. After that, he had protection in the silken scarf which he wore as a gas mask. So far as the snakes were concerned, he doubted that any of them would stalk him. Snakes were generally harmless, if not threatened, with a few rare exceptions. The *kraik* was not one of those.

Wentworth knew the pattern of the tumblers in the safe. That was part of his training. It took him less than three minutes to turn out the combination. He whipped open the door, and there was a sharp hiss of released gas! Wentworth held his breath, rapidly snatched out the books, stripped every compartment and knotted the contents together

with a strand of the Web. Not until then did he move toward the side door of the room which opened into the hall.

He breathed shallowly through the neutralizing folds of the scarf. A lockpick soon unfastened the door. Hand on the knob, books tucked under his arm, Wentworth paused to draw an automatic. As he checked, a thread of light, as brilliant as steel, slitted in through the keyhole. The crack at the bottom let in a wedge of light. They were waiting for him out there!

The *Spider* looked down at the light. In order to throw that pattern, it would have to be directly across from the door, and at the level of the keyhole! Wentworth smiled thinly. He presented the muzzle of his automatic to the thinnest-part of the door... and squeezed the trigger. He did not wait to check results. In the same instant, he whipped the door open and leaped out of the doorway!

The light was out, but new illumination sprang instantly in the corridor. It was the flare of many guns! Their bullets crashed and tore at the door; at the frame of the entrance. Two pocked the floor. But the *Spider* had gone through fast and low! He rolled, got his shoulders on the floor... and his gun blasted. In that first flicker of exchanging lead, he slammed two bullets home behind the gun-flame which spotted the ambushers.

Instantly, he lunged toward the spot where they had been. Behind him, the floor was clawed to bits by screaming lead. There was a door ahead of the *Spider;* one door and one only. He was plunging into a dead end. He knew, in that grim minute, that the trap had been deliberately designed for that purpose. The wall of flame from the front part of the hall had been impenetrable; the guard to the rear, weak.

For an instant, the *Spider* delayed. He pressed hard against the wall and sent his bullets screaming into the press of the attack. His lead flew true; it always did. But the gunfire did not abate. He knew then, past any question. Those men were protected behind barricades of some sort. He had no choice.

Wentworth jerked open the door, saw steps slanting downward. He leaped halfway down, flung himself flat on the steps and from that protected position, continued to pour out lead. He cast a swift glance behind him. The basement was without a flicker of illumination; not even the gray of a window showed.

The muzzle of a machine gun was thrust around the door jamb. It spewed out lead that cut the air within inches of Wentworth's head. He smashed a single bullet into the muzzle. The compensator was torn loose; the barrel driven back out of sight. The *Spider* thrust away an empty gun, drew out another. With this in hand, he vaulted over the railing and landed soundless in the basement below. His flashlight played swiftly over the place. It was a small cellar, barely large enough for the furnace and the coal bin. He could defend it against an army, but not against poison gas.

The *Spider* laughed softly to himself. He bounded across the basement to the laundry room. As he peered up the chute, there was a sudden racketing burst of gunfire above. Wentworth staggered back. He was not hurt, but only one thing had saved him... the body of the captive which he had dangled in the chute! He whirled and raced to the coal bin. The coal chute entrance was walled up solidly with concrete!

THE gunfire had ceased. He heard a clang of steel and knew that the stairway entrance was sealed. There were scrambling noises in the laundry chute, where they were pulling out the body of their fellow assassin. Wentworth shrugged slightly. He was trapped, but that had happened to him before. He had the books of the gang, and he would escape with them. Also, he had learned that the overlord of the gangs kept close contact with the Wissouri City mob! Not otherwise could this elaborate trap have been planned and carried out by a mob, necessarily disorganized by the disappearance of Max Vellie!

Wentworth crossed to the furnace and pulled open the door. It had a huge firebox. He set methodically about building a hot fire. If they tried poison gas, he would set up a powerful ventilation system! He doubted if they could pour enough gas into this basement to overcome the draft he could set up! For the rest, he would wait. Despair was foreign to the *Spider*. The awareness of the gravity of his situation showed only in the quickness of his movements; the alertness with which he listened and kept watch.

He only hoped that Nita van Sloan, who would drive to this locality when she had finished an errand on which he had sent her, would be content to wait also. As long as she was outside, and free, he had a chance. Wentworth settled himself as comfortably as possible to wait. He had sent Nita to attempt to persuade the Rileys to leave the city for a place of safety. It had not been easy to decide what place would be safe from the gangs, so widespread were their operations. But, so far, California seemed free of their incursions. So far!

There was a new sound in the laundry chute. Wentworth moved toward it warily, gun in his fist. He did not think they would send anyone down to attack him, but—he caught his breath on an oath. A woman's legs had thrust out of the bottom of the chute. An instant later, she dropped heavily to the floor and Wentworth caught her swiftly away. It was Nita van Sloan!

There were tears of anger in her eyes, but her voice was calm.

"They've got the boy, too. Jim Riley," she said. "They had set a watch over the Riley home, and caught me there. I should have been smarter, and—"

With a small, muffled cry, Jim Riley was dropped down the chute. He landed in a heap, sprang up and shook his fist at the unseen tormenters overhead. Only one sound came down to them. It was a shrill, senseless giggle. Nita shuddered.

"The most horrible little man," she said. "They call him the Weasel. He's in charge, apparently."

"The Weasel!" Wentworth said, softly. "He was in a madhouse for the criminal insane!"

He had an arm about Jim Riley's shoulders. "We'll get you!" the boy was shouting. "We'll get you, the *Spider* and me!"

The words were like blows to Wentworth. He could not let even Nita know how planless he was; or how helpless their situation. There was a thud under the chute, and Wentworth whipped them back. A solid white cube, a foot through, had been dropped down the chute. It was powdered crystal, tightly compact, and slow white fumes wisped from it.

Another cube thudded down, and another. A wave of cold crawled across the floor.

"Out of here," Wentworth ordered shortly, and swept Nita and the boy toward the furnace. His eyes were cold and fierce as he stared at the laundry chute. He might be able to contrive a plug for that chute, but nothing that they couldn't instantly break loose from above. If they failed in that, they could open a hole. Best to let it fall in that one place.

Nita's voice sounded stifled, "That looks like dry ice."

"It is," Wentworth told her.

The fire in the furnace roared deeply. The pressure gauge on the steam was rising.

Jim Riley laughed, "Ain't they crazy, thinking they can freeze us out when we got a fire!"

"Sure. Sure, they're crazy," Wentworth agreed absently. His eyes were on Nita's.

Nita said quietly, "That white vapor... carbon dioxide?"

Wentworth nodded shortly. The thuds of falling cubes continued. The white vapor was crawling across the floor. The draft from the furnace caught it, sucked it in through the open bottom door. The flames dimmed a little as it went through. Wentworth slammed the furnace doors, cut the draft. The warmth was more valuable than the draft right now.

Carbon dioxide was not a poison gas, but it was heavy and asphyxiating. In less than an hour's time that deluge of dry ice would fill the basement to suffocation, put out the fire. The cold would find little work left to do.

Nita van Sloan looked at the *Spider* with eyes that showed no fear. "Is there *any way* we can make sure that the F.B.I. gets the gang books?" she asked, quietly. She glanced at Jim Riley, and then toward the chimney. It was a large, old-fashioned flue. It wouldn't accommodate a man, but a boy—

Wentworth smiled at Nita. She had found a way, and an excuse, to save the boy. After that, they could worry about themselves. *After that*— Wentworth's eyes were grim as he opened the draft door of the furnace again. He took up a cake of the dry ice in a shovel and put it under the firebox. The coals darkened rapidly.

He knew that he was lessening his own chances; his and Nita's. He went and got another cake of the dry ice.

CHAPTER TWELVE
Death by Degrees

THE fire was snuffed out, so that it did not even smoke. There could be no smoke where there was no combustion, and the carbon dioxide gas took care of that. Presently, the smoke pipe was cold enough to detach from the vent hole in the chimney. Wentworth set to work to enlarge the opening. He had the poker and shaker-bar for tools.

While he worked, Nita van Sloan knelt beside Jim Riley. "We are going to trust you to save us and the city," she said, "We have the evidence that will destroy this man, Max Vellie, and his whole gang. We've got it with us. We think that chimney is big enough for you to climb up it, and carry this evidence with you. We're not sure. It will take a lot of courage, and a lot of strength."

The boy looked where the *Spider* was ripping loose bricks, working slowly and quietly, so that there would be no alarm. His eyes grew large.

"Gee!" he said. "Gee! You mean I'm going to have a chance to help the *Spider?*"

Nita crushed him in her arms, let him go quickly. Boys didn't like to be babied. Nita went on talking to him quietly, telling him that he must, on no account, go to the police.

"Sleep at my apartment tonight and then, first thing in the morning, go to the offices of the *News-Times* and tell them everything you know. Max Vellie is locked up in one room of my apartment. You can tell them about that, too. But only to the newspaper men, at their office, and... not until morning."

She showed him the books then. "You'll have to climb up the chimney first, then haul them after you," she explained. "We have a way of getting out, but we'll have to fight, and we don't want to risk any damage to the books."

Wentworth had finished opening up the flue now. It was amply large for Jim Riley. It was almost large enough for Nita, but not quite. The boy looked at the opening a moment with large shining eyes.

"This is going to be fun," he said. "Look, before I go to the newspaper office, don't you think I ought to call the G-men?"

Nita looked at Wentworth, and the *Spider* nodded slowly. If they hadn't got to the apartment by then, they never would. Best to set up whatever guarantees were possible both for the prosecution of the criminals and for the protection of the boy.

"Yes, phone directly to Washington," Wentworth said. "Here is the number to call. Tell them everything you know. All right, Jim, on your way. You can haul the books up after you. Don't make any noise. When you get on the roof, you'll find it easy to climb a fire escape to the tenement roofs. Keep out of sight and go straight to the apartment."

JIM RILEY nodded solemnly, and Wentworth shook hands with him, started him on his climb. Nita van Sloan moved into the circle of his arm then and they stood and listened to the faint sounds as the boy climbed by the rough projections of the inner wall of the flue. Little runlets of soot slid down every now and then. The length of silken rope, coiled in the opening, jerked and raised itself slowly like a thing of separate life.

"Keep watch," Wentworth instructed Nita briefly. He sprang to where the dry ice was piled. It was deathly cold there. The walls were frosted, and the carbon dioxide made his lungs pump more rapidly, made him conscious of the heavier pound of his heart.

Moving swiftly, Wentworth sprang into the adjoining room and turned on water faucets in the laundry tubs. He did not turn them on strongly, lest the noise cause an alarm. Then he bounded back into the furnace room. His feet were already numbed with cold and he leaned against the wall while his lungs slowly worked back to normal.

Nita called softly, "He's almost up!"

Wentworth nodded. He ripped off his silk-lined cape and fastened it over the lower half of the door, hooked it over nails. Then swiftly, he shoveled coal against it to hold it solidly against floor and door frame. He was building a makeshift coffer dam.

Nita uttered a glad little cry. "He's up!"

Wentworth crossed to her side, saw the silken rope was fully extended, saw that the books were starting on their journey upward. His lips were grim. With that act, he was setting a time-bomb to explode—if they died. But Wentworth had not given up hope. He stayed at the chimney for only a few moments, then he turned abruptly away. He took the poker and slicing bar and, in a remote corner, began to study a bricked up window.

Nita joined him. She shivered a little. It was growing much colder in the basement. The water pipes overhead were frosted.

"Is there something I can do?" she asked quietly.

"There is," Wentworth told her. "There's a

drainage pet-cock on the furnace boiler. Take my hat and fill it with water. Dribble it over my cape there by the door, and over the coal. It will freeze and make the dam I have built more effective."

"Dam—" Nita looked toward the entrance of the laundry room, heard the water running in the tubs. "Water won't absorb much carbon dioxide except under pressure, will it?" she asked doubtfully.

Wentworth said, "No, but when it overflows the laundry floor, it will cover the dry ice cubes, freeze, and if the dam is made tight, it will seal in the carbon dioxide. It will be cold; damnably cold. But if it works, it will at least gain us a little time. Meanwhile—"

Wentworth began to work the poker point in the mortar between two of the bricks. It was like rock. The scratches of the steel plate seemed feeble, and he dared not make any noise which would betray his purpose.

From the laundry room, there was another series of thuds. The killers were dropping down more dry ice!

JIM RILEY was tired and hot when he reached the top of the chimney. The soot was thick all over him. It was in his nostrils and in his eyes. He hung his arms over the side of the chimney and for a while he just didn't have the strength to get up on top. He couldn't see very far, it was so dark, but the wind was pretty strong.

Finally, he got a leg over the side of the chimney and groped for the silk rope about his waist and hauled up the books. They were awful heavy. Once or twice they caught and he was scared. He was more scared than he had been climbing up the chimney. Finally, he had the books resting on the edge of the chimney in front of him and he could look around. He wanted to get the soot off his face, but he was soot all over. He just had to stay that way. He looked around. That was when he really got scared. Chimneys didn't look high when you saw them from the ground, but this way it was high. It was terribly high.

He was about twelve feet higher than the peak of the roof; and then the sides sloped down almost as steep as walls. And way, way below was the street. Jim looked the other way. There was that building the *Spider* had told him about, and the fire escape. It was across empty space, though. About a mile of empty space, it looked.

Jim hung on very tightly to the chimney and to the books. They couldn't get lost, because they were tied to him by that silk rope. He just sat there, like a cat that has climbed up a telegraph pole and doesn't know how to get down. He didn't yowl, but tears began to slide down his cheeks.

"You darned old baby, you!" he told himself angrily. "Here the *Spider* gives you a job to do and you sit down and cry. You darned old baby, you!"

But he couldn't seem to pull his other leg out of the chimney. Every time he tried, it seemed like his leg just clamped down tighter. He began to feel cold. It was a long time before he thought about the rope, then he was afraid to untie it for fear he'd lose the books. But he got out his Boy Scout knife and cut off a piece. He tied the books to his belt with the short end, and then he began figuring how to tie the long piece to the chimney so it wouldn't slip. It would be a very tough task.

Now that he was doing something, he felt better. He got the silk rope tied around the top of the chimney, above that ledge of bricks near the top. He didn't think it would slip up and over, not if he was careful. He got it all tied and he dropped the loose end over the side and it slid down the roof and caught in the gutter. Right quick then, before he could start thinking about it, he turned over on his belly on the edge of the chimney.

The books dangled from his belt and they jerked at him, almost pulled him loose. He felt behind him for the rope and got his fingers in the loop, and he scrambled for the rope with his feet. It felt awful tiny when he got it between his legs. He wrapped it around his leg two or three times, moving his feet awkwardly. Then he just lay there. He lay there for a long time and tried not to remember how steep the roof was, or how far down the ground was.

"You darned old coward!" he muttered.

He slipped over the edge.

THE rope burned his leg, and his arm felt like it was almost pulled out of joint when it stretched out straight. The books jerked and swung, fiendishly trying to pull him loose. He swung there and clawed for the rope with his other hand. He got it finally, and then right quick he grabbed with his other hand.

And then he was on the ridge-pole. He was going awful fast, and he tried to slow himself down. He stubbed his toe against the slates, and suddenly his toe caught something and held. It was a piece of metal turned up from the roof. There were rows of them. They were to hold snow. He lay flat on his face there, one foot braced against the snow block and twisted his head around to look behind him. He was awful close to the edge of the roof and the fire escape looked a mighty long way off. In fact—an impossible distance!

He looked at the gap and clung more tightly to the rope. His foot was tired of holding to that snow cleat. He tried calling himself a coward, but it didn't make him mad anymore. He buried his face on his straining arms. He started to think about his Dad, but he couldn't, on account of Dad was gone. And then a face did swim up in front of his eyes that he could think of. That was the *Spider*. The *Spider* hadn't treated him like a kid. He had shaken hands and said he was depending on him. It was as if the *Spider* was talking to him now, telling him what to do.

All he had to do was to slide down to the gutter and get his toes in it. The gutter was plenty strong. Then he could hold onto the rope and stand up right straight. If he did that, he could reach out and get hold of that fire escape ladder. Then it would be easy to step across the opening.

Suddenly, it all seemed awful easy. Jim Riley took his foot off the snow cleat and slid down to the next one, and the next one, and the next. And then his toes curled into the rain gutter. It was heavy and wide. He looked out across the gap, and the ladder was pretty close, after all. Gee, it was easy when you knew how. Especially when a guy like the *Spider* told you how.

Jim held onto the rope and, first, he got his feet flat in the gutter. Then he sort of crouched there, holding onto the rope. It was a little bad there, when he had to take one hand off the rope and grope out toward the ladder. But then his fingertips found the steel rung and after that it was easy. The books jerked at him a time or two but any boy could climb a ladder. He went up to the roof of the next building.

DOWN in the basement, Nita van Sloan lifted her head and opened her eyes.

Inwardly, she felt a release of strain. Nearby, the *Spider* was pecking at the mortar between the bricks. It was very slow work, but Nita felt suddenly almost happy.

"I'm sure Jim is all right now," she said cheerfully.

Wentworth smiled toward her. "Of course," he said. "I followed him—mentally—every inch of the way. You don't know how much courage a boy of twelve can have. Jim has plenty."

As he spoke, he pried and the first brick came out. "That's the hardest part," he said softly. "Now I can use a lever on the others!"

There was an ice dam across the door of the laundry. Water was flooding out slowly over the floor. When it neared the deadly cubes, it began to form an ice skim. It was terribly cold. Nita realized that she felt sluggish and heavy. She could see her breath. There was something like breath along the floors, too, a swirling, rising mist of carbon dioxide gas. At his work, Wentworth was panting heavily.

Nita realized then how slight a chance they had.

What could be done had been done. If there were more time... she moved toward Wentworth, and stumbled as she walked.

"I'm cold, Dick," she said thickly. "Can't I help?"

Wentworth looked at her swiftly, stared at the small hole he had made in the wall. He whipped out an automatic and thrust it into her hand.

"Watch the steps," he said curtly. "To hell with noise!"

He picked up the heavy bar and began to wrench and strike with savage fury at the bricks. He tumbled down a few more. He staggered as he whipped the bar up to ram again at the obstinate wall. The blow was ineffective.

Wentworth leaned his shoulder against the wall and rested through a long and precious minute. Nita stood close by, her eyes on the steps. The gun seemed too heavy for her hand. Wentworth pushed out from the wall. This time, he aimed and struck very deliberately. A brick in the outer wall was knocked out... a gush of fresh air poured in. It felt hot and sultry and fog formed about the opening; frost settled on the bricks.

"Get a breath of fresh air, Nita," Wentworth said, and heard his voice, thin.

Nita was propped against the wall, her head sagging. "What?" she asked faintly.

Wentworth peered at the hole he had made. He managed to dislodge another brick, but the deadly gas, like a sentient thing, was sucked more swiftly toward them now. In an hour's work, he might open a hole large enough for escape. In another hour... Wentworth felt a wild impulse to laughter surge through him. Nita was slumping toward the floor!

He caught her up and held her face where she could breathe the fresher air near the opening. One-handed, he set about loosening her coat. If he could fasten the tail of it high on the wall, it would hold her, by her arms, above the deadly gas. Then he could go on working.

Upstairs, the Weasel got to his feet. "Time to take a peek at our babies," he said. "I got a periscope I can slip down the chute. If they ain't dead, they're so groggy it won't make much difference. We'll go down and finish them off." He giggled.

He had a gun in his fist.

Wentworth did not see the periscope as it was lowered to peer toward him; nor hear the curse of the Weasel. The others winced when the Weasel swung toward them, his teeth like fangs.

"We gotta get down there quick, while he's groggy," he said, shrilly. "He's got a hole in the wall. We can get him while he's dopey. After he gets better, all of us together couldn't take him!"

Wentworth was dazed, scarcely able to think. He leaned against the wall. Now and again, he stirred himself to peck feebly at the bricks. The jarring

ring of steel as the gangsters loosened the door at the top of the steps penetrated to his consciousness only dimly. He turned his head slowly, saw the white fog of the gas shift toward the steps. Even then, thoughts came through to him sluggishly.

Slowly, his lips parted. It was ghastly, but it was a smile. He had won! He had done what he had hoped to accomplish: to force the enemy to come to him! He had won... but could he still fight?

He dragged out his automatics. He leaned his shoulder against the wall. His body protected Nita. On the steps, he heard the creeping feet of the killers!

CHAPTER THIRTEEN
Bitter Battle

THE criminals had extinguished all light behind them. Wentworth long ago had ceased to use his own flashlight. The hole he had punched in the wall was a dim gray patch against the blackness. There were only sounds to guide the *Spider*'s battle, and the criminals would have a target as soon as he fired!

The criminals had overlooked one thing: when they opened the door, they created a draft. The chimney opening sucked at the gas. In through the wall opening, fresh air rushed. But the bulk of the gas moved toward the steps. The men there began to breathe more rapidly under the stimulation of the carbon dioxide. They could not control it. And the fresher air swept over Wentworth like a cold shower, pumping oxygen into his lungs, sweeping the sluggishness out of his poisoned blood.

Still, Wentworth waited while the killers crept down the steps and moved toward him. They wanted a clear target; probably they would switch on lights. But the *Spider* also wanted clear targets. He wanted no hidden gunmen on the steps who could burn him down while he battled the others. So both sides waited.

Off to his right, there was the faint rasp of leather on concrete. In the corner straight ahead, there was the harsh rapid breathing of a man. The others were grouped in between. His lips parted still in that cold smile, the *Spider* flung down the gauge of battle!

His two automatics swung into line. They blasted in the same split second. Then he seized Nita in the crook of his arm and leaped with her toward the furnace. The blaze of the guns slashed the basement with red fire. Bullets clawed at the brick wall where he had crouched. The lights came afterward, as dazzling as an explosion. It showed four men crouched about the foot of the steps. It showed two others motionless on the floor.

It did not reveal the *Spider!*

From above, the Weasel's voice shrilled at them. "Behind the furnace, you fools! Rush him!"

Those four men tried to rush the *Spider*. They spread and charged in from two sides. Each of them ran into a solid wall. That wall was less than a half inch in diameter, but it had behind it the shocking power of smokeless powder, and the unerring aim of the *Spider!* The bullets of his forty-five caliber automatics smacked each of them in the forehead, with the regular rhythm of drum beats. Four shots, and four men went down in succession. Only one of them moved after that. His feet stirred a little before he was still.

Even as the last two shots rolled out, the *Spider* was out from his hiding place. He charged like a panther across the floor toward the steps. He heard the Weasel's shrill cry of warning, and knew that the man was watching him by some secret device. The killers heard the Weasel and obeyed him. They swung at the steel door that closed the steps. They had it three-quarters closed when the driving impact of the *Spider*'s charge smashed against it.

One man was hurled against a wall six feet away, and dropped in a limp bundle to the floor. Two others were thrust savagely backward. The steel door struck them, drove them against the wall... and the *Spider* was out! Guns converged on him. In an instant, the hallway was a living hell of flying lead. The two men behind the steel door fought to get at their guns. Pressure on the portal pinned them to the wall, but they struggled. They braced against that pressure. And the bullets drove the *Spider* back!

Wentworth swore and ducked back to the cover of that door. He snaked the unconscious man across the threshold so that his body would prevent the door's full closing. Through the foot-wide opening, he kept his watch. The killers who poured out their hate-sped lead against him were behind barricades. He could not dislodge them... but their bullets could not reach him! He kept wary guard because of the two men who were behind the steel portal. They were trying to push it shut, but they were only bruising the body of the gangster on the floor. Then a gun-muzzle poked around the edge of the door!

Wentworth waited tautly. The muzzle burst with flame, and the lead howled past the *Spider*. It tore into the ceiling of the steps. The *Spider* waited. The man fired twice more, then he thrust the gun more openly around the corner. This time, the muzzle bore directly on the *Spider*... but the man's fist also was exposed. Wentworth squeezed the trigger of his automatic!

THERE was a scream, and the gun fell. The man scrambled out from behind the door and, dancing

(Facing page) Four shots—and four men went down!

in pain, raced down the hall. The merciless guns of his companions cut him down.

Abruptly, there was a scream from the basement! It was Nita's cry of warning. *"They're coming down the chute!"*

Then came the oath of a man and the heavy sound of a body falling. In the darkness, without weapons, Nita had gone into battle! He heard the quick thud of her feet as she mounted the steps.

"I stopped the first. Others are coming," she panted.

Wentworth thrust a gun into her hand. "Hold this door!" he instructed quietly.

Then he raced downward into the dark. A side-leap, and the gun that blazed hurled its lead past him. He made no answer, sprang to the spot where he had dropped the iron shaker-bar of the furnace. The thud of men dropping down the laundry chute came swiftly. There were at least three of them, besides whatever number had descended before Nita gave warning. The *Spider* sent his whispering laughter into the darkness... from behind the furnace. Guns blazed at him! He nodded. Five guns had spoken. He would assume that all had fired!

The *Spider*'s movements were silent as the creature whose name he bore. The iron bar in his hand, he moved to the attack! And he had a strong advantage over his foes. He knew every inch of the basement, and exactly what obstacles were there; the location of the walls. They knew they were seeking the *Spider,* and that was all.

The *Spider* waited until he was close to the sound of their breathing. Then he laughed again, leaped lightly aside. Their guns blasted. They were huddled together, in terror. He lashed out with the iron bar.

The chattering terror of their guns, their screams and the thud of the iron bar mingled into a hell of battle in the confines of the basement. The wall gave back the sounds until it seemed an entire army fought on each side, instead of one crudely armed man against five equipped with automatics! The *Spider* was everywhere at once. He struck, leaped aside, struck from a new angle. More than once, the bullets of the killers smashed into the bodies of their own companions.

From above, his keen ear caught three shots from his heavy automatic. Nita was fighting, too! That knowledge lent desperation to his struggle. He redoubled his efforts. In a space of seconds, the fight was over and Wentworth sent his whisper ahead of him as he ran up the steps. It should be possible now for him to climb the chute, take the enemy in the rear.

Nita spoke without turning her head. "There's a man out there who pretends to be Jackson," she said. "He says he has polished off all of the men. They aren't shooting. I think it's a trick."

WENTWORTH peered along the hallway, trying to see against the blaze of light that focused on the door. That light died suddenly. He could see three dead men in the hallway then. He could not see the man who claimed to be Jackson.

Wentworth lifted his voice. *"Tambotoi!"* he called, using the same French phrase that he had shouted at Jackson in the battle which had initiated the warfare.

For an instant, there was silence, and then a voice called back, hesitantly. *"Va... chez... moi!"*

Wentworth laughed. "It is Jackson!" he said. "No one else could know what I said to him in that saloon."

Against the dimmer light of the corridor, Jackson showed himself now. He came forward steadily, hands half-raised. "We've got to get out of here," he said. "A rat of a man dodged out of the house as I came in. He got in a car and shoved off, but I heard sirens. Maybe you can afford to be arrested. I can't."

Wentworth led the way in a swift race toward the front door. He stopped only once, as he went out. There was a glass panel there, still unmarked by bullets. In the middle of that pane, he set... the seal of the *Spider!*

It was moments later that they leaped into the *Spider*'s car and Jackson wrenched it skillfully into a dark street, cut through a private drive... and was gone.

He spoke jerkily: "I got Miss Nita's address here from Marianne. Kid there with a batch of books. Didn't want to believe me, but finally told me where you were. Guess I wasn't needed."

"You are needed," Wentworth told him quietly. "We'll need a small army before we're through. What about that murder charge in New York? How do you stand?"

Jackson laughed harshly. "I haven't got a prayer of beating that!"

Nita glanced suspiciously at Jackson's profile. She was crowded between him and Wentworth on the seat. Wentworth said, "We'll beat it."

Nita laughed, softly. "Ronald Jackson, on your word as a soldier and a gentleman—"

Jackson stiffened. "That's the truth," he rumbled.

Nita laughed again. "Dick, Jackson didn't wait to see whether he could beat that murder charge. He thought he was needed here. He came!"

Wentworth glanced from Nita's smile to the set and sheepish look on Jackson's face and knew that she had spoken the truth. Humility touched Wentworth like pain. Jackson had thrown overboard his life's ambition, and his very life, because he wanted to serve the *Spider* and his cause.

He said, quietly, "Jackson is a soldier."

No further word was spoken. Between them,

thanks would have been foolish, even a little insulting. Wentworth flicked on the radio and heard the chatter of police calls. The air was alive with their sirens. Jackson wove a twisted way through the city; ultimately landed them at the back entrance of Nita's apartment.

They went in secretly, swiftly... and stopped inside the door. The apartment was a wreck. In the midst of it, the books in his lap, Jim Riley had fallen asleep.

With a muffled oath, Wentworth sprang to the door behind which Max Vellie had been locked. The door swung open to his touch. But the gang had not rescued Max Vellie. It was quite obvious that the Overlord of the criminals was in charge.

Max Vellie's throat had been cut. Even as Wentworth stared into the room, even as he grasped all that the murder implied, there was a thunderous knocking at the door!

"Open up!" a voice ordered harshly. "Open up! We got the building sewed up and you can't get away!" *The police!*

CHAPTER FOURTEEN
Out of Defeat

A GRIM smile spread across Wentworth's lips at the challenge of the police. A force of crooks!

"We can't complain that the criminal Overlord refuses battle," he said, lightly. "Apparently, he has found out about the books and has sent the police to take charge of them. They would be perfectly safe with the police. Plainly, the books will show bribes and graft!"

Jackson had a revolver in his fist. "Grafters, eh?" he said, quietly. "Then we fight?"

"We fight," Wentworth agreed, "but not that way."

There were heavy blows on the door now. Fortunately, it was metal faced for fireproofing. Nevertheless, it would not resist the attack very long.

"We have to escape, "Wentworth instructed steadily. "Jackson, you will carry Vellie's body. Nita, take care of Jim and the books. Here are two smoke bombs." He opened a suitcase against the wall, which he recognized. It was a suitcase of supplies that was taken always, when possible, on the *Spider*'s crusades. "You will all go into the other room. I will let the police in here and create such a diversion that the guards will be sucked in. That will give you your opportunity. Take it, for the whole success of the campaign depends on those books reaching the proper hands. After you've made your getaway, I'll escape. You will keep your radio turned on and hunt me out. You know the signal."

Jackson said, "Hell, Major. I'm done for anyway, with that murder charge hanging over me..."

"Orders!" Wentworth said quietly. "Nita, each moment's delay makes my own task more difficult. Leave, please."

Without a word, but with a blown kiss, Nita went into the room where the dead gangster lay. She had Jim Riley and the books. Jackson, reluctantly, followed.

The instant they were through the door, the *Spider* sprang into action. From the suitcase, he whipped out a fresh cape and hat. He started a fire-bomb in the suitcase and laid it near the windows, so that the smoke presently would roll out. Then, quietly, he took his stand against the far wall, and waited for the police to drive the door in.

It was dark in the room save where the fire was flickering up smokily among his supplies. An axe blade penetrated the door, and when it was withdrawn a wedge of brighter illumination lay across the floor. The *Spider* relaxed all his body and sucked slow, long breaths.

Then, as the door shook in its sockets, he crossed to the steam radiator and wedged one of his automatics between two sections, its muzzle pointed upward. It was the work of an instant to attach a strand of the Web to the trigger, draw it down under the radiator and across the floor to the opposite wall. He shoved a heavy upholstered chair into a position that half concealed the radiator and the gun. That was all his preparation.

As he reached a protected corner, the door flew open. The police fanned away from the possible line of fire.

"Surrender!" a man's voice called harshly. "If we have to come in, we'll come shooting!"

The *Spider*'s mocking laugher floated out. He pulled his other automatic and, bending forward, sent a bullet crashing into the hall light. Instantly, a machine gun was loosed in the hallway. The streaming lead sawed across the doorway, made a ruin of the opposite wall tore stuffing out of an upholstered chair, crashed out a window. The *Spider* waited.

As the gun cut off, three men vaulted through the door and flung themselves to the floor. One of them crouched against the wall within two yards of Wentworth! Without a sound, the *Spider* rose to his feet. He jerked the lanyard, and the automatic across the room belched out. The policeman whipped up his gun and blazed away, and the *Spider* drove two rigid fingers into his throat. The man did not even gasp as his body went limp. He flopped to the floor.

To the others, in the room, it would seem that the *Spider*'s bullet had dropped him!

THE machine gun slashed out again from the doorway. It clawed at the chair behind which the gun was placed. Wentworth glided, unseen, toward the doorway. The man with the machine gun sidled in, still loosing short bursts toward the chair. Once more, Wentworth jerked the lanyard and, again, struck out with prodding fingers! The machine gun clattered to the floor. The policeman fell across it!

There were still two police in the room. They were crouched behind furniture, throwing bullets toward the chair. All their attention was focused there. One of them twisted his head and saw the two sprawled bodies on the floor. He let out a yelp of fright.

"Hey!" he called. "Hey, Bill and Mike are down! Come on! Rush him!"

Once more the eerie laughter of the *Spider* sounded in the room. Wentworth muffled it with his hands, sent it into a corner of the ceiling. It was impossible for them to tell its source. For a moment after it sounded, there was dead silence in the darkness lit only by the flicker of the fire, by the gun-flashes of the police.

Suddenly, four more men leaped through the doorway with blazing guns. Two of them went prone on the floor and began to crawl to the attack. One of the others sprang to the cover of a chair. The fourth was crouched beside the doorway. The *Spider* jerked on the lanyard, two, three, four times. The gun was empty now. At the fourth shot, he struck down the man beside the door... and ducked out through the opening!

There was one man outside the door. He opened his mouth to cry out, but the shout was lost in the fury of gunfire within. The *Spider* jarred his chin upward with the heel of his left hand, struck strongly with his right. The man slumped to the floor. In two leaps, Wentworth reached the kitchen door of the apartment, opened it.

At the same moment, he heard Jackson's hoarse voice below. "Watch those guns! They got Bill! Can't you see I'm carrying him?"

The *Spider* darted down the first flight of steps, raced to a window in the front of the building. Jackson was hurrying across the sidewalk with Vellie's body on his shoulders. Nita and Jim Riley were not in sight.

Jackson reached a car, heaved the body in. Three police converged on him. At the same moment, Nita darted from the doorway! Her swift, striking hands, using the same jiu-jitsu blow that Wentworth had employed, knocked down the first policeman before he knew what was happening. Jackson whirled and crashed his fist to the chin of a second.

The third man danced back, gun leaping to his fist!

From the window, the *Spider* threw a careful bullet. The gun clashed from the policeman's hand. His face jerked up, incredulously, and Nita reached him with striking hands in the same instant. Jackson leaped behind the wheel; Nita swept Jim Riley into the rear. Police were running to intercept them. The *Spider* opened up a rapid, high fire. It hit no one. It whistled dangerously close to three. The police scattered, and the car went through.

THERE was a shout behind Wentworth! His flicking gaze caught a reflection in the window glass. A policeman poised with a machine gun ready to blast! But the *Spider* was in motion at the first impact of the man's shout! He went straight out the window!

An instant after he cleared the sill, the machine gun hosed its death stream through the window!

Policemen in the street stood with hanging guns—and gaping mouths! They saw the *Spider* dive head-first out of the second story window of the building! It looked like suicide; like certain death! He sailed gracefully, hands straight before him as in a dive. His cape streamlined behind him. Even the machine gun fell silent. The policeman darted to the window, leaned out, staring.

The *Spider*'s dive suddenly changed into a graceful somersault. His out-reaching hands closed on the heavy telephone cable which looped from pole to pole. His body swung down, up and over... and he was dropping straight down to the roof of a parked police car!

The beat of his feet upon the roof of the car jerked the police from their daze. Their guns came up. But the *Spider* had used the car roof only as a springboard. He went off the car roof in a back-flip, flung himself behind the wheel! The machine gunner jerked up his weapon. The police ran forward, firing. The *Spider* kicked the motor to life, wrenched the car onto the sidewalk.

Between him and the charging police, there was a line of parked police cars. Within a second, or less, the machine gunner was checked, too. He was a right-handed man. It was not possible to lean out the window and fire to the right at a sharp angle with any accuracy. The stolen police car gained speed. Its siren began to scream. It plunged along the empty sidewalk, debouched into the side street and took the turn on two screaming tires. The car heaved into the air, almost overturned. But the *Spider*'s skillful handling straightened it out, sent it hurtling away.

He had a head start of seconds on any pursuit. For the *Spider* it was enough. He flicked on the radio, and through the excited voice of the police announcer, there came a series of metallic clicks: Morse code.

"N on Barrington," came the slow beat of the dots and dashes. Wentworth whipped the wheel over and drove due east. He cut south, and was paralleling his original line of flight. Within minutes, he changed direction again and flashed across the street on which was Nita's apartment. It was five minutes later that he began to bore northward. The clicks had changed now. They were, *"E to river."*

Ten minutes later, Wentworth made rendezvous with his allies on a dark warehouse-lined street near the river. He walked up to their car with quiet, assured haste.

"Nita, you will start the Rileys, including Jim, for the west coast," he directed. "Friends of mine there will see that they are established. Jackson, photostat every mark in those books, three copies. Mail one to the governor, with my card enclosed. One to the F.B.I. in Washington. Retain one. The books themselves will be turned over to police in the morning, with appropriate fanfare. I'll take charge of Vellie and the cars."

Jim Riley smiled brilliantly into the *Spider's* face. He was black with soot. The traces of tears striped him like an Indian.

"Gee, *Spider*," he said, and swallowed hard. "That was fun."

CHAPTER FIFTEEN
Crime Pays

AT EIGHT o'clock, the uniformed police lined up for inspection in all the precincts of Wissouri City. An order was read to them: *Get the Spider!*

Police captains stood before their men and harangued them on this all-important duty.

"You will have double patrols today," they said, sharply. "Allow no suspicious incident to go uninvestigated, and remember that the all-important thing is: *Get the Spider!*

"Last night, single-handed, he killed eleven men. There is no question of his guilt, and no question of bringing him in. You understand? He had the gall to leave his seal to claim the murders as his own. He is armed, tricky, dangerous. Shoot on sight! There will be promotion and a bonus for the man who gets the *Spider!*"

The men went out on patrol and by eight-thirty, headquarters and the precinct stations had only their normal complement of men, except that reserves were held in readiness to rush wherever help might be needed.

In his office, Chief Drinker was a desperate man. He had made every effort to recapture the books, and he had failed. God alone knew what was in those books. The Mayor was on the phone every five minutes, demanding action. For all Drinker knew, the Mayor's name might be in there, too. With Vellie gone, Drinker didn't know what to do, or whom to call. Vellie had disappeared as completely as if the air had swallowed him.

During the night, there had been an even forty robberies. There were reports of a score of stolen cars. The detectives put on train and plane stations reported that known criminals and gangsters were pouring out of the city.

Drinker was a man of clichés. He muttered, "The rats leave a sinking ship."

At eight-thirty, four newspaper men alighted from cars in front of police headquarters. Two of them had cameras and they stayed near their cars, waiting. The two police on guard outside the doors stared at them curiously. Presently one of the cops came down the steps.

"You can't hang around here," he ordered. "Move on."

The newspaper men laughed at him. "Go tell Chief Drinker we're from the *News-Times*. We like Chief Drinker, sometimes. But I think the boss is about ready to start a clean-up campaign. Now, you go ask Chief Drinker if he wants us to move on."

The cop hesitated. He had his orders, but Chief Drinker changed orders without warning. A cop hardly knew what to do. He might get suspended for following orders the wrong way. The cop shrugged and went back to his post outside the door.

At eight-thirty-nine, a man walked around the corner and came straight toward police headquarters. He was just an ordinary looking man, except that he moved with a crisp efficiency and had a military erectness about him. His eyes looked neither to right nor left. He was smoking a cigarette. As he reached the newspaper men, he flicked his cigarette into the gutter. His eyes merely brushed over the photographers, and the reporters.

He walked straight up the steps of headquarters, like a man who had business there.

It was two seconds before eight-forty. A car turned the corner and slowed down in front of police headquarters just as the man nodded to the two police guards and reached his hand for the door. The cops looked toward the car, and the man who stood between them reached out a sudden hand toward the guard on his right. He seized the man by the collar and hurled him against his companion. He had a gun in his fist.

"Just stand there, you two!" he ordered. His voice was quiet, but there was a force in it.

The door of the car opened, and a man stepped out. It was possible to see now that he wore a long black cape, and a black hat that shielded his eyes. He moved unhurriedly, but with a swift efficiency that saved seconds. From the back seat of the car, he took the stiff form of a man whose arms were bound about his hunched-up knees. Between knees and chest were wedged a half dozen fat bookkeeping binders. He set that man in the middle of the steps of headquarters, and as he did so, the man's head rolled back. The cameras were clicking steadily, recording every movement.

One of the reporters whistled softly. "Good God! Vellie, dead! That's the *Spider* seal on his forehead. Look, *Spider!*"

"I am, as you see," the *Spider* said quietly, "a little pressed for time. Those books in Vellie's lap are the books of the gang business. They also include the police who have been receiving graft, and the city officials. Here is a prepared statement for you gentlemen." He handed them three closely type-written sheets.

The man who had held the police prisoners was backing down the steps. The *Spider* pivoted and sprang behind the wheel of the car. As he sped away, the other man leaped into the rear. The sedan whirled the corner as one of the police guards fired wildly. The camera was still engaged in snapping pictures. It was thirty seconds past eight-forty o'clock.

THE FIRST newspaper extra hit the street at nine-seventeen. It contained only a brief flash and a two-inch black streamer across the top. The front page was made over at once and more details added. They picked that up on the same run and called it the second extra. Within an hour, the first smashing picture of the *Spider* delivering Vellie and the gang books to headquarters was spread across the front page. There was a fuller story, and the beginning of the *Spider*'s statement.

The telegraph wires, at that time, had already flashed thousands of words on the story, and other newspaper presses over the country were rumbling with their first extras. Governor Hansen of Wissouri had, by mail, photostats of the gang books and was swinging into action. Chief Drinker had made his break for freedom. He got as far as the airport. There were detectives on guard there, but they only saluted. He was still their superior.

Drinker ran toward the plane he had chartered. He was being assisted to climb into the cockpit when a powerful car leaped from the taxi parking ranks and raced toward him. Drinker didn't hear it because of the roar of the plane's engine. He flung a leg into the cockpit, and a satisfied expression crossed his face. He had enough money in his satchel to last a long time. He had planned all this a long time ago.

He turned his head to grin back sardonically at the city that had treated him so well. He saw the car and a scream tore from his throat. The pilot turned his head, ducked low. There were two machine gunners in the car. The sedan stopped to give them full opportunity to aim, even though the range was less than twenty feet.

The two machine guns chattered for fully ten seconds. In that time, each of them fired sixty bullets. Most of them found their mark.

The sedan whirled and streaked away from the plane. One detective ran out of the administration building of the airport. A burst of machine gun bullets scoured toward him. He flung himself flat and covered his head with his arms. When he looked up, the car was a half mile away and traveling fast.

In the rear seat, the Weasel patted his hot machine gun and giggled. "Did you hear baby speak her piece?"

Not even the airport officials thought anything of the small sport plane that was hanging in the sky. The pilot seemed as if he had been about to land, and then had changed his mind. The gangsters in the car didn't notice. There was almost always one of those light planes floating in the neighborhood of the airport.

Even if the killers had known that the pilot was a woman, they would have attached no significance to it. They would have had to know that the woman was Nita van Sloan. Even then, they couldn't do anything about the fact that the airplane was following them.

THE newspapers were delirious over the clean-up. It would be statewide. They didn't mention that the crime wave was nationwide, although their wires brought them an unceasing flood of the facts. In fact, there was so much of it that crime was no longer news. After a certain number of holdups, robberies and racket killings are headlined, they cease to be novel. The public's taste in such matters is soon jaded. It takes something spectacular to make headlines, something unusual. Besides, this crime wave was competing with urgent war news.

Two men in particular were discussing the matter. They were in a dilapidated car heading northward along secondary roads. They had been stopped twice by state police, but one of the men was a master at disguise; and the other knew how to obey orders. They kept rolling northward.

The radio in the car was nothing unusual. Even if the police had heard the series of dots and dashes, it would have meant nothing to them. Besides, the messages in code didn't come very often, and didn't say much.

"*Ten m south of Willetsville.*" And presently, "*West at W.*" After a while, "*N on 34.*"

"Roll it," the *Spider* ordered softly. "They're heading for Mobiletown. We'll have to be there ahead of them. And Nita will have to land soon for gas."

His voice was grim and Jackson nodded crisply. "Nice clean-up back there in Wissouri City," he said.

Wentworth laughed shortly. "I thought I was curing the pneumonia; I only knocked out a headache. The ramifications of this thing are nationwide, perhaps worldwide. There are a dozen states, a hundred cities as badly overrun as Wissouri City. By the time I can clean them all up, the old ones will have started up again.

"I've got to locate the brain of this organization and destroy it! So far, I have only the evidence of my reasoning to indicate there *is* such a man: I've seen his operations. I know one of his direct underlings: The Weasel. Meantime, crime is paying big dividends... and undermining the entire nation. How many such exposes as that back in Wissouri City do you think the public morale can stand?"

"The people are all right," Jackson said.

"Yes," Wentworth agreed. "Of course the people are all right. They are always all right. John Schmidt in Munich doesn't want to invade Russia. It won't pay him, personally, any dividends. Koto Sama in Tokyo doesn't want to invade the United States. John Doe doesn't want to leave Roxbury to fight anywhere. They do what they do because they trust their governments. When people in the mass cease to trust their governments, collapse follows, whether by revolution or by pressure from outside. That was what happened in France. That is what will not happen here!"

Jackson said, "That makes it bad."

Wentworth's smile was tight against his teeth. He kept a sharp lookout on the road ahead and behind as their speed increased. Yes, the battle grew more difficult. It was not possible to say that the Overlord was performing his criminal exploits with any intention of helping the enemy. But if the thing had been deliberately planned in Berlin or Japan, it could not be better executed. A man did not have to know Hitler in order to do Hitler's work. He could hate Hitler with all his spirit, and still do Hitler's work—if he followed personal greed instead of the best interests of his nation at war!

Abruptly, Nita's voice broke out of the radio. "Attacked by machine gun plane!" she called. "Will try for landing!"

After that was only silence.

CHAPTER SIXTEEN
Gang Chattel

NITA VAN SLOAN had one advantage in her battle with the machine guns of the gang plane: her craft was slow. Consequently, the other machine was handicapped in getting home a telling burst of bullets. Twice, she dodged the killer plane. Then she flipped her own ship on its back and spun for Earth.

Her only chance, she knew, was to pretend distress, and then land in a small field where the faster, heavier craft could not set down. Even so, she would need to be close to cover. Her maneuver had taken her over such a field; little more than a cleared wood-lot in the forest.

The machine guns yammered again, and then the plane was following her down. The bullets tore at her right wing, crawled toward the cockpit. The fabric began to tear, ripped loose a huge section. The tips were vibrating wildly, and threw their tremor through the ship.

With a grim set to her firm jaw, Nita bailed out. She simply hurled herself against the cabin door and was catapulted into space as the bullets tore through the spot where she had been sitting. She was close to Earth; terribly close. Nevertheless, she delayed the yank on the ring which would open her parachute. At the last possible moment, she pulled the ring.

The gang plane zoomed up and swooped back toward her and her still spinning plane, ripping toward Earth. The killer ship still poured its lead into her doomed craft. Smoke spouted from it, then a lick of crimson flame. That much Nita saw, and then the strong, comforting yank of her parachute took hold. She could no longer see the assassins. She had no time for them, anyway. She was within a scant hundred feet of Earth and falling swiftly. She braced herself, and the Earth leaped up to meet her. The fall was hard, dragging. Nita bounded to her feet, dived for the cover of nearby trees while she struggled with the parachute harness. She freed herself, reached the trees.

Bullets slammed down through the foliage like a strong hail. Twigs and leaves fluttered down about her. Nita pressed her body close against the bole of the tree. Once more, the hail swept down around her. Something like a sob pushed up into her throat—a sob of anger.

Abruptly, Nita understood their purpose. They did not actually hope to kill her. They were pinning her motionless while men came to capture her! With that thought, Nita broke from the protection of the tree and raced off through the woods. She knew there was a concrete highway no more than two hundred yards to her left. She did not know whether men were dropping by parachute to take her, or whether the airmen could communicate with the car she had been following. But if she were to escape, it must be by way of that road!

Nita had covered half the distance to the road, when a man's voice rasped: "All right, sister. Get them up!"

Nita threw herself to the ground, rolled to the protection of a tree. She came up on her knees, gun ready... and a pistol muzzle pressed coldly into the back of her neck. At the same moment, she spotted two other men with their guns steady upon her.

NITA lifted her hands slowly, let the gun fall from her fist. The two men came out from behind their trees and came toward her steadily, grinning. She heard a giggle behind her and realized it must be the Weasel; he whom Wentworth called a homicidal maniac!

If anything, that knowledge intensified Nita's determination. Her rising hands leaped suddenly into action. She jerked head and body aside, seized the gun-wrist behind her and wrenched forward from the waist! The Weasel cried out shrilly. His feet were whipped from the ground and described a high parabola as he sailed toward his two fellows!

Nita snatched up her pistol, dodged behind the tree and fired in the same swift action. Her bullet took one of the men under the chin, and then a chopping, vicious blow caught her across the base of the skull. Her body went limp. Her senses went from a blaze of white into grayness that swiftly turned black. She realized she had made the fatal blunder of not spotting all of her enemies before she struck. There had been two men behind her.

It was the aching stiffness in the back of her neck that was her first sensation. After that, she

NITA VAN SLOAN

realized she was in a car that moved swiftly through city traffic. Before she fully recovered, she was being carried roughly from the car into a house. She was dropped upon a chair and the fall made her feel sick. After that, there was no more movement. Gradually, she swam back to consciousness. She was helped by a sharp and painful knife-prick in the throat. Her eyes flew open... and she heard the infantile and ghastly giggle of the Weasel.

A man's passionless voice said, "That will do."

Nita's eyes flicked toward the sound. She couldn't see the whole man, could merely feel his bulk behind a bright light that focused down on a desk, showed only his hands clearly. The hands made her shudder. They were white, well-tended, and the fingers were flexible. Between the knuckles were tufts of hair that were black and wiry and curled slightly.

"You are one of the *Spider*'s agents," the passionless voice said quietly. "You have put me to considerable trouble. I have not quite decided whether you are worth more to me living than dead."

The Weasel giggled. "Leave me kill her, Chief?" he said. "Just leave me—"

There was no answer, but the silence was cold with menace. Nita van Sloan shifted her position in the chair a little. She could feel the menace, and she knew that the man before her had spoken the literal truth. But if he expected her to plead for her life, he was wrong.

Deliberately, Nita van Sloan put a smile on her lips. Not provocative, or pleasant; merely a smile of strength. It said better than any words what she felt: whichever way the verdict went, she would not quail. She knew the mysterious speaker was he whom the *Spider* called the Overlord of Crime.

"If I keep you alive," the voice went on, steadily, "you will be a burden. From the record, your captivity will do nothing to slow down the *Spider*. He has no regard for hostages, and rightly so. On the other hand, you are as effectively out of the fight alive as dead."

Nita van Sloan had a curious sensation of being a spectator at her own trial. She strove to hold that detachment... and meantime to penetrate the screen of light and find, in this man, something that she could identify for the *Spider*, should she escape. There was nothing except those hands, and they were too prominently displayed. She suspected that there was falsehood in those hands. She did not think they would help in his ultimate identification.

"What's it going to be, Chief?" The Weasel was eager.

BEFORE he could answer, a phone whirred on the desk. A hand picked up the instrument and disappeared with it into darkness.

"Yes," the man said, and waited. "No, do not kill him. He will lead you to the *Spider*. When he does, kill him and every other living being around him. Wait until he is in this city, if possible. If you fail, you may expect the *Spider* to raid headquarters here with the intent of destroying it completely. You may report to me... what? Yes, Manitoba."

The phone went back into its cradle. The calm voice went on, summing up for the defense and the prosecution. "The *Spider* and Jackson have eluded us so far. The police will he watching for them both. It is possible that I can use you for bait."

Nita said, dryly, "It's extremely doubtful."

Her thoughts were racing. It was plain to her that the Chief had received word that Ram Singh was driving toward the city. He was due. The Chief was making the cleverest use of his knowledge. It behooved Nita to do the same. She opened her purse and took out her lipstick, while the Weasel leaned toward her with the knife. Placidly, she used powder and rouge. She did not drop the lipstick back into the purse.

"I want to look my best when you kill me," she said steadily.

Against the tapestry of the chair, she was scrawling with the lipstick. The dimness of the room helped her.

"So you wish to die?" the man asked, incuriously.

Nita lifted her left shoulder, moved her left hand. It would distract attention from what she was doing. "No one wants to die," she said, "but I am ready."

Nita was using her only weapon, psychology. This man was clever, and therein lay his pride. He night be clever enough to penetrate her idea; possibly not. If she made up, think he had reason to kill her, it might arouse his perversity. Also, a man who had the Weasel as a servitor would have a certain deep streak of cruelty. Cowardice would not intrigue him; but he might wish to try her courage.

The man said, "Are you sure you are ready?"

The Weasel giggled and his hand tightened in readiness about the knife.

Nita folded her hands in her lap. She let the smile quiver off her lips, then bravely put it back. She forced voice out clearly; but with strain:

"I am ready!"

Silence then, while the Weasel poised the knife and looked toward those hands under the light. Nita knew then, as she was supposed to know, that if he lifted those hands, she died.

There was no question in her mind that the Chief had decided the trouble of keeping her alive was scarcely worthwhile. Her only weapon was this psychological trick she had attempted; to encourage him to believe he could torment her mentally.

She said again, "I'm ready!"

The smile was a stiff mask for her face. She let

her eyes almost close, but still she could see those hands. If they moved, she would make an effort to overpower the Weasel, vain though she knew it would be. If the hands moved—

CHAPTER SEVENTEEN
Battle Stations

IN A luncheon diner on route 34, Wentworth picked up a fragment of information about Nita. He asked no questions, but none were necessary. People were talking about the fact that an airplane had been shot down over the woods a few miles north of there.

"Spy, most likely," the counter man said. "No, I ain't been up there, but some state cops was. They didn't find anything except a wrecked plane, and a parachute, and a dead man. They wasn't talking much."

Wentworth sped grimly north with the knowledge that Nita, at least, had not been left dead in the woods. If they had bothered to carry her off, she must have been alive.

Jackson had a scowl. "I suppose we're going to have to ring Ram Singh in on this rescue party," he said, reluctantly.

At any other time, the words would have made Wentworth smile. Jackson and Ram Singh were rivals in their service, continually jabbing at each other, and each willing to die at need to save the other. But the rivalry persisted.

"If he has arrived," Wentworth agreed quietly, "we will need force. But Jackson, this is not primarily a rescue party. We are going to smash gang headquarters in Mobiletown. From the identity of some of those who were killed in Wissouri City, I know that the gang leader in Mobiletown is Big Hara. He's the next man we're after... and a clue to the identity and whereabouts of this damnable criminal boss!"

They sped into the southern limits of Mobiletown, but not on route 34. It was too likely to be watched by the Snake men. Dusk was swimming into the streets now. They were nearly empty of traffic in the pause that comes between the after-work rush and the theatre crowds. They rolled more slowly downtown.

"Drop me at the railway station," Wentworth ordered quietly. "I'm going from there to police headquarters. You know where to pick up Ram Singh. If he isn't there, leave a message: I'll spell it out for you." He gave Jackson a message of a half-dozen Punjab words. "That will bring him to us if he comes in time."

Wentworth took a taxi directly to police headquarters. He had a briefcase in his hand. He wore glasses, and behind their enlargement, his eyes seemed bland and boyish. There was a certain exaggerated quiet about his manner; a studied authority.

"Chief Rainer," he told the desk sergeant, "or one of his deputies. But I'd rather see Rainer."

"What's your business?" the sergeant asked, officiously.

"It's private," Wentworth told him, almost gently. "And official!"

To Chief Rainer, Wentworth presented his credentials as an agent of the F.B.I.!

"I have a warrant," he said quietly, "for the arrest of Big Hara for income tax evasion. I'd like as many men as you think the job will require. Also, some information on his probable whereabouts."

Rainer's face wore a grim smile. "I haven't got that many men," he said flatly. "I've been trying to get something on Hara for a year. The courts throw out the cases."

Wentworth smiled happily. "They won't throw this case out. If that's your situation, you'd better not call any men. Hara might be tipped off. Just tell me where to find him."

Rainer's smile faded. "Do you want to commit suicide?" he asked harshly.

Wentworth just continued to look at him with his eyes big and young behind his glasses and Rainer leaned his elbows on the desk and clasped his hands.

"I'll tell you where Hara is to be found," he said, "and I'll send a squad with you. A riot squad."

The phone bell whirred on his desk, and he snapped up the instrument. "Shooting where? The Indigo! All right, get over there and take plenty of men!"

He slammed up the phone. "That's the way it goes," he said angrily. "The Indigo is our biggest hotel. A gang just shot up the lobby. God knows how many people will be killed."

Wentworth's expression did not alter. It was to the Indigo that Jackson had gone to meet Ram Singh!

"You were going to give me an address," he reminded Rainer.

The chief swore. He gave the addresses at which Hara might be found.

"If this is a gang job—one of his jobs—you won't find him at his headquarters. He'll be out with seventeen witnesses."

BUT IT was toward the headquarters of the Hara gang that Wentworth sped as soon as he left police headquarters. He did not wait for Jackson, or Ram Singh. Nothing he could do about that, now. If they had been taken prisoners, they would be carried to headquarters. And Wentworth thought Hara would be there. It seemed obvious that Jackson's entrance into the Indigo had touched off that shooting affray. Hara could have no advance notice of when it would occur.

The car he had rented served him as a dressing room. From the briefcase he took out cape and hat and makeup kit. It was the *Spider* who would raid Hara's headquarters tonight! Seconds later, Wentworth was sliding soundlessly along the wall of the warehouse designated as headquarters. The few windows were high up and steel-barred. The building filled an entire block, and there were no overlooking structures. Three times, as he slid along that building's side, Wentworth spotted lookouts on the roof. They did not see the black shadow that was the *Spider*.

There was a padlocked elevator door in the sidewalk. The *Spider* swiftly picked the lock. There was no sound as he slipped under the half-raised door and let it ease back into place again. He was on the overhead brace of an elevator. He dropped lightly to the floor, and was among stacked piles of cartons, crates and barrels.

In a box-made cavern, the *Spider* rapidly laid a fire. He set a candle among the tinder and lighted it. It would be some minutes before the candle burned low enough to ignite the pile. He glided on and found the inside elevator shaft. Its counter balance guides provided him with a ladder. He went upward.

At each floor level, he paused to listen. It was at the top that he checked and, after a wait, nodded in satisfaction. He continued his climb to the penthouse which enclosed the elevator machinery. There was a trapdoor there for workmen. He went through, and was looking out over the roof through a narrow window. There was a neat roof bungalow and its widows were brightly-lighted. The silhouettes of patrolling guards showed against the sky.

IN THE main room of the penthouse, Big Hara stood on wide braced legs. He fitted his name. His legs were massive, but proportioned well to a thick, heavy-shouldered body. His head, only, was small. His eyes were quick and lethal. Four of his men were with him.

"I've had a tip an F.B.I. man is coming here," he said, roughly, "and in the middle of it, you pull that shoot-up at the Indigo!"

"Orders, Hara," one of the men said shortly. He lifted a hand and showed a snake-ring.

Hara groaned. "All right. All right. So it's orders, and I take the rap. I can beat it, but you oughta give a guy some notice. Did you get the *Spider*?"

The man with the ring lifted his shoulders slightly. "We mopped up everybody in sight," he said. "The funny guy with the turban, and a guy who spoke to him. And just for good measure, everybody else in sight. We oughta have got the *Spider*."

Hara said, "Good God! Good God! Listen, you fools, I have to live here!"

The man with the snake-ring took an easy step forward. "Why, Hara?"

Hara's voice was edged. "What? What do you mean?"

"Why do you have to live... *anywhere?*"

Hara took that more quietly. His small eyes raked the man from head to foot, and a funny small smile came to his mouth. "Listen," he said softly. "I was in this town, and in this racket, before the Snake ever came along. I'll be in it when there aren't any more snakes. I was wise enough to get out of the prohi racket when things went sour, and—"

The Snake-man said, "Look, there's only one boss. You know that. It's got to be like that. If we run things right, we can take over the whole country, the whole world. What do you think Hitler is? A gangster, isn't he? Right now, he's the boss of Europe! All right, and he ain't so smart. He had to go in and smash things up. We don't work that way. We take over a little at a time. Let somebody else think he's bossing things, so long as we know we take the gravy! We run the world! You don't want to deal yourself out of anything like that. Now, if you do—" The man grinned, and his voice fattened, "if you do, it can be arranged."

The three men at his back were spread out, and they had Hara pinned against the wall. Bullets would strike him from three angles at once, and he wouldn't have a chance. He knew it.

Hara said, slowly, "Sure. I get your point. But figure this thing out. We gotta have somebody to take the rap at the Indigo. That's the only way to play it smart. The cops gotta make some arrests after a shoot-up like that!"

The Snake-man shook his head. "Nope. This man Jackson is an escaped murderer. That dark-skinned guy is nobody. And the *Spider* is wanted by the cops. They ought to pin a medal on us."

The voice that spoke had an edge like a file. "Where do you want the medal pinned?" it asked.

The voice came from behind the four Snake-men. It was whispering and sinister, and there was a hard laughter behind it. Only Hara could see the place from which the voice came. His small eyes flicked that way, and a pallor crawled over his face.

He gagged before he got out words. "The *Spider*!"

His words were choked off by a rolling blast of gunfire!

CHAPTER EIGHTEEN
A Slim Thread

THOSE four men were killers and they had the thought of death in their minds. It is doubtful if they reasoned. There was a challenge and, to the Snake-man, Hara was a part of the challenge. His first bullet took Hara in the middle of his expansive stomach, and the other guns blasted in unison.

Hara went down with four bullets through him even as the killers rounded to battle the *Spider*. The black hunched figure, shrouded in the long cape, was crouched just inside an open window. There was a heavy automatic in each fist. The four men were scattering, leaping, dodging as they whirled to throw their lead at him. But there was a hard and wary smile on the tight-drawn lips of the *Spider*.

His two guns lifted and blasted as casually, it seemed, as a man shooting clay pigeons with a shotgun. The accuracy of his bullets was unerring. Each gun spoke twice. Over his shoulder, there was a smashed scar in the wall where a gang bullet had struck. But after his fourth shot, there was no more firing. The four were dead. The *Spider*'s technique was the same as that of the United States Marines. They had always held that a few men who were deadly accurate could stand off ten times their number.

The *Spider* moved swiftly across the room, then. He stooped to imprint his seal upon the leader of the Snake-men, to look rapidly through the contents of his victims' pockets. The man had scrawled a notation on the back of an envelope. It read: "Wissouri City." Wentworth shook his head over it, impatiently. He could hear men shouting somewhere in the house. There had not been time for them to discover the fire, except by accident. He glided to the door, listened there for a moment; unlocked it. Then he faded into the shadow behind a big chair, set in a corner facing the desk.

After a space of minutes, four men burst into the room with guns in their hands. They stopped short at sight of the dead. The man who stole cautiously forward was bandy-legged, the movements of his head as quick and vicious as a snake's. He winced at sight of the *Spider* seal, then sent his quick stare probing over the room.

"The *Spider*'s been here," he said, his voice dead flat, grating. "Mort, get on the phone and report."

The man called Mort, thin as death, moved sideways toward the phone on the desk. "Where do I report?" he asked, uncertainly.

The leader swore at him in the same flat voice. "Call the Weasel, tell him the *Spider* killed Hara and I'm taking over."

Mort picked up the phone and said into the transmitter, "Look, I want the Weasel. Oh, Wissouri City, hunh?"

Behind the chair, Wentworth narrowed his eyes in disbelief. It confirmed the notation he had found in the pocket of a Snake-man, but still he could not credit it. The Weasel had skipped out of Wissouri City just one jump ahead of a clean-up. He was a well known criminal. It would be folly to return.

Something had bothered Wentworth since he had crouched in his hiding place. He felt this uneasiness, and could assign no reason for it. He tried to put it out of his mind, watching the killers, waiting for the call to go through. It was unusually delayed for a call over so short a distance. Abruptly, he swore under his breath. He knew now what it was that obtruded on his attention. It was perfume: Nita's perfume!

He threw his sharp glance at the wall beside him, but that led only to the roof. There could be no hiding place there: But the scent was very strong, powerful. Almost as if perfume had been spilled— Wentworth almost laughed aloud. He knew now that Nita was alive, and had her wits and courage about her. That perfume had been spilled, deliberately! Nita had known he would follow and had left a signal to show that she had been here! He leaned toward the chair. Yes, that was the source of the perfume. Not very long ago, Nita had sat in that chair!

A SAVAGE impatience rose within the *Spider*. He had been a little too late then to overtake her. Had the Overlord, the Snake, been in this room, too? Wentworth's lips drew tight against his teeth. He was closing the gap between him and the man!

"This is Mort, Weasel," the man spoke into the phone. "The *Spider* bumped Hara and Zieger is taking over. Okay? Hell, I don't know nothing about him being shot up. There was a blow-off at the Indigo today, and some guys was killed. But this just happened. We heard the shots, and we're looking for the *Spider* now. Okay, Okay."

He hung up, drawled at Zieger, "He says okay." Zieger's eyes were questing over the room. "He came in that window there. Mort, get out of it and look around. You, Smack. Get out through the door. Harry, watch the other door."

Zieger moved over where Hara had fallen; stood in his position, and looked around. "The Spider did his shooting from right by the window. There's a bullet hole in the wall. He had to put this seal on. He's been looking through that mug's pockets. He hasn't gone far. Harry, phone downstairs and tell them to plug every door. The *Spider*'s inside this building!"

Behind the chair, the *Spider* smiled, grim acknowledgement of the man's keenness. He lifted one automatic and put a bullet through the lightswitch. There was a flare of brilliant fire, and then the room was dark. Zieger whirled around. Wentworth heard the rasp of his feet on the floor.

"He's in this room!" Zieger exclaimed. "Every man of you stay where he is!"

There was a gun-crash, fire splashing the darkness, and a bullet thumped into the chair behind which Wentworth crouched! Zieger had figured well! The man's voice ripped out:

"Behind that corner chair! Open fire!"

As he spoke the last word, he opened rapid fire, and the *Spider* stood up, taking the chair with him, and ran straight at the blazing gun! The shock of the collision scarcely shook Wentworth. He let the chair go down with Zieger, heard the man's gasp of pain... and struck straight down. Zieger made no more noise.

Bullets were raking toward the spot now, yet so swiftly had the whole thing occurred that Wentworth was already away. He crouched behind the desk and scooped the phone off its top. Under the cover of the racketing gunshots, he spoke to the man who answered.

"Give me the long-distance operator," he ordered, his voice like Zieger's.

The operator said, "I'll make the call, Zieg!"

Wentworth swore at him with a savage violence "Do as I tell you and keep your ear off the wire, get it? This is personal, me to the Snake!"

When the long-distance operator came on, Wentworth's voice was entirely different. "I want to know the charges on that call just made over this wire." He masked the flashlight in his fist and read the number on the phone disc. The operator reported back and Wentworth asked for the number and exchange.

The guns were still blazing crazily in the darkness. A man cried out hoarsely as his ally's bullet caught him. He fired back in a greater frenzy. Behind the desk, the *Spider* laughed, and its eerie mocking flatness carried menace to the men in the dark. Now, suddenly, the hall door was ripped open and a man bolted that way. He was followed, an instant later, by another. There were left only the unconscious Zieger and the wounded man who cursed hoarsely and continued to shoot impotently into the darkness.

The *Spider* reached him by a circuitous route and knocked him out, then he turned his flashlight on the chair in which Nita had sat. It was just possible she had left a message. There was something red on the tapestry and, for a moment, fear gripped him. Then he saw that it was lipstick. She had written *Manitoba*.

Wentworth flicked his light on Zieger and saw that, in the darkness, he had not struck quite true. He had wanted to keep the man alive. He had slain him instead.

THE *Spider* glided back to the window by which he had entered. There was a sharp tang of smoke on the air. The hall light was hazed by smoke. He did not think that the gang guards had succeeded in "plugging the doors." Wentworth laughed silently and, at the roof's edge, he paused a moment. His silken Web sailed out into the air and noosed a chimney pot near the corner of the building across the street.

For an instant, the *Spider* poised on the balustrade, then he leaped out into space. His spring whirled him down and around the corner of the building. As he surged upward again, he swung his body forward and landed lightly on the gutter of the opposite roof. It was a work of moments to regather his Web and hurry toward a roof scuttle.

In the warehouse headquarters of the Hara gang, the flames had reached the windows.

Less than an hour later, having ascertained that Jackson and Ram Singh were alive, but wounded, in a hospital, Wentworth lifted a rented plane from the runway of Mobiltown's airport. Once more his impersonation of an F.B.I. man had stood him in good stead. He had a fast plane that should put him close upon the Snake's trail within a few hours. A thin smile curved Wentworth's lips. Zeiger's call to headquarters had been fortunate for him. Through it, he not only knew the city to which the Snake had fled, but would be able to learn his address when he arrived.

"Wissouri City" in the spoken code of the gangsters apparently meant New York City!

At any rate, it had been to New York that Zeiger's phone call had reached, and his man had talked to the Weasel at an address which Wentworth placed on the lower East Side! Where the Weasel was, the Snake would not be far away! Nita's clue confused him a little. He could not puzzle out the meaning of that word "Manitoba" which she had scrawled on the chair tapestry. He had stowed the thought away in his mind for future reference. It might mean that Nita had been carried to the province of Manitoba in Canada, but he doubted it. At any rate, the *Spider* was not primarily intent upon rescuing Nita. His first duty was to find and destroy the Snake!

As soon as the city had dropped behind, Wentworth leveled the plane off and thrust the throttle wide open. The powerful motor ripped the ship across the sky. The broad middlewestern states slid under his wings at furious speed, and in an incredibly short time, he was vaulting the Alleghanies and straightening out on the last sharp dash to New York City itself.

It was when he was within a fast half hour's race of the city that he became aware of another plane bulleting toward him at a higher level, and from the direction of the city itself. At first he gave the ship, dimly discerned against the moonlit sky, only a cursory glance. Suddenly, he realized that the ship had changed its course and was slicing straight toward him! Their combined speed was enormous and, within seconds after he had sighted the craft, they were plunging head-on toward each other!

Wentworth remembered that Nita's plane had been shot down. He pointed the nose of his ship upward steeply, and, at that moment, the other craft opened fire! Wentworth saw the entire front of the plane flicker and blaze with guns! It must be either an Army or Navy ship to carry such fire power! Fully eight machine guns were blasting. At the nose, there was the bloom of cannon fire!

Wentworth's upward leap had been quick, but not quick enough. That tremendous burst of lead struck the tail of his ship like a hurricane... and the tail was lopped off as cleanly as an amputation. The motor whirled the remnant of a plane like a dervish. Wentworth cut the gun, dived over the side while there still was time. Overhead, the killer plane performed a zoom and whipped about to slash once more at the falling ship. It exploded under the full impact of the guns. The winds flailed loose and the air was filled with fluttering bits of debris. Among them, Wentworth was a falling dark blur.

The suddenness of the attack, but more than that, the virtual certainty that it was an Army-piloted plane shook the *Spider*.

He peered below him and, suddenly, the sky was illuminated by a bright flare, dropped by his assailant. Against that his parachute, which he soon must open, would stand out enormously. There would be enemies waiting for him then!

The *Spider* grasped his ripcord ring. It was time. As his body steadied in the tight grip of the harness, he whipped out his guns. Enemies would be waiting, but would they be the Snake's killers, or federal men? If it were agents of the government below him, his chances of escape were not one in a thousand. For, against them, his guns were useless! The *Spider* did not fight the servants of his country!

THE men on the ground were ready and waiting for him. They seemed to have calculated in advance just where he would fall. Machine guns and revolvers and shotguns covered the *Spider*. The circling plane dived down and swept upward again, ready at need. The wind of its passage postled the parachute. The flare still flung out its brilliant light.

Wentworth slipped his guns back into their holsters and reached up to the parachute shrouds. All that he could do, at this time, was to land among those waiting men, spill his parachute quickly... then trust to circumstance for his chance. He was certain now that these were officers of the law!

An instant later, he struck the ground. Expertly, he spilled the parachute, threw off the straps. Flashlight glare struck him from four angles.

"Just hoist your hands and keep them there," a man ordered quietly. "You're under arrest."

The *Spider* made no answer, but lifted his hands. He was debating swiftly. If they would listen to him, he would guide them to the Snake headquarters. Otherwise, he must escape as the opportunity offered. The *Spider* had been arrested before! So he thought, but knew that he was bolstering his hopes against despair. He knew they would be unlikely to listen to his story; and if they were careful, his chances of escape would be slim. He heard behind him the footsteps of the man come to disarm him.

The blow that smashed across his skull from behind took the *Spider* completely by surprise. It blacked out his senses, but even as he pitched limply forward, his brain flashed a single thought: "Not the law! *Snake-men!*"

CHAPTER NINETEEN
Crime Marches On!

THE touch of her door knob brought Nita van Sloan sharply to her feet. She was not bound but there was nothing in the room that could be used as a weapon. The Weasel stood on the sill.

"Come on, babe," he said. "I guess it's time."

Nita van Sloan said nothing, but she was quite calm as she walked through the door and, ahead of the Weasel, moved along a brightly lighted hallway. The Snake had kept her alive with the foreknowledge of early death hanging over her. He had summoned her a half dozen times like this. Each time, she had walked down that hallway with a certainty that this meant death... and each time, she had presently been sent back to her room again.

Not many men could have stood that walk to death, the last long mile, for six times. Six times, the summons at the door, the slow gathering of the vital forces, of courage screwed up to the breaking point... and then let down. But Nita walked it steadily, with her head high, though strain had cut a thin line about her mouth.

The scene never changed. Always there was that blackened shadow of a man behind the light, always those two awful hands under the light. Twice now, there had been no word from him at all. She was thrust into a chair and, for minute after minute, they sat there, captor and victim, while death stood at Nita's elbow. With all her studied strength, Nita clung to her inner core of courage and calm readiness. She knew that if her courage wavered, the Snake would kill her. He had a cruel curiosity as to how long she could resist the poison of fear.

So Nita, presented this sixth time, put her gallant smile upon her lips and, without orders, dropped into the chair to confront her tormenter. The strain was plucking at her nerves. When the Weasel giggled at her elbow, she started violently, and thereafter twisted her hands tightly together in her lap. Her body screamed for relief; anything to stop this torture. Break and achieve death! But Nita clung on, because it was her code to do so. If an opportunity to escape should come to her, she would seize it. And there was always the chance that the *Spider* would come, even though the clue she had left him was a false lead. For they had come to New York, not to Manitoba.

The Snake's voice was, as always, flat and without emotion. "We have captured the *Spider,"* he said. "His two men were shot in Mobiletown, but he dodged the trap. We did not catch him until he was almost in New York. Then we shot him down. I rather fancy he thought he was being arrested. He did not fire a shot."

Nita's hands were suddenly still in her lap. Could she believe this killer? She gave him no answer except a skeptical laugh. She felt the Weasel move closer, could sense his eager knife. The Snake made no answer to her laughter, only she saw that his hands were very still. They were compressed. They were pink and white with pressure. Only where the crawling black hair was, they showed no result of a man's tension or anger.

They sat so, and the slow minutes dragged past. A phone bell whirred and a hand moved to scoop up the instrument. He said, presently, "I am waiting."

For once, there was expression in his voice. It was evil with triumph!

Nita shivered. Unless the man was putting on another act to shatter her nerves, he had told the truth! There were slow steps in the hallway, heavy as if men walked with a casket. The door was opened and three men came in, carrying a fourth, feet first. She could see the feet, and the multiple wrappings of rope around the lower legs. That was all. Then they threw the man to the floor, within a few feet of her.

The face was disguised. It was possible to see that now, with the pallor of unconsciousness under the makeup. It was the *Spider!* Nita's heart cried out to him, but she only forced a laugh.

"You've been fooled again," she said lightly.

THE Snake made no answer. The three men stood back against the door and the wall. Wentworth was wrapped in rope like a cocoon. If he moved a finger, that would be the limit of his freedom. Nita saw suddenly that he was moving... one finger! It tapped against his leg in swift dots and dashes.

"Play him," the *Spider* signaled.

Nita leaned forward to peer more closely into Wentworth's face, and a smile curved her lips. She was suddenly relaxed and ready. It seemed madness that the presence of this man, helpless as a paralytic, should give her such fresh courage. She thought that, even if he were dead, she still would draw courage from him. So, clever actress that she was, she overdid her relief.

The Snake laughed dry acknowledgement of her effort. "That was the confirmation that I needed," he said flatly. "Now's the time to bring him around."

The Weasel stepped eagerly forward, but one of the captors was before him. Presently, under his ministrations, the *Spider* rolled his head. The finger against his side was tapping again now, steadily. *"He has some use for us or he would not have kept you alive and bothered to capture me. Be bold. We will conquer!"* It was like a voice of courage whispering in her inner ear. Suddenly the imminent shadow of hooded death, which she had emboldened herself to face, was no longer fearsome. She knew it was still near, but now the man she loved was with her.

"Come, *Spider."* The Snake's voice was acid. "Surely, your great brain is able to overcome a mere tap on the skull?"

Wentworth's head rolled toward the sound of the voice. He could see nothing, because the desk was between him and the hands; the face was in black shadow. He could only see its loom, but the outline was fatly huge. Wentworth smiled, slightly.

"A nice little trap," he said, "and neatly staged. I must compliment your men on their execution. You apparently have a use to which you expect to put me, eh?"

Even bound and helpless upon the floor, he dominated the situation. He had taken the lead away from the Snake. But the man only laughed, like a dry rattling of pebbles.

"You came back too suddenly, *Spider,"* he said, carelessly. "I perceive that you were conscious before we 'revived' you."

Wentworth said, "Of course."

It was as cautious and deadly as the first lunges and parries of two expert swordsmen. *The Spider* knew this was no ordinary gangster who could be goaded into swift, confusing angers. He was struggling to identify something about the voice. It had a peculiar tonelessness, an absence of inflection that might be studied; or the speech of a man of many languages, to whom English was not native. There was no trace of an accent, aside from that.

Nita interrupted gravely, "I'm sorry I misled you with my planted clue, *Spider."* Wentworth smiled up at her. "You did not. It was cleverly done."

The Weasel leaned toward them, and his face worked. "You talk too much," he said, viciously. "I could fix you so you didn't talk so much."

The *Spider* said, curtly, "I thought you specialized in killing unconscious men, Weasel, with other men's guns! I'm still too dangerous for *you* to work on."

The Weasel fairly chattered with his rage. "I can kill you! I don't like them unconscious. I—"

"Weasel!"

THE voice was like a crack of a whip, but Wentworth's eves were lidded, well-pleased. He had not been able to goad the Snake, but he had made him utter a word that was not completely under control. And now he knew what language was native to the Snake!

He said, "You should keep away from Canada, Snake. Up there, they shoot your kind."

The Snake said, "Canada? Ah, yes. You are too clever, *Spider.* You cause me to question the wisdom of using you, as I had intended."

"I beg of you," Wentworth's voice was heavily satirical, "use me as you will."

Nita did not understand that exchange. She saw that Wentworth had penetrated some secret of the Snake and that it had been cleverly done. The Snake's voice was underscored now with cold hatred.

"I shall accept, my dear *Spider.*" His voice sounded thicker. "It is, after all, a very small service. You see, New York has resisted all my effort, and that resistance is centered in one man. You shall help me to trap and destroy that man. Afterward, I shall leave you there to take the responsibility, so that the police will not so soon seek us out. Their morale is too high now. We must first destroy that."

Nita felt the tension crawling back along her arms and thighs. The illusion of fresh strength was fading; the feeling of their complete helplessness weakened her. But Wentworth only smiled and turned to her.

"I do believe the man thinks he can hold you hostage for my good behavior," he said, dryly. "Imagine his keeping you alive for that!"

The Snake said, "I will not be goaded. We who are sure of our strength do not need to defend ourselves."

Wentworth's smile widened, for the assertion was, in itself, weakness. The strong are silent. The Snake slapped his hands down hard on the desk, came to his feet. But still that black shield of shadow lay across his face.

"I promise you only this!" There was a suggestion of a "w" in his pronunciation of promise. "Certain death for you both, under certain circumstances. If you fail me, the woman shall live for a while."

Wentworth nodded easily. It was the old threat, but its antiquity did not lessen its force. "The identification now is complete," he said. "Now, who is it you are hoping to assassinate? I must know that before I can prevent it."

The Snake laughed, and this time there was a hard, sure violence in his speech.

"The man who will die," he said positively, "is Commissioner of Police Kirkpatrick!"

CHAPTER TWENTY
Bait and a Trap!

COMMISSIONER KIRKPATRICK realized that he was finished for the day. All that could be done to protect the city for the night had been done; the day's spate of crime was under control. He had a feeling of work well done. His men werze swift and energetic at their jobs. Their morale was splendid. A faint smile stirred Kirkpatrick's lips. Other cities might yield again before the pressure of gangsters and racketeers, but in New York, the line of the law stood firm. That efficiency was the reason that he was kept in office through changing administrations.

He cleared the last report from his desk, thrust a long-barreled revolver into its holster and locked the drawer. He plucked a flower from a vase on his desk, and slid it into his buttonhole. His hat now—

The phone on his desk whirred. He hesitated, then scooped up the instrument.

"The *Spider* speaking," a flat whisper beat against his ear. "I have evidence that will clear an innocent man of a charge of murder. Meet me in ten minutes at your office and I will surrender the evidence to you."

Kirkpatrick's voice was strong and challenging: "I make no appointments with criminals. I give you no safe conduct. If you come here, it is at your own risk! I warn you every effort will be made either to capture or kill you!"

The laughter of the *Spider* answered him, and the wire went dead. Mechanically, Kirkpatrick reached to the annunciator box on his desk, pressed a cam.

"I have had a call from the *Spider,* saying he will be in my office in ten minutes," he said. "Get out the reserves and sew this building up tight. Throw a cordon around the block."

He released the cam. Slowly, he reseated himself, put the flower back in the vase. He drew his revolver out of his holster and laid it on the desk under his hand. He began to swear, softly, but vehemently.

"Dick, Dick," he said, "why do you place me in these situations!"

Despite many factual proofs to the contrary, many perfect alibis, Kirkpatrick's conviction that Dick Wentworth was the *Spider* still persisted. One large reason was that Kirkpatrick knew no other man of sufficient integrity, courage and ability to perform as the *Spider* did! Kirkpatrick knew the *Spider* well, from their many battles. He knew Richard Wentworth even better. They were both of the same steel.

That was not evidence you could take into court, of course. Kirkpatrick smiled grimly. There was a part of him that was glad of the fact, but it would never swerve him by one hair's breadth from the sure course of his duty. He clicked open the gate of his revolver and slid a sixth shell into the chamber. He spun the cylinder, carefully laid the gun down, again under his hand.

He was ready... for the *Spider*—whoever he may be!

ON THE roof of police headquarters and on the roof across the street from headquarters, the trap of the Snake was ready. There were five machine gunners across the street, with their weapons trained on Kirkpatrick's office window. The *Spider* himself, helpless in his ropes, was on the roof. Yet he was calm, composed.

Presently, with his robe about him, the *Spider* would be lowered to Kirkpatrick's window. When the Police Commissioner came to the window, both would die under the belching hot deluge of machine gun bullets!

It was a simple trap. There were ninety-nine chances out of a hundred that it would succeed. Wentworth, lying there on the roof, knew that the hundredth chance depended upon him. They had told him nothing of their plans, but he had gauged them easily. They jerked him to his feet, and tied him very cleverly. Each wrist was bound so that it had a few inches of play, no more. His feet were invisibly lashed together. The loop of the Web was under his arms, going straight up behind his head.

There was no way he could reach the rope by which he was lowered. They gave him no chance to attempt anything on the roof, but swung him instantly out over space. Then they leaned over and placed an empty automatic in each fist.

"Hold them, *Spider!*" The Weasel spat in his face. "I have my knife in my hand. At the first false move, I will cut your rope. If you so much as whisper, I will cut your rope. Your fall will bring Kirkpatrick to the window where we can shoot him!"

Wentworth did not speak. The rope began to slip over the edge, and he was lowered rapidly toward Kirkpatrick's window! The *Spider* had made no plan, could make none. If it would save Kirkpatrick, he would willingly commit some folly to make them cut the rope. It would not help. He threw a glance across the street. There was a single thread of light shining steadily. He guessed its significance. When he had dropped low enough, that light would go off as a signal.

The *Spider* clutched his useless guns. He was spinning slowly at the end of the rope. He reached out with a gun and dragged its muzzle against the wall to keep his face turned outward. So that he could watch that shred of light up above. Until that light went out, some of the men would be busy

with the rope. He peered upward. The Weasel's vicious silhouette was there against the sky.

Wentworth's lips creased in a cold smile. How swift were the Weasel's reflexes? How quickly would he react to a "false move?" The Weasel was in charge. He would have to glance at that light across the street occasionally, to tell the men when it was time to stop lowering. On such small things as that, Wentworth was building a plan which might save Kirkpatrick's life. It was the hundredth chance. Of his own survival, there was not one chance in a thousand. If he succeeded, he would still be a helpless prisoner in the hands of the police!

The *Spider* laughed soundlessly. Odds a thousand-to-one! Well, he had fought longer odds... and won! But he knew he was pumping false courage into his nerves. He did not need it. He made his gamble with his eyes wide open. If he saved Kirkpatrick, it would still be a victory!

He was only a foot above the window of Kirkpatrick's office now. He did not change his position, back to the building. He did draw his knees up, so that his legs were doubled tightly, so that his feet rested lightly against the wall. He would make his gamble the instant the light above flicked out. When that happened, the Weasel would order his men to cease lowering. Wentworth did not think that the Weasel would do that without turning his head. Having that thought in his mind, the Weasel would have difficulty in reacting quickly. That was Wentworth's hope, Wentworth's gamble.

He was still beside the window. They would swing him over it at the appropriate minute, but not too far, for they would want a clear shot at Kirkpatrick! The *Spider*'s head was tipped back, watching that thread of light. Abruptly it went out. The *Spider* unwound like a released spring. His feet drove against the wall and thrust him far out at the end of his silken rope.

How quick was the Weasel's reaction time? If he cut the rope too soon, the *Spider* would sail outward to crash to death in the middle of the street! He was still swinging outward, turning so that he would face Kirkpatrick's window as he moved back. He reached the end of his swing, and there was that still moment of waiting before gravity overcame his momentum and pulled him back toward the window. It was just at that pause that he heard a hoarse shout!

THE Weasel had spotted his action now! Wentworth turned and was sailing back toward Kirkpatrick's window! He flung one of his guns before him, heard it crash the window glass. His voice rang out clearly:

"Keep back, Kirkpatrick! Trap! Assassination!"

He felt the rope sag, but still he did not fall. The

stout silk had defied the first slash of the knife! He was no more than six feet from the window now. Five feet, four... he could see Kirkpatrick through the glass, and he repeated his cry of warning. And then the rope let go.

If Wentworth's arms had been free, he could have reached out and grabbed the sill. It was going to be as close as that! His feet were thrust out before him. They would strike the wall and flip him over backward.

... In a convulsive effort, Wentworth wrenched his body in mid-air, using the momentum of his swing. He started a slow, torturously slow somersault. His feet were drawn back, even with him now. He was bending forward. The windowsill was only two feet away, only inches away—

With frenzied effort, Wentworth whipped his legs up and over. His forehead hit the sill of the window. Even that faint leverage he used, by jerking his head sharply forward with all the power of his neck muscles. His feet came over slowly, balled tightly. He felt the hot-cold slash of broken glass... and then he struck the floor inside the office.

"Keep away from the window, Kirkpatrick!" he gasped. "It's a trap!"

He rolled frantically back to the protection of the wall, and at that moment, the machine guns cut loose. One was directly across the street, but the others were ranged out to each side so that they converged on the window at a wide angle. It had been cleverly planned, perfectly executed... except that the Snake had not held a stopwatch on the Weasel's reaction time.

Kirkpatrick was at his desk, shouting into the annunciator. Even there, the bullets almost caught him. They cut a destructive swathe across his blotter. His flower vase became a thousand fragments; his telephone was smashed into junk. Crouched against the wall, under the window, Wentworth found what he sought... a jagged knife of glass. His hands had a few inches of freedom, and it was enough to enable him to cut his ropes.

He had escaped the trap at the window, saved Kirkpatrick... but he was still a prisoner of the police. He could not have used weapons against the police, even had he one with bullets in it. What made the situation even more difficult was that Kirkpatrick and the New York police knew that the *Spider* would not fire on them.

Freed of the ropes, Wentworth crawled under the window where the machine gun bullets still streamed. He was behind Kirkpatrick as the Commissioner straightened from the annunciator. With a deft wrench, he disarmed Kirkpatrick and thrust him back against the wall.

"You know I won't kill you," Wentworth said in the *Spider*'s voice, "but I'm going to knock you out

if you open your mouth. Listen! I did not telephone you. That was the man who is at the head of all the crime in this country, a man called the Snake. He used that phone call, and me, a prisoner, in an attempt to assassinate you." There was a heavy knocking at the door. Wentworth spoke more rapidly. "I can lead you to the Snake. Nita van Sloan is his prisoner. I'll give you my parole not to attempt to escape until the Snake is captured or dead! You know I have never broken my word. Will you accept?"

Kirkpatrick's jaw was set hard and there was stubbornness in his brilliant blue eyes.

"Wait!" Wentworth urged. "Which is the greater danger to your people and your nation: The *Spider*, or the man who is victimizing the entire nation, and destroying the morale of the people when every ounce of courage and effort is needed for war? I know your ideals and your integrity. They are the reason you were going to be killed.

"But which is worth more, Kirkpatrick? Your integrity... or your country?"

Kirkpatrick's jaw still had a rock-hard set. The hammering at the door was louder.

"Get those men on the roof!" Kirkpatrick ordered harshly. "Throw the cordon wider. There are machine gunners on the roof across the street!"

His eyes were stern upon those of the *Spider*, only half-seen under the brim of his black hat.

"I make no compromise," he said harshly. "You will go with me as my prisoner, not on parole. You will do this because you, too, love your country and will serve her at all costs."

The *Spider* had won all that he had hoped to win. He knew Kirkpatrick and how to maneuver him. He stepped back a full pace and presented the revolver, butt-first.

"I accept," he said quietly. "There is no time to be lost. We will need about twenty well-armed men, and a speedboat or two."

Kirkpatrick's eyes narrowed. "Where is this criminal, then? Who is he?"

"On the interned steamship, *Manitoba*. He is the enemy's secret agent whom the police, the Army and Navy Intelligence, and the F.B.I. have known was in this country and have not been able to find. His name is legion."

CHAPTER TWENTY-ONE
Race Against Death

THREE of the gunmen who were on the roofs were slain by the police. Two more were wounded. The Weasel was not among them. That made the need for haste triply imperative. The big police car charged through the city with its siren silent. Behind them rolled four carloads of police, armed with rifles and machine guns. Two speedboats were waiting.

Kirkpatrick turned uneasily to the *Spider*, who was handcuffed to a detective. "Isn't there a chance that Nita van Sloan will be killed by this man you call the Snake?"

"A very good chance," the *Spider* answered, quietly. He said no more, but kept his eyes fixed straight ahead. He was cold with the certainty that the Snake would do exactly that, or else attempt to use her as a hostage when the police struck. He would have some warning from the Weasel. How much warning would depend on the speed of the police and their means of communication.

Kirkpatrick said irritably. "There is no way to do it except by frontal attack! I cannot delay, or give the man an opportunity to escape, in order to save anyone's life."

The *Spider* was courteous, "Certainly not."

Kirkpatrick had not attempted to strip off his disguise. In his own mind, he knew this man beside him was Wentworth, though there was no resemblance, either in carriage or speech or any other particular. And now there was another unspoken thing between them. Wentworth had saved Kirkpatrick's life and had escaped himself only by the narrowest fraction. Now the woman he loved was in peril.

Kirkpatrick said, slowly, "I will attempt a silent capture of the ship, and appoint certain men to race for the cabin. That is the most I can do. But if they are already warned, that will not be successful."

"Yes," Wentworth agreed, "it depends entirely upon the identity of those certain men whom you appoint to attempt to save Miss van Sloan."

Kirkpatrick frowned and was silent while they left the cars and rapidly filled the two speedboats that were waiting at the pier.

"You will follow my boat," Kirkpatrick ordered one of his subordinates. "No lights. As quiet as possible."

The speedboat purred out from the dock, its powerful engine throttled low. Kirkpatrick sat once more beside the *Spider* and the man who held him prisoner. The commissioner's silence told the *Spider* that he had won. He would be free to race ahead and save Nita. It made his own capture more binding. He would not violate his parole.

The chop of the harbor waves began to slap the boat more rapidly. A gust of spray stung their faces. The prow lifted and began to plane. They were going fast now, into the teeth of the wind. Presently, when they were nearer, they would slow down. One of the harbor police came back and saluted.

"Small speedboat racing ahead of us, sir, in the same direction," he reported. "Can we overtake it?"

The man shook his head doubtfully. "We may be a little faster, but there isn't much farther to go."

Kirkpatrick made his sharp decision. "Full speed. Damn the noise. This will be close and fast." He turned to Wentworth. "I will accept your parole for the duration of the battle. At the battle's end, you will surrender to me."

The *Spider* said, quietly, "You have my word for that."

THE detective looked up with startled eyes as he was ordered to unlock the handcuffs and give the *Spider* ammunition and his two automatics. Wentworth loaded the clips with steady fingers and his eyes ranged ahead toward the rusty-sided steamer. The small speedboat scuttled in under her stern and disappeared.

Kirkpatrick was risking his entire reputation in order to afford him this opportunity to save Nita. But that very fact laid an additional bondage upon the *Spider*. He had given his parole to surrender when the battle was over. He must do more than that. He must go docilely to police headquarters and allow himself to be locked up! Otherwise, Kirkpatrick would be ruined!

Wentworth slapped the clips into the butts of his automatics, heeled back the slide to jack a cartridge into the chambers, added an extra cartridge to the clips. He spun the guns into his holsters. His movements were as deft as oiled machinery. He did not look at the guns. The detective watched him with a mounting awe.

The ship was very close now. Wentworth turned his head. "I want a grappling iron thrown over that railing," he said. "Slam in at full speed, and throw that iron. You'll find some sort of ladder over the side."

Kirkpatrick nodded and gave the order quietly. "Signal the other boat to take the starboard side. We'll go past portside at full speed."

One of the harbor police crawled up on the forward deck, stood straight up against wind and sea to swing the grappling iron at rope's end. Wentworth stepped up behind him, picked up the coil of rope and twisted it about his left hand. As they charged past the steamer, a man sprang suddenly to the railing of the boat, and jerked up a submachine gun!

The *Spider's* right hand moved like a flick of a whip. He drew and fired in a pause as brief as a heartbeat. The machine gunner was hurled backward, and the next instant the grapple rang on the railing. The *Spider* was peeled off the forward deck of the boat. His body swung far forward along the side of the ship. He spun like a trolling spoon. His cape ballooned, then wrapped around him. His body bounced against the rusty steel plates, spun higher.

His upreaching right hand snagged the railing and, an instant later, he vaulted lightly to the deck. The police in the boat had that one glimpse of him, and then, with a black swirl of his cape, he had plunged from sight.

"God help him," Kirkpatrick muttered. "He is a man."

The detective said, fervently. "I'm glad it ain't me he's after!"

THE Snake had left the cabin of the ship. With Nita helpless in the grip of two men, with the Weasel crouching ahead of them, they raced along the forward deck. When Nita saw what was there, she began to struggle against the men who held her. There was a small sea-plane, cocked back on a catapult boom!

The Snake reached out and jarred the base of her skull with his fist, and her body went lax. Nita felt herself thrown into the forward seat, strapped back against the headrest. The Snake took the controls.

She heard the Weasel, shrill with fright. "Hey, ain't there a place for me? Ain't there a place—"

She heard the Snake say, "Certainly, my friend."

A gun crashed, and the Weasel screamed.

Then the Snake's voice went on calmly. "You have your orders?"

The men saluted. Their guttural voices were steady. "We shoot you off, then explode the ship."

"Good!" the Snake said quietly. "Let go as soon as the motor starts. It's already been warmed up."

Nita was fighting desperately to regain full consciousness. The starter whined. The motor exploded into life and, from its sound, it was already warmed up. The Snake shouted his order, and at that moment, guns began to speak on the deck of the ship. They were heavy booming shots, such as a forty-five caliber automatic would make. They spoke of certain doom.

Nita twisted about her head. She saw that both of the Snake's men were down. She saw the black shape of the *Spider* leap tremendously into the air toward the plane! And one of the Snake's men, on the deck, crawled over and laid his hand on the lanyard that would fire the plane from the catapult.

A shriek lifted in Nita's throat. She saw the *Spider* land asprawl the ship's tail, spraddling it like a horse. Then the sudden harsh impetus of the catapult slammed her back against the headrest, and she saw no more. The plane made its short race, motor bellowing wide open. It dipped at the beam's end,

sagged toward the dark waters. Its motor howled, and the propeller clawed the air. But the tail was heavy, weighted down. The pontoons hit the surface of a wave. It bounded wildly upward, and then Nita heard the crash of gunfire behind her. She twisted about, freeing herself of the straps. The Snake had a gun and was firing straight back at Wentworth, who straddled the tail.

It was incredible that he could hold on that way; incredible that the Snake could miss at such short range. But the plane slapped from wave to wave. Nita sucked in a deep and desperate breath. She got to her knees and drove her knotted fist against the base of the Snake's skull. His head jerked forward. He wrenched the gun about, and Nita struck again. This time her stiff, prodding fingers hit the right nerve centers!

The Snake's head wrenched back violently. His mouth popped open... and the plane, instead of skimming the next wave, stubbed its pontoons deep into it. The ship's tail flipped high and Wentworth lifted like a gaunt and awkward bird. Nita felt herself thrown, too. The impact of the water was incredible, like the slap of a big hard-rubber club. Her senses reeled. She felt herself sinking, remembered to keep her mouth shut, to hold her breath. She tried to fight her way upward, but still she was going down, down. A panic fear pounded up into her throat. She conquered that... and knew, suddenly, that she was rising again.

When her head broke water, she still could not move, but she tipped her head back and breathed shallowly. She watched the waves and timed her breathing. Presently, she was able to move her arms and legs. She heaved high on the top of a wave, looked around her. There was some wreckage of the plane nearby, but the ship itself had vanished! And the Snake was unconscious, strapped into the cockpit.

Nita stared toward the rusty old steamer, heaving short at its anchor chains. It seemed an incredible distance away. Weariness crowded through her. She knew now that Dick had lived at least to save Kirkpatrick; to lead this rescue. She knew that the Snake was dead. It was enough. Dick... but Dick had been hurled a hundred yards through the air, by the flip of that plane's tail. She had been thrown only a short distance.

Terror struck her. She began to swim with a swift racing crawl away from the boat. Somewhere out here, Dick might be lying unconscious, or sinking. Abruptly, from the crest of a wave, she saw a man swimming toward her. He was moving with a competent flash and sweep of his arms. Behind him, his trudgeoning feet made the faintest of wakes.

His head flipped up. He saw her. "Back to the ship!" he called clearly. "Back! They've planted a mine in that ship! It may blow up at any moment. There are twenty men aboard, and Kirkpatrick!"

NITA turned and, side by side, they raced back toward the *Manitoba*. They were fully a half mile away. Swiftly, Wentworth began to draw ahead of her. He had shucked off his outer clothing and his body sliced the water like a shark. There was a superhuman power in the way he swam; in the swift lift and sweep of his arms, the tireless beat of his feet. Nita did not struggle to keep up with him. Her weariness was gone now with her fears and she swam easily, but without taxing herself too much.

Minutes before she reached the stern of the ship, she saw Wentworth's lithe body swing upward on the rope still attached to the grappling iron. She heard his shout sail downwind.

"This boat is mined!" he called, and urgency edged his voice like steel. "All hands off! All hands overside! Abandon ship! It will blow up in seconds!"

He saw police racing toward him. Kirkpatrick was walking steadily beside a stretcher on which someone lay unconscious.

"Hurry!" Wentworth shouted. "This ship is mined, I tell you!"

Kirkpatrick's voice took up crisp command, and the police spilled overside swiftly. The stretcher, however, was lowered carefully to the speedboat. Wentworth dropped down one of its ropes as Kirkpatrick slid down the other.

"Miss van Sloan's in the water astern," 'Wentworth said crisply. "Port side."

The speedboat backed a dozen yards and picked up Nita. But Kirkpatrick was crouched beside the stretcher. Wentworth saw now that the man who lay upon it was the Weasel. There was a great spreading stain upon his chest. He coughed, and his voice was a whisper that was interrupted by seeping blood. Wentworth moved toward the stretcher and heard the Weasel's words slip out one by one, with the last beats of his heart.

"That guy, Jackson, ain't guilty," he said. "I did them kills. The Snake made me. The Snake made me do everything I did."

"Tell me more about Jackson," Kirkpatrick said quietly.

The Weasel grinned. "Slick, that was. We had a dame put on a hat like Jackson's wife, and then two guys snatched her into the barroom. But Jackson knocked those two kicking, like he was supposed to do. Then we came in; beaned Jackson, killed the two guys with Jackson's gun and planted it. Whole idea was... keep *Spider* here in New York!"

There was a policeman taking down what the Weasel said, in shorthand. At the bottom of every page, the Weasel scrawled his name. They'd get as much as they could before the Weasel died. Wentworth did not go to Nita. He drew on a coat that a policeman supplied and found the detective.

"I haven't had a chance to surrender to Kirkpatrick yet," he said. "But you better put on the cuffs."

As the detective snapped the cuffs, there was a tearing explosion behind them. The *Manitoba* lifted bodily from the waters. Flames towered toward the sky, and the waves were flattened by the beat of the concussion. They were half-stunned by the violence of the explosion. Before they could do more than realize what had happened, the waves had closed over the ship.

THEN Kirkpatrick was standing over the *Spider*, looking down at the handcuff that linked him to the detective.

"The Weasel is dead," he said. "We got a pretty good lot of stuff from him. Enough to confirm everything you told me, *Spider*, and a lot more. The Snake shot him, so he talked."

The *Spider* nodded soberly. "The Snake went down with his plane. There'll be some cleaning up to do, but with the head lopped off, the gangs will split apart. Divide and rule." He smiled up, thinly, into the face of Kirkpatrick. "It was the enemy's old trick. Undermine the confidence of the people in their government, make them afraid of each other, greedy, full of hate." He nodded. "It's worth it, to me."

Kirkpatrick turned abruptly away, but not before Wentworth had seen the shadow of pain in his eyes. This, Wentworth knew, was the most difficult task the Commissioner of Police had ever had, to take the *Spider* to a prison from which he would emerge only to die in the electric chair!

Kirkpatrick called back, "He's released from his parole now, Green. Watch him!"

Wentworth's smile was warm. Kirkpatrick had stretched his conscience to the breaking point to say that. He knew that the words were as good as an invitation for the *Spider* to escape. But the *Spider* sat placidly beside his guard, and went with an equal placidity to his cell. Once the door clanged on him, he was free to escape... if he could. For then, no one could say that he was free because Kirkpatrick had accepted his parole.

"Ask the warden to send me some clothing," he told the jailer. "I'm stripped down to my underwear under this coat."

The *Manitoba* lifted bodily from the water!

The jailer grunted, "Ain't supposed to supply clothes."

He went off, and Wentworth's smile was quizzical now. Though he was the *Spider*, they had not thought it necessary to search him when they saw him in his dripping wet underwear. They had registered and fingerprinted him, and charged him formerly with suspicion of murder. And then locked him in the cell. But they should have searched him. It was a part of the *Spider*'s need always to be able to force or open locks, and so, in the leather girdle he wore under his clothing, he carried appropriate tools.

When the jailer returned grumpily, with clothing, he thrust it toward the figure he could see just inside the bars, in the dimness of the cell. The figure's back was turned toward him, shoulders broad under the blue police coat.

"Here's your clothes," the jailer said impatiently.

No one answered him. He poked the blue coat, and the figure swayed out from the bars, heavily thudded back. He saw then that there was a rope, made of torn fragments of a blanket, and knotted to the bars. The jailer frenziedly unlocked the door, ran inside... and two hands reached out and took him. The prod against nerve centers was hard

enough to put him out. The *Spider* slipped his arms out of the noose of the rope, laid the jailer on the bed and covered him up. Rapidly, he put on the clothing, the blue coat, the uniform cap of the jailer. He would need the lock-picking kit before he was out of police headquarters.

IN WENTWORTH'S apartment, to which she had sped, Nita van Sloan paced the floor uneasily. Here, she had access to all the *Spider*'s implements and devices; here she had plenty of cash available.

But what could she do at the present time to rescue Dick Wentworth?

She started at the ringing of the door bell, ran to open it. Commissioner Kirkpatrick walked in.

"Where's Dick?" he asked quietly.

Nita van Sloan looked at him, and her lips wanted to tremble, but she could not allow that. She said, lightly, "He went West to work on those same cases that the *Spider* was so successful with, Stanley. I'm expecting him almost any time now. I tried to get him by phone, but the hotel said he had checked out He's probably flying east right now." Kirkpatrick took out a notebook and pencil. "What hotel is that?" he asked.

Nita told him, "The Monterrey, in Wissouri City."

She had made that call as a cover. Everything she could do to protect Richard Wentworth's double identity she would perform until such time as it was no longer necessary—either because he was known, or had escaped.

Nita stood very still at the thought of that possibility of escape. But how could it be expected? Dick had got out of many tight places, but she knew well how they would guard the *Spider.* Kirkpatrick was at the phone in the hall.

"Police business," he told the operator. "Check against it at headquarters. tomorrow. Stanley Kirkpatrick speaking. Put through a person-to-person call to the manager of the Monterrey Hotel in Wissouri City, Wissouri."

He turned from the phone and, at that moment, there was the rattle of a key—or perhaps it was a lock-pick—in the front door. It swung open, and a man walked in. He wore a soft felt hat set jauntily on his head, and the tailoring of his suit was perfection. There was a topcoat over his arm, gloves in his hand, and a cane tucked under his arm. He turned as he came in, taking the key—or the lock-pick—out of the door, concealed in his hand.

"Bring the suitcases in here," he said.

A taxi driver slid them across the floor, accepted the man's tip. "Jeez, thanks, governor!" he said. He touched his hat and went back to the elevator.

Not until then did the man in the doorway turn toward the room, and then his face lighted in a smile.

"Why hello, Kirk! Nita!" he cried. "This is great! A welcome home reception. You disappeared, Nita. I was worried. Did I make you angry or something?"

HE WALKED toward Nita and took her close in his hard-muscled arms, but it was not a kiss. Nita whispered that Kirkpatrick was phoning the Monterrey Hotel in Wissouri City,

Kirkpatrick shook hands with him "Just back from the West?" he asked lightly. "What train?"

Wentworth shrugged at Nita. "It's the police

habit," he said. "Really, Kirk, it's making you impossible as a friend." He was feeling in his vest pockets, and he brought out a Pullman envelope, with ticket stubs in it. He handed it with a bow, and a click of his heels to the commissioner.

Kirkpatrick glanced at his watch, strode to the telephone and called Grand Central Station. When he came back, his lips were grim to hide a smile.

"Nice timing, Dick," he said "You had just enough time to arrive from the Streamliner. A little leisurely, perhaps, but enough time."

Wentworth smiled at him quizzically. That lapse of time had been necessitated by getting someone who looked approximately like him and buying the Pullman receipts from him.

"Your gloves," Kirkpatrick said sternly.

Wentworth handed them over with a shrug. "Is it permitted to ask just what I'm accused of this time?" he asked.

His gloves were excellent, but apparently had seen some use. So it was with the suitcases, hat, top coat. Kirkpatrick threw up his hands.

"All right," he said. "I quit." He called long distance. "Cancel that call to Wissouri City."

He looked back from the darkened hallway to where Wentworth stood beside Nita "I've done my duty," he said. "I could say that you must have a cache of clothing somewhere in the city, and that you probably bought that Pullman stub, but I can't prove a thing. It's peculiar about that. I never can prove a thing." He snapped up the phone again, glowering at them. "Now I'll receive the report," he said harshly, "that the *Spider* has escaped from jail!"

He turned his back and Nita crept into Wentworth's arms, and he held her very tightly. It was only then that the walls of his home seemed to close about him again. It had been a long time since either of them had known... security.

Kirkpatrick's voice boomed from the doorway "I can hardly believe it," he said sarcastically, "the *Spider* has just vanished into thin air! Nobody even saw him leave the jail!"

He went out and slammed the door.

THE END

THE WEB by Will Murray

Our selections for this third *Spider* volume both date to 1942, and have never been reprinted in any form.

In 1942, America was at war, and *The Spider* pulp magazine was in its ninth and penultimate year of publication. The hundredth issue had recently been published, and Norvell W. Page continued to work hard keeping the series vital and fresh, concealed by the impenetrable house name of "Grant Stockbridge."

As with any long-term pulp fiction writer, during the course of his *Spider* career, Page had many times recycled plots, or seen his plots recycled by other *Spider* writers. Now, those other ghosts had fallen by the wayside, and with the field cleared, Page was free to push the series into new directions.

Our first selection, *Return of the Racket Kings*, is actually a rather retro story. During the 1920s into the early 1930s, Norvell Page has been a newspaperman and a crime reporter on several newspapers around the country, finally quitting the *New York News-Telegram* in January 1934 to devote himself to full-time fictioneering. Thus the expatriate Virginian witnessed firsthand the wave of lawlessness created by organized crime figures that attended the misguided experiment called Prohibition.

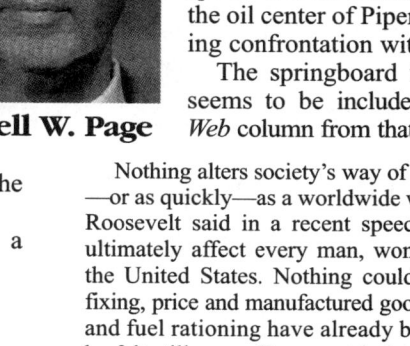

Norvell W. Page

In 1935, Page reflected on those days with a strange nostalgia:

I don't know why it is, but men who aspire to write the Great American Novel always become newspapermen. I did, too, and for the last twelve years have been sliding about the country doing one dirty job after another. I didn't know, when I was patting corpses familiarly on the shoulder in the morgues, that it was all going to come in mighty handy someday. In fact, when I began to write fiction finally, I chose the one part of these United States I knew absolutely nothing about: the West. I wrote Western stories and, what's worse, sold 'em!

One day the editor who purchased them looked at me sourly and said, "Why don't you write about something you know… like gangsters." Well, he paid for that remark—for I've been writing detective stories ever since. Amazing how many midnight murders can chill your blood after a lapse of many years when at the time they happened it was "just another stiff." And we newspapermen grumbled about leaving our cans of coffee in the press room and rushing out into the night. We thought that was work. I could get wistful about newspaper *work*, and I would swear that when I sidle into a police headquarters press room and whisper, "I'm an old newspaper man myself," my voice is positively *mournful*..

No doubt that nostalgia prompted Page to pen *Return of the Racket Kings* with its evocation of those seemingly invincible crime lords of yesteryear.

Since this is 1942, and *The Spider*'s circulation is being chipped away by comic book superheroes like Superman and Batman, not to mention *Spider* knockoffs such as Alias the Spider and the Spider Widow, Page concocted a supervillain of the type that once ran riot through the four-color presses during the Golden Age of Comics.

The Snake belongs to the genre of *Spider* villains of the early 1940s who included the Fox in *Revolt of the Underworld*. He's on the outlandish side, even for *The Spider* magazine, a clear caricature of a human evidently modeled after the exaggerated comic strip supervillains like those the Human Torch and other superheroes battled endlessly.

Our second selection was inspired by America's need to protect its critical oil resources during a time of war. *The Spider and the Flame King* takes us to the oil center of Piperstown and a blazing confrontation with a fantastic foe.

The springboard for this wild tale seems to be included in *The Spider's Web* column from that issue:

Nothing alters society's way of life as drastically —or as quickly—as a worldwide war. As President Roosevelt said in a recent speech, this war will ultimately affect every man, woman and child in the United States. Nothing could be truer. Wage fixing, price and manufactured goods freezing, food and fuel rationing have already been felt and will be felt still more. Every patriotic American recognizes these measures as necessary and vital to prosecute a war designed to save the world from slavery. No true patriot objects. Yet, as incredibly shocking as it may seem, there are those individuals who already are taking advantage of present conditions to prey upon the unsuspecting public!

Here are a few examples which show how quickly the criminal element has grasped the opportunity to operate illegally:

Oil is one of the most essential products in the world today, not only to move fighting forces, but merely to maintain production levels in manufacturing and transportation. Yet thousands of gallons have been stolen from tankers which, after undergoing a perilous voyage, have finally been tied up safely in their docks. The procedure has been for the thieves to moor a lighter to an adjacent pier, run a hose underwater across the narrow intervening space, secretly hook onto an outlet and pump from the tanker to the lighter even as the tanker is being unloaded into other lighters and tank cars!

It has never occurred to tanker skippers that such an audacious theft could be accomplished. Steps to prevent this have been taken. But no one knows how many thousand gallons of oil have thus far been stolen. Will this oil be refined in secret refineries, and bootlegged to those willing to pay the price now that fuel rationing is necessary in the Eastern states?

After almost a decade, the men behind *The Spider* magazine had found a new scheme for the *Spider* to smash. It was not easy. The conventions of the magazine forced their editorial thinking along narrower and narrower lines.

During the 1930s, the *Spider* rarely ventured outside of Manhattan and his home state of New York, but as the 1930s turned into the 1940s, more and more Richard Wentworth took up the challenge of small-town crime. It was another strategy to change the ordinary—or should we say *extraordinary*?—routine of the *Spider*.

When World War II broke out in Europe in the Fall of 1939, America had a new worry: Spies, saboteurs and so-called Fifth Columnists. *Spider* readers began clamoring for Richard Wentworth to take them on.

By 1940, Norvell Page and his editors finally succumbed to the drumbeat demand. Page produced the first war-themed *Spider* entry, *The Spider and the War Emperor.* Six months later came a tale Page entitled *"Spider* Against the Fifth Column," which his editors retitled *The Spider and His Hobo Army.* In the following issue, the Master of Men battled Axis agents operating in Colorado in *The Spider and the Jewels of Hell.*

Thereafter, the Master of Men took time out from crushing homegrown crime to rooting out Axis and other subversive threats against America. After Pearl Harbor, he tackled the occasional Japanese menace.

But some *Spider* fans were not satisfied. From the outbreak of war in Europe, a new cry was heard from loyal *Spider* fans. The first shot fired was a letter from reader Dwight Braley, which appeared in the January, 1940 issue.

The papers are full of stuff about the Second World War. I think there must be other readers who, like myself, would like you to publish a war story now and then in *The Spider.* The *Spider* devotes his life to fighting crime, so why couldn't you have a war hero—preferably an air pilot—who considers war the greatest crime of mankind, and strives constantly to make this conflict a war to ACTUALLY end all wars?

The new conflagration was only weeks old at that point. Editor Loring "Dusty" Dowst replied cautiously:

It's like this, Dwight: we're giving the war story angle some pretty careful consideration. Right now, it is so hard to get authentic news on the war that it would be nearly impossible for an author to secure the facts necessary to give his story a convincing ring. Most war stories (dealing with this new war, we mean) would therefore have a synthetic flavor. Still, it is not impossible for a writer to fictionalize a war situation and make it sound real, if he is extremely careful. We'll think about it some more—and stand by for some comments from you readers.

As Dowst wrote four issues later:

A young man from way down in the Canal Zone tells me that he agrees with

NEXT MONTH

The SPIDER breathes the death-tainted air of a city swept by Bubonic Plague, in—

WINGS OF THE BLACK DEATH!

. . . An Epic Tale of Panic, Death and Titanic Struggle

Like the consuming flames of a prairie fire the dread news spread: "The SPIDER" has gone mad! He will massacre us all!" But Richard Wentworth, never more sane, gambles life itself in his desperate, night-and-day battle to save the city which, in blind panic, curses his name. Trapped between police and underworld he fights grimly on, determined to clear the city of its man-made plague and to exact full payment for the dead who "lie unburied in its streets."

• • •

Go with the SPIDER on this, the greatest and most deadly of his adventures!

Share with him the thrills of his two-edged battle against law and crime!

Watch, as a city in despair flees the unseen death that walks its unlighted streets!

READ THIS
GRIPPING FULL-LENGTH NOVEL IN THE DECEMBER ISSUE OF

THE   **MASTER OF MEN!**

. . . FOR SALE ON ALL NEWSSTANDS NOVEMBER 5th . . .

Coming soon in *The Spider* Volume 4

Dwight Braley about the *Spider* going to war—but not with the Underworld!

Nehemiah Brown wants the *Spider* to pit his strength and wits against the world's greatest modern-day despots; he wants Dick Wentworth to wage battle in the trenches of Europe! Does anybody back Nehemiah Brown on that? I am not keen on that idea—because Richard Wentworth has devoted his life to fighting Crime—not the would-be rulers of a new Europe, even though some of them may be considered criminal. Still, if enough demand should come in, Grant Stockbridge might be prevailed upon to try a war story featuring the *Spider*. I will add that the demands would have to be overwhelming!

Evidently, the demand was underwhelming, because former Major Richard Wentworth and his erstwhile sergeant, Ronald Jackson, although decorated veterans of World War I, did not reenlist, never mind rushing off to Europe to take on the hated Axis.

Still, the *Spider* and his team did their part on the home front to help keep America's shores safe. *The Spider and the Flame King* is a prime example of that. Although Fifth Columnists are not involved, the targeting of an American oil field by a supercriminal was another example of a shifting focus for criminal enterprises in wartime and the *Spider*'s ever-evolving campaign against the crime lords who continually rose up to challenge him.

Illustrators J.T. Fleming-Gould and Joseph A. Farren

The year of 1942 was a time of great change for *The Spider* magazine. Harry Widmer replaces Loring Dowst as editor. During this period, long-time interior illustrator John Fleming-Gould left the title after nine years. He had illustrated every *Spider* story since the first issue in 1933. The artist who did *The Spider and the Flame King* is unidentified, but stylistically the illustrations appear to by Joseph A. Farren, an illustrator whose work also graced some of Johnston McCulley's Zorro stories in *West*.

As a bonus, we are also including a rare *Spider* short story, "Blood Bond," which originally ran in the June, 1942 issue, which fills in some of the backstory of the *Spider* cast of characters.

Now, go into battle with the *Spider*, Master of Men, in the riveting tale Norvell W. Page originally titled "The Flame King." •

The Spider
and the
Flame King

111th Novel Based on the
Notebooks of the *Spider*

By Grant Stockbridge

DANGER
EXPLOSIVES
NITROGLYCERINE

If you lived in the oil-field city of Piperstown, you'd be afraid to open the door of your own home ... for nitro hell might explode in your very face. You'd dread stepping on the starter of your car. You'd cringe from opening your own breadbox. You'd know fear such as only the wanton cruelty of the Flame King could strike into your heart. And you'd blame the *Spider* for aiding in these atrocities... for the *Spider*—who fought alone to save life, property, and oil for our war effort—was blamed by the police for every new outrage. And the Flame King rode high on his self-made flood of black gold and red blood!

CHAPTER ONE
Death Road

WHERE the road that snaked up Arroyo Diablo squeezed between two house-big boulders, the three men had placed their car broadside. It blocked the road. They hunched silently against the boulders in the blackness of the moon-shadow, and only one of them smoked. The intermittent red glow glinted on the machine gun across his knees.

It was desert-still. A cricket kept up a persistent shrill and, oft against the saw-tooth skyline, a coyote pointed its nose at the moon and howled. Then a faint and distant drumming brought new tenseness to the waiting trio. The sound grew louder. It was a big car, coming fast.

The man with the machine gun got to his feet and the cigarette brightened in a last long drag. The redness showed the glint of his bullet eyes, the hacksaw thinness of his mouth. Then the point of fire arched to the ground and was stamped out. There was an oil smooth click as the machine gun was cocked.

The big car was a Daimler limousine. The thunder of its powerful motor beat back from the arroyo walls. Its driver wore a turban and his eyes shone happily above a thicket of beard. Ram Singh sang just under his breath, a rumble of sound drowned in the motor's roar.

In the rear of the limousine were a man and a woman. The man was keen-faced; and his repose was like a sword in its sheath, carrying the hint of swift action and sudden death. He smiled faintly now at the whisper of Ram Singh's song. The girl beside him smiled back.

"You men!" she scolded. "You never sing except when you're fighting, or getting ready to fight!"

Richard Wentworth laughed to hide the mounting tension within him. Reason and intuition both told him of danger. He drew Nita against the tweedy roughness of his shoulder. "We fight in a good cause, Nita," he said. "Somebody has turned hell loose in this oil field. I've heard some strange and terrible things."

Nita sighed. Wherever criminals preyed on people, there Richard Wentworth hastened, a lone wolf of justice whom criminals feared and the police tried to destroy because he held their pettifogging law in contempt. His was a higher, more terrible justice— the justice of the *Spider!*

"I never could make out, Dick," Nita said, "whether you are the *Spider* because you like to fight, or fight because you are the *Spider!*"

Wentworth forced himself to forget danger. He bent toward Nita, his eyes merry. "Do I kiss you because I love you," he whispered, "or do I love you because—"

The scream of the Daimler's brakes whipped Wentworth erect. In the tunneled glare of the headlight was a car broadside across the road. One man stood in their path, a palm raised to stop them. He seemed alone, and the deep mutter of the Daimler's engine killed sound, but Wentworth's keen eyes detected movement in the moon-shadows. Men were on both sides of the car, not approaching, but wary and alert. Wentworth unbuttoned his coat, rolled his shoulders. It freed the butts of the twin automatics beneath his arms. His voice was barely audible, but distinct.

"Sit tight, both of you," he said. "Ram Singh, be ready to kill the lights if I signal. Nita, lock the doors after I get out."

Nita's hand slid from his arm to her handbag, made sure that the light automatic was there. "Police?" she asked.

"No," his voice was sharper. "Driller Scott is in danger. They must be already at his house." He stepped to the ground, carelessly slapped the door shut.

"I say, there," he called, "what's the trouble?" He made his voice light, and a little frightened, but his eyes were probing the shadows. One man was off to the right, crouched behind a rock. Looked like a sub-machine gun he was holding. The smile that moved Wentworth's lips was harsh and stern. He had thought that his presence here was, as yet, unknown. He had hoped to get information from Driller Scott before the battle started.

"Road's closed," the man in the road answered shortly. "Turn around and beat it."

Wentworth's manner was deceptively mild as he moved into the full glare of the headlights. He no longer had any doubts as to the identity of these men. They were connected with the criminals who had been spreading devastation in the oil fields— devastation and death. Behind the *Spider's* eyes was a grim smile. With danger came opportunity; he would extract information from these men.

His voice was still mild, "I say, that's really too inconvenient! We were on our way to visit an old friend. Perhaps you know Mr. Driller Scott?"

He could hear better now that he was away from the engine mutter. There was a faintest whisper of leather on sand. The men were closing in on his flanks with guns ready. That was what he wanted. Excitement began to make Wentworth's pulses drum long, slow, heavy throbs. He liked a fight. He was the *Spider.*

"Look, bud," the man reached out and tapped Wentworth on the chest. "I said, *'Beat it!'*"

WENTWORTH laughed. He snapped the fingers of his right hand. As the extinction of the headlights jerked a hood of darkness over the scene, he leaped past the crook. His left elbow hooked under the man's chin. He twisted his body and heaved and the man sailed through the air. The crook's yell lifted, sharp and frightened. There was a slamming crash as his body smacked into his own car, and after that he was silent.

With a soundless leap, Wentworth sailed wide of the road. He turned in the air, brought up against the big boulder on the right—and his twin guns were in his fists. So swift and unexpected had been his attack that he was in position before the first streamers of gun-flame lashed out toward the spot where he had been.

He triggered both guns together. The echoing crash of the shots rolled down the arroyo. Afterward, there was only the quiet mutter of the Daimler's engine.

"Lights, Ram Singh," Wentworth's voice was casual from the dark, casual but a little strained with the tightness of his breathing.

Wentworth propped up the bodies of the two gunmen he had slain. He set them against the boulder on the right. On their foreheads he put the glittering scarlet signature of his crusade—the *seal of the Spider!*

He gestured sharply to Ram Singh, and the Daimler rolled forward. Wentworth darted to the side of the man he had thrown. With effortless ease, he heaved the man's body to his shoulder, trotted to meet his limousine.

"Push that car into the ditch," he snapped. "And then drive like hell!"

He tossed the unconscious crook to the floor of the tonneau. The smile on his mouth was thin, stern. This road block could mean only that the criminals already had gone after Scott. The *Spider* must strike and strike swiftly.

His smile changed, softened as he turned back to Nita. Her eyes were bright, excited. There was a small gun in her fist. "I don't blame you for loving to fight!" she said, breathlessly.

"An annoying interruption," Wentworth's voice was light in spite of the brilliant gleam of his eyes. "We will need about three minutes to cover the four miles to Driller Scott's home, and meantime..." His arms reached for Nita. "We were discussing kisses."

The tires on the crook's car exploded as the Daimler nosed it into the ditch. Then the big car leaped forward, while Ram Singh's song of battle competed with the deepened roar of the engine. He swayed slightly behind the wheel. Even the heavy limousine slewed wildly on the curves. The tires sucked and screamed. The wind hissed angrily about the perfect streamlining.

Nita was held tightly by Wentworth's arm about her. The wild swaying of the car did not seem to touch him, as if he were too powerful, too sure, to be moved by anything that would affect ordinary men. But she had seen him in the past, struck low by murder bullets. Nita shivered.

Wentworth's keen mind ranged ahead. "Don't know the lay of the land," he said. "No time to spy it out. I'll have to smash into it and play them as they fall." He laughed sharply.

Without any warning, the crook on the floor lunged to his knees. He gripped the coat-rail, leveled a revolver at Wentworth's stomach.

"Stop this car," he ordered harshly, "or I'll blow you wide open!"

CHAPTER TWO
Flame Warning

RICHARD WENTWORTH nodded gravely at the man and kept his arm clamped hard around Nita van Sloan. "Are you sure," he said, "that you don't need hospital treatment? After the bomb exploded, we thought it was best to get you to a doctor quickly. What doctor would you prefer?"

The man blinked uncertainly. "I'm all right," he said flatly. "Stop this car!"

Wentworth shook his head. "You know how it is, after a bomb explosion. Men who were fatally injured have been known to run a half mile. You probably don't feel the full effects of the wounds yet. What's that doctor's name?"

"Sawyer could—" He broke it off, eyes narrow.

"Don't try that stuff on me! Damn it, you do as you're told!" The leveled gun jutted.

They were out of the arroyo now and rolling over level sagebrush plain. Only another mile and a half, a swoop into another arroyo, and they would be at Driller Scott's house.

Wentworth wagged his head admiringly. "Can't fool you," he said. "As a matter of fact, what I really want to do is to talk to your boss. You wouldn't care to tell me his name, would you? After all, you're in charge. There's no reason why you shouldn't talk. Your boss and I have some business together."

The man said, "Damn you to hell. I—" His finger tightened on the trigger!

Wentworth laughed. "I forgot to tell you, my friend. I took the bullets out of your gun."

He reached over and took the revolver out of the man's limp hand, then prodded two stiffened fingers sharply into his throat. The man's head jerked back and, senseless, he slumped down on the floor.

"So Doctor Sawyer is involved with the criminals," Wentworth said. "Make a note of that, Nita." He touched a button and the window beside him slid open. "It's time to create a diversion," he said. "We're within gunshot sound of Driller Scott's place now."

He lifted the crook's revolver and fired five deliberate shots into the night sky, then tossed the weapon away.

"You told him the gun wasn't loaded!" Nita whispered. "The way you behaved, I didn't think it was, either. Oh, Dick!"

Wentworth smiled at her, ruefully. "I thought of taking out the bullets, but he *might* have examined the gun before he went into action. In which case he wouldn't have talked so easily. It was important that he talk, and talk fast. Forgive me for exposing you to the danger."

The Daimler dropped its nose and swooped into the arroyo like a dive bomber. Motor and wind sound mounted. Just below the lip on the far side of the arroyo were the warm yellow lights of the windows of a house. Nita twisted her hands together. Dick was taking wild chances tonight, but he was not a man who would endanger her needlessly. The pressure was desperate. She knew from this that the man to whose home they were racing was in sharp danger, and that it was vital he should be saved.

But Dick Wentworth would take the same chances for any innocent person.

He was like that. Nita glanced at him, seeing the clear strength of his profile against the snow-whiteness of the sand beneath the moon. In no other way, except his anxiety for her, had he given any evidence of the tension and the danger.

His voice was detached now. "You're going into the house alone," he said. "Criminals and killers are there. Don't let them know that you suspect them. You fired the shots because you wanted to attract their attention. You wanted to be sure to get your bid in for Driller Scott's well before he sold. You understand that he is about to sell, that this is why the men are in his house. Your top price is a half million. The money is in the Arkanzona National."

He leaned forward and opened a compartment in the back of the front seat. There was a black bundle there, and he tucked it under his arm. Nita caught her breath. The *Spider* was going into action!

"Ram Singh!" he called. "Swing one of those hairpin curves too wide, so that you're forced to back up in order to make it! You're on guard!"

He turned to Nita then and his smile was gentle. "It's for a man's life dear."

"I'm not afraid," Nita's voice was quiet, "when I know you're near."

His kiss brushed her lips and then, as the car backed away from a curve swung too wide, he vanished into the shadows at the roadside.

There were four men in the drawing room of Driller Scott's home. Three of them had guns in their fists and the fourth was bound immovably to a straight-backed chair. There was a thread of blood from his mouth corner, but defiance glared from his blue eyes. His hair was a grizzled thatch.

One man turned sharply from the window. "It ain't Doc Sawyer and the girl, Mack," he said, harshly. "It's a big car. Couldn't make the turn and had to back up for it."

The man called Mack gestured with his gun. "Get him out of sight. Gag him. Then cut around front. Stay out of the way and listen for what I say."

Scott said, "You rats better run for cover while you got time."

A fist smacked against his mouth again and, swearing, he was tipped back and dragged out of the room. His swearing stopped suddenly. Mack crossed to the window, and his eye caught a red gasoline can they had brought with them. He caught it up hurriedly and set it in a closet before he went back to the window.

The limousine was pulling to a stop and the turban of the chauffeur made Mack narrow his eyes. He stared while the man helped a girl out of the car, then sprang back behind the wheel and sat there. The girl came on alone toward the house.

Mack crossed the room in a bound. "Girl with a chauffeur," he snapped at his two men. "If things go sour, get that chauffeur. We'll probably have to burn the whole damned bunch of them."

He went back into the front room and crossed toward the main door, opened it as the girl reached out a hand to tap. She smiled at him brightly.

"I hope I'm in time," she said.

Mack said, with restraint. "In time for what? Come in, won't you?"

The girl stepped past him. "Are you Driller Scott?" she asked.

Mack veiled his eyes to hide their satisfaction. "Scott's my name," he said.

Nita van Sloan watched him secretly when she gave her own name, but it was not apparent that it meant anything to the man. She saw that he had a gun in a holster under his left arm, and that he was keyed up and nervous. Also, he did not fit Wentworth's description of the oil prospector, Driller Scott.

The rug showed that a heavy chair had been dragged across it on two legs toward a door that now was closed. On the rug was a single gleaming drop of blood.

Nita knew her peril without question. For just a moment, she wished that she had brought Ram Singh into the house with her. Nita peeled off her gloves. She made a slow business of it, and presently she would thrust them into her purse. Her gun was there. She wanted to time her movements so that she forced affairs to a crisis at the same moment.

"I represent Richard Wentworth," Nita said quietly. "We want to buy your oil lease, Mr. Scott. I understood that someone else was bidding for it, and wanted to get my offer in."

Mack studied her from under lowered lids. His face was sharp and there was brutality in the harsh line of his mouth. He said, shortly, "Sorry you had the trip for nothing. The lease is not for sale."

Nita smiled and looked about the room. There were photographs of oil derricks and gushers on the walls, and one, startling and in color, of a flamer. The furniture was heavy and plain. Over the broad smooth boards of the floor was a rug and several coyote furs spread around.

"I had thought you were an older man, Mr. Scott," she said. "I realize that young men rarely wish to sell. They prefer to take their own gambles. But I am prepared to make a generous offer, on behalf of Mr. Wentworth. The cash is at hand. In the Arkanzona National."

The man shook his head. Impatience was on his face. He had allowed himself to be called Scott. Suppose now they allowed this girl to leave, and then she reported that she had seen "Scott" and described him? He moved carelessly toward her, drawing out a cigarette case.

Nita had her gloves off, her purse open. "I understood, for instance, that you had a daughter of twenty. You certainly *seem* to be under forty—Mr. *Scott.*"

Mack laughed, disarmingly, and offered his cigarette case. Nita had her back toward the fireplace now. She tucked her gloves into her purse—and drew her automatic!

"Stand just like that, Mr. Scott," she ordered,

and coldness underlined her words. "And don't make either sudden moves or loud noises. I'm nervous, and I might shoot—by mistake."

Out of her eye corners, she could see the door toward which the chair had been dragged. "It remained shut and Mack's jaw had sagged. Nita pursed her lips and uttered a low, piercing whistle to bring Ram Singh into the house. At the same instant, she heard a muffled shout outdoors and the crash of a gun.

Her eyes flicked toward the window, through which she could see the car. Mack hurled the cigarette case at her face and charged in fast behind the missile.

CHAPTER THREE
Prisoners of Doom

NITA VAN SLOAN whipped up her gun and snapped a bullet past the ear of the charging man. She could have killed him with equal ease, but the destruction of human life, any life, was a thing to which Nita had to nerve herself. She had not thought it would be necessary in this case, and so she shot deliberately wide.

Mack did not hesitate. He had counted on just that feminine weakness. An instant after the gun-blast, he rammed into Nita with his shoulder, wrenched the gun out of her hand and hurled her back against the fireplace. Her head struck the stone mantel. She wavered, slumped to her knees. Mack reached the window in a long bound, jerked up the gun and fired through the glass.

"Bring him in here!" he shouted to his men outside.

He was back over Nita before she could gather her whirling senses. Minutes later, a man struggled into the room dragging the unconscious body of Ram Singh.

"He killed Jim," the man gasped. "He just picked him up and broke him in half! He'd of had me, too, but—"

"Save it," Mack rasped. "Dump him on the floor. Get Scott."

Nita saw blood on the side of Ram Singh's head. Mack had been fingering a length of rope. Suddenly, he noosed it over her head and cinched the other end high behind her on the stone mantel. He left her struggling against the noose while he bounded across the room and came back with the big red can of gasoline. Nita fought free of the rope, but he had accomplished his purpose. He stood warily wide of her and the limp body of Ram Singh. A gun was ready and vicious in his fist. The other man was struggling with the chair to which Driller Scott was bound, dragging it back into the room. But Mack's face was flushed and there was a glitter in his eyes.

"All right, babe," he said softly to Nita. "You're going to die. Make up your mind to that. You can talk and go out quick with a bullet through your heart, or you can keep your mouth shut and burn alive. I don't give a damn which."

Nita drew in a half dozen long breaths to steady herself, to clear her mind, but still she did not speak. Her brilliant eyes flashed over the room. Scott was looking at her, frowning. The criminal who had hauled him in dragged a sleeve across his forehead, stood breathing noisily.

"Spill the gasoline around, Jake," Mack ordered.

The man crossed to the red can, but not alertly. He was tired.

Nita was careful not to look toward any of the windows. Dick Wentworth was somewhere near. The affair had gotten out of hand with the attack on Ram Singh; or rather with the bullet fired through the window by Mack.

Nita calmed herself. "I told the truth," she said. "I came to buy the Scott oil lease, but I knew you were lying. There's been a lot of crooked work going on in the oil fields. You didn't expect me not to carry a gun, did you?"

Scott finally managed to wrench his face free of the gag. "Mack, I'm going to kill you for this," he said hoarsely.

Mack looked at him and smiled faintly. "Not you, Scott," he said. "Not anybody. There's not going to be any evidence at all. But the oil rats will learn not to poke their noses into the back country—after they hear what happened to you."

Scott started to swear in a heavy voice. "You think I kept my mouth shut, do you?" he demanded.

Nita said, quickly, "What did you see, Mr. Scott?"

"Guns," Scott said shortly. "Men using trench mortars to blow up a hillside."

Mack hit him across the mouth. "Who did you tell, you old fool?"

Scott spat in his face. "Try and find out!"

Mack reached out for the gasoline can, and spilled some on Scott's shoes. "We can wait until Beulah comes home," he said, softly, "and ask her."

Scott said, hoarsely, "She doesn't know! I swear she doesn't know!"

JAKE said, nervously. "Look, Mack, we better hurry this up. Doc Sawyer and the girl will be coming back before long. I don't know how this dame and her chauffeur got past the Twin Rocks, but they did and somebody else might come. We gotta hurry this up! To hell with the old guy. Suppose he did talk to somebody? They'll keep their traps shut after they hear what happened to *him*. We gotta get out of here!"

Mack's teeth were bared in a grimace like a wolf. "All right, all right," he said.

Deliberately, he gun-whipped Scott. As the oil

man's body jerked and sagged in its bonds, Nita leaped forward. She snatched up the oil lamp and held it above her head.

"Now then—" she whispered fiercely — "get your hands up or I'll toss this lamp into the gasoline! You won't have time to get away! Drop your guns!"

Mack lifted his gun deliberately, and his purpose was clear in his eyes. He was going to shoot—and take his chances on the lamp and the gasoline. Nita saw it, knew that her threat had failed... and at that moment laughter sounded in the room!

It was cold laughter, sinister and full of menace— *the laughter of the Spider!*

The voice that spoke was in the same pitch, mocking and challenging. *"Shoot me first, Mack!"* it said, *"Shoot me—the Spider!"*

Mack whipped around toward the sound of the voice. The gunman, Jake, hurled himself behind a heavy chair and clawed at his gun. In the doorway of the room from which Scott had been dragged crouched the *Spider!* His figure was shrouded in a long black cape and, under the broad brim of his hat, his face was stern, ruthless as the pale glitter of his eyes. There was an automatic in each fist!

Frenziedly, Mack began to hurl bullets at that mocking, threatening figure! The *Spider's* twin guns spoke together. A bullet caught Mack's right arm. It was jerked backward by the impact of heavy lead. His body pivoted with it, twisted, awkward as death, and his flailing arm struck the lamp from Nita's hand!

Frantically, Nita leaped backward. She saw that the *Spider's* second bullet had lanced through the fabric of the chair to kill Jake. Then the *Spider* was springing forward, but he would be too late to catch that lamp. Nita flung herself at Ram Singh, seized him by the shoulders and sought to drag him out of danger. It was a heavy task. She had scarcely begun when the lamp burst on the floor. There was an instant of darkness, and then a furiously eager tongue of flame leaped upward.

IN AN instant, the staggering figure of the killer, Mack, was enveloped in dancing red. It scorched up his legs, wrapped about his body, struck like twining snakes at his face! Screaming, the man hurled himself at the window!

There was no time to pursue him. The flames were spreading with the swiftness of a powder train. Wentworth caught up Ram Singh and rushed him into the hallway, pivoted back to seize the chair to which Scott was still bound. Nita was beside him and together they heaved him out of the immediate path of danger. It was fast and furious work, done in short relays—drag Ram Singh from the immediate threat of the flames, then jerk the chair and Scott—back a few paces. It had to be that way, or one would be caught.

But presently both men were outside. It was already too late to save the house. The flames had swept through the entire main room, were bursting through the ceiling, crawling into neighboring rooms. Wentworth cut the ropes from Scott, carried him to his own car and settled the unconscious oil man against the cushions. His face was grave as he studied Ram Singh's wound. It was serious. He gently put him into the car.

Nita spoke in a muffled voice. "I smothered the flames on Mack, but he's already dead."

Wentworth jerked a nod. "Get behind the wheel, Nita," he ordered crisply. "Drive fifty yards down the road and wait."

Nita felt numb. Her hands fumbled at the mechanism of the heavy car, but she got it in motion. Horror had her by the throat. Abruptly, the glare of headlights struck her in the eyes. She slammed on the brakes and another car stopped, nose to nose with the Daimler.

Two men raced toward her, and there was a girl behind them. They converged on Nita, and a flashlight washed her in brilliant light, swept into the tonneau of the car.

"Mr. Scott!" one of them cried. "What in the name of Heaven—"

He whipped open the door of the tonneau and bent over the prostrate form of the oil man. The girl squeezed past him, and Nita knew that this must be Scott's daughter, Beulah.

Nita said hurriedly, "Three men attacked him. They were going to burn him up in the house, but

we—I got him out. I couldn't stop the fire."

"Where are the three men?" the voice of the man who was bending over Scott was harsh, skeptical.

"Dead," Nita said.

The girl, Beulah, said, "Oh, Jerry, *do* something. Help Dad!"

The man drew the girl back, his arm clamped hard about her shoulders. He said slowly, "Beulah, dear—"

The girl gasped. Her face was white, drawn, and her eyes showed the sudden shock of fear. "Jerry!" she cried. "Jerry Sawyer! He's—He's *dead!*"

Dr. Sawyer's voice had a rasp. "He is. And this young lady who *rescued* him from three murderous gentlemen has some heavy explaining to do! She knows something about those men at Twin Rocks who were killed by the *Spider!*"

Nita saw, suddenly, that he had a gun in his fist and that it was pointed at her. Suspicion of this man leaped into her mind. In the back of the car, captive, was one of the killers from Twin Rocks, and that man, pressed by the *Spider,* had mentioned a Dr. Sawyer. What Sawyer had said indicated he had known their prisoner was on guard at Twin Rocks.

Nita was abruptly certain that Sawyer was an ally of the criminals!

Dr. Sawyer took a step toward Nita and the gun snouted very accurately at her head. "Get your hands up!" he ordered.

CHAPTER FOUR
Race With Death!

SLOWLY, Nita van Sloan obeyed the doctor's command. Her knee rested against a button which would slap shut the window at her side, and that window was bulletproof. But the way ahead was blocked by their car—and she could not leave Dick Wentworth behind her!

Abruptly, Nita's attention centered on the car ahead of her. It was parked on the steep hill, headlights blazing into her eyes. It had just swept around a curve when it had confronted her. She could not be sure, but she thought she had detected furtive movement down there.

Calmness settled over Nita van Sloan. She said, quietly, "The leader of the three criminals was called Mack. One of his men was Jake, and another Jim. They were going to leave us unconscious in the house and set it afire. My chauffeur fought them and was wounded, but it gave me a chance to do something about it. I'm sorry that Mr. Scott is dead. I did the best I could for him."

Sawyer laughed, harshly. "I'll say you did! A bullet right through the heart!"

Nita frowned. One of Mack's wild shots must have struck the oil man. There was no question now

about the movement in the car ahead of her. As she watched, the headlights began to move away from her.

The other man with Sawyer cried out sharply, "Hey, did you set those brakes?"

Sawyer's head whipped toward the other car, and Nita kneed the button that slapped the bulletproof window shut. Her foot drove in the clutch, and she released the brake, all in one swift movement. The back door was still open. As the heavy Daimler surged forward, it struck Sawyer, spun him to the roadside. A touch on the brake slammed the door shut... and then, to the right running board, sprang the *Spider!*

"Step on it!" he snapped.

Guns cracked out behind them, but the Daimler was already sweeping around the curve of the road. The narrow, twisting way required all of Nita's concentration. She gripped the wheel hard with both hands and used gas and brakes skillfully. Moments later, they swept out of the last curve, heeled far over, and the heavy car bit into the straightaway. Nita relaxed slightly, threw a strained smile at the *Spider* beside her.

"As fast as you dare," he said. "We have more work to do!"

From his pocket, he took out a soiled and scorched piece of paper, spread it on his knee. "Mack's orders," he said, shortly. "It says, *'Burn Scott, Guard flamers, P.G. 61!'* That was Mack's next job, and it was tonight!"

Nita said slowly, "What is P.G. 61?"

"Oil well is my guess," Wentworth said quietly. "We have to identify it first." He turned and smiled at her. "Quick thinking back there, Nita. Sorry I had to wreck their car, but there wasn't time to argue with this thing looming. When an oil well is set afire—" his jaw set sternly.

Nita shuddered slightly. The wells of this area were rich in natural gas, which was piped off separately. It took very little deliberate tampering to set one aflame, and once it was ignited the oil was set off, too. It would come with a push and a roar—death. Heat like the flaming interior of a star.

She said, "That was Dr. Sawyer and Scott's daughter, Beulah. I don't know who the other man was. Scott is dead."

WENTWORTH'S nod was grave. "Yes, I know. One of Mack's bullets, but it would be hard to prove. Not much chance we won't be identified. Ram Singh is conspicuous and I have to get him to a doctor. Your face was brightly illuminated. I don't know how widespread the criminal influence is here. They may have the police in their vest pocket."

The gray earth was a blur under the headlights. The ranks of sagebrush wheeled past dizzily. Wind and motor roar hammered at them. Abruptly, Wentworth began to strip off the *Spider* disguise. "We'll have to chance it," he said grimly. "Straight to the hospital. I'll get hold of the local law officials. They'll know what P.G. 61 is."

They swooped into Arroyo Diablo. The echoes built up the engine roar. Nita lifted her voice. "They wanted to kill Driller Scott to shut his mouth! He saw them using trench mortars in the back country to blow up a hillside. I don't understand why—"

"Practice range," Wentworth snapped. "I heard Scott was excited about something he found in the back country. They must be using those trench mortars to blow up wells. That makes it tougher."

They swept on toward Twin Rocks and, as the headlights washed over them, Nita uttered a gasp and stood on the brakes! Huge boulders had been rolled into the road. There were men behind them with rifles and shotguns. Bulletproof glass cannot stop rifle bullets!

"Steady!" Wentworth snapped. "Around the left-hand rock. The way is fairly clear. Spotted it earlier tonight!"

But the car had been doing better than eighty. A turn can't be made at that speed. Nita kept the brake hard down, watching the left-hand rock, watching the men in the road. Whatever she did had to be done fast. If she gave the bullets only a slanting surface— She waited while the car weaved and bucked wildly against the brakes. She let it seem that the Daimler was almost out of control. That way, when she left the road, they might be fooled for a few seconds.

She wrenched the wheel to the left and she screamed! She sent the sound of it, shrill and terrified, at the police to delay them for a few precious moments. As the big car lurched from the road, bounced violently over the shallow ditch, she jammed the accelerator to the floor again. With a bellow, the motor took hold. The wheels spun dirt and sand a score of feet into the air. The car lunged, with mounting speed, toward the far end of the rock.

"Swing wide!" Wentworth snapped. "There are boulders just around the corner."

Nita feathered the wheel to the left. Gunfire burst out behind them. A hammer blow struck the top of the car. There was suddenly a hole in the windshield, through which the wind screamed. Then the headlights swept around the end of the house-big boulder. A gasp crowded words from Nita's throat. It seemed to her that the sagebrush flat beyond was solid with boulders! Everywhere her eyes searched, the way was blocked.

"To the left of those two boulders," Wentworth's voice was quiet in her ear. "Then sharp to the right. About fifty yards then, and there is another sharp turn to the left around three boulders in a clump."

The steadiness of his voice had its effect and Nita began to ply brake and throttle, hands firm and quick on the wheel. She threw it hard over around the twin boulders. The car heeled and the treacherous soil crumbled under the tires. She blasted them out of the skid with the accelerator. The fifty yards to the triple rocks was past in a flash and she threw over the wheel again. There was a ringing crash as they sideswiped a towering rock. The rebound tore a fender with a scream of tortured steel.

Ahead was a fairly clear way through the scattered boulders, like a ski-slalom course, zig-zagging between jagged monsters of rock. So far, there had been no further shooting. The rifleman had not yet had time to shift their positions. Nita strained to pick a clear way, to keep the car free of the boulders.

"Headlights out!" Wentworth snapped.

Without delay, and without question, Nita obeyed. Things had to be like that when split-seconds could spell the difference between life and death. Her dazzled eyes peered frantically for the boulders in he pale wash of the moon. The car lurched wildly as it caromed off a rock. Behind them, rifles began to crack. But there were no hits. Nita's eyes were adjusting now. The moon-shadows helped, underscoring the position of boulders on the flat Earth.

Suddenly, with a heavy lurch, the car bounded over the ditch into the road. She swung over the wheel a last time and ground the accelerator to the floor. Behind them, a car was seesawing frantically to pursue. The Daimler laid its belly to the road and streaked for the oil city of Piperstown, its motor howling with power.

THEY were six blooks from the white-frame hospital when Wentworth motioned Nita to turn the corner and stop the car. "We'll have to separate here," he told Nita quietly. "I'm going to leave our captive, along with Ram Singh and Scott's body, at the hospital. Either he will escape, in which case you will follow him; or his friends will come for him—in which case you will learn something. When you can, return to your rooms at the hotel."

Stopping the car, Nita turned and placed her hands on Wentworth's chest. "I don't like the way things happen here," she said simply. "They move too fast. The police and the criminals may not cooperate, but so far as we're concerned they might as well be partners! It's dangerous, Dick!"

"It is," Wentworth nodded, his blue-gray eyes smiling into hers. "But it's not as dangerous for us... *as it is for the criminals!*"

There was a smile on his lips now that boded ill for the enemy. Nita nodded jerkily and climbed out into the darkness. Instantly, the big car leaped away and Nita ducked into the shadows between two frame shacks that were workers' homes. She was not a moment too soon. Two cars, full of men, raved up the street, but their pursuit seemed to be blind. They blasted past the hospital without pause.

Nita stepped out of the shadows and hurried toward the building, saw Wentworth check the big Daimler before the emergency entrance.

At the hospital, Wentworth rapidly marshaled help and carried into the hospital the three men from his car: Driller Scott, dead; Ram Singh, severely wounded; and the captive killer, unconscious. In the surgery, the sole intern on duty was bandaging the shoulder of a man, pale under his tan, who sat with head tilted back limply against the wall.

Wentworth helped a porter carry Ram Singh to the operating table.

"Two men with bullet wounds, Doctor," Wentworth said quietly. "I'm afraid one of them is already dead."

The doctor said, shortly, "One moment and I'll be with you."

The man in the chair opened his eyes and looked at Wentworth.

The doctor finished the bandage and said, "All right. I'll be around to see you tomorrow, Whitey. Better stay in bed a few days." He turned to Wentworth. "You'll have to stay till the authorities arrive. Where did all this shooting happen?"

Wentworth, watching his face, said, "Arroyo Diablo. I think one of the men is known as Driller Scott."

The doctor nodded, but his face didn't show anything.

The man, Whitey, had made no move to get out of the chair. Instead, he spoke with sudden harsh power.

"Get your hands up, stranger!" he ordered.

Wentworth's head jerked around, and he saw that the man had drawn a revolver and was pointing it very directly at Wentworth's stomach!

"You're a police officer?" Wentworth asked.

"Yeah," drawled Whitey. "I'm a deputy, and the only shooting there's been out in Arroyo Diablo was some guys being killed by the *Spider*. He killed them all, so you got to be on the other side. You got to be one of the *Spider*'s pals!" He didn't move his pale, narrow eyes from Wentworth. He jerked his head at the doctor. "Doc, you call the office and tell them," he said. "You move a finger, stranger, and I'll blow your belly out through your backbone!"

CHAPTER FIVE
Gun Talk

THE intern swore and strode out of the surgery. Wentworth bent his cold gaze upon the deputy and his gun. "So you're one of the crooks?" he said softly.

The man started, winced at the shoulder pain.

"What the hell are you talking about?" he snapped.

Wentworth slid his cigarette case from his vest pocket, snapped fire to a smoke with his lighter. "Deputies have the road blocked at Twin Rocks," he said quietly. "Previously, it seems, the *Spider* killed two men there, but there has been no shooting since then. So, you must have been there with the crooks in order to know anything about it. In other words, *the Spider shot you!*"

Wentworth was balanced on his toes, the cigarette in his fingers. His blue-gray gaze probed searchingly into the face of the deputy. The deputy's pallor increased. There was a slow narrowing of his eyes, and his gun hand grew more rigid. Wentworth nodded at him, deliberately forcing the issue.

"I shall report these facts to your superior," he said softly.

The deputy's gun jerked in his hand under the sudden, hard squeeze of his trigger finger! But Wentworth was ready. The cigarette snapped from his fingers and smacked the deputy, Whitey, between the eyes.

The bellow of the gun was tremendous in the narrow confines of the surgery. Behind Wentworth, as he toe-pivoted his body, there was the crash of glass. He lunged and had the gun, shucked out its cartridges and handed the weapon back in swift sequence.

"Now then, Whitey," he said, flatly, "you're taking me to the office. At once."

Wentworth whipped out his own automatic and thrust it into his side pocket, kept his hand on it. "Let's go, Whitey," he commanded.

The doctor bounded back through the door. "What the hell goes on here?" he demanded. "This is a hospital!"

Wentworth was back in his original position. Whitey still held the revolver and the doctor could not know it was empty. Whitey tongued his lips and fear was greenish in his face.

"I—" he hesitated. "I had—a little trouble. We'll go, doc."

The intern glared at them, shrugged. "No more noise!" he ordered sternly.

Whitey lurched to his feet and Wentworth moved to his side. A keenly observant man might have detected that he was the captor, not the prisoner, but the doctor was already intent upon Ram Singh's wound. Wentworth silently directed the deputy out of the hospital and toward his own car. There was no time now to make other arrangements.

"You must precede me, sir, as my guest!" Wentworth's lips wore a smile that was belied by his eyes. "You and I must have a nice long chat!"

Whitey obeyed dazedly, slumped into the front seat beside Wentworth. "You will direct me to P.G. 61," Wentworth ordered.

Whitey said thickly, "Go to hell!"

RICHARD WENTWORTH

It was the final test. Wentworth knew now that the man definitely was one of the criminals. He whipped the car away from the hospital, but only for a short distance. Then he checked, and gave his whole attention to the deputy. He took his gun out of his pocket and ground its muzzle into the man's side, below the ribs.

"Get out," he ordered.

"No!" Whitey's voice was thin, frightened. "No!"

Wentworth grimaced, "I do hate to mess up my car. However—" He let his eyes narrow and harden. It was an expression Whitey would recognize— Whitey who knew killers, Whitey who was a killer.

The deputy squealed for mercy. "It's an oil well," he gasped. "P.G. 61 is a well. I don't know which one. Hell, there are hundreds of them. How would I know?"

The man was terrified. Wentworth recognized the truth. "Someone knows," he said. "How do we find out?"

Perspiration was heavy on the deputy's face. He was gasping for breath. "Legs Jackson, he'll know," he said. "He keeps the maps and all. That's his job. He'll know."

The house was a dozen blocks away and Wentworth drove swiftly there. He reached over then and prodded Whitey's throat, compressing certain nerve centers. The deputy's body jerked, then went limp. He was good for a half hour or so.

Wentworth raced up the short walk to the wooden porch, rapped sharply on the door.

IT was a while before a door, in the back of the house, opened to let light into the hall which Wentworth could see through the glass panel. A girl came lightly to answer his knocking. Light blazed on the porch, then he was looking into the girl's face. She was Mexican. Her black hair was sheeny and neatly coifed. Her dark eyes swept him over in demure appraisal.

"Señor?" she murmured.

Wentworth's bow was gallant. "I must see Mr. Jackson at once, on urgent business," he told her.

From the lighted room in the rear, a man's voice called out deeply. "What is it, Carmen?"

When Wentworth stepped into the room, he was immediately aware of the bulk of the man who sat behind the desk. His shoulders were enormous, and his hands, resting on the desk, were the powerful members of a working man, not one who kept records. His head was bushy, and there were scars on the cragginess of his face.

His eyes were cold. "Beat it," he jerked at the girl.

Her voice was a musical murmur, and the door closed. Wentworth said quietly, "I want to locate a well called P.G. 61. It is of utmost importance, and time is short."

The man, Legs Jackson, regarded Wentworth levelly. "That's my job," he said, but without moving. "What's up?"

Wentworth decided on shock tactics. He smiled. "I understand," he said quietly, "that some criminals are planning to set the well on fire. I thought it possible it could be prevented. Have you any idea why a deputy named Whitey should try to keep me from doing that?"

Jackson's two hands were on the top of the desk. They flattened, and his huge shoulders tensed. Anger was a flame in his eyes. Suddenly, he heaved himself forward! It was exactly as if he were going to leap over the desk. But the straightening of his arms lifted his body upward. Wentworth saw that his legs had been amputated close to the hips!

But instead of attacking, Jackson was flipping over a series of maps, pivoted on vertical leaves against the wall. He had only heaved himself up so that he could set his truncated body on top the desk. The short stubs of his legs held him erect. His rough voice grated out:

"P.G. are the initials of the Porcupine Grinnell wells. Sixty-one..." He peered at a map, ran a stubby finger over it. "It's about thirty miles from Piperstown, off the Arkanzona city road. I'll go with you."

He scooped a pair of abbreviated crutches up from behind the desk and fairly dove onto them. His movements were almost acrobatic, sure, tremendously powerful. That single, diving swing on his crutches took him to the door.

"Carmen!" he bellowed as he flung into the hall. "Call Grinnell and tell him the crooks are going after well Sixty-one. Make it fast!"

Wentworth's swift strides scarcely kept pace with the crippled man.

Jackson whipped open the front door. "The sheriff's men are crooks," he said shortly. "Can't depend on them." He stopped, peering toward the car. "That looks like Deputy Whitey."

"He won't trouble us," Wentworth said quietly.

He jerked open the door of the car, then checked. Jackson blew out his breath in sudden, strange laughter, "Not us, or anybody ever again," he rasped, "but why did you have to cut Whitey's throat?"

Legs Jackson's right hand had flicked from his crutch to the waistband of his trousers. There was the butt of a gun there. Wentworth saw the movement, but ignored it. His eyes were questing swiftly over the shadows round about. Whitey's head had been almost severed from his shoulders by a circling knife wound. Someone had simply reached in through the window and gashed the unconscious deputy! The enemy moved fast—and ruthlessly! The criminals had unhesitatingly murdered one of their own men in order to hang the blame upon Wentworth.

And, somewhere in the night, Nita was alone and on the trail of one of these criminals!

"Have you a car?" Wentworth asked, his voice quiet. "It won't be possible to use this one, and there is no time to lose." Jackson grunted, "You're pretty cool."

THAT was all he said before he had jerked his own car out of the garage and, Wentworth beside him, was hurtling through the city streets. He manipulated the car easily by means of special levers.

"I suppose the story is you've been framed," Jackson's heavy voice was a sneer.

Wentworth's voice was cool, "What would you say were my chances of making the Piperstown law officials believe that?"

Legs Jackson chuckled. He didn't look at Wentworth. The car was already through the city, roaring out into the country. The smell of oil was acrid and sweet on the air. A black skeletal derrick flicked past.

Wentworth was not thinking just now of his own peril. The murder of Whitey had placed him at the mercy of this man, Legs Jackson. Only he—and the murderer—had seen Whitey dead. No one else would ever discover the crime. Wentworth had made sure of that. It was always necessary for Wentworth to be prepared to destroy his car, so it was equipped with a device for destroying it with flames. Before he had left the Daimler, he had activated the device—and by now the Daimler, and what was inside it, was a charred ruin. It was ruthless, but it was necessary. It was possible Whitey's remains would be identified—but it was unlikely.

What occupied Wentworth therefore was not the murder, but the vicious and cold-blooded acumen of the criminal gang and their leader. True, they had been prepared to burn Driller Scott alive in order to eliminate a witness, but this was the murder of an ally for no other purpose than the incrimination of Wentworth!

And Legs Jackson had been *amused!*

This was a hard country and death was no stranger; still, the reaction of Legs Jackson was that of a warped mentality. The man's emotions were as crippled as his body. Humanity had gone out of him.

Jackson said, shortly, "What's the dope on this well?"

"It's going to be set afire," Wentworth told him, "probably by a shell fired from a trench mortar."

Jackson was plainly startled. His head did not jerk about toward Wentworth, but it started to. His huge hands threatened to crush the steering wheel. A glowering anger reddened his scarred face.

"How in hell do you know that?" he demanded.

It was the wrong question, as Wentworth instantly recognized. Doubt should have been the man's reaction, or amazement, but he wanted to know—how *Wentworth had found out!*

Wentworth's jaw set grimly. Was every man in this city an ally of the criminals? Or was he wronging Legs Jackson? Certainly, the man had been eager enough to rush to the well.

Watching the man covertly, Wentworth said, "I went out to see Driller Scott tonight. He knew about the mortars."

Jackson muttered, "Driller Scott, hunh?"

Abruptly, he wrenched the car toward the ditch, then back into the road again. He was already rolling at top speed. As he straightened out, there was a terrific explosion behind them! The car leaped wildly and Legs Jackson ripped out a frantic oath!

"By dam'!" he rasped. "They're shelling us!"

CHAPTER SIX
Living Flame

A SMILE curved the long line of Wentworth's lips. It was possible that they were being shelled, but unless the enemy had orders to destroy every car that moved along this road, it was difficult to understand why they had been fired upon.

Legs Jackson was fighting the last ounce of power out of the car. He feverishly fingered the levers of the machine. Behind them, there was another blasting explosion

"They have the road ranged, it seems," Wentworth said quietly. "Can we cut across country?"

Jackson grunted and his heavy shoulders flexed as he whipped over the wheel. He was a blunt and powerful figure; the absence of legs was a shock. Such strength and dominance seemed strange in a cripple. He handled the car now easily as it took the ditch and slanted across a long bend in the road.

"We're getting pretty close to the well," he shouted above the engine roar. "What do you want to do?"

"First, warn away all workers," Wentworth said shortly. "Then we'll hunt down the mortar and the men who are operating it."

Jackson bent over the wheel, his craggy face set.

The car lurched wildly, but he clung to his speed. They flashed past an oil derrick and a man ran out of a shack and yelled something. A gun flashed in the darkness. Just ahead of them, the land swooped down toward a gully and Jackson was forced to cut back at right angles to the road.

"Land's getting pretty rough now," he said. "Hills from here on."

Wentworth's forehead was dented by a knife-gash frown. They had already traveled a greater distance than the range of the ordinary trench mortar could cover. This meant that there were two mortars, one to cover the road, and one to destroy the well.

They were on the road again now and their speed increased a little.

"About two miles to go!" Jackson called. "One on this road, one to the east."

Wentworth took out his automatic, As soon as it was possible that the men at the well could hear him, he would start shooting. It would help to pull the workers at the well together, for a quick getaway. Abruptly, Jackson reached to the brake lever. The car lurched wildly against the controls, skated broadside into the turnoff, then straightened out with a howling motor.

The machine bucked wildly, leaped the hummocks. The tires guttered and howled. Wentworth braced himself rigidly and Jackson, despite his grim grip on the wheel, was jerked from side to side. Wentworth reached out the window and fired three shots. He paused and fired three more. It was the danger signal, the call for help which westerners would recognize. Impossible to reload the automatic in this wild jouncing. They flicked past a well derrick, and a light came on belatedly in the watchman's shack.

A hundred yards farther on, Jackson jerked into another, still rougher road. It swooped downward and, atop the next ridge, a derrick stood out blackly against the sky.

"That's it," Jackson gasped.

There was no light. They had not heard, or else had not heeded, his gunshots. Reluctantly, Wentworth drew his second automatic and hurled three shots into the night. The car thumped into a gully at the bottom of the rolling hill, slewed sideways and began to labor in second gear. The wheels spun in the sand and, with racing motor, the car advanced by inches.

Suddenly, there was a burst of flame fifty yards down the hill from the well. Bristling bayonets of white stabbed up into the night. The rolling concussion beat against the car. Smoke built a black column. The flying wheels of the car finally took hold, sent them surging upgrade. Still, there was no light in the well shack. On they raced. Two hundred yards, one-hundred-fifty, a hundred... Another shell burst

on the hill, and this one was nearer. A fragment screamed overhead. Legs Jackson's face was pale now, but there was no wavering in his driving; no lessening of speed. The shells were not the only danger. If one hit the well while they were at this range, they were doomed. That first rolling blast of flame would mushroom out for hundreds of yards!

Abruptly, splinters of flame spat at them from a cluster of rocks. Bullets slammed into the car. Powdered glass spat back into Wentworth's face, and it seemed that the bullet hole came afterward.

"Stop!" Wentworth snapped at Jackson. "I'll get out. Turn around."

"Friends!" Wentworth shouted toward the gunmen. "Friends!"

The guns blasted again, as the car whipped its back toward the ambush. The front wheels thumped into a ditch, and the engine stalled. The silence was sudden and enormous.

"Grinnel sent us!" Wentworth shouted again into the darkness. "There's a gun shelling the well. It will blow up. Get in the car and run for it!"

Punctuating his words, there was a shocking wave of concussion from the hilltop. In a gush of flame, the workers' shack lifted into the air and disappeared. Steel fragments howled like devils through the night.

Three men came like moving shadows from behind the rocks, but they came forward cautiously. Jackson got the car started again; the tires screamed as they bit at the road bed. The sedan heaved back six inches and would do no more. It pranced there, tires skidding futilely. The stench of burned rubber rose.

Wentworth sprang out and put his weight on the rear bumper and the tires bit, suddenly hurled the car backward. Wentworth was almost thrown. Suddenly, the three men were around him with ready rifles.

"Get into the car!" Wentworth snapped.

HE LEAPED toward the front seat himself, flung open the back door. One of the men half-moved to intercept him, but the drive of Wentworth's command struck him. They were not soldiers, accustomed to discipline, but the impact of that order came from a man accustomed to command. They began to obey before they realized the origin of the impulse. He was the Master of Men!

"Fast!" Wentworth snapped. "Your rifles can't stop a shell!"

The three men tumbled into the car and Jackson slapped the throttle wide. Like a released arrow, the car streaked down the hill.

From the back seat, one of the men demanded, roughly, "What the hell goes on here?"

"Save it!" Wentworth snapped at them.

He was twisted around in the seat, gazing backward. Those shells had drawn progressively nearer the well. They had crawled upgrade from the West—from the direction of the main road. Unless the well-wreckers had a high observation post, they must be shooting from a place in sight of P.G. 61. The car hit the ditch at the hill's bottom. The springs cracked, and they lurched drunkenly. A hoarse cry came from Jackson's lips.

"Can't steer!" he shouted.

Wentworth clamped his own powerful hands on the wheel, and felt the locked rigidity of the jammed wheels.

"To the left," he commanded.

Together, they threw their force upon the wheel. The wheels yielded with a jerk, and then jammed immovably. But they were pointed uphill.

"Keep going!"

The sedan kept to the road for a flew yards, leaped the ditch and slammed out across the eroded slope of the hill. Fifty feet farther on, Jackson slammed on brakes moments before the car rammed into a boulder. As if that touch had been the contact, the night was turned suddenly into lurid day! The world was engulfed in flame, and heat struck like a sledge. A man screamed; the sound was thin and awful in a vacuum filled with intolerable fire.

It was over in an instant. The flame sucked back to its source, and then reached up for the heavens in a soaring geyser of liquid blaze. It stabbed up, up as if to pierce the arch of the skies, crimson and gold and blue, exquisite and terrible.

On the slope of the opposite hill, there was a blackened car. It was plainly picked out by the brilliance of the light, by the blackness of the shadow beyond. On the ground was the charred ruin of what had been a map. Sagebrush smoked and the acrid scent of it was strong, but not so strong as— other smells.

There was a long minute of utter stillness save for the fluctuating living roar of the flame. Wind began to stir on the hill. It kicked up little runnels of dust. A rag on a bush fluttered and whipped. All around the well, the wind was stirring, running uphill into that heart of flame, spurting upward. It increased with each moment. It was hot, intolerably hot. The shadows danced and quivered. The light shimmered. It was as if a sun twinkled.

There was movement within the wrecked car. The right door started to open, hesitated, then was swung wide. The wind sucked at it. Flutters of dust swirled about its edge. Wentworth stepped out of the car. He stood, gripping the doorpost. Around his feet, the dust curled. The thin grit gnawed at his ankles. He looked into the car. Jackson lifted his shaggy head. It was singed, and the flesh of his face looked stiff.

Wentworth said, thickly, "One man tried to get away on foot. Being in the car saved us."

The others were stirring now. Wentworth staggered as he moved toward the front of the car. The right front fender was bent down against the wheel. That was what had jammed the steering. Wentworth set his fingers under the edge and at first his touch was futile. He abruptly braced his shoulders, his back arched—and the fender came up.

He weaved back to the car.

"Let's go," he said thickly, "Damn it, Jackson, let's *go!* The murderers who did this are over on the highway!"

Jackson fumbled life into the motor, backed away from the rock. The air was a torment to the lungs. Even the car seemed sluggish. They trundled uphill and, slowly, coolness crept upon them. Wentworth shielded his eyes from the flame of the well, as he looked back toward the hill on which it stood.

"Half a mile down the highway," he muttered. "That high spot—" He swore suddenly. The light of the blazing well had picked up a glittering point of reflection at the point he had selected. The well-wreckers were still there!

"Faster!" he called to Jackson. "Faster! Those devils are still on the main road!"

Jackson reached out and killed the motor. "To hell with it," he said thickly. *"To hell with it!* I've had enough."

Wentworth stared at him, and the man's face was working. His hands were massaging his thighs, and his eyes were stretched wide. They were streaming tears!

"That's the way—" he said, wildly—*"that's the way I lost my legs!"*

For an instant, Wentworth's eyes softened—but for only an instant. "Out!" he snapped. "Out!"

Jackson fumbled open the door and heaved himself to the ground. He looked pitiful, tiny in that immensity of sand and fire glare. The remaining two men reeled out after him. Wentworth did not debate with them. Instead, as the last man pushed his fumbling body out of the car, Wentworth slapped at the car's levers—and sent it ripping forward into the night!

The killers were there on the road. They had the implements of modern warfare, trench mortars and bombs. Probably others. Wentworth knew that, but he did not hesitate.

Singlehanded, his face set in a thin and mocking smile, the *Spider* raced to the attack!

CHAPTER SEVEN
Into Danger

IN PIPERSTOWN, Nita van Sloan kept her

NITA VAN SLOAN

watch for the criminals whom Wentworth had taken, unconscious, to the hospital. It was a scant fifteen minutes after Wentworth himself left the place that she saw the man she was watching slide furtively out of the hospital and hurry away into the darkness afoot.

Nita set out at once on his trail. The streets were dark and that made her task easy, but her quarry went directly toward the brighter section of town. He looked back several times, but Nita was too familiar with her task for him to spot her. She scarcely needed to think about it.

Actually, her mind was concerned with Dick Wentworth and the battle they had come to fight; the perils they already had encountered. They were both identified in connection with the murder of

Driller Scott and, in a town this size, their arrest was only a matter of time.

Nita checked in abrupt dismay. The man she was following had entered an office building and abruptly she realized the meaning of those green lights beside the door. He had gone to the police!

Nita shook her head. What was more likely was either that the man himself was a member of the force, or else that he had gone to see some particular policeman. Those gunmen who had ambushed them on the road would not be city police, but sheriff's deputies, for police authority did not extend so far.

In the shadows, Nita threw a quick glance about her. She realized as she did so that she must have sensed someone following her, but the shadows yielded no secret. She thought she heard a low, warning whistle. It was not the *Spider*'s signal. Her instinct then had warned her when her conscious mind had been busy with other things, and she had been right. There was someone on her trail.

Nita hesitated, fingering the automatic in her purse. She stepped across the pavement to a shop window and, in its dark reflection, kept watch on the street behind. For moments, there was nothing, and then the flitting figure of a man darted from the shadow of a post to a dark doorway. Nita smiled, settled her hand more comfortably about the gun. She had a mission to perform for the *Spider*, and no one was going to prevent her successful completion of that task.

Someone came out of the police headquarters, not the man she sought and Nita pretended to take fright. She turned and hurried back down the street into darkness. As soon as she was out of the light, she turned and doubled across the street.

There were other men besides the one she had spotted, otherwise there would be no need for a signal. Therefore, she kept away from any place that might conceal an enemy. Her trailer was trapped in the doorway. Nita ran a little, until she was close against the wall into which the doorway cut. She was out of the man's sight now, and, on silent feet, she raced straight toward him.

She was still a dozen feet away when there was a flicker of light in the doorway and a man, lighting a cigarette, stepped into sight. His face was washed with yellow light for an instant before he flicked out the match and tossed it into the street. Nita's breath caught in her throat. *The man was Dr. Sawyer!*

But there was nothing furtive about the doctor's movements as he stepped out of the doorway and turned, walking briskly—toward police headquarters. Was he the man who had followed her? Or had he merely been in that building and, coincidentally, chosen that moment to step outside? Nita was strongly suspicious of coincidence. Sawyer went up the steps into police headquarters also!

The rasp of a furtive footstep behind Nita did not make her whirl. Instead, she ran straight ahead— toward the doorway. She heard a man curse. Nita had her gun out now. She flung into the protecting niche of the door. She was aware, too late, of another figure hidden there. A rough hand clamped on her gun-wrist, and a man's arm reached out to capture her!

Nita van Sloan was glad in that moment that Dick Wentworth had insisted on long and arduous training in self-defense when she had set her mind on sharing his perils. Instead of resisting that tug on her wrist, Nita drove forward into the man with all her weight and strength—and the jerk on her wrist to help. She jabbed up her elbow and crooked it before her face like the ram of a ship.

Her elbow caught the man in the mouth, drove his head back against the brick jamb of the door. There was a muffled curse; the grip on her wrist loosened. Nita struck again, instantly, slapping the solid barrel of her gun against the man's jaw.

She whirled about just as the second man charged into the entrance way of the building. Fading aside from his lunge, she let her foot drag in his path. His shoe struck her ankle with vicious force, but he stumbled. As he reeled, off-balance, Nita struck again. The gun thudded against the base of the man's skull, and he went down on his knees. Then, as if weary, laid down his face on the cold stone.

Up the street, a police whistle screamed!

Nita gasped out a sob of disappointment. She had been seen! She took a quick step backward, and her ankle sent agony sharply through her leg. There would be no running on that ankle. There was only one thing to do. If she were quick, it might work.

Nita cried out faintly, "Help! Help!"

SHE staggered out of the doorway, let her bad ankle go under her and slipped down on her knees on the pavement. Her hands clung to a telephone post. Out of her eye corners, she watched the policeman run toward her. He ran heavily, an old man. So far, there had been no response from police headquarters. It was just possible that they had not heard. If no more came out, if she could overcome this last man— she could perform her mission for the *Spider*.

The cop was almost upon her now—and still no one showed at the door of police headquarters. Nita tensed her muscles, and then she saw the policeman's face. It was a kindly face, with heavy white brows, and there was pain in it.

"Now, now," he said. "it's all right, lady. Papa Carew is here. They won't hurt you again."

"Those men!" Nita gasped.

His arm went around her. "What did they try to do, lady?" he asked gently. "Who were they?"

His kindness did what nothing else could have accomplished. Nita nerved herself, but she could not take violent action against this gentle policeman who called himself "Pop Carew." She could, perhaps, send him to the doorway, and—but she could not run.

She heard the man gasp, "Glory be!" He blew shrilly again on his whistle and kept it up. And he was no longer close, where she could take action, even if she could bring herself to it. He had, she knew, seen the two men lying in the doorway. Her chance had come—and gone.

"Glory be," he said again. "*Two* of them! What did you do, use a knife? I'm thinking they're the ones who need help, not you!"

Police boiled out of headquarters and there was no alternative for submitting to arrest. She had just time to slide her automatic out of sight in the gutter before two of them had her by the arms and jerked her to her feet.

"A strange town," she said sardonically. "I'm attacked by two men, and you arrest me. Bring them in, too!"

The policeman, Pop Carew, was beside the thugs now. "Just knocked out," he said, with relief in his voice. "I thought she'd knifed them. Give me a hand."

They made a curious procession back to the green lights of police headquarters, two inertly carried men and the limping girl. The sergeant was waiting on the step and turned back only when they were near. He climbed up behind the desk.

"Okay," he said, "what's the charge?"

That was the moment when a door into the big barren office was opened, and a girl stepped through. There were three men behind her, and one of them was Dr. Sawyer. The girl was Beulah Scott!

She stared and then she ran forward, caught Nita fiercely by the shoulder.

"You!" she said. "You! What did you do with my father?"

There was no use in denying the identification. She glanced at the men behind Beulah. One of these men undoubtedly was the police chief of Piperstown. That would be the beefy man with the fat-crowded eyes, because he was extremely deferential to the taller, older man who walked beside him.

Nita said, quietly, "I took him to the hospital, along with my chauffeur."

"You murdered him!" Beulah cried.

Nita looked into the girl's blazing face. It was a small face, and its contours should have been gentle, but her dark eyes were glittering with anger, and her soft lips were drawn back from white, regular teeth.

"I'll discuss that when you're calmer," she said, still quietly.

The police chief shouldered his way forward. "Who are these two men?" he asked, and his tone was bullying. "Did she kill them, too?"

Pop Carew came forward. He had an enormous stomach and his face was red and round. Except for the absence of a beard, he was a jovial Santa Claus, but he was worried now.

"I made the arrest, chief." He saluted. "I heard her scream and saw her stagger out of a doorway and fall. When I got there, she was on her knees and these two men were stretched out in the doorway, knocked cold. She said—"

The chief turned toward Nita. His feet were small and his movements quick in spite of his beefiness.

"What's the story?" he demanded harshly. "These two men are detectives."

Nita laughed. "Did you train them, chief?" she asked. "You should, in the future, tell them that it is customary for police officers to announce their identity before they attempt an assault upon an innocent bystander."

"You're wanted for murder," the chief said bluntly. "You're known to be dangerous."

"Show me the warrant!" Nita challenged. "I don't know just what you're trying to do, but I do know this: there has been no warrant issued for me, and those detectives were not searching for me on those grounds. Beulah Scott has only now identified me, and she was conferring with you in your office. There wasn't time for those two men to have received a description. Therefore, chief, you're trying to cover up for your men. What you're trying to cover up, I don't know." Nita turned a scornful shoulder on him and faced Beulah.

The girl's anger was under control now. She was looking in bewilderment from Nita to the police chief.

Nita said, "Your father is at the hospital, with my chauffeur. There was a third man in the car who, I believe, is one of the criminals who killed your father. I waited to see what would be done about him and, presently, he walked out of the hospital. I followed him, and discovered that I was being followed. Those two men—" she nodded to where the two assailants lay, still unconscious, with Dr. Sawyer bending over them— "attempted to attack me. I defended myself. That is all."

The chief had an ugly smile. "I suppose the man you were following got away?"

Nita smiled sweetly into his face. "As a matter of fact, chief," she said, "he came into police headquarters. Perhaps he was another of your detectives?"

The chief's smile pinched out. His mouth was small and looked rigid. "You're lying," he said flatly. "You're lying, from start to finish. Driller Scott is not at the hospital. You burned his body when you burned your car!"

NITA'S eyes widened as she stared into the man's face. He believed, at least, that he was telling the truth. Therefore, Dick Wentworth's car had been found, destroyed by flames, and with a—a *man's body in it!*

Dick had driven away in that car, Dick—but he wasn't dead. She *knew* he wasn't dead. He couldn't have been killed without her feeling it somehow in her heart. Her voice was quiet. "Why not call the hospital?" she suggested.

The man who had come out of the office with the others had remained in the background, but he had been keenly interested in all that had taken place. He stepped forward now, gravely.

"I am Mayor Grinnel," he said pleasantly to Nita. He turned to the chief. "Rounder, before you go any farther with this, why not call the hospital? I am inclined to believe this young lady's account of affairs, and I would like very much to know the identity of the man she followed to police head-quarters. Who is he?"

The sergeant, still behind the desk, shook his head blankly. "I don't remember anybody coming in," he said.

Beulah Scott said, "There was a man with her at my father's house. We didn't see him, but he got our car out of the way so she could make a getaway."

Nita had been waiting for that, and dreading it. The sergeant was calling the hospital, and he would learn that Dick Wentworth had been there.

Nita said, quietly, "Yes, the man with me was Richard Wentworth, my fiancé. From one of the criminals, he learned that an attempt would be made to blow up an oil well tonight, and he was intent on preventing it."

Mayor Grinnel's face flushed. "There have been too many oil wells destroyed lately," he said. "Why didn't Wentworth come to the police?"

Nita shrugged. "They would have had no jurisdiction," she said.

Mayor Grinnel started to speak, and didn't. Nita met his eyes directly, without defiance, but with knowledge in their depths. It was as if she said, "Do you trust your police, now?"

Grinnel gestured impatiently, "What well was this?" he demanded.

The sergeant leaned across the desk at that moment. "She's telling the truth about that, all right," he said in a puzzled voice. "The doc hadn't reported because he was so busy. He was operating. Driller Scott is there. He's dead. There was a Hindu there, too, badly wounded and he's disappeared. Near as the doc can make out, this Hindu, with a wound that

might kill him, got up and walked out of the hospital."

Nita winced as she heard the story. Ram Singh had—walked out of the hospital. He couldn't be in his right mind! He would be helpless, an easy prey to criminals or police. But she dared not ask the police to search for him. In his present state, he might tell—anything!

At that moment, the front door of headquarters was smacked open and a boy of about fifteen ran in, panting. He darted straight up to Mayor Grinnel.

"Dad!" he gasped. "Dad!"

Grinnel caught his shoulder, in anxiety. "What's the matter, Roy?"

The boy swallowed, grinned. "Nothing, nothing at all. Gee, Dad, the radio says the *Spider*'s come to town! Boy, would I like to talk to *him*! I didn't really think the cops would know anything about him, but maybe they could tell me about how he got away from them. He always gets away."

A smile moved Nita's lips as she looked at the boy's excited face. He was pudgy and his voice broke in his excitement.

Mayor Grinnel swung on Police Chief Rounder. "I wasn't informed of this," he said harshly.

Rounder shrugged his shoulders. "News to me," he said. "Maybe he ran into Sheriff Burton's men."

Roy Grinnel bobbed his head excitedly. "Yeah, that's it. He bumped off two crooks out by Twin Rocks. They're trying to say he killed Driller Scott, but they're nuts. Driller Scott was a swell egg and the *Spider* don't kill guys like him."

The mayor said grimly, "We'll talk about that some other tine. Run along home now, Roy." His eyes cut back to Nita's face. "You were going to tell me about this oil well that's supposed to be blown up."

Nita said, "Yes. The well was designated only as P.G. 61."

Grinnel started, "The hell it was! That's *my* well!"

Roy giggled, "Don't worry, Dad! The *Spider* will get them!"

CHAPTER EIGHT
Into Battle

WENTWORTH'S car skidded wildly as it looped out into the main highway. A mile down the road, the well-wreckers' sedan was just getting underway. It was a big car. It would be powerful, and the machine that Wentworth drove had taken rough treatment. Once the crooks got going, he would not stand a chance of overhauling them. They must have already spotted him.

Wentworth slapped his hand down on the horn-button and held it there. As the sound of it reached the other car, it hesitated visibly. Wentworth had a thin smile on his lips. Flight had been in the minds of the crooks. They thought they had been spotted as the well-wreckers. But the blast of his horn upset that concept. For the horn didn't say, "I'm chasing you!" It said, "Get out of the way, and let me by! I'm in a hurry!"

The car hesitated while the crooks debated. It was foolish to attract attention to themselves by racing away if they were not being pursued. And, while they hesitated, the horn kept dinning in their ears, drawing nearer. The car behind had swung over to the extreme left of the road. For moments it looked as if it would race past—and then, it cut sharply across the road toward the crooks.

There were sharp curses of surprise. One of the four jerked up a gun—and it was too late! With a grinding screech of torn metal, the car smacked into the left front wheel. Immediately, they were locked in a grotesque waltz. The cars made a wide, looping whirl, bounded over the ditch and slowed to a halt amid the sagebrush. The crooks were shooting now, pumping lead into the car that had rammed them. They were cursing, fighting their way out of the wreckage.

The driver raced his motor, trying to jerk clear. The wheels spun up a great cloud of dust. It was all brilliantly illumined by the blazing well. Two men were out of the car now. They dodged around the wreckage, closing in on the car Wentworth had driven, firing through the windshield, through the side panels, seeking their victim.

No shots answered them. They ran forward, yanked open the door. The car was empty. They staggered back, dodged suddenly flat on the earth. Still, no shots answered them. They peered back toward the road. The motor howled; tires threw up clouds of dust. The air was full of the dull thunder of the blazing well.

Off on the highway that led to Piperstown, head-

lights were suddenly brilliant. Three cars, in a close train, were racing toward the scene at top speed! The crooks leaped to their feet and raced back to the cars.

"There's a mob coming!" they yelled at the driver. "Three car loads! We got to get out of here!"

They cut down the motor to idling speed. The three of them crawled out hurriedly to inspect the jammed cars. The wheels were interlocked.

"Get out the mortar," the leader snapped. "We can't get this loose in time. We'll have to blow the hell out of that mob! Hurry it up!"

The three men skated in the loose earth as they darted to the trunk of their car and threw it open. They dragged out the heavy barrel of the gun, the tripod. One of them caught up a shell and held it ready.

"*Freeze!*" ordered a cold voice from behind them. "Freeze—or *die!*"

A bullet cracked past their ears and starred the rear window of the car. Another bullet plucked a man's hat awry on his head.

The men twisted their heads about uncertainly. They saw a man's head and two guns, just above a clump of sage. He was alone!

"*Take him!*" the leader's order was a whisper.

Like one man, they dropped their burdens and hurled themselves forward. One of the guns behind the sagebrush spat. The leader arched backward. He went down on his face with his feet in the air. The other two froze in their places, and after that there was silence in which the leader's convulsive feet made a faint scrabbling sound. It didn't continue long. The drum of approaching motors beat through the continuous thunder of flame. Presently, brakes screamed, and there was the racing thud of men's feet.

Mayor Grinnel came around the wrecked cars with a gun in his fist. "What goes on here?" he rasped.

Wentworth rose from the sage, guns still carefully ready in his hand. "Mr. Grinnel, I presume?" he said politely. "I have the honor to surrender to you the three men who just blew up your well with that trench mortar. Unfortunately, one of the gentlemen committed suicide."

"Suicide?" Grinnel gasped.

Wentworth's smile was pleasant. "Why, yes," he said. "I ordered him to stand, and he preferred to charge a pointed gun. I'd call it suicide."

Grinnel said, flatly, "You're Wentworth?"

His men moved forward and took hold of the two well-wreckers. Wentworth saw badges glitter. He came toward them.

"You got my message then?" he said.

Grinnel's eyes never left him. "I received no message from you."

"Freeze!" ordered a cold voice behind them. "Freeze—or die!"

Wentworth shrugged. "From Legs Jackson's girl, Carmen. He told her to phone you before we left his house. I'm afraid you owe Legs a new car, Mr. Grinnel. I had to wreck his to catch these men. He, and two of your well-workmen, are over there on the turn-off. One of your men was killed. Legs and I got here just in time to warn them, but after the shelling had started. The car stalled, and one of your men got out of the protection of the car. He was burned."

Grinnel blew out a tight breath, looked toward the tower of flame that was destroying hundreds of dollars' worth of gas and oil every minute. Wentworth followed his gaze.

"If I may suggest," he said quietly, "a shell from the gun, properly placed, might snuff that out."

Grinnel asked slowly, "You can handle it?"

Wentworth laughed. "I have had some experience with the weapon."

He crouched over the mortar, heaving it up on its tripod, but his eyes and his mind were not on the task. There was something about Grinnel's manner that was as good as a warning. The two well-wreckers were sullenly silent, in the hands of the police.

Grinnel spoke just behind him, "You left your car at Jackson's place?" He made it casual.

Wentworth answered in the affirmative without looking up. "Get everyone out from in front of the mortar," he directed.

His eyes were on the calibration of the mortar, but his mind was only half attentive. Grinnel's question indicated knowledge of the fire, of the corpse in the Daimler. It argued that Grinnel had some connection with the police. Wentworth frowned. He was marooned thirty miles out of Piperstown, and the only cars here were those of the police who had come with Grinnel. The man had said he received no warning, yet he had arrived far sooner than would have been possible, even had he been told immediately when the first shot was fired. There were no phones out here.

Had the crooks notified him, then?

"Carmen called you?" he asked.

Grinnel said slowly, "I was not at home. I don't know."

But somebody had warned him. There were only two possibilities. Either the crooks had warned him what was to happen—or *else Nita had!* Wentworth straightened and peered toward the flaming well, apparently estimating distance. He had a deep crease between his eyes. He knew suddenly that Nita must have been picked up by the police and been in a position of having to tell their story. She had not come in the cars, or she would be here. Therefore, Nita must have been placed under arrest.

Wentworth nodded. He picked up the shell and dropped it down the barrel of the mortar onto the firing spike.

The blast of the mortar was deafening. All eyes followed the lobbing flight of the shell as it reached out toward the blazing well. It went very high, out of sight. Then, abruptly, there was a sharp explosion and the flame went out! It was an almost incredible performance. It meant not only perfect control of the shell, but accurate knowledge as to how to place that shell in order to accomplish its purpose. The man who had fired that shell knew oil wells!

Suspicion suddenly snapped taut in Grinnel's mind. He whirled about, gun in hand—and Wentworth was no longer by the mortar. He was not in sight! As Grinnel stared, bewildered, there was the abrupt roar of an automobile motor on the highway. A car streaked off over the road to Piperstown!

CHAPTER NINE
Fugitives

THE police sergeant felt uneasy. He had three patrolmen in the outer office and three more detectives behind the chief's door, but he felt uneasy.

"Look," the sergeant spoke to them doggedly. "Did you ever hear of the *Spider?*"

"Sure, Millikan." The cop didn't grin. "What makes you think he's after you? I hear tell he only kills crooks."

Sergeant Millikan turned a slow, dark red. The three cops suddenly guffawed. The sergeant said, heavily, "All right, so it's funny. Including Driller Scott, there's been seven guys killed tonight that we know of. Lord knows what's happened out at that well. Two of the dead ones had the *Spider* seal on them. Maybe you can make out like you don't think there's reason for the *Spider* to come to this oil field. There's been too much death and destruction. We're cops and we're supposed to stop things like that. Why ain't we done it?" The sergeant glowered at them. "Well, Dinkler?"

The cops weren't amused anymore. The one he addressed spoke slowly. "Most of them things happened in the county. Sheriff's job."

When the outer door opened, the men whipped around that way. Dinkler half drew his gun, and Millikan pushed back his chair, both hands on the high desk. The man who had stepped inside the door looked at them cheerfully.

"You boys seem nervous," he said, ironically. His face was keen, pleasant. Only his gray-blue eyes were chill. He walked up to the desk and leaned across it. He spoke in a low tone, and flipped open a wallet to expose it briefly to Millikan's gaze.

Millikan's face showed a sudden vast relief. "Oh, sure," he said. "Sure, come with me." He glanced toward Dinkler. "You keep watching for the *Spider.*"

The man in civilian clothes, walking lightly beside the sergeant, let them hear him laugh. He clapped a hand on the sergeant's shoulder. "So the *Spider* is making trouble for you, is he? Well, take my advice. Don't try swapping bullets with him. *He never misses.*"

The tension of the cops increased and Sergeant Millikan glanced nervously at every shadow as he led the way back toward the cells. "Sorry I can't bring the woman out to you," he said apologetically, "but I got my orders."

The man beside him said, easily, "We all have to follow orders or get bounced. Most cops want to be honest, like most men. When they got crooked bosses, it's tough."

Milliken said, quickly. "Our chief is honest."

The man laughed dryly, "So you're afraid of the *Spider*?"

Sergeant Milliken was jittery so his tone to the turnkey was peremptory. "We're going in to talk to the woman."

The turnkey unlocked the door, handed his keyring over to the sergeant. As they went past the turnkey, the man in civilian clothes suddenly jerked up his right fist. It caught the turnkey unprepared, jarred the senses out of him. At the same instant, his left hand gouged a gun muzzle into the fat around Millikan's loins.

"Step fast, sergeant," he said, gently.

Millikan squealed at that jab in the back. His face twisted about, pallid and suddenly flabby.

"Think you'll know me next time, sergeant?" the man asked.

The sergeant's lips were dry. He licked them. "N-no," he stammered.

The man laughed again, and this time the sound of it was flat and menacing. It was a whisper of laughter that did not reach far, but made Millikan shiver. He fumbled badly, unlocking the door of Nita van Sloan's cell. Nita rose stiffly to her feet. Her eyes went past the sergeant to the man behind him, but she did not smile. She only veiled her eyes quickly, and some of the tension went out of her.

"If you would do me the honor," said the man smoothly. "I'd like very much for you and me to take a little walk."

"Oh, sir!" Nita said. "I couldn't think of it—without permission."

"The sergeant has given his permission, madam," the man said, "Haven't you, sergeant? In fact, he's going to sit up for you—in your room. Inside, sergeant!"

Nita stepped out deftly as the sergeant was thrust into the cell. The man stood close against the bars, looking at Millikan. He nodded. "I'm under the impression, Sergeant Millikan," he said, "that you are by nature, a silent man. I'd hate to be mistaken in my estimate of you, sergeant. You *are* a silent man?"

Millikan chattered, "Ye-yes!"

The man nodded, "Then stay that way for at least ten minutes. I do love consistency of character. You'll want your receipt."

He handed through the bars a white oblong of pasteboard, bowed to Nita. "After you, my dear," he said.

Inside the cell, Sergeant Millikan sat down suddenly on Nita's bunk. His shaking hand could not hold the card any longer and it fell, fluttering to the floor, but it fell face up. In the dimly lighted cell, it seemed to blossom in red. It glittered vermillion and menacing—*the seal of the Spider!*

As Wentworth ushered Nita into the main room where the cops stood guard, he turned and called back over his shoulder, "What did you say, Sergeant Millikan? Oh, all right, then we won't wait."

He nodded brightly to the policeman, kept his hand clamped on Nita's arm as if she were a prisoner and walked right out through the main doors of the police station.

Seconds later, they were in the car parked at the curb. They shot away fast. The car screamed its way around a corner and raced for the darkness of the town's outskirts.

Nita said, slowly, "It's bad, is it, Dick?"

Wentworth's voice was normal now, his disguised face very stern. "With crooked police," he said shortly, "any kind of charge is bad. We can't afford to delay now. We can't fight this case successfully except by cleaning up the town."

"It's worse than you know," Nita said, gravely, and told him how the wounded Ram Singh had disappeared from the hospital.

"Now, why—" Wentworth exclaimed, "He must be out of his head, or else he felt that he was a danger to us. We dare not notify the police. This is a blow."

His lips tightened and he checked the car in a narrow dark alley between some wooden shacks. "You'll have to leave town, Nita," he said. "I can't protect you. I can't protect Ram Singh. This fight is already crucial—a fight to the finish!"

Nita's chin set stubbornly, "You're alone," she pointed out. "I'm almost as good at disguise as yourself. I know this is a small town, but I can manage it. There's only one kind of person here who won't attract much attention." She nodded toward the shacks. "Mexican *paisanos*. It would be a good cover for you, too. And you'll need one. Unless you intend to blow this thing up tonight?"

"Not much chance," Wentworth said, shortly. "I'm going to try to force a showdown. I guess you're right." He grinned at her with sudden boyishness. "I'm glad you're staying."

His arms tightened about her and Nita was,

afterward, breathless. "Maybe I'd better go!" she said, but she laughed softly.

THERE were seven men in the adobe shack. No one was behind the bar. Presently, the smallest of the seven men rose and took a jug from behind the bar, brought it back to the others.

"Better go slow," he said. "If I know the boss, we got work to do."

"Giving orders, Poker?" another man snapped.

The small man shrugged and dropped into his chair. He turned his own earthen mug bottom up. "I'm not giving orders," he said easily, "but we've lost a lot of pals tonight. I don't want to be one of them."

He tapped a finger on the tabletop. "Two at Twin Rocks. Three at Scott's. One at Legs Jackson's house. One killed and two arrested out at the well. That's nine."

"Getting yellow, Poker?" the man who spoke was flushed, and his speech was sloppy with liquor.

"I'm not getting drunk, Fats," he said with studied intent.

The big man pushed himself to his feet. "You saying I'm getting drunk because I'm yellow?" he demanded.

Poker's smile was thin and stiff as iron. "*You* said it," he snapped.

Fats moved a hand slowly toward the gun under his arm, but Poker suddenly slapped his mug down hard on the table.

"Cut it out!" he snapped. "We're all edgy. Who wouldn't be, with the *Spider* in town! But we ain't got enough men to start killing off each other. I say, 'Wait for the Flame King!'"

The other men mumbled at Fats and he said, "Guess you're right." He sat down. "But I ain't afraid of the *Spider*, nor a dozen like him!"

Poker just looked at him. The others didn't speak. When the door of the place opened suddenly, they all started to their feet, grabbing for guns. Then they settled down, slowly.

Fats gasped: "The Flame King!"

The man who came through the door had to duck his head to enter. He was tall, but his shoulders were in proportion; so was his head. He walked across to the table with ponderous slowness and stood over it. He had a black handkerchief over his face. Behind the eyeholes, his eyes glittered like hidden snakes.

"Getting nervous, boys?" he asked roughly. There was a slight impediment in his speech, so that it was almost a lisp. He laughed, hoarsely.

Poker was the only one whose face remained the same.

"Ain't it about time you took off that mask, boss?" he asked.

The Flame King reached out a hand and his fingers clamped around Poker's neck. He lifted him out of the chair and shook him gently. Poker's hand clawed toward his gun, and he was shaken so violently he couldn't reach it. His eyes goggled, his tongue squeezed out. The Flame King dropped him, and he landed on his chair and sat there, gasping, shuddering.

"I'm still running this show," the Flame King lisped. "I pay the bills. Anybody who doesn't like it can get out... the way Poker almost went!"

Fats shivered, "It's okay, boss," he muttered. "Sure, it's okay. Only, there's been a lot of the boys killed tonight. You pay the bills, so—" He spread his pudgy hands.

The Flame King snickered. "You cheap gunnies! You're a dime a dozen. Think you're the whole works, do you? You're just a very small twig on the tree. I've got—" he bit it off. "That's none of your damned bushinesh. I've got a job for you, if you got enough guts. There's a bonus—five hundred each."

Fats' face lighted. "Sure, boss!"

The Flame King's hidden face turned toward him. The laughter in his eyes was evil. "I think you'd better all go to give yourself courage," he said. "Get Poker's telescope rifle. Get a two-quart can of nitro."

"*Two quarts!*" Fats gasped. "Good Lord, are you going to blow up Piperstown?"

"Jusht the hoshpital," the big man said softly. "Lean that two quart can against the wall under the hospital office window. Get off as far as you want to, and then blast it with the rifle. The gate light will give you enough light to see by."

Fats pushed himself to his feet. "Two quarts of nitro," he muttered. "Two—No, sir. Not me. Not for—"

The Flame King didn't strangle him. He had put a hand on his shoulder, and one under his jaw and wrenched. That's the way a lion kills a deer. The effect of that sudden wrench is to snap the vertebra of the neck, cleanly and sharply. Death is immediate.

Then the Flame King stood on widely braced legs and just looked at them. The sound of his nostril breathing was raspy. The black handkerchief sucked in and out.

He said, "Anybody elsh?"

The men did not speak, or even move. They did not seem to breathe.

"In exactly one hour," the Flame King said softly, "I'll expect to hear the nitro. Let's go."

He turned and walked, with the same leisurely ponderousness as before, across the adobe shack and ducked out of the door. The darkness swallowed him.

Poker made a sudden grab for the tequila jug, didn't bother about a glass. He tilted his head back and the jug gurgled.

That was the only sound in the room until one man giggled.

"Two quarts!" he said. "Hell, there won't be enough left of that hospital to cover a dime."

CHAPTER TEN
The Trap

THE hospital was wrapped deep in sleep. Even the little crippled boy in the ward had finally drifted off, and the nurse sank down into her chair in the hall with a sigh of relief. She was young and she had a smile in her eyes. She picked up her book of charts and began to check them over—and the light flashed on over a door at the far end of the hall.

Nurse Higgins whispered a small, "Damn!"

She rose nevertheless and walked briskly toward the room where young Mrs. Wallings was. These young mothers were all alike, worrying about the infants all night long. Even babies had to sleep, but not Nurse Higgins! Oh, no! But Nurse Higgins was smiling when she went into the room.

The hospital was peaceful, full of grief and of happiness like a human heart.

Outside the hospital, a car drew to a halt at the curb. There was something weary about Dr. Sawyer as he put briskness into his pace. His black bag was a fixture in his hand. He walked into the hospital, and the orderly at the switchboard stirred from sleep.

"What's brought you down, Dr. Sawyer?" he asked.

"Emergency," Sawyer said shortly. "Call Higgins and—" He stopped suddenly, staring at the orderly. "What do you mean 'What brought me?' You put through the call to me, didn't you?"

The orderly flushed. "I'll call Higgins," he said.

Sawyer looked at him strangely, then swung off toward his office at the corridor's end. He supposed that the orderly had slipped off for a smoke or something and Higgins had put through the call herself. He went into his office, began to peel off his coat and shirt. He crossed to the corner and washed his hands with a brush, scrubbing studiously at the blunt nails of his powerful hands.

Outside the door, Nurse Higgins paused to put her cap into the exact right posture. She wished that rouge or powder was allowed. She opened the door and stepped in.

"Orderly said something about an emergency case you're expecting, doctor," she said. "What preparations do you want? Shall I call Dr. Young to assist?"

Sawyer turned slowly. "Say that again," he instructed.

Nurse Higgins flushed slightly and repeated. Dr.

Sawyer picked up a towel and dried his hands. His blue eyes were suddenly angry.

"If this is somebody's idea of a practical joke!" he snapped. "Four o'clock in the morning, and—" He stopped at the bewilderment on the girl's face. "There was a phone call about fifteen minutes ago. To my home. *You* said there was an emergency case here, brain operation. You described it as a deep depression above the left squamous."

"I did not!" Nurse Higgins was indignant.

"So there's a joker." Dr. Sawyer nodded. He seemed quite calm, but the glitter in his eyes was angry.

There was a step outside the door, a firm knock, and then the door opened. Mayor Grinnel stood on the threshold. He looked sharply from Sawyer to the nurse, then nodded abruptly. He didn't speak.

Nurse Higgins stammered to Dr. Sawyer, "I'm sorry, sir, about the call. I know nothing about it."

Sawyer grinned at her. "Forget it. Well, Mayor Grinnel, what can I do for you?"

Grinnel waited until the door had closed on the nurse, then he sat down heavily, "All right," he said. "Spill it. This is a hell of an hour to call anybody out for anything. But if it's important I certainly want to hear it."

Sawyer let the towel hang at his side. There was a touch of color on his tanned cheekbones now, and his lips were thin. His voice was chill, very formal. "Would you mind, Mayor Grinnel, telling me just what happened?"

The Mayor looked up at him sharply, saw anger in the doctor's face. He frowned quickly. "You called me twenty minutes ago and asked me to come down here. You said you couldn't leave because of an emergency case, but that you had something to tell me that couldn't wait. About the crimes in town tonight. You were afraid to talk over the phone."

Sawyer's voice suddenly lifted, "There's some damned trickster around! Somebody deliberately tricked both of us."

"Pardon me, gentlemen," a voice spoke lightly, *"I called you both here!"*

Grinnel's head whipped around. Sawyer swung toward the door of the small adjoining laboratory. On the threshold stood a man robed in black. His face was shadowed by a broad-brimmed hat, but his eyes glittered. They were cold and full of menace. His hands were not in sight. He made them a slight bow.

"I," he said, still softly, "am the *Spider.*"

Sawyer rasped, "Damn you, I'll—"

A hand appeared and gestured him to silence. That hand held a heavy automatic.

"I'll do the talking—for a while," said the *Spider.*

A MILE away a group of six men walked toward an automobile. They walked as if the ground were fragile and might open beneath them. One of them carried a rifle with a telescopic sight. Another carried a two-quart can, very carefully, in his arms. They moved slowly, until they were beside the car. Then one man got inside and held out his arms gingerly, and the two-quart can was deposited in them.

"We got ten minutes to go," said the smallest of them. "Go slow!"

It was Poker and his voice was hoarse. He twisted his neck, winced at the pain.

"Go slow!" another man whispered.

The *Spider* looked at his two prisoners and allowed a faint cold smile to move his lips.

"Grinnel," he said, "one of your wells was set afire tonight. Sawyer, your prospective father-in-law was killed tonight. These are the immediate evidences of a wide area of crime. Grinnel, yours is the seventh well set afire. There has also been the explosion of two nitroglycerine trucks, a round dozen murders and a lot of unexplained assaults. Sawyer, you know that Scott saw something in the back country that caused him to be killed tonight—for fear he'd talk.

"I'm going to lay before you gentlemen certain facts:

"Item, the sheriff's men tried to stop the car bringing Scott's body and a prisoner to town. They tried with guns.

"Item, that prisoner, released, went to police headquarters.

"Item, the woman who was following that prisoner was attacked—by two police detectives!"

Grinnel shifted his feet, frowning. His regard did not move from the *Spider*'s face.

"Sawyer," the *Spider*'s eyes flicked toward him, "you supported an accusation of murder against that woman, *when you knew better*. Why?"

Dr. Sawyer's jaw set so that muscles worked along the bone. "There was enough evidence against her," he snapped.

The *Spider* nodded at them. "Shall I tell you two gentlemen what you should have decided for yourselves long ago? There is a racketeer operating in your town and in the environs. He is big time. His racket is to 'protect' your oil wells. He is called—the Flame King. Sawyer, you accused the woman because you were afraid to do anything else."

"I'm no coward!" the doctor snapped.

The *Spider* smiled faintly, "But you didn't want the thing that had happened to Scott to happen also to Beulah."

Sawyer's eyes fell. "There was plenty of evidence," he said, but it was a confession.

"Grinnel!" The *Spider*'s voice made the mayor start. "How much protection money did the gang demand from you?"

Grinnel said, "Not one damned cent. I don't know what you're talking about." He said it angrily and positively. "They blew up my well tonight, and they used a trench mortar to do it. We've got two of the men down at the sheriff's office, and we can't get a thing out of them. You may be right. I'm not saying you aren't. But they haven't asked me for any money—and they better not!"

In the dark, a half block away, the car containing the six men tooled cautiously to the curb. They went once more through the elaborate business of passing the two-quart can from hand to hand.

Poker said, "Take it slow. I'd rather be two minutes late than drop that can, wouldn't you?"

A man said, softly, "D-don't—d-drop it!"

In the hospital office, Grinnel said, savagely, "You're implying the police are crooked, in cahoots with this—this Flame King!"

The *Spider* said, "That's right. The police, or some of them, *and* the sheriff's office. You're mayor of this town, Grinnel. I don't know why you took the job. Most men seem to enter public office in order to do one of two things: gather prestige or loot. They seem to forget that the only purpose they should have—is service to the public!"

Grinnel said, harshly, "It costs me money to hold this office, and I'm not looting the public!"

"You aren't serving them!" the *Spider* said curtly. "You may think the mayoralty is unimportant. Most people seem to think public office is unimportant, and anybody is good enough to run the government, until trouble comes. Then they howl to High Heaven! The people are to blame, for picking unwisely, for actually not giving a damn. But, since you're in office, Mayor Grinnel, you're going to do your job well—or you're going out of office, suddenly."

Grinnel came slowly to his feet. "I don't need you to tell me my duties!" he said harshly.

"Who is responsible to the people for protection of property and life?" The *Spider*'s voice was harsh. "Who is responsible for the police force? Wake up, Grinnel! The mayoralty wasn't created for your benefit! It's a post of service. I have small patience with those who use the public service for their own benefit, Grinnel. When I lose that small patience—"

Grinnel was fighting mad. He even took a step toward the *Spider*—and saw that the *Spider* was smiling!

"Good," the *Spider* said softly, "so you're thinking now! That's what I wanted. *Sawyer!*"

The doctor jerked at the sharpness of his voice.

"Sawyer," the *Spider* repeated, "that prisoner tonight said that, if he were hurt, *you would fix him up!* I hope, Sawyer, that he didn't mean you were the gang doctor. I hope he didn't mean that. But— *watch your step!*"

Outside the window, two men were advancing on their knees, and one cradled a two-quart can under one arm. One of them lifted his head to peer toward the lighted window.

He whispered. "Good Lord! *There's the Spider!*"

The other man's head jerked up, and he saw a black-robed figure spring from the window. The man leaped to his feet, clasping the shiny nitroglycerine can in his arms.

"Don't shoot!" he gulped. "This is nitro!"

Abruptly, his body jerked backward at the waist. His arms flung high and a choked scream pushed out of his mouth. There was no sound of a gun, but he had been shot through the back.

The nitroglycerine can arched into the air toward the wall of the hospital!

At the same instant, a gun blasted from the hospital window, and the *Spider* felt the lead take him heavily in the shoulder!

CHAPTER ELEVEN
While Hell Waits

THE bullet threw the *Spider* off balance, but he used even the force of that impact, as a jiu-jitsu expert uses his opponent's strength. He pivoted and flung himself frantically toward the hospital to catch the can of nitroglycerine.

"Nitroglycerine!" he cried out sharply. "Hold your fire, or it will blow the whole hospital to bits!"

He saw, framed in the window, the hunched figure of Dr. Sawyer, gun hand outstretched. But the *Spider* could pay him no farther heed. He was putting all his strength into the dash to catch that can of nitroglycerine before it smacked against the wall and exploded! A bullet whipped viciously past him, smacked the wall, and bored straight through. It had been aimed, he realized, not at him, but at the can of nitro! And that shot had come from

somewhere in the night, the same silent gun that had killed the man who carried the explosive!

"Lights out!" the *Spider* gasped. "There's a sniper shooting at the nitro!"

He saw Sawyer push back from the window sill, body off balance. His face was distorted by horror, and all his movements seemed incredibly slow. The *Spider*'s own race against death seemed that way to him. He had taken three great bounds and now, desperately, he hurled himself into the air toward that arching can. His left arm refused to answer the command of his brain. The bullet shock had paralyzed it. Wentworth's fingertips strained toward that tumbling cylinder of death. They just brushed it, set it tumbling, interrupted its course. But still it was plunging toward the wall!

Wentworth fell back to earth, lunged against the wall and got his hand between it and the can of nitroglycerine. He batted it away from the wall. He juggled it into the air, staggered after it. He made a cradle of his cape and, as the can plunged down once more, he caught it. Falling to earth, he twisted and brought his body between that fearful explosive and the shock of the fall.

Overhead, another bullet snapped past. Mercifully, the lights inside the hospital blacked out at that instant. The *Spider* lay, panting. He had the nitroglycerine now, cradled in his good arm. Destruction had been averted. Something struck the ground beside him. The rifleman was still sniping in the dark!

Wentworth reeled to his feet and hurried away through the darkness. His feet fumbled. He was aware now of shouts and the beat of running feet. But the moon had set; his black robes blended with the darkness.

Abruptly, he was aware of a figure running toward him from ahead! His gun was in his hand— but he did not fire.

A voice called out to him softly, and it was the voice of Nita van Sloan.

"This way, Dick," she whispered. "The car isn't far away. But hurry!"

Her arm went strongly about his waist. The *Spider*'s jaw was set sternly. The pain of the wound was washing over him now in pulsing waves of heat. The cumulative fatigue of the night gnawed, too, now that agony had weakened him. He ploughed doggedly on.

The car was suddenly before him, and the *Spider* crawled in with the nitroglycerine still in his arms. "Bridge," he mumbled at Nita. "River. Have to dump this nitro."

Nita bit her lips, but she did not seek to disobey the order. She started the car and, running dark, shot off into the night. To reach the river, she must traverse the center of Piperstown, and the police would be on guard. Nevertheless, it must be done.

The *Spider* had the can wedged between his knees now and, with a knife, was carefully opening it. Flung into the river, it would be harmlessly dissipated. Nita shuddered. Not *flung!* It would have to be lowered, very gently.

Dick was knotting an end of the silken rope that was called his Web about the can. His head was held erect by an effort. She could see how thinly his lips were set.

"There's a sniper loose with a high-powered rifle," his words came out with slow precision. "He tried to explode the can with a bullet. You'll have to watch out for him."

"No one is following, yet," Nita said, reassuringly.

"No need to follow," the *Spider* pointed out. "They can guess I've headed for the river and bridge."

Nita bit her lip. Dick's voice was not much above a whisper. That wound must be severe. She had to get him to cover quickly—and there was no protection. She had found an empty house in the slums of Piperstown, but it would not serve for many hours. And there was still the nitroglycerine, the police—and the sniper.

THE pursuit was organizing now. She saw headlights slash past on a cross-street and pulled sharply over the curb and into the shadow of a house. The car shot by the street, and she heard no scream of brakes. She waited for moments before she drove on, cautiously. Speed was important, but she was on a back street. It was unpaved, full of holes and hummocks. And they carried death in their laps.

On a parallel street, she heard two cars roar past at high speed. They were headed toward the bridge. Were they going to post a guard, there? The river was still a half dozen blocks away, but it would have to be the bridge. The margins were marshy, grown thick with reeds. And they not only would have to go slowly over the bridge. They would have to stop and, cautiously, lower the can.

Dick's movement drew her eyes for an instant. He was drawing off his cape, binding it around the can. Well, that would reduce its visibility and make the sniper's task more difficult.

She turned toward the bridge street and, short of the corner, stopped to reconnoiter. She ran on foot and peered toward the bridge itself. There was a guard there, gun in hand! It was the only bridge. She ran back to the car.

"Never mind the guard," the *Spider* told her. "Drive slowly, straight toward the bridge."

The guard stepped into their path as they approached and held up his hand. Nita stopped at the *Spider*'s order, and the guard came cautiously toward them,

The *Spider*'s voice ripped out with sudden force.

"I have a can of nitroglycerine here. Stand aside!"

The man swore, sprang toward the car with his clubbed gun uplifted, but Nita stepped on the accelerator. The man would not dare to shoot. Out onto the span she spurted and, in its middle, she moved close to the right-hand rail. As she braked to a stop, the *Spider* boldly flung the can into space!

For a moment he let it draw on the Web, and then he snubbed it with a careful hand. Clear of water and bridge, the can swung at the end of the rope. Its gyrations would make it a difficult target, but this would have to be fast, fast! He let the line pay out through his fingers, not too swiftly. A bullet rang on the steel railing of the bridge. The sniper was at work again!

Suddenly, Wentworth slashed the silken line. *"Drive!"* he snapped.

With a gasp of relief, Nita poured gasoline to the motor and the car leaped like a released catapult! The opened can of nitroglycerine was safely sunk in the river. Nita drove wildly, lights out, slammed careeningly into the first cross street.

On this side of the river, there were only great storage vats for oil, a pipeline pumping station—and the slums where the Mexican laborers lived. Two thousand people dwelt here in shacks of wood or adobe. There were saloons and gambling halls. There was a plain little box of a church. Here, Nita had found a leaky hut where they might hide—she hoped.

Nita helped Dick Wentworth into the place and dressed his wound. There was no furniture. He stretched out on the earthen floor and Nita stood, looking down at him, tormented by fears and doubts. With abrupt resolution, she strode out of the place and went to the car. Dick was helpless, at the mercy of the first criminal or police officer who came along. She dared not allow them to suspect that they were in this small village. There were no more than five or six hundred houses. A posse could search them in short order. They had only one protection. The Mexicans, like all oppressed minority groups, clung together. It was unlikely that they would carry tales to the police.

Nita set the car in swift motion and rolled, silently as possible, back toward the highway. There were two guards on the bridge. They had set up a blazing searchlight. Nita looked at them, and set her jaw resolutely. She had rigged up a dummy beside her, so that there seemed to be two persons in the car. She herself wore the *Spider*'s hat. She got out her automatic, tucked it under her thigh, and then she sent the car roaring out into the highway, charging straight toward the bridge.

Her headlights blazed into the eyes of the police guards. That was her only hope! The men on the bridge sprang to cover behind the steel girders of

the bridge. Their guns winked with powder flame. Nita felt the shock of the bullets strike the car. The windshield suddenly had holes in it, and the particles of glass stung her face. But she slammed straight into their fire!

Nita crouched as low behind the wheel as possible. As the car blazed up the ramp of the bridge, she ducked entirely out of sight, driving blindly, holding the wheel straight. There was a crescendo blasting of the guns, and then the car slammed into something that stopped it dead!

Nita was jerked forward violently against the steering post. The car wrenched backward. She heard triumphant shouts from the guards. They had blocked the bridge, though she had seen no barricade. It must be a chain, but it was one that the car could not snap.

Grimly, Nita wrenched the wheel hard to the right and jammed on the starter, on the accelerator. The car leaped—toward the railing of the bridge!

There was a crash, a rending snarl of torn metal. The car hesitated sickeningly, then the front wheels dropped into space. The guards were running toward her, shouting. Nita heard the hand of one of them hit the back of the car. At that instant, the sedan teetered slowly forward.

Its rear lifted higher, higher. Nita felt herself lifted toward the roof. The car had turned completely over! It struck the black waters of the river that way. The current caught it, tumbled it over on its left side as it went under.

CHAPTER TWELVE
Hell Town

DR. JERRY SAWYER lifted his head wearily when his office door opened. The quickening day already had sucked the vitality out of his lights, was a bright gray outside his windows. It was Beulah Scott and her face was as wan as the overcast sky, but there was satisfaction in the set of her soft lips.

"The *Spider* is dead," she said flatly, "that settles that!"

Jerry Sawyer reached forward and snapped off the desk light. "It's not as simple as that," he said, dully.

He met Beulah and put his arms about her, but his smile was grave.

"The *Spider* was here last night," he said. "Not many hours ago. There was an attempt to blow up the hospital with nitroglycerine. It wouldn't have left a living thing in a half block or so. The *Spider* prevented that."

"He killed my dad!"

Jerry Sawyer led her to his chair, and perched himself on a corner of the desk.

(Left) At that instant, the sedan teetered forward...

He said, "Beulah, I don't believe he had anything to do with your father's death. I've always thought of the *Spider* as a crook, but what he said here last night didn't sound like it. He talked sense."

Beulah shrugged a shoulder impatiently. "Well, he's dead, and that settles it. Now we'll have peace around here. I think he's a crook, and I think he's been blowing up oil wells and all that."

A small muscle quivered in Sawyer's jaw. He looked at Beulah curiously. "Who told you that?" he asked.

Beulah flushed slightly. "Don't you imagine I can think for myself?"

"You do all right," Sawyer acknowledged with a smile, "but that isn't your idea. You don't bother about crime. Who said that, Chief Rounder?"

"Suppose he did!" Beulah was angry. "He's done more to catch father's murderer than you did!"

"It's his job," Sawyer pointed out, equably. "It was also his job to stop the destruction of oil wells. He knows the crooks operate out of Piperstown. If he doesn't know that, he's the only one in the city who doesn't know it. I think Chief Rounder is just looking for an easy out. The *Spider*'s dead, and so he can hang everything on the *Spider*!"

"Why not tell him so?" Beulah taunted.

Jerry Sawyer took the girl's shoulders in his hands. "I don't know what's eating you, Beulah," he said, "but I can tell you this. I'm having no part in this racket business. Last night, this hospital and all the patients were almost killed. I'm going to keep hands off!"

A memory prodded at Sawyer's mind. The *Spider* had said that sloppy law enforcement was the people's fault. Sawyer's mouth turned grim. To hell with it. He was a doctor and he'd stick to his business. Let the police look after the crooks.

"You're afraid!" the girl cried at him.

Jerry Sawyer said shortly, "I am! It's my job to save lives, not to destroy them! With the *Spider* alive, we might have had some chance, but now—"

"You're a friend of the *Spider*!" Beulah stormed. "That's why you don't want to fight the crooks!"

Sawyer said, reasonably, "Look, we're both tired. Let's postpone this."

Beulah's voice lifted, "You're defending the man who killed my dad! You're the friend of a crook like the *Spider*! I—I never want to see you again!"

She ran out of the office. Jerry Sawyer took a long stride after her, then he checked. His hands fell laxly to his side and presently he turned back to his desk. To hell with it. He was no crusader. He was a man with a job to do. Crusaders got killed, like the *Spider*. Let somebody else do it. Sure, it was wrong, but he had his living to make. Maybe next election, they'd get an honest government here.

Mayor Grinnel started awake in his chair. His son, Roy, was grinning at him anxiously from the doorway and Grinnel looked about him without comprehension. He remembered then that he had come straight home from the hospital, sat down and fallen asleep.

"Look, Dad," Roy said. "Guy on the radio said the *Spider* was dead. It isn't so, is it?"

Mayor Grinnel said, harshly, "Lord, I don't know!"

It was as if the *Spider* stood before him once more, telling him sharp truths about his negligence and his responsibility. Dead? Grinnel had a hard time conceiving of that vital man as dead, but such things happened.

"Can you find out, Dad?" Roy asked.

"What?"

"About the *Spider* being dead, can you find out?"

Grinnel looked sharply at his son's face and saw that the boy was fighting against grief. His eyes had a watery look.

"What's the matter, Roy?" Grinnel got up and put his arm about his boy's shoulders. "Suppose he is dead. What's that to you?"

Roy Grinnel looked at the floor. "He's a swell guy," he said gruffly. "He fights for people and he kills crooks. They never can lay a finger on him. He slides out of things, just as easy. But he likes kids, and he takes care of poor people. He's a swell guy."

GRINNEL'S fingers tightened hard on his son's shoulder. He had received that same impact of integrity from the man himself. He had been angry at the time, but it takes truth to make a man angry and, afterward, he had realized that the *Spider* had told the strict truth. He wasn't taking proper care of his job. He had allowed the police to be slipshod, and the well bombings had gone on. The fact that it was all outside the city proper didn't matter. The crooks must be here somewhere.

"I'll call up for you, son," Grinnel said and crossed to the phone to ring police headquarters.

He was still feeling angry. He had put a good man in charge of the police. That ought to be the end of the matter. A mayor couldn't be held responsible for every crime that was committed in the town and the surrounding country.

"Grinnel here," he said shortly. "What's this about the *Spider*?" He listened, then asked, "Rounder there? All right. Tell him from me to stick around. I'll be down in a half hour."

He hung up and faced his son. "There doesn't seem to be much doubt about it, Roy," he said gently.

Roy looked at him, his eyes widening. He turned abruptly away and went out of the room sharply. Mayor Grinnel lifted a hand to stop him, and didn't. He stood looking down at the floor, quarreling with his anger. What the hell did the kid know about it? The *Spider* was a crook, like any of the rest of them. He shook his head impatiently. Suppose the *Spider* didn't talk like a crook? That was just front.

A half hour later, he got out of his car and went into police headquarters and he was still angry. He went in the chief's office that way. Rounder didn't get up from behind his desk.

"How'd you make out on your well?" he asked.

"Men trying to cap it now," Grinnel said and flung himself into his chair. "That blow-up last night is going to cost me about ten thousand dollars. I'd like to get my hands on the men that did it!"

"He's dead," Rounder reached to his desk and got a cigar, clamped it between his teeth. *"Spider* didn't last long in *our* town."

Grinnel said shortly, "Don't talk like a damned fool. You know the *Spider* didn't blow up those other wells, nor mine either."

"I think it would be smart," Rounder's voice was low, "to keep on thinking the *Spider* did it."

Grinnel felt tightness crawl through him. He could still shiver over that nitroglycerine last night. But his anger grew warmer. He held it down.

"Meaning what?" he asked, sharply.

"Nothing." Rounder's face was bland.

Grinnel said, "Rounder, don't try anything on me."

Chief Rounder smiled, teetered in his chair, chewed on the cigar. His eyes were masked in fat.

Grinnel's mind flashed back to the *Spider's* words of the night before. *"There's a racketeer operating here."*

Grinnel said, "You've got an oil well or two, Rounder. They haven't been bombed."

Rounder said, softly, "That's right. I'm smart."

"What the hell do you mean?" Grinnel was on his feet.

Chief Rounder wasn't disturbed. "You say that blowup last night cost you ten thousand. You've got a lot of wells. It wouldn't take many blowups to wipe you out. One blowup would ruin me. So I play smart."

Grinnel controlled his anger. "So you pay protection money to the Flame King."

Rounder shrugged. "I hire men to guard my wells. It's expensive, but I haven't had any explosions."

Grinnel's anger was red before his eyes. His fists were knotted, but Chief Rounder continued to teeter in his chair. It made a little squeak each time. Grinnel looked down at his fists. The whole picture was pretty clear now. Rounder was looking after his own property, actually paying protection money. So he walked softly where the Flame King was concerned, for fear his wells would be blown up. People would be saying that he did the same thing.

"Where did you get your guards," Grinnel said slowly. "It looks like I better have some, too."

"Hidalgo Protective Association," the chief answered.

Grinnel exploded. "You trying to tell me that

because you have a couple of sleepy Mexes watching your well—How much?"

Rounder shrugged. "Why don't you call them?" he said. "Rates vary, I guess."

Grinnel came across to the desk. "Rounder, you're going with me to pay a personal call on Hidalgo," he said. "We're taking a squad of men with us and we're going to blow that place wide open! I'll be damned if any racketeer is going to run my town!"

CHIEF ROUNDER continued to smile. "No we're not, Grinnel," he said. "And I'm not resigning, so don't ask me. I like the way my wells are guarded. I like it just fine."

Grinnel said, "Damn you, Rounder!" He started around the desk, and the chief took up a revolver out of his drawer. He did it casually, but his fist was hard on the butt, and the muzzle didn't waver. His eyes showed suddenly, flat and brilliant.

"Don't try any rough stuff, Grinnel," he snapped.

Mayor Grinnel was a big man. He had heavy shoulders and his hands were powerful. They clenched now, but he controlled himself.

"So it's like that, is it?" Grinnel ground out.

"Exactly like that." Rounder was suave. "Nobody is being hurt except a few big boys who own wells."

"There have been twelve murders," Grinnel snapped. "And they weren't big boys."

Rounder shrugged. "Somebody spoke out of turn, probably. I like things the way they are. I think we better keep them that way."

Grinnel took two steps backward, then swung toward the door.

"Wait a minute, Mr. Mayor!" Rounder called out. "I wouldn't try anything rash. You've got more oil wells."

Grinnel said, grimly, "I'm mayor of this town, Rounder. Not you. There are more than enough people here who see things the way I do. I wouldn't give much for your chances of escaping a lynch party."

Rounder lurched to his feet, his heavy face graying. "Wait a minute, Mr. Mayor," he said again. "Did you ever hear of—hostages? And what they do to hostages in Europe?"

Grinnel looked at Rounder. He walked back to the desk. "Maybe you better explain what you mean," he said.

Chief Rounder smiled at him and put the cigar back in his mouth.

Grinnel leaned across the desk. "I said, *'Explain!'"*

Rounder sat down. "I think we understand each other," he said. "You're mayor. I'm chief of police. You run your business and I'll run mine. But keep on your side of the line, or—" He shrugged, but the revolver was under his hand.

Mayor Grinnel straightened. He went out of the office without speaking and his thoughts were whirling crazily. A man spoke to him in the main hall and he looked up, startled. Then he smiled, it was Detective Sergeant Burroughs. He was an old-time law officer. With a man like him as chief of police—

Grinnel glanced behind him toward Rounder's office, then stepped close to Burroughs.

"Come to my home as soon as you can," he said, under his breath.

Burroughs' eyes narrowed, but he only nodded curtly. Grinnel went out and got into his car and drove home. He drove savagely. He slammed into the house—and suddenly he was afraid.

"Where's Roy?" he snapped at his housekeeper.

The Mexican woman lifted her big dark eyes and smiled. "He left right after you telephoned him, *Señor,*" she said.

"After *I*—" Grinnel went pale. He staggered a little as he went across the room and sank into a chair. Chief Rounder, or the Flame King with whom he was allied, had moved swiftly. Good Lord, where could he turn? He had friends. He began to recapitulate. There were, perhaps, five men to whom he could go to in this town and talk frankly. Five men, all oil well owners. And all of them had had one explosion; just one and no more. *And all of them used Mexican guards now!*

Mayor Grinnel cursed bitterly as he realized the meaning of that fact. All of them had thought it was wisest to pay the Flame King. Grinnel was alone then, alone in his battle against the crooks—and Roy was in danger! Perhaps, Burroughs and he could work something out. Burroughs was an honest man, fearless, and he didn't own any oil wells. Burroughs was his only chance, now that the *Spider* was gone.

Mayor Grinnel winced suddenly. The windows of the house had rattled in their frames and there was the distant thud of an explosion! He pushed to his feet and his eyes swept around him almost wildly. That meant some new horror.

The telephone shrilled and Grinnel reached it with a reeling stride and snatched up the instrument. Chief Rounder's fat voice vibrated against his eardrums, and Rounder sounded frightened.

"Grinnel, something's happened," he said. "Listen, don't try anything! Burroughs just got his. He stepped on the starter in his car and it blew him up! There ain't enough of him left to scoop up in a dipper!"

Mayor Grinnel suddenly felt tired and old. His shoulders sagged. "All right. But send my boy home, Rounder. Send Roy home."

Grinnel groped to replace the phone in its cradle. He lifted his big hands to his face. What could he do? He was alone.

CHAPTER THIRTEEN
"Kill the *Spider!*"

RICHARD WENTWORTH swam back to consciousness in the hot swelter of noonday. He was feverish, but there was water beside him. He drank of it slowly, stared about the shack in which he lay. His wounded shoulder was neatly bandaged. It was stiff and sore, but he pushed himself to his feet, swayed dizzily.

There was only this one room. He peered cautiously out of the window openings and knew that he was in the Mexican slums. Nita was nowhere in sight. He settled down to wait for her, but the long afternoon wore itself out without a sign of her. The streets presently filled with screaming, romping children. School had let out. And Nita did not come.

He thought about Ram Singh, and worry furrowed his brow.

In the next house, a girl began to sing. She had a clear, rich voice, warm in her throat. When she broke off the song, it was with a laugh. Wentworth smiled, and was glad that the criminals who were preying on the countryside had not yet dampened the happiness of these people.

If Nita did not come by the time darkness set in, he would leave a message she would understand and get on with his work. Worry prodded at him, but he stilled it. Nothing had happened to Nita.

The slow crawl of hours increased his tension. Once he heard the singing girl and a woman talking excitedly in Spanish and strained his ears. It seemed there had been an explosion near the City Hall. A policeman had been blown up in his auto. *El Señor* Burroughs. The way they spoke of the man held respect.

Wentworth's eyes narrowed as he listened. The murder of a policeman did not fit into his suspicions about the conduct of the police in Piperstown. But there would be honest men on the force. Wentworth swore softly. Actually, that murder reinforced his suspicions. Since the *Spider* had brought the war to them, they were closing up the ranks. It was always that way when danger threatened.

The weary day dragged itself out. Wentworth was dimly aware of a weakness that was part hunger and part the wound. His clothing was stained and stiff. He had no others, and his hotel rooms would be watched. He took out an automatic and, with slow hands, checked its loading and mechanism. That completed his preparations for the night.

He thought another call was in order upon either Dr. Sawyer or Mayor Grinnel. It was only through one of them that warning of the meeting at the hospital could have been given—through one of them, or through his home. He frowned, remembering the ruthless savagery of the huge quantity of nitroglycerine that had so narrowly been prevented from destroying the hospital.

Didn't that one fact clear both Grinnel and Sawyer of any suspicion? Or did it merely mean that there was a traitor in the organization who wanted to remove the chief? He bowed his head in thought. Ram Singh had disappeared... and now Nita.

Dusk quieted the children in the street and, next door, a guitar began to twang. Presently, the girl began to sing softly. Wentworth peered out the window. A boy, on a bench against the wall, was plucking the guitar. The girl began to weave her arms to the rhythm. She stepped lightly into a dance. There was nothing formal or studied about it. She was young and her happiness expressed itself in this way. Wentworth smiled. In the back of his mind was worry and grimness, and thoughts of death and justice. But it was for people like this that the *Spider* fought for: the happiness of plain people.

There came, through the night, a long-drawn call. It was high and thin. The guitar stopped on a twanging discord. The girl froze in the midst of a dance step. In the doorway of the hut there appeared a man. He was barefooted, and his clothing was worn but clean.

"Los ladrones," he said, harshly. "The thieves! Get inside, Pepita."

The girl went inside, taking the guitar. The boy stood beside his father, and their faces were as blank as wood.

On Wentworth's forehead a frown had gathered. A car had turned into the end of the street and it jounced slowly, with comfortable springing, over the unpaved roadway. It came on steadily and Wentworth drew back from the window. His hand slid to his gun. The fact that a signal had been given meant that this was no rare occurrence. It did not mean a raid by thieves, but a visit from someone whom the Mexicans considered thieves.

The big car stopped before the shack next door, and one man got out. He was a big man, heavy in the shoulders and tall. He walked ponderously toward the hut and stood looking at the Mexican in the doorway. The man looked back blankly.

"Better come along with me, Miguel," the big man said harshly.

"For why, *Señor* Rounder?" the Mexican asked.

There was firelight within the hut, and its flickering redness shone through the doorway and illuminated the beefy face of the police chief. He had a gun in his hand.

"Sergeant Burroughs was murdered today," he said. "You did it, Miguel."

The Mexican gasped. *"Por dios!"* he gasped. "It is not true, *Señor!* I, Miguel, have killed no one!"

Chief Rounder continued to look at him.

Lamentations burst out within the shack. A girl's voice spoke rapidly while a woman sobbed.

"I'd hate to make a mistake," Rounder said, slowly. "The townspeople are pretty sore. They're apt to lynch anybody I bring in."

Miguel fell to his knees. *"Por dios, Señor,"* he whispered. "I know nothing! I did nothing!"

"Well, now, I don't know," Chief Rounder went on. "You don't like me, I know that, Miguel. And it might be you intended to kill me, and not Sergeant Burroughs. You haven't liked me ever since I asked you to let Pepita keep house for me. You haven't been real friendly since that time."

MIGUEL crossed himself slowly, and got to his feet. "It is true," he said stonily, "I killed Sergeant Burroughs, who is my friend. I killed him by mistake for you."

Pepita burst out of the house. "No, father!" she cried. "No. I will not let you! It is a trick, but I will not let you! I will go! What does it matter?"

Chief Rounder had not smiled, but his small eyes glittered on the girl. She was lithe and beautifully formed. Her black hair was a glistening veil across her shoulders. She stamped her foot in the dust.

"I will go!" she said.

Chief Rounder nodded slowly. "Well, now," he said, "if I could prove to the townspeople that you were friendly-like, they probably wouldn't think you were guilty. Maybe that would be a good idea."

Miguel reached out and struck Pepita across the face. "Go into the house," he said calmly. "I will not have—"

Rounder took him by the throat and lifted him off the ground. He shook him—and he had a gun in his right hand.

"You shouldn't strike a lady, Miguel," he said.

Pepita tugged at Rounder's shoulder. "Please," she whimpered. "Please, do not kill him. I will go with you! I swear it!"

Chief Rounder dropped Miguel to the earth, and faced the girl. He looked at her, and she shrank back. But her eyes did not falter.

"I will go," she said, her voice low but clear. "To save my father, I will go."

Inside the house, the woman wailed. Miguel lay in the dust, and his son knelt beside him. Rounder gestured the girl to his car, and then he squeezed his huge body in behind the wheel and drove slowly away. His beefy face was satisfied, and his eyes glistened. He glanced at the girl and began to drive faster.

When he reached his home, he slammed into the drive and jammed on the brakes. He turned again toward the girl, reaching out—and he froze like that. Color drained from his face. A gun muzzle was nuzzling into his right ear!

Out of his eye corners, Rounder could see the face of the man who pressed the gun against his head. It was a passionless and ruthless face, as remote, and as unswerving, as a face of stone.

The man spoke, and his voice was strangely gentle, "Go home, Pepita," he said. "You and yours are safe. You will not be troubled again."

The girl's slim hand crept to the catch of the door, but neither man was looking at her now, and the voice spoke with a new tone, bitter and thin with menace.

"Chief Rounder, is it murder to kill a snake?"

Abruptly, a narrow beam of light reached out and struck the windshield. Its heart was shadow and that shadow-shape was a spider with sprawling legs and ready fangs!

Chief Rounder moaned, *"The Spider!"*

Pepita sprang from the car and ran with a swift and desperate silence away into the night.

CHAPTER FOURTEEN
"I saw the *Spider!*"

BEULAH SCOTT was not on her way to see Chief Rounder when she drove past his house, but the street led to the hospital. Nevertheless, she looked, in gratitude, toward the home of the chief of police. After all, his men had been responsible for the death of the *Spider*. They had avenged her father.

She looked, and she saw the car in the driveway, with people in it, and then she saw a focused beam of light strike the windshield from within—and she saw and recognized the signature of the *Spider!*

Her first reaction was to stop; her next was to put on all speed and summon help. She had believed the *Spider* dead, but that signature could mean only that he was alive. Not only alive, but he had Chief Rounder a prisoner. Beulah did not think beyond that point.

Beulah Scott sped through the city toward the hospital. Her eyes were strained wide and her hands gripped the wheel of her car with white tension. Hatred was in her heart, and a little fear. It was incredible that the *Spider* should be alive, but he was. Would the police believe her? They would have to! But would they?

Beulah whispered, "Jerry! Jerry Sawyer!" The police would listen to *him!* She could convince him.

She raced on. The hospital was only a half dozen blocks away now. She slammed up to the emergency entrance, ran her car onto the grass plot and hurried toward the door.

Her face was pale and intent, and all her young body was instinct with driving anger and hatred. She was like a graceful wild thing, beautiful but dangerous.

And with a wild creature's singular purpose, she ran down the hallway of the hospital. It did not seem strange to her that Nurse Higgins only glanced at her and hurried on toward the switchboard, nor that an orderly stood against the wall with a white and frightened face. She thrust into the doctor's office and Jerry Sawyer was seated behind his desk with an angry and bitter expression on his face, and both fists clenched.

"Jerry!" Beulah gasped. "Jerry, the *Spider* is alive! I saw him!"

Jerry Sawyer looked at her with an effect of not seeing. He didn't answer. The telephone shrilled and he snatched it up. "Hello!" he snapped. "An ambulance case? Where? Market and Poplar? All right, send out the wagon. Dr. Elms will go. I can't. And get that call through right away, Higgins!"

"Hello, Beulah," he spoke then to the girl. "This town is going crazy! That's the third man today we've gone out for, beaten up by thugs! And five people injured when that store was blown up. And now, tonight—"

Beulah interrupted. "Jerry, listen to me! The *Spider* is alive! I saw him!"

Sawyer said, savagely, "Good, I hope he cleans up these crooks!" He stood up and his voice held outrage and fury. "Those fiends came into my hospital tonight and killed one of these poor devils who was beaten up today! They cut his throat! Damn them, I'll—"

"But I'm telling you, Jerry! I saw the *Spider!* He's behind this! He's the one who is doing all this! He killed Dad, and—"

Jerry looked at her then, and incredulity touched his face. He came around the desk and took Beulah's shoulders in his hands. The girl wrenched away impatiently.

"You've got to call the police and tell them about the *Spider!*" she said. "They wouldn't listen to me. They think the *Spider* is dead, but I saw him. He's at Chief Rounder's house, and he's got Chief Rounder a prisoner! He's going to kill Chief Rounder if they don't get there and get there fast!"

Jerry Sawyer snapped, "Nonsense! The *Spider*—" He stopped then, and his eyes were narrowed and intent. Slowly, he nodded his head. "Why not?" he said. "Why not? The *Spider* told us that the Flame King had this city by the throat, and I didn't believe him. But it's been proved today. All these assaults, that store blown up, this murder here in my hospital! Those things couldn't exist if the police weren't in on it. No racket can continue until the police let it." He laughed sharply. "Let Chief Rounder worry about the *Spider!*"

THE telephone shrilled and Sawyer snapped it up. This time, it was police headquarters and he told them about the murder in the hospital.

"Damn it!" he rasped. "I tell you, it was murder! Do you think I don't know when a man's throat has been cut! What's the matter with you down there? I've had eight cases here today where criminals injured people. Your own man, Burroughs, was blown up. And you ask me if I'm sure it's murder! Get over here and get here damned fast, or I'll raise a stink that will blow the lid off this town!"

He slammed up the receiver and Beulah snatched at his arm. "You didn't tell them about the *Spider!*" she cried.

Once more, the look of incredulity passed over his face. He tried to take Beulah's hand, but she snatched it away,

"Beulah," he said. "Don't you understand? The *Spider* is fighting the people's battle; our battle. It's impossible that he should have killed your father. He's fighting the criminals—and if he's after Chief Rounder, that's swell. He probably knows that Rounder is the man who is tied up with the crooks. I tell you, all these things couldn't happen if the police weren't in with the crooks. Look how they behaved when I reported this murder here in the hospital!"

Beulah had backed away from him. "You're a friend of the *Spider!*" she said slowly, unbelievingly. "You'd protect the man who killed my Dad! And Dad was your friend, too! Jerry, if you don't pick up that phone and call the police, I'm through with you! I'm through with you, forever!"

Sawyer's face was grave, but it grew grim at her threat. "Call them yourself," he said shortly. "I have business to attend to."

He stalked out of the office. Beulah stared after him for a moment, but her anger was still untouched, unappeasable. It was the *Spider*'s fate, as it is of all great men, that he engendered either great love or great hatred. There was no middle ground.

Beulah caught up the phone to call police headquarters.

CHAPTER FIFTEEN
Trapped!

THE *Spider* saw Beulah Scott's car hesitate and then race on. He could even guess the reason, but it did not alter his plans. He had formed them swiftly when he had learned the identity of the bully who was imposing on Miguel and his family. It had been easy to slip into the back of the car and remain hidden while Chief Rounder drove swiftly toward his home.

"We're going into your house for a little chat, Rounder," he said, raspingly. "Or, if you'd prefer, I can kill you here."

Chief Rounder fumbled open the door and walked with the ponderous stiffness of a dead man into the house. The *Spider* moved behind him, gun ready. Their footsteps were hollow on the porch and on the bare polished floors within.

"The telephone," the *Spider* commanded. "Call Mayor Grinnel and get him over here, immediately."

Rounder said, thickly, "Suppose he won't come?"

The *Spider* laughed. It was a low sound but Chief Rounder shuddered. He picked up the phone.

"Come over to my place right away," he said, when he had reached Mayor Grinnel. "No, I'm not telling you why, but get over here and make it fast. Listen, I've got something to talk over with you. We—we're both in a jam." He hung up and dared not turn to face the *Spider*. He lifted a ponderous hand and dragged his sleeve across his forehead.

"He's coming," he said thickly.

The *Spider* drove him to a heavy winged chair by the fireplace, let him turn on a single lamp beside it. Once wedged into that deep chair, Rounder was almost as helpless as if he were bound. The front door was open. The *Spider* stood in the shadows across the room and his gun was as steady as rock. They waited.

Rounder's courage came back slowly. "You can't get away with this," he growled. "I've got good cops in this town. We'll hound you to death!"

The *Spider* gave no indication of having heard.

Rounder moved his shoulders a little, eased forward slightly in his chair. By degrees which he thought imperceptible, he got his feet close under him, tensed his thighs. He talked to distract attention from his movements; he gestured hugely with a thick, powerful hand.

"I'm the head of the police of this town, and you're interfering with our efficiency," he said. "You're probably in with the crooks who are trying to take over the town. You act like it. But you can't bluff me. I'm going to clean out every rat in this town, you included."

He was almost ready now. He moved his left shoulder in a shrug, and his coat swung free of his body. The *Spider* was a fool not to have taken his gun. He could get it out and shoot an instant after he smacked over the light. And still the *Spider* gave no indication of having heard anything he said.

"If you're really the sort of man you're supposed to be," Rounder went on persuasively, "if you really fight criminals, you ought to help me instead of pulling a stunt like this. That Mex girl is a valuable witness and her old man did have something to do with Burroughs' death. I was just getting her away from the family to threaten her and make her tell what she knows. You know how these Mexicans are."

He was ready now. A quick flip with his left hand would knock out the light. He would be out of his chair and shooting before the *Spider* knew what was happening! Rounder's fat-crowded eyes rested with candor on the *Spider*'s face.

The *Spider*'s gun crashed loudly in the room.

And the *Spider* smiled at him! His lipless gash of a mouth made an ugly crease across his ruthless face, and the *Spider* deliberately lifted his gun and put it back into its holster under his arm! The cold and implacable eyes of the *Spider* rested on a spot between Rounder's eyes.

Chief Rounder felt the sweat start on his forehead. The *Spider* not only hadn't been fooled by his talking to cover his movements, but the *Spider* was inviting him to shoot it out! *The Spider intended to kill him!*

Rounder gasped and slumped back in his chair, understanding now why the gun had been left in his holster, understanding also that the *Spider* had already judged and condemned him. He was doomed! He had just one chance. Apparently, the *Spider* didn't want to kill him in cold blood, and so was anxious for him to make a move in self-defense. If he remained perfectly still, if he did not provoke the *Spider* at all, perhaps the *Spider* would not kill him.

The *Spider* chuckled.

Chief Rounder's spirit was broken. He cowered.

Outside a car turned into the drive and stopped. Presently, footsteps came across the porch, the footsteps of two persons. But one pair of feet was light.

"Come in!" a voice called, and Rounder shivered. It sounded exactly like his own.

MAYOR GRINNEL strode into the house, and his son, Roy, trotted beside him. They came forward toward where Rounder sat and it was the chief's terrified gaze that turned their eyes toward the *Spider.*

Roy cried out, delightedly, worshipfully, "Oh, swell! It's the *Spider!* I knew they hadn't killed you, *Spider!*"

Mayor Grinnel's haggard face seemed suddenly relieved. His lips relaxed from their harsh bitterness.

He said, quietly, "Thank God!"

Rounder was waspish. "You damned fool! He called you here to kill you!"

Grinnel glanced toward him and anger crept back into his eyes. "Death is too good for you," he rasped. "Why do you think I brought my son along with me? Because there's no other way to protect him from you scheming coyotes!"

The *Spider* felt, for the first time, a surge of hope. He had descended upon so many cities, cleansing them, wiping out the criminals who victimized the peoples. It was a necessary service, but it was only a part of what was necessary. Beyond that there was the uprising of the people, the awareness to their own danger and their own responsibility. There was the need for honest officials to carry on the work. Now, it seemed, Mayor Grinnel would fight.

"What are you going to do about it?" he demanded coldly of the mayor.

Grinnel laughed harshly. "Do? What can I do

alone? I went to Rounder and he threatened my son's death. He was taken away for awhile, then restored to me as a bribe. I was afraid to go to see men, for fear they would be killed. I phoned four men, and what has happened? Two of them are dead. The detective I trusted above all others is dead. Two other men were beaten and put in the hospital. And tonight—" Grinnel's face twitched—"tonight my housekeeper opened the door of her closet, in her room. And there was an explosion that killed her!

"For some reason, they don't want to kill me, merely to terrify me. So they deliberately killed—my housekeeper! A woman who has served my family faithfully for years. They destroy *her!*" He shook his two clenched fists. "What can I do?"

The *Spider* felt the slow and awful tide of his just anger rise in his breast. This sort of thing had happened before, would happen again whenever the cleansing out of criminal elements began. They struck out wildly in all directions, spreading death and terror.

Roy grabbed his father's arm. "What are you afraid of, Dad?" he asked. "Isn't the *Spider* here with us—and on your side?"

The two men looked at the boy and the shining faith, the worship in his eyes as he gazed from one to the other was a thing that hurt like a knife. Both men knew the peril and the slimness of their chances, but things were so simple for the boy. He was the *Spider,* wasn't he? Well, then—he'd win!

Mayor Grinnel's eyes met those of the *Spider,* but there was no hope in the mayor's face. He had tried all he knew, and it not only had failed, but men had died.

He said, without hope, "There is no way."

That was the moment when Chief Rounder made his play. He was driven to desperation, for his dominion had been shaken. Chief Rounder batted out the light and flung himself violently from the chair. His gun leaped to his hand, crashed in the darkness!

He thought himself free from observation, reasonably safe. The *Spider* had never relaxed vigilance—but he stood in such a position that if a bullet missed him, it would kill the mayor or his son! He dared not risk even his sure lead upon a moving target with other lives at stake. So the *Spider* held his fire, and hurled himself violently against Mayor Grinnel and his son. The impact of his charge drove the two off their feet. The *Spider* spilled with them, and his wounded shoulder stabbed him with weakened agony so that his senses reeled.

Chief Rounder came forward on his ponderous legs, firing as he came, driving lead toward the dark moving mass on the floor. Roy cried out in a gasped scream—and the *Spider*'s gun crashed!

THE hulking figure of Chief Rounder leaped backward, crashed into the wall. It was motionless then. In the room where hell had exploded, there was silence. Then there was the clatter of a falling gun. Afterward, Chief Rounder pitched straight forward. His fall shook the room.

Outside, a police whistle screamed!

The *Spider* pushed to his feet, and the flicker of his flashlight struck across Mayor Grinnel where he knelt over his son. Wentworth bent swiftly, seeking the bullet wound that had felled the boy. He looked down into the white face of the boy, twisted with pain. The wound wasn't serious. It had torn through the fleshy part of his thigh.

The *Spider* said, quietly, "The man who hurt you is dead, Roy."

Roy smiled, and his face was bright in spite of the pain. "I knew you'd take care of me," he whispered.

Mayor Grinnel surged to his feet. *"Spider,"* he rasped. *"I'm fighting!"* The police were pounding across the porch. Their flashlights scorched into the room, through the windows.

The *Spider* said, "I knew you would, Mayor Grinnel. Call a mass meeting and tell the people the truth. They can't kill a whole town! You'll have to protect yourself."

"I will!" Grinnel rasped. "Now get out of here before the cops take you."

"Lead them against me," the *Spider* said. "Don't let them know we're partners!"

Lights blazed suddenly in the room. All about the house there were the shouts of the police. They had taken time to sew the house up tightly. Men stormed into the drawing room—and checked as they saw Chief Rounder's body, and the vermillion seal of the *Spider* upon his forehead!

Mayor Grinnel had his son in his arms. But the *Spider* had disappeared!

IN A driveway half a block from Chief Rounder's home a shadow paused briefly, then darted swiftly toward a coupé parked at the curb. Behind him, as he sprang under the wheel of the battered coupé, the *Spider* could hear the police spreading out, could hear Mayor Grinnel's voice shouting stentorian orders. The *Spider* prodded the motor to life, whipped away from the curb as the cry went up in back of him, and bullets pinged on metal.

When he reached the bridge that led back to the Mexican slums, Wentworth saw the torn gap in the guard rail which had been roped off. He checked, then sent the coupé for the gap while he dropped to the roadway. He was frowning as he drove himself to a hard lope toward the other end, toward his hiding place. The crash and deluging splash as the car took the river did not make him turn his head, but he was worried. What car had plunged through the guard

rail? Nita had taken the car away the night before, so that he would be safe in hiding. Obviously, she would have tried to lead the police away from his trail—and there was a gap in the guard rail!

Wentworth was in more than physical torment as he drove himself along the unpaved slum street toward the shack where he had hidden. He fairly flung himself through the drooping door—and then relief left him weak. From the pallet where he had lain, Nita van Sloan climbed easily to her feet. Wentworth braced his good hand against the wall for an instant before he went to her and gathered her hungrily into his embrace.

"Little fool," he said gently. "I saw that gap in the guard rail!"

Nita laughed up at him, "It worked!"

"Where have you been all day?"

Nita made a face. "Hiding in the mesquite two miles below the bridge. I was pretty badly shaken up, and—and, Dick, I almost didn't get out! It took me all that time to get ashore and, after that, it was daylight and I had to wait.

"Are you hungry?" she asked. "Those blessed folks next door brought food. It seems that somebody called the *Spider* has saved them from dishonor, from worse-than-death, from ten thousand devils and hell-fire. Or something. And, for some reason, they think that you and the *Spider* have something in common."

The *Spider's* eyes were grim. "Unless we smash these criminals, there will be many Pepitas!"

He told her then what had happened and of Mayor Grinnel's plans to call a mass meeting of the citizens and arouse them against the Flame King, even if he had to establish vigilantes.

"Once that threatens, the police will support him fully," Wentworth said, "but if they can kill Grinnel, or intimidate enough people—" He brushed it aside. "We will conquer!"

Nita van Sloan, watching him, made her lips smile, but she knew that it was a forlorn hope that Wentworth expressed. One man only stood between the people and criminal slavery!

"You must rest," she said, quietly.

At that moment, the girl, Pepita, burst in through the door. *"Señor!"* she cried. "Ah, *Señor. Aronya! Los Ladrones,* they come!"

Wentworth was on his feet. "The police?" he asked sharply.

The girl nodded violently. Her black hair swung. "They are closing all the streets, *Señor!* They are searching every house! You must go, and go quickly. They will kill!"

Wentworth reached the window in a stride. What the girl had said was true, for a police car was drawn up broadside across the end of the street, and a squad of men was quickly searching the houses.

It would not take long. The houses were so small. He felt Nita at his side.

"Go to the river," he directed her quietly. "I will lead them another way."

"But, Dick—"

Wentworth's sharp gesture cut her short. "You must find a disguise and get into the telephone exchange here," he said. "Preferably, get a job. It may be that they have tapped the wires of Grinnel's home, but I think that it is more than that. I think that the criminals maintain a surveillance on the whole city through the telephone exchange. That was the way they got advance warning of my presence at the hospital when they tried to blow it up. That was the way they knew to crash in on Rounder's home last night, after I had escaped the police. That is the only way in which they could have known what men to kill after Mayor Grinnel tried to assemble some support. I will let you know how to reach me."

Pepita spoke softly. "I have a friend who works there. I will carry messages!"

Nita put her arm about the girl's shoulder and Pepita drew shyly close to them.

"It is time to go," Wentworth said quietly. He smiled at Nita, and she kissed him quickly. She went with Pepita to the door and they crossed the street leisurely, then ran toward the river. Wentworth took out his guns and, with the help of his awkward left hand, checked the loading. Then he took deliberate aim at the headlights of the car which illumined the street, and began to shoot.

CHAPTER SIXTEEN
One Man Alone

MAYOR GRINNEL installed a cot-bed in the chief's office at police headquarters and kept his son with him. Grinnel himself did not leave the office, but took over Rounder's job and authority. He had sent his men to search the Mexican slums as the least likely district in which they would find the *Spider*—and they had found him! Fortunately, the *Spider* had broken through their lines and escaped, but Mayor Grinnel's stock had gone up with the police officers. Grinnel smiled grimly. He needed every ounce of prestige he could squeeze out of the situation!

At noon, Grinnel assembled the bulk of the police force of Piperstown in the main room of headquarters. He took his stand behind the sergeant's desk, a brick wall at his back, and his hand on a gun tucked into his trousers. He grimly looked over the men.

"Most of you are honest men," he began abruptly, "but some of you are crooks. I don't know which ones. I don't want to know. But I'll kill any man who even looks as if he were going to draw a gun!"

As he spoke, he drew his own long revolver and thumbed back the hammer. Men's bodies grew stiff, and every eye focused on Mayor Grinnel. Expressions turned wooden.

Grinnel nodded at them, "Yesterday, Sergeant Burroughs was murdered. So was Chief Rounder. There have been a dozen other men killed within the last forty-eight hours. This is only the climax of a series of crimes—murder, and destruction of oil wells. You know the history. For whatever reasons, crooks have been allowed to get hold of the city, completely. You thought you were safe, you men who have let this happen, but the events of yesterday prove you were wrong. I allowed myself to be tricked. I thought that Chief Rounder was honestly trying to catch the crooks. Instead, I find that he was their partner! So I'm just as guilty as any one of you!"

Suddenly, a boy's cry rang through the building—the voice of Roy Grinnel! "Dad!" it called. "Dad, *help!*"

Grinnel leveled his revolver, "Don't any man move!" he ordered and his voice croaked in his throat.

There was an instant heavy crashing of gunfire down the corridor from the main hall, and then silence. After a space of a minute, a uniformed policeman staggered out through the swing doors of the corridor. There was blood on his head.

"Two men tried to kidnap your son, sir," the officer said thickly. "We killed them both. They got Jeremy Martin."

Grinnel nodded stiffly. "I'm promoting you, Sullivan. Go back to your post."

The patrolman Sullivan saluted, and the doors swung shut behind him. They creaked a little. That was the only sound save a heavy shifting of feet among the waiting men.

Grinnel cleared his throat. "That's the sort of thing we have to fight," he said harshly. "I'm going to clean up this town! You men can fight with me, or against me—but this town is going to cleaned, up! Now, then! I'm asking no questions. I want ten men to stand guard around this building. I'd prefer single men, who can't be reached by threats to their families. The rest of you are on twenty-four hour duty until this job is done! And don't think the crooks can stop this by killing me. I've made arrangements, and my murder will be the signal for the Governor to send in troops!

"Here are my orders:

"Every man goes on patrol in pairs. I've posted your assignments. I hold each two men responsible for any crime committed on his beat. The orders are, 'Shoot to kill any man seen attempting a crime!' But if any officer shoots an *innocent* man,

I'll personally spring the trap that hangs him. You know the crooks of this town. You have your orders. This is war!"

He slammed his fist down on top of the desk and the taut men started as if at a shot.

"I'm calling a mass meeting of the men of this town tonight," he went on. "I'm forming them into vigilante committees and I'm arming them! You will spread the word of this meeting everywhere you go. You newspaper men who are here, I request you to record this fact and to publish it. At eight o'clock tonight, at City Hall. All men who want a clean town, who want to live and work out their lives in peace and freedom will come. If there are too many for the hall, we'll hold the meeting outside.

"I want the meeting like that, overflowing. This is a town meeting out of the past. This is the men, of Piperstown asserting their democracy, their right to rule." Mayor Grinnel's smile was stern and bitter. I will regard any man who fails to support this movement as a crook or a weakling. "He who is not for us, is against us! That is all! Dismissed!"

SERGEANT MANN found his name on the bulletin hoard and it directed that he report to Mayor Grinnel. Sergeant Mann was a little confused. He had done his duty, he knew, but perhaps he had not done it thoroughly. It was his job to enforce the law, but he also must receive orders and obey them. If he had put the latter over the former, it was because that was the emphasis which Chief Rounder had placed upon it. But he acknowledged to himself now that his conscience had never been entirely easy. He had stilled it with the old plaint, "A man has to earn a living." He had known that it was not an answer. And now Mayor Grinnel wanted to see him!

Sergeant Mann went toward the chief's office on heavy feet. He felt resentful and angry. There were a lot of other guys who had done worse than he had. Why was he being called on the carpet? He wasn't going to be made a goat!

There were a dozen or more police officers in the hallway outside of the chief's office, into which Mayor Grinnel had gone. They were uneasy and resentful as Sergeant Mann was.

"What's up?" Mann asked. "You been in yet?"

Shakes of the head, shrugs, sullen looks answered him. They all were conscious of guilt, and none of them had gone inside. But to Sergeant Mann's knowing eye, none of these was among the chief offenders. Mann felt his anger growing warmer. His jaw set, and he walked up to Grinnel's door and knocked peremptorily. Men in the hall started at the thunder of that knock.

Grinnell's voice was quiet, "Come in!"

Sergeant Mann opened the door wide. He hesitated, then stepped inside and closed the door.

Grinnel's desk had been shifted to a blank wall, clear of the window. Over the window, he had set a basket grill so that nothing could be thrown in through it. Sergeant Mann sucked in his breath sharply. He crossed to the desk.

"You wanted me, sir?" he asked.

Grinnel nodded, looking at him with steady eyes. Mann flushed under the stare, but his gaze did not waver.

"Call the others in," Grinnel said abruptly. "I have nothing to say to you that cannot be said to all."

Sergeant Mann frowned as he strode toward the door, but he didn't say anything when he had opened it, just jerked his head at the men. They trooped in stolidly, sullenly, resentfully. When the door was closed, Grinnel got to his feet.

"I have chosen you men for special duty," he said shortly, "because I believe in your integrity. There are sixteen of you. You will work in pairs. I have eight letters here to be delivered to eight key men I want to speak at the mass meeting tonight. When you have delivered the letters, you will stay on guard with those eight men and come with them to the mass meeting tonight. These are posts of danger. The crooks have taken to killing men with nitro bombs set up as booby-traps. Be on the alert for such traps. Check cars for bombs before you start them. Watch for bombs hooked up with doors and drawers. The lives of the men you are sent to watch, as well as your own, are at stake. I know how to reward those who do their job well. Here are the letters. Sergeant Mann, distribute them. That is all. Dismissed."

The police trooped out of the office like kids let off from punishment. Sergeant Mann chose Patrolman Wilkins to accompany him. They went out of headquarters together and Mann said, "We're taking the letter to Boss Fletcher,"

Wilkins whistled, "The Mayor is going to town, ain't he? Fletcher hates him like poison."

Sergeant Mann shrugged. "Lets hoof it," he said.

THEY had a dozen blocks to go, through the heart of the town and into the fringes of the residential section beyond. They were keyed up. Sergeant Mann felt tautness in his muscles and his skin. He fetched a long breath like a sigh, "This is going to be tough," he muttered.

The blast of a big steam shovel, just starting an excavation near the City Hall, made him start like a bullet in the back. He and Wilkins grinned at each other, a little shame-faced, but it did not relieve their tension.

The scream of a siren made them wince. Down the street rolled a police motorcycle, barely crawling, its siren going steadily. Behind it was a bright red truck. It looked like a small ice cream truck, with doors and locked handles, but it didn't carry confections. In big white letters on its side were the words:

Danger! Explosives!

In smaller letters, under it, was the single word:

Nitroglycerine.

It was a common enough sight in oil territory. When the drill had sunk deep enough, they dropped the shining cans of hell-stuff down the shaft to blast the solid rocks apart. Twenty quarts. Forty quarts. Even when the stuff let go a half mile beneath the Earth's surface, you could feel the jar like hell coming through.

The man behind the wheel of the truck was white-faced and frowning with strain. He wore a convict's suit, and his left wrist was handcuffed to the wheel.

"Nitro is ugly stuff," Wilkins muttered.

Sergeant Mann grunted, "Suppose you was a murderer and had the chance to drive a nitro truck instead, like he does. Would you do it?"

Wilkins said, "I don't know. Some of those killers last right long behind the wheel. When it comes, it comes sudden."

Mann laughed harshly. "Yeah!"

It wasn't the nitro truck they were thinking of. It was what would happen to them, if the crooks tossed a half-pint of the stuff at their feet! Wilkins' boyish face was pale.

"Maybe it takes less nerve to drive a nitro truck than it does to walk the last mile," he said.

"You only walk the last mile once," Mann argued stubbornly. "You may drive your forty quarts of nitro a dozen times, but every time it *could* be the last. No thanks. If it comes to that, I'll burn." He laughed, sharply. "Not that I'm figuring on doing either."

But they were driving with nitro now, and they knew it. If the crooks were going to try to blast any man, it would be Boss Fletcher.

Wilkins licked his lips. He couldn't drop the subject. "I saw where one of those trucks let go once," he said.

"*'Where'* is right," Mann said "A big hole in the ground."

Wilkins shook his head. "They found one piece—a mile away. After a while they figured it had been a hubcap plate. Forty quarts would just about stretch Piperstown out flat."

They walked on, not talking, both men staring ahead, putting their feet down doggedly. Wilkins cleared his throat.

"Shut up!" Sergeant Mann snarled.

A sudden slap of air gusted into their faces; their eardrums ached with a sharp blast. They ducked. Sergeant Mann threw himself flat, then got up shakily. A woman was screaming now. They ran to the corner, and looked down the side street. There was the wreckage of an automobile a block away.

The front of a house had slumped down into the street.

"It's started," Wilkins said. "Maybe we ought to check up."

Sergeant Mann said, flatly, "We got our own job to do. Come on."

They didn't say anything more as they went toward the home of Boss Fletcher. They didn't need to. Their thoughts were just one word: *nitroglycerine.*

CHAPTER SEVENTEEN
Terror Town

BOSS FLETCHER read the mayor's letter and looked up into Sergeant Mann's pallid face. Fletcher took out the butt of his cigar and looked at it with distaste.

"All right," he said. "Have a seat, sergeant. You look scared."

Mann said stolidly, "Sergeant Burroughs got blown up yesterday."

Fletcher was putting the cigar back to his mouth. He stopped and threw it into the wastebasket. "All right," he said angrily. He reached toward the humidor on his desk for a fresh cigar. Sergeant Mann pounced on his hand. "Sorry, sir," he said hoarsely. "But when did you open that thing last?"

Fletcher swore. "A half hour ago," he snapped. "I've been right here, ever since. Who in hell do you think is going to plant nitro in my humidor? Who would have the nerve to do it?"

Sergeant Mann wiped his forehead with a bandana. Fletcher opened the humidor with an impatient gesture. It was empty. He laughed sourly at Sergeant Mann.

"This wouldn't be some trickery of Mayor Grinnel, now, would it?" he asked. "We're on opposite sides of the fence. If there's real danger, I don't mind, but damn it, this is going pretty far!"

He got up from his desk and waddled across toward the steel filing cabinet in the corner. Mann stared at him with hopeless eyes. What the hell could you do? If every drawer might be a trap, and every door a danger? Stooping over the file drawer, Boss Fletcher hesitated—then he snatched it open quickly, as if that would solve the matter. He took out a fresh box of cigars and moved toward the desk. He lifted it and shook the box. He smelled it. He grinned at Sergeant Mann.

"This box hasn't got anything but cigars in it," he said flatly.

Mann said, "I ain't arguing, Mr. Fletcher. I saw a guy's auto blow up this morning. It took out the front of a house, too. I didn't see the man."

Fletcher sat down at his desk and eyed the cigar box, which he placed, exactly and carefully, in the middle of his blotter.

"This is nonsense, you know," he said flatly, but he didn't open the box. He carefully picked up the stub from the wastebasket. He laughed sheepishly as he clamped his teeth on it.

"Well, it's only for one day," he said. "I guess I can take it. I tell you, sergeant, I'm just going to sit tight. I'm not going to open another drawer, or another door. I'm not going to do anything. Now, let's see what they can do about that!"

The telephone shrilled, and he started and swore. He pulled the instrument toward him, and scooped it up from its cradle.

No man has ever lived to describe what happens when a pint of nitroglycerine lets go in a small room. They've picked up the pieces afterwards, of course, and that gives some idea. Things get blown to pieces.

That was what happened in Boss Fletcher's office. It was blown to pieces—

OSCAR STEIN was not an important man in town; not important to anyone except himself and his family, and perhaps his customers. He operated a butcher shop. There were only three people in the small, clean, sawdust store this afternoon, but they were all talking about what Mayor Grinnel was doing. It sounded like a good thing, if it could be done. They were a little cautious about even saying it was a good thing. They looked over their shoulders when they said it.

"Nice day, Mrs. Johnson," Butcher Stein said, "and what can I do for you today?"

"Well, now, if you've got any pork chops—"

Butcher Stein smiled all over his red face. "I have the best!" he said, and chuckled. "Nothing but the best!"

He moved comfortably toward the big refrigerator in the rear. He hadn't been in there since he had reopened the shop after lunch, but there was no reason why he should hesitate. He didn't even think about opening the refrigerator. He was thinking about the pork, and he had already decided just which loin he would take down when he wrenched the handle of the refrigerator door.

He swung the door open, and he saw something fall toward the floor. It was a small shiny can, and it had been poised up there above the door so that when it was opened, the can would fall.

Butcher Stein saw the can falling. He made an involuntary stab at it with his hand, and his blunt, clean fingers just touched it and sent it harder than ever against the floor.

DR. TERRY SAWYER swung down angrily from the step of the ambulance and gestured sharply to the orderly. "Get these patients inside," he said. "Get that woman into the surgery first. I'll have to amputate."

He slammed into the hospital and his voice reached out crisply to the orderly at the phone. "Well?" he snapped.

"I've got calls in for half the doctors in town," the man said alertly. "Haven't got hold of any yet. They're all out on calls, or up to their necks in their own offices. I've heard three more explosions. Here's a call—Stein's Butcher Shop blew up. Somebody buried in there, it seems. They can hear her screaming. Near as we can get it, there was four people in the shop. Woman next door is hurt. Boy in the street got a cracked head. Police have called three times for the wagon."

Two policemen walked into the corridor, and one of them thrust a letter at the doctor. Sawyer thrust it angrily aside, his face red.

"I haven't got time to read letters now," he snapped, and turned to the phone orderly. "Call Mayor Grinnel, and tell him I've got to have more doctors here... and I've got to have cars to bring in the injured. Tell him to call the defense drivers, or the air raid wardens or the Red Cross or something—only make it fast."

One of the cops said, "We're supposed to guard you, doctor. Mayor's called a mass meeting against the crooks. He's afraid you'll get bumped."

Dr. Sawyer's face was grim. "All right. I'm going into the surgery to amputate a woman's leg. Come along."

The police looked sick, but Sawyer didn't wait. The phone orderly called after him. "Another explosion, doctor! Ten injured! They say—"

"Tell the driver," Sawyer snapped. "You two cops go along. You can do some good that way."

The two policemen hesitated, walked slowly after Dr. Sawyer. They looked into the receiving room and what they saw made them sick. They went through hurriedly toward the ambulance at the door, and the driver came after them.

"All right, boys," he said. "We've got to make this fast."

He jumped up behind the wheel and stamped on the starter.

MAYOR GRINNEL caught up the phone in the chief's office, and his face was glistening with sweat. The man's voice that rasped over the wire was hysterical.

"All right," the mayor said wearily. "Is Dr. Sawyer all right? Well, I'm thankful he's safe. Send a crew of men to brace up the hospital wall where it's weakened. I've already called in the emergency services, and cars should begin arriving at the hospital any minute now."

The mayor hung up the receiver and sponged at his forehead with a handkerchief that was already gray with sweat. On the cot against the wall, Roy lay

THE SPIDER AND THE FLAME KING   109

with his eyes closed. Under Grinnel's hand was a sheet of paper. He picked up the pencil and heavily drew a slanting line across four other vertical lines. That made ten explosions in the last three hours. The phone shrilled again hysterically, but he ignored it, staring straight ahead of him with grim and bitter eyes.

Was it worth it? Was anything worth this wanton murder? What could he do to stop the slaughter: offer to resign? Send radio messages into the air, offering to surrender to the Underworld?

There was a trampling of feet outside his door, the sound of a scuffle. Grinnel caught up his revolver. The door punched open. Three men came in, their faces angry. They were men to whom he had sent letters, important men to whom the people would listen.

Chan Murdock, the president of the Arkanzona National, strode across and stood glaring at him. "You've got to call it off," he said harshly. "Damn it, I tell you, you've got to call off this meeting. This is more than flesh and blood can stand!"

Grinnel said slowly. "You want me to surrender to the crooks?"

Murdock pounded the desk! "I want this murder stopped!"

Grinnel got to his feet. The phone was still shrilling. He had the gun in his hand, but he hit the desk with it like a gavel.

"I am stopping the murder," he said harshly, "in the only way it can be stopped! By uniting the citizens against it!"

"The citizens are dying!" Murdock threw the words at him, "*You* keep safe enough!"

Grinnel nodded his long head at the banker. He took up the phone, not fumblingly, but with wooden hands. He was beaten. If the people would not support him—

"Mayor Grinnel," he said, into the transmitter.

The voice that spoke was low and calm, and had a driving force like bullets.

"Three of the bombers are here," it said. "They are alive but helpless. They were planting a bomb in Murdock's office. Send your men for them, and let the people know."

"*Who* is this?" Grinnel demanded.

Thin laughter answered him—*the laughter of the Spider!*

"I'll be with you tonight, Mayor Grinnel," he said, and the connection went dead.

Mayor Grinnel laughed into the face of the banker. He punched a button on his desk, and a policeman came in at the door.

"Go to Murdock's office at the bank," he said. "You'll find three prisoners there. Nitro bombers. Take an open car, and drive them slowly through the streets on your way back. If anybody makes any move at the car, shoot him down!"

He tucked his gun into its holster.

"Want to go with me? Murdock?" he said. "It may not be safe."

CHAPTER EIGHTEEN
Mass Death

THREE times that day, the *Spider* seized nitro bombers and turned them over to the police. Once, he shot it out with them. In the end, he flung himself flat behind a window ledge and put a bullet through a small shining can in the hand of one of the men. And that was that.

There was a lull in the bombing after that and Piperstown licked its wounds. The men who prepared for the mass meeting that night were grim and their hips bulged with their guns. The crooked boss had made the mistake that Hitler had made when he thought that bombings would destroy the morale of the fighting English. These were not English. They were Irish and Polish, Dutch and Spanish by their names; but their forefathers had freedom burning in their hearts, and so they were Americans.

They walked along the streets in tight, angry wedges, meeting block by block with neighbors, posting their own guards at home to supplement the police. They didn't talk much, because angry free men are like that. Their feet made calm, flat noises on the pavements. Their voices made drawling thunder in the dark. They moved with the easy alertness of hunters, guns ready to their hands. The frontier was not fifty years behind them here, and many had shaken hands with death this day.

Death walked with them this night.

On Elm Street, one man stepped on the starter of his car and was blown to kingdom come. On Third Avenue, a man tripped over a wire stretched across the walk, and he and three others died. On Sycamore, a gun stabbed redly in the dark, and two men spilled across the sidewalk, and one held a small shining can in his palm. When the marchers found them, there was a scarlet *Spider* seal upon their dead faces.

But the *Spider* could not be everywhere at once. He fought, and the police fought, and the citizenry fought, but here and there a bomb went off and men died. The shock of those blasts shook the night air. It did not shake the purpose of the men who converged on City Hall Square.

Fires broke out, too, in the residential districts. Chan Murdock's home went up in scarlet flame and boiling black smoke. A wing of the hospital burst out with crimson fire, but it was smothered quickly. Mayor Grinnel's house was wrapped in an oil-fed blaze. But no man even turned aside to watch, and the *Spider* found three more killers and sent them, dead, to grace the mass meeting with crimson seals upon their foreheads.

When the hour came, the square was black with silent men. They stood and faced the broad steps of City Hall and, just as the big clock in the tower boomed out the strokes of eight, floodlights blazed there on the steps and Mayor Grinnel stepped out through the double doors. He was alone.

The crowd met him in silence, as thick as the night.

"I'll make it short," Grinnel began without preamble. "When I called this mass meeting, I turned loose hell on the city. I asked eight men to stand here with me tonight and talk to you. Three of those men are dead, and six of my police died with them. You know why?"

"Down on your face for your life, mayor!"

The voice that cried the warning carried like a trumpet. The echo of a gun blast beat back from the fronts of the buildings that faced on the square. A figure like a great winged bat swept down from the roof in a long arc, and a gun blazed in each of his fists. From a window, gunfire answered him. But Mayor Grinnel did not fall on his face. He went backward, twisted awkwardly as a broken doll.

The gunfire ceased, and the black figure that was the *Spider* came to a rest on the sill of a window three stories above the street. He stood there through a long moment, then his face stared whitely down at the huddled mob in the square. There were four thousand men, and there were probably four thousand guns.

A girl cried out shrilly in the crowd. "It's the *Spider!* He's the crook! Kill him!"

THE *Spider* looked down on them, passionless as a god, aloof, waiting. He saw the girl who cried and knew it was Beulah Scott. He saw her fling up her hand to shoot at him, and still he did not stir. The gun spat, and a man twisted the gun out of her hand. On the portico of the City Hall, three men were bent over Mayor Grinnel.

"He's alive," one of them called. "He ain't hurt bad."

Something like a cheer went up from the men, but it was muffled and deep. It might have been a growl. Mayor Grinnel tried to get to his feet, fell back limply.

The *Spider* stood on the windowsill and lifted his hands. His folded cape fell back from his arms. The vagrant moon pushed through the clouds and gave him a pale spotlight. He faced the men of Piperstown, and his voice rolled out over them like doom:

"You've known death today. You've seen criminals try to kill the man who led you, Mayor Grinnel. You've seen your friends and your loved ones die. The criminals are hidden, sly, deadly. It will cost lives to find them out."

A growl came up from the waiting men, from the thousands of upturned faces, white as an angry sea. There was a cold smile on the *Spider's* lips.

"Everyone of you has suffered from these criminals!" the *Spider's* voice lifted like a trumpet. "Everyone of you has been victimized in rackets, and it did not seem worthwhile to fight, or you were afraid! You were afraid because you thought you were alone, because you suspected the police, and your officials. But the mayor has given his testimony of faith!"

The growl was louder now, breakers on a rocky reef, The *Spider* waited while it rose and fell again, rose and was sustained and died. Behind him, in the room where he had killed the mayor's assassins, a girl cried out the *Spider's* name.

The *Spider* twisted about his head tautly. "Pepita!" he said. "In Heaven's name—"

"Ah, *Señor!*" the girl gasped. "They have taken her! They have taken your lady!"

Nita! They had taken Nita van Sloan! The *Spider* made his voice calm. "She had found out something." he said. "What was it, Pepita?"

"Madre de dios!" the girl sobbed. "I had forgotten. The *Señorita*—She say, The nitro truck! They will explode it in the square!"

"The nitroglycerine truck?" the *Spider's* voice was dead and flat. A fully loaded truck, exploded here, would flatten half the town, would blast it off the face of the Earth, would slaughter thousands! "Where is it coming from?"

"Señor, I do not know, but it comes fast, fast!"

Silence now in the square. The thousands were waiting for his words, but he dared not tell this horror. Panic would sweep them. They would kill each other in their terror, and in the end they would not be saved.

The *Spider* dropped his words quietly.

"Many of you know one of the criminals," he said, harshly. "Men who have come to sell you protection, men who have come to collect your money! Go and get them! You are sworn deputies under the law! That was what Mayor Grinnel intended. Go and get the crooks and go swiftly! They will run like rats. They will be dangerous as cornered rats! Go faster than they! *Go get them!"*

He leaped into the room and caught Pepita's shoulders in his hands. He had to know more about that nitroglycerine truck. His memory flashed back to the afternoon, and a white-faced convict behind the wheel of a scarlet truck, carrying a load of death. How would they get a man to drive a truck to destruction! But that was easy, damnably easy. They would lash him in place so that he could do nothing but steer, and then they would jam the throttle wide open, and disconnect the controls! Death, hurtling at wild speed through the streets, and a terror-crazed man who could only steer and pray!

"How did the lady find out?" he snapped at the terrified girl.

"The phone," she gasped. "She listen over the phone!"

"Think!" the *Spider* commanded, and his voice was cold and quiet as a winter night. "Think, did she say where that call came from?"

The girl's eyes flared wide. "Ah, yes! I had forgot! It was a call from—*from Arroyo Diablo!*"

From north of the city!

"They came and took her then," Pepita whispered. "I was talking to her, and she turned and fought them like a tigress and all the while she called to me. "Run! *Run!*" Pepita sobbed. "I ran. I ran and left her—"

You did right," the *Spider* said. "Go now. Hurry to your home, as fast as you can run."

HE THRUST the girl out of the room and sprang back to the window. The men had not yet left the square. Here and there a compact group tramped off with the resolute march of men who knew their goal and would not be turned aside, but the vast bulk of them still were there. The *Spider* raced down through the building, and there was cold sweat upon his forehead.

How did a man stop a runaway truck without wrecking it? How did you stop a runaway truck that a sharp jar would change into hell's own juggernaut of destruction? If he could get aboard the truck—

The criminals would have foreseen that danger. They would not have been content with binding their captive driver helplessly; they would have disconnected the brakes, ripped out the gearshift. They did not intend the truck should stop, save in one way—in a blast that would be felt for a hundred miles, and would be remembered for a hundred years! A blast that would destroy a city! A blast that would take ten thousand lives!

The *Spider* darted out of the building, and a man shouted at him. The *Spider* raced on. Suddenly, from the roof of a building, a machine gun began to speak. The bullets ploughed up the asphalt in the *Spider*'s path, jerked toward him. He sprang wildly to the left, then reversed his leap. He reached the cover of a doorway, and the muzzle of his automatic ranged upward. Lead scattered, white-hot, upon the concrete. Cement powder, like smoke, dusted in its path. It crept nearer, probed for the doorway. The *Spider* fired once again.

The machine gun was silent—and the *Spider* raced on. A revolver spat at him from the roof now, but he ignored it. These killers certainly had not been told of the nitro truck, but he already knew how merciless the Flame King could be! He whipped around a corner, and a car roared into action on the side street. It streaked toward him, with flaming guns!

Something like despair seized the *Spider* then. It was not that he feared death, but every moment was so vitally precious. Every second that hell-bearing truck was racing nearer, nearer. And the streets were full of men. They could not possibly be cleared in time.

The *Spider* raced straight toward the charging car, and his guns flamed in his hands, spat out their lead in a drum roll of death. The car swerved wildly. A tire blew out. Steam geysered from the hood. A man screamed. Still, the *Spider* raced on, and his guns did not cease. When he went past the car, nothing in it moved, or stirred. Something dripped slowly to the pavement.

He cut another corner, and now he was racing toward the street along which the nitro truck must come if it charged in from the Arroyo Diablo road. But, how to stop it, how to stop it? He burst out into the street... and he heard the far-off wail of a siren. It was thin, piercing, never-ceasing—a scream that held the desperation of madness.

It was the siren of the nitroglycerine truck!

The *Spider*'s eyes cast wildly about. Across the street was a high board fence and, above it, a wisp of steam showed against the night... a wisp of steam, and an upright steel beam, a tin-covered roof. It was a steam shovel.

With a laughter that had its own share of despair, the *Spider* hurled himself across the street. It was a chance in a thousand, a chance in a million. But it was the only chance!

The siren was louder. Far off along the tree-lined avenue, he could see the red headlights of the nitro truck. It was coming terribly fast, this hell-laden juggernaut of destruction, as if eager to maim, to slaughter, to wipe out a city of living souls!

And the *Spider* flung himself at that high board fence and prayed that there was still enough steam, and that he had the skill, and that he would be in time—a million-to-one.

CHAPTER NINETEEN
Hell Driver

BUT even that chance of a million-to-one was against the *Spider*. For a man sat in the cab of the steam shovel. He had a big revolver in his right hand, and a pint liquor bottle in his left. He had the pint tilted and was taking a swig for himself. The *Spider* didn't know if the man was a friend or a henchman of the Flame King.

There was no time to make a cautious approach to find out; there was not even time to hazard a guess. The *Spider* rushed boldly across the clearing, his cloak bat-winging out behind him. And it was the tilted angle of the pint bottle that concealed the *Spider*'s approach until he was almost abreast of the steam shovel cab.

The man in the cab pulled the bottle from his mouth. A curse spattered liquor from his throat. His right hand leveled with a jerk. The *Spider* had no choice. It was kill or be killed—with the lives of thousands hanging in the balance.

The *Spider*'s automatic ran out a red tongue into the night. His slug ploughed into the man's throat. The man's last, convulsive movement was to drag a shiny little can from his pocket. Then he died, clutching the can, and falling from the cab down to the Earth.

Under that falling body sprang the *Spider* to cushion the drop. And the *Spider's* desperate fingers darted out to seize the shiny can. His hand wrapped around the can and the dead killer's clutching fingers. With his other arm he let the man ease to the ground.

Then the *Spider* swiftly opened the lethal can and let its liquid hell seep into the earth.

Leaping to the cab, the *Spider* ripped at the controls of the steam shovel. Luckily, its half-ton scoop was tucked up against the beam. He threw the steam into the caterpillar drive and, with a coughing, groaning complaint, the thing shuffled toward the street. There was no ramp. The pit was only three feet deep, but the steam pressure was painfully low; terribly low.

The shovel cleared the earth and burst out the board fence. Somewhere, a man was shouting. From a rooftop, fifty yards away, a gun blasted. The bullet rang on steel. The *Spider* scarcely knew it. His eyes were on the bank of the pit. The caterpillar tread clawed into it, and the earth yielded. The tread clawed for another hold—

The siren of the nitro truck was audible even above the clatter and the hiss of steam!

The steel treads bit on the edge of the concrete, and the front of the steam shovel lifted perilously. The heavy beam reached backward. This machine was never made for such work. It would over-balance. Desperately, the *Spider* shifted controls and shot out the shovel as a counterbalance, jerked back the power into the treads.

The steam shovel continued to tilt backward. Men were running toward him now. There were more guns. A madness of guns burst over the square. Were they criminals, or were they the vigilante? No way of knowing. But death could sit on any leaden slug, even though fired by a friend!

The treads had heaved the shovel up almost vertically now. Grimly, the *Spider* kept the power in the treads. He was balanced, wavering. In a frenzy of motion, he locked the treads and shot power into

the shovel. He waved it like a baton, swung it violently toward the street, and as violently checked it. That accomplished what nothing else would have done. The mechanical giant slashed forward, toward the street!

Then another heart-tearing waste of steam and time while he shifted power once more, set the caterpillar treads revolving. He was past the fence. He peered desperately up the street. Three blocks away, and roaring at the speed of an express train, the nitro truck hurtled toward him! Men saw it now, and screamed. They whirled and ran, wildly, crazily—futilely.

And the steam shovel waddled like a complacent dowager, taking its time, not yet at the curb. The *Spider*'s hands hovered over the controls. He could gain no more speed. The steam dial was subsiding, the pressure dying. His head was twisted stiffly toward the onrushing destruction. He saw it flash under a street light, and he saw the face of the driver!

Death laid its icy hand on his heart then, and for a space of a held breath, he could not move, nor think.

It was no convict who was handcuffed to the wheel of the nitro truck! It was a woman! *It was Nita van Sloan!*

NITA VAN SLOAN stared with blank eyes of dismay at the crowded square before the City Hall. The howling motor had rolled up a fearful momentum. She dared not attempt a turn. It would mean a crackup—and the instantaneous destruction of the city. For herself, she had long ago given up hope, and formed her resolution. The river was not far ahead. If she could reach it without a crackup, she would dive the truck into the river. It meant her own death; she could not hope to free her handcuffed wrists from the wheel. She might be able to wrench it loose, but she had no real faith in that possibility.

And now, the square. It blocked the end of the avenue along which she raced. There was a walkway, flanked by benches that led straight across. Near the center was a fountain with a cast bronze statue. She might be able to swerve past it. The curbs and the benches might not blow out the tires. If she could get past the square. there were only ten more blocks before the river. Nita thought of the river almost with relief, though it would mean her own death.

That was her plan—and then she had found the square jammed with thousands of men!

A sob of horror swelled into Nita's throat. Almost, she whipped the truck wheel over to slam it into a wall and end this fearful torment. But no such easy way was to be allowed to her. She must drive the truck straight ahead, through the man-jammed square and beyond it into the river. No matter how many of those men were killed by the juggernaut's charge, it would be fewer than would perish if the truck blew up.

She must hold her mind clearly on that knowledge, hold the wheel steadily down that narrow walkway, swerve around the fountain and streak on for the river. She must see the terrified white faces of men before they died under her wheels. She must feel, and fight, the jar and wrench as the truck struck and smashed over their helpless bodies. And she must keep her eyes open to the horror and remain coolly competent to drive that last frantic mile to the river.

The scream of the wind matched the scream of the siren. The red headlights luridly lit the street, like a foretaste of hell. Nita swayed rigidly behind the wheel and, hands locked solidly to control the fearful speed, waited prayerfully for the moment when she must kill tens of men to save tens of thousands. Some of them had seen her now and were stepping leisurely from her path. But they would not move in the square. They would not realize, until too late, that she would have to plough through the walks!

A shout rose in Nita's throat. "Oh, please!" she cried. "Oh, please, get them out of the way!"

Abruptly, Nita's attention was snapped toward the board fence that flanked the street to the left. She was still a mile away from the square—a mile that she would cover in exactly sixty seconds—when she saw the fence flattened into the street and glimpsed the steel monster waddling up out of the excavation. She watched it without understanding, with an intense fascination because it helped her to escape the memory of what lay ahead!

HAD someone been forewarned of the danger of this death on wheels? Was it possible they thought this merely a runaway truck, and did not know that its contents were liquid destruction? Men were running toward the steam shovel now, firing as they charged. And the leviathan caught its balance skillfully on the edge of the excavation and waddled forward.

So far, Nita knew she would have no trouble in dodging the machine. She even leaned a little forward over the wheel, as if to urge her truck faster. It would be a close thing, as close as possible, but she still thought she could get past it all right.

To Nita the driver of that steam shovel was mad. He was pushing himself right into the path of destruction. The men who had been firing guns suddenly recognized the nature of the truck. She saw their mouths stretch in terror though she could not hear their screams. They fled wildly—but not the men in the square.

They were more thickly packed now, surging in her direction. For the first time, she wondered— would the truck plough through their bodies? Suppose the shock was enough to set off the nitroglycerine?

Nita groaned, all her attention set upon dodging past that lumbering steam shovel. A strange calm had descended upon her. Agitation comes from conflict, and there was no longer any conflict within her. What she must do, she had accepted, and she would achieve. It was in that detached coolness that she glanced at the operator of the steam shovel.

She screamed then. Dick—Dick Wentworth was at the controls!

A shuddering rigidity of despair locked all her muscles, and in those few seconds, the last yards of distance between them were eaten up by the howling insensate speed of the engine. Dimly, Nita saw that Dick was signaling to her. He was sweeping his hand down in a straight, unswerving line. He wanted her to *miss* the steam shovel, to go past in front of it.

The great shovel had been wrenched around, far to the right, cocked like a hammer to strike. What did he hope to do? Nita fumbled and cut off the siren. It was the only way she had to signal. She would obey. Death was very close. Those packed ranks of men were only a hundred feet beyond the shovel. If Dick's plan, whatever it was, failed—

But Nita was past thought now. She looked across the swiftly closing distance to the face of the man she loved, to his eyes, and she smiled. Martyrs died like that, gazing into the face of the Unseeable. But Nita was looking on the *Spider.*

She held the wheels rigidly straight, slashing on at fearful speed. She heard the blast of the steam just before she went past, saw the great steel beam, the clawed hammer head of the shovel swing to meet her. A scream clogged her throat—but she held the wheel straight.

For an instant, the heavy swing of that crazy machine almost matched the speed of the truck. But the red truck was almost past, and still the *Spider* had done nothing. It was past, and still the crazy leviathan merely pivoted on its base, as if in clumsy salute.

At the controls, the *Spider* was rigid as stone. His eyes stared with dead-man fixity. He had only this one chance, and if the timing were wrong by even a heartbeat, he failed. Slaughter came after.

The truck was past, and the long steel beam was pointing in almost the same direction, down the street. Suddenly, steam gushed. The *Spider* had wrenched on the levers, kicked the heavy pedal. The fiercely clawed scoop shot forward, racing the truck, snatching at it. An instant, it seemed, and the hammer head would smash the rear of the truck, and explode its hell! An instant, it seemed the shovel would miss altogether. Then the broad blades of the claws whipped under the rear axle of the truck, and lifted.

.There was a rending scream of steel, the howling fury of a racing engine. Then the truck went on. The back of the truck was perceptibly lower. The rear wheels canted at a crazy angle inward. The smoke of burned rubber spurted under them. From the prongs of the shovel, something dangled like a toothpick between careless fingers. The *Spider* had torn the rear axle out of the truck!

A wheel came loose now from the truck, lowered one side to the ground.

It lurched once more, shed its second wheel. The freed wheels bounded eagerly forward, bouncing like a child's hoop. They raced past the dragging truck, spurting ahead like motorcycle outriders, vanished into the darkness beyond the red headlights.

Gouts of sparks spurted from under the skimming rear of the truck. It rocked wildly, but the street was smooth. Blood on her forehead, Nita fought the steering gear, balancing each swing and lurch. The truck was in a long curve now, and she could not check it, could not change it lest it overturn. The curve became sharper, dangerously acute. Abruptly, the whole deadly crimson load of nitroglycerine swung about in a spinning glide.

The front tires went, and still Nita fought the wheel. She was rolling forward now. The motor was dead. There was no sound except the slobbering of the blown-out tires, the tortured rasp of dragging steel. It died slowly. It became a rumble. The tires thumped, came up heavily, thumped once more. There was silence. Not ten feet from her windshield, men stared, white-faced, frozen, immobile.

In that still and incredible moment, Nita van Sloan realized that the truck was motionless, that it was not going to explode. There was, after despair, after the turmoil of hell, only silence.

It held and Nita felt the stiffness go out of her. She did not faint. She slumped back against the cushions, and the world wheeled around her. But she saw the faces of the men before her change, saw them turn from frozen terror into rage. She saw the first slow forward sway of the mob. Their eyes were on her.

Nita jerked herself erect. Her wrists tugged futilely at the wheel to which she was manacled. Her body understood even while her mind rejected the thought.

In their unreasoning terror-heated rage, the mob blamed her! They were roaring toward her to kill her!

CHAPTER TWENTY
The Slaughter

A SMILE touched Nita van Sloan's lips, a smile of incredulity, that held its trace of bitterness. She had been able calmly to contemplate her own death in order to save these people. She had planned it that way. And now they wished to destroy her! For that fleeting moment, she knew in her own heart, in her own person the feeling that must often reach the *Spider,* hunted while he served.

It was only a moment, then clarity again crowned her thinking. She looked swiftly to the doors, but they had been locked by her captors when they handcuffed her to the wheel. No glass had shattered in the furious activity of the wreck. But that was natural. If the stoppage had been violent enough to break glass, it would have exploded the nitroglycerine.

The mob reached and engulfed the truck. A furious hand wrenched at the handle of the door beside her, and it came off in his hand. Through the windshield, faces washed in scarlet light were awful in their rage. Mouths cursed her and reviled her, and the sound of it came through only dimly.

Then a man lifted a revolver and leveled it at her through the glass! In the same second, he squeezed the trigger—but a man beside him struck up his fist, just in time. The man struck viciously at the gunman.

Through the glass came one word, *"nitro!"*

A sudden wash of relief flushed over Nita. No, they would not shoot at her, lest the bullet go astray and explode the nitroglycerine. They could not reach her. One man battered at the glass of the window beside her, but the glass was tough. It cracked after a while, but it did not break. They shouted at her, and shook their fists. But they could not reach here... *yet.*

Nita closed her eyes and bowed her head, and her lips moved silently. She dropped a veil between herself and the menace round about. Suddenly, new sound crashed through the muted mob roar. It was the clatter and clank of steel, and the spatter of gunshots. Nita wrenched about in her seat, saw the massive approach of the giant steam shovel. The men gave way sullenly before it.

Nita saw the shovel head swing toward her, handled as deftly as a surgeon's scalpel. It thrust in the glass beside her, and she shrank aside from its savage blades. But, behind it, she could see the *Spider*'s smiling eyes. Then the blades hooked into the wheel which held her prisoner; hooked and lifted two inches. The wheel snapped. She was free!

In a long leap, the *Spider* was beside the truck. He had an automatic in his fist, and its blunt nose was pressed against the side of the truck!

"If we die," he called in the trumpet of his voice, *"we won't die alone.* One bullet into this truck will take care of all of you!"

A shivering moan ran through the mob. Nita was dragging her way out through the window of the truck. She held the steering wheel in her hands, and felt a wild impulse to laugh. She knew now that fear had left her in the instant when she had seen the *Spider*'s face, and she realized under how great strain she had carried on through those last mad moments.

The *Spider* lashed at the mob with his voice. "Fools!" he cried. "Do you think this woman wanted to drive the truck? The controls were smashed. She was handcuffed to the wheel! She is your friend, the enemy of your enemies! You have a job to do that you still have not done! There are men to capture and punish! The gangsters who had slain your friends and your loved ones! Go get them! They are the men who tried to destroy your city!"

THERE were men in the mob who heard the *Spider* and felt the force of his truth. There were others who were still wild with terror and blindly anxious to destroy the thing that had threatened them. Voices lifted among the mob, and men quarreled with their neighhors. In that flat moment of pause, the *Spider* scooped his arm about Nita's waist.

"Run for it," he whispered. "That excavation. The way is clear. I can't hold the mob long. Gangsters are among them. *Run, Nita!*"

He leaped to the hood of the truck, and his black cape flaunted behind him. He flung out his arms and stood there, the calm, poised Master of Men.

"There are those among you," he said harshly, "who serve the Flame King. There are those among you who take orders from the murderer who planned all this. *You fools! Don't you see that your master intended you to die, too?* This truckload of nitroglycerine was to blow you to kingdom come—and *leave him with all the loot!*"

He stood there, calm, scornful, commanding, with his cape flowing in the stirring wind of night, his face washed by the reflection of crimson light from the car's lamps. There was complete silence now among the mob. He had them in hand. He stretched out his arms.

"What are you waiting for?" he cried, his throat suddenly hoarse. *"Go get them!"*

There was a cry now from among them, a cry that grew into a roar. It drowned out the distant crack of the rifle. The *Spider* felt the blow of the lead in his thigh. It drove his leg out from under him. He wheeled, arms fanning for balance; pitched to earth. Desperation stabbed through him. A single rifle bullet, into this truck...

Against the numbing shock of the wound, the *Spider* drove himself to his feet. His guns were in his fists, crashing. The first two bullets blasted out the red headlights. He canted up the muzzles of his automatics, and the street lights on the corner were gone. Darkness clapped down on the street, and the moon's face was hidden in the clouds. He had made the shooting fast but he had lost his control of the mob. With the unreasoning madness of stampeded cattle, they thought that he was shooting at them, or fleeing them!

He heard their roar, and the stamp of their feet. But the *Spider* knew from what direction that rifle shot had come. He turned and plunged across the street, toward the pit to which he had sent Nita. The rifle shot had come from there! At each step, his wound shot agony through him; he shut his teeth and raced on, desperate. He saw the long spurt of rifle flame leap toward him from the darkness. His automatics were ready—and yet he held his fire. Nita was there somewhere.

He heard the sound of a blow, a muffled woman's cry... and then, incredibly, the deep rumble of a voice speaking Punjabi—rumbling a hillman's oath!

THE *Spider* reached the edge of the excavation and saw Nita struggling to her feet, helped by a thin and tottering Ram Singh!

Wentworth leaped down beside the Sikh and Nita. Nita was laughing shakily. "He was going to kill me. Ram Singh came just in time—"

The man lay on the ground, his neck broken.

Ram Singh said, *"Sahib,* I am ready for battle. I have been in some Mexican's hut. I do not know him, but he is a good man and took care of me. He said I walked in and asked for help."

There was a smile on the *Spider*'s grim lips. "Good," he said. "I can use you." He hurried them across the excavation toward the back street.

"The plan has gone up in smoke," he said shortly. "Terror smoke. Only one thing will work. Nita, can you identify any of your captors?"

"If I saw *him* again. Yes, in spite of his mask." Nita's voice held a shudder. "He was a giant, nearly seven feet tall. I never saw such shoulders in my life, and he squeezed the life out of a man with one hand! And laughed while he did it! Even his walk was horrible, slow and ponderous as if he owned the Earth!"

"He was at the telephone exchange?" Wentworth asked, frowning.

"No, no. They took me to him, the men who came there. But they were nothing. Only hired gunmen."

They were out of the excavation now, hurrying along the back street toward the telephone exchange.

"You're wounded!" Nita gasped.

Wentworth jerked a hand impatiently. "Get us a car, Ram Singh," he said, and turned to Nita. "Someone at the phone exchange betrayed you. Who could it have been? Did anyone leave the hall just before you were attacked? It would be, probably, a woman; one of the regular employees, possibly an important one. She would be on duty in the afternoon and at night. That was when the calls were overheard. She would be the means by which the Flame King maintained his surveillance over the city."

Nita had drawn his arm across her shoulders. She winced at his obvious pain; she gloried in his weight upon her strength. She did not notice the gall of the handcuffs.

"Yes," she said swiftly, "I did notice a girl leave before I was attacked. She was a Mexican."

"You don't know who she was?"

Nita shook her head, setting her teeth against the strain in Dick's voice. "We could find out, I think."

The *Spider* rasped, "We will!"

The mob roar was a swollen angry sound, punctuated by gun shots. It was not drawing nearer, but it was not far away. The door of the phone exchange was locked, but the *Spider*'s slim lock-pick forced it open. They went up the stairs heavily. A gun blasted from the shadows above, and the *Spider*'s automatic spat like an echo.

A man pinwheeled out from behind the wall. He slipped to his knees against the wall, and then pitched sideways across the steps. He rolled down slowly. They let him slide past, went steadily onward.

"That shot may bring the mob," the *Spider* said shortly. His breath was rigidly controlled against the stabs of pain. They went together into the main hall of the exchange. Nita van Sloan went forward then. She took the arm of one of the girls in her hand, and the girl looked down at the handcuffs, at the dangling wheel, and smothered a scream.

"The supervisor who left just before I did," Nita said quietly. "What was her name?"

The girl stammered, "Carmen? Carmen Veldez."

A glitter leaped into the *Spider*'s eyes. He turned to the steps again and Nita rushed to his side. They could hear the shouts of men more clearly now. The shot had brought the mob!

"What can we do?" Nita gasped.

We go through," snapped the *Spider*. "We're going to get the Flame King!"

"But the mob—?"

The door at the foot of the steps pushed open slowly and, gun in hand, the wounded Mayor Grinnel stepped into the hallway. He looked up and saw the *Spider*.

"I'm arresting you," he said, harshly, and lifted his gun.

CHAPTER TWENTY-ONE
To Destruction!

THE *Spider* neither slowed nor hurried his descent of the stairs. His arm, about Nita's shoulders, clamped her close to him. In her heart, Nita prayed. She knew what she meant to do. She would throw herself on Mayor Grinnel, cover that gun with her body.

Abruptly, she felt the relaxing of the *Spider*'s grip. She felt a change in the tension, and she stared down the steps. There was a small Mexican girl behind Mayor Grinnel. She was barefooted, and her dress was torn. Her eyes were merry in spite of the worry on her face—and slowly, broadly, she winked! It was Pepita!

The *Spider* looked into Grinnel's face and the man shook his head slightly, jerked it toward the door where the mob howled.

The *Spider* said, "Very well, Mr. Mayor. I surrender to you. I hope you have a car. I don't want to walk through that mob."

Grinnel said, "I have a car."

Wentworth stooped toward Pepita. "Find a big dark man with a turban and a beard. He will have a car. Tell him it is all right. He is to follow us, very carefully."

The girl nodded and vanished through the door.

The mob howl rose crashingly as they stepped across the sill, and Mayor Grinnel's gun blasted into the air, his voice cracked like a whip. Then they were in the mayor's car, and it surged forward through the thick of the maddened crowd. At the last moment, Pepita ducked in beside the *Spider.* Fists were shaken, and a few stones thudded against the car, but it pressed on, turned a corner, gathered speed.

The *Spider* leaned forward, "Mayor Grinnel, we want to go to the Black Bottom mine. Beyond Arroyo Diablo, isn't it?"

Grinnell nodded. "Yes. Why?"

"We'll find the Flame King there," the *Spider* said, and his voice rasped. "He'd have to get out of the town when he sent that nitro truck here to blow Piperstown flat. It's plain they have nitro stored somewhere, and the best place would be underground. He owns that mine. He'll be there."

"*He*—owns—that—mine?" Grinnel said it very slowly. "Damn it, man. *I* own that mine!"

There was an aching silence in the car then, while it drilled northward through the city, toward the road that led through Arroyo Diablo.

"Your purchase is recent," the *Spider* said. "You haven't taken it over yet, have you?"

Grinnel was fighting some sort of battle within himself. "Yes," he muttered. "I felt sorry—damn it, *Spider*—it's impossible!"

"It's the only thing that is possible," the *Spider*

said flatly. "Driller Scott was killed by them, because up in the hills he had seen them practicing with a trench mortar. The hills are beyond Arroyo Diablo. So far as I know, there is no other mine up there, and no other mine owner."

The car began to roll faster. The motor hum deepened and there was the hiss of the wind. "So that's why Scott was killed," he said. "Yes, I can believe that."

Silence then, and the Arroyo was open before them. They swooped into it. No moon shadows tonight. Everything was shadow, save the white tunnel of the headlights.

Nita said, tautly, "There are *two* cars following us!"

The *Spider* made no comment and the car was howling now with speed. Above the noise, Mayor Grinnel called back. "I'm asking the governor to turn out the troops. I didn't dare use the telephone. I don't dare do anything in Piperstown. It belongs to—to this man you call the Flame King."

The *Spider* made no answer and they were slamming over the twisting road. After they passed Twin Rocks without challenge, he relaxed a little. He slit his trouser leg, and examined his wound by his bouncing flashlight.

Nita said, "These handcuffs—take them off me, Dick. I'll dress your wound."

His lockpick served again, now that there was time, and he freed her. His leg was stiffening. His teeth showed between his taut lips. He looked away from what Nita was doing and saw Pepita's shining eyes upon him.

"I found the man with the beard," she whispered.

The *Spider* smiled at her.

"You brought the mayor to help us, Pepita," he said. "What can I do for you?"

The girl shook her head, "No, *Señor*, it is I who am in your debt!" Her Spanish was flowery, and her dignity complete. She was a princess conferring a favor. They said no more. The *Spider* knew that—for Pepita, as for himself—the service was its own reward.

The car was surging into the hills now. "Only a mile to go," Mayor Grinnel called back.

THE *Spider* nodded, and drew out his automatics. His leg felt more comfortable now. He stuffed fresh cartridges into the clips, holstered the guns. They swooped over the crest of a hill, slowed and turned sharply into a mountain track. The car sighed and heaved; the motor blurted in second gear.

"I see no tire tracks," Grinnel called back doubtfully, "but the trail is rocky. Perhaps I wouldn't."

Nita whispered, "I think those two cars are still behind us! I saw headlights flick across the rocks we passed."

They rounded a rock, and the brakes slammed on. "Trail washed out," Mayor Grinnel said. "That settles it!" He pointed off into the darkness. "The mine shack is there. No lights."

The *Spider* climbed painfully to the ground. "I'll go on afoot. There must be another trail in."

Before he had taken a half dozen strides, Nita was beside him.

Mayor Grinnel hobbled up. "I'm in this to the end," he said grimly. "Pepita, you've done enough. Stay with the car."

"Must I, *Señor?*"

"You must!"

They went off into the darkness, two wounded men and an unarmed woman. It was a painful and endless trek through the blackness of the pit. Rocks rose, menacing, in their path, and stones turned underfoot. It was eternity before they stood at the entrance of the slope that struck into the hillside. The shaft entrance was above, and this was what they sought. The roadway here was smooth, and it bore the mark of truck tires.

Mayor Grinnel got out his revolver. "I think this is my job," he said, flatly.

But the *Spider* laughed, and curiously fatigue and pain were gone from his voice. He said lightly, Mr. Mayor, you cannot deny me the *coup de grace!* Nor can I deny you? Shall we go to the kill together?"

Grinnel frowned, "We may be killed as well as kill."

"Just so," the *Spider* was amiable, "I insist upon the honor, sir."

He strode before Grinnel into the mouth of the cave, and he limped scarcely at all. He was the knight riding to a pleasure joust, and gallantry sat upon his shoulders. Almost, it fooled Grinnel, then he swore and started after him, swiftly.

"He wants to save us from danger," he snapped. "I—"

A gun blasted in the darkness, and a voice roared out. *"Nitroglycerine,* fools! If you shoot, you'll blow up the mountain side! There are gallons of it!"

THE *Spider* laughed somewhere in the darkness ahead, and Grinnel felt Nita press past him and steal forward. Grinnel was not a cowardly man, but this death that waited in darkness made him cold. Yet these two pressed on! Grimily, the mayor followed, halt and slow because of his wound, but with his revolver grimly gripped. When the full shock of the words reached him, he dropped his gun and shuddered. A gun was worse than useless. It was suicide!

All was blackness. There was a wall at his shoulder. He could hear the faint hurried breathing of Nita van Sloan.

"Spider," a man's rough voice came. "I do not

trust you in the light, and in the darkness, I cannot shoot you. But neither can you shoot me, because the lining of these walls is nitroglycerine. But both of us aren't going out of here alive."

"Gallantly spoken," murmured the *Spider*. His voice was a whisper that came from the walls and had no direction.

The speaker cursed from the darkness. "You're too smooth," he said harshly.

The *Spider* laughed, and that was a sinister sound in the thick black air, for it seemed the walls of the mine laughed with him.

"Since my guns are useless," the *Spider* whispered, "and since you dare not show a light in order to shoot—for I could shoot you out from among a hundred cans of nitro without touching one—I make a suggestion."

He waited. There was no sound save heavy breathing, and that, too, seemed to come from all the walls. The *Spider* shifted his weight cautiously to his good right leg so that he could move swiftly. He remembered the picture that Nita had drawn of this Flame King, seven feet tall and able to squeeze the life out of a man with one hand. Such men were vain of their strength.

The *Spider* smiled and there was a reckless glint in his eyes. "Suppose we throw away our guns," he said casually, "and fight it out—man-to-man?"

Nita said, "No! In heaven's name, no! He's a giant!"

"That suits me, fine!" the harsh voice of darkness answered, and there was gloating in the sound.

The *Spider* tossed a gun into the middle of the floor, then waited. "A thought occurs to me," he said, quietly. "There are a couple of crimes charged against a friend of mine. Since you intend to kill us all, you wouldn't mind clearing my conscience, would you? I have defended this man. I think that you are really responsible for killing Driller Scott, and for the death of that deputy in Wentworth's car in front of Legs Jackson's house, weren't you?"

Silence for a while then. There was a curious noise of something heavy and metallic falling to the ground; it was repeated, and the man in the darkness grunted.

"I did them," he said. "Now I'm going to do you in." He chuckled. "I guess I ought to warn you. I got a friend here with me, with a gun. If anybody makes a false move, it's going to be too bad! I can't die but once, and the nitro will take care of all of us very nicely! I'm fighting you, *Spider,* single-handed. Get it?"

The smack of a gun falling in the floor answered him, and after a moment, another gun fell.

The *Spider* said softly, "May I have the honor of the first attack, or will you?"

No voice answered him, and the *Spider* stepped

"You cannot shoot me," he mocked.

"The walls are lined with nitro! If you shoot—you'll blow up the mountain."

lightly, silently two paces to his right. His left foot scraped a little because of his wound. He lifted his brows, mockingly, at the darkness. He crouched like a sprinter on the mark, and waited.

The attack came with the sudden silence of a bullet from the dark. A heavy body struck him, shoulder high, and two great hands snatched at him. But the *Spider,* a sprinter from the mark, ripped out of his crouch—and the driving force of it hurled his opponent back. But a hand had fastened on the *Spider*'s injured shoulder, and the other hand was crawling toward his neck.

They brought up hard against a wall of stone. There was a grunt and the hands jerked free. Wentworth pivoted and drove his fists into the man's body. Five times he hammered home the punches before a fist drove against his chest and sent him tumbling backward.

Before he could regain his balance, the bulk of the man struck upon his chest. Hands seized at his throat, caught his head instead and held. The thumbs were under his eyes, and the fingers cupped behind his ears. The thumbs slipped upward. Flesh rolled over the bone; the skin tore. Flat on his back, the *Spider* drove his linked hands up between those stiffened steely wrists. He did not jar the hands loose.

The *Spider* bridged, and with a tremendous heave of his legs that tore loose the wound, he flipped straight up and over. As he fell, he jerked up his knees and felt them jar against the man's skull. The hands were torn loose from his face, but one of them locked upon his nape and began a horrid pressure.

NITA had spoken truly of the strength of this man. In an instant of time, pain like fire was lancing into the *Spider*'s brain! The thumb and fingers were encroaching on the jugular vein beneath the ears. Once they clamped shut, consciousness could last for only seconds. The *Spider* moved his left hand lightly, and the fingers just brushed his enemy. Instantly, a hand closed on that wrist, wrenching, twisting, trying to grind it apart by sheer force.

The *Spider* had his target now. He rolled and struck with all the power of body and arm squarely between those arms, not too high, not too low. His knotted fist slammed in under the Flame King's chin! The hands tore loose from his wrist and neck. In the darkness, there was a horrid, gasping, breathless sound. The *Spider* was on his knees, slamming out with his fists. He was overanxious. His blows rained on lifted arms. An answering blow, haphazard in the dark, sent him sprawling.

He surged back—and could not find his foe. He listened, and heard that painful, labored gasp again, heard a faint whimpering sound, as if an animal sought to speak and could not. Wentworth dived toward the sound. He struck a broad back, and was

tumbled off. Once more the frantic, tearing hands hunted for his throat. They fastened on his upper arm and sought to tear the muscles out of the flesh. The other hand battered and prodded, seeking a death grip. The *Spider*'s blows rained on the man's face and head, and the groping, tearing hands did not falter. There was a whimpering like an eager dog.

The *Spider* checked his blows for an instant, let his body go limp. With a harsh gasp of eagerness, the man sprawled toward him—and the *Spider* met him with an elbow cocked before his face. With all his force, he drove up to meet the killer. There was a violent blow on his elbow. He raked it upward, and whipped over his right hand under that guard.

There was no voice sound after that, only a flopping awful scrabbling noise. Then the whimper. It was retreating toward the spot from which the first sound had come. It seemed to be trying to make words, and the words failed.

Then, abruptly, in the thickness, the *Spider* laughed.

"You may show a light, Mayor Grinnel," he said. "The Flame King is dead, and his 'friend' is my captive!"

A woman protested feebly, "I have no gun! I was supposed to push the nitro cans over! But I wouldn't have done it. I swear, *Señor,* I would not have done it!"

Light reached out from a flashlight and the *Spider* limped out from behind a stack of shining cans with a Mexican girl firmly clasped in one arm that held both her hands prisoner.

"Carmen!" Nita gasped. "Carmen Veldez!"

"Phone operator extraordinary," the *Spider* said to Nita. "And also housekeeper for Legs Jackson. It's a common enough name down here, but after I linked it with your description of the Flame King—"

GRINNEL'S light focused on the floor. The man there was uncouth and huge. His shoulders were monstrous, but his trouser legs—were empty! They made a curious flat pattern on the dusty floor.

"Artificial legs," the *Spider* said shortly. "He took them off before the fight. Remember, Nita? He walked slowly and ponderously... never saw such shoulders in your life. No wonder! Legs Jackson has been *walking on his hands for years.* He was vain of their strength. He made himself very tall, because otherwise his shoulders would have betrayed him, they would have been out of all balance. He's your monster! He's your Flame King!"

Grinnel said, dazedly, "But, Good Lord! He was— Well, he lost his legs in a fire at my well, but I've always taken handsome care of him. He seemed to like me. He was almost servile in his gratitude—"

"To hide his hate," the *Spider* said shortly. "It was a fair fight, I think. He had no legs, but I have a bum leg and a bad shoulder, and his strength must be twice mine."

"Fair!" Grinnel gasped. "Fair! Good Lord! I've seen him bend a gun barrel with his hands! A murderer, and you worry about it being *fair!*"

The *Spider* lifted his brows. "After all, Mr. Mayor," he said lightly, "one has one's code."

He laughed, but no one joined him, for he had spoken no less than the truth. He was a man who lived by his code, and no man had a higher!

Nita said, a little pettishly, "You might let that woman go now. *I'll* keep her in hand."

There was a blaze of light in the doorway, and behind it they could see a girl with a gun in her hand. It was Beulah Scott. The gun was pointed, and Beulah came slowly forward. She walked like a dead woman, and it might be that there was death in her eyes. But the gun fell suddenly from her hand and she walked forward and dropped to her knees at the *Spider*'s feet, and bowed her head.

"I came here to kill you," she whispered. "But I did not understand! I did not know there was— there could be—I didn't know any man could be like you! I was there all the time. I could have stopped the fight, but I wanted you to die! *I wanted you to die!* I am ashamed!"

The *Spider* raised her gallantly to her feet. "My dear," he said gravely, "if the men of this town had half your courage, the crooks would have been driven out long ago. I see no need for shame in courage." He did not tell her that Ram Singh was behind her—and that he would have killed her at need! The *Spider,* as always, was prepared!

The girl's head lifted, and suddenly she laughed. "Why, you even give me back my self-respect!" She flung her arms about the *Spider*'s neck and kissed him.

There were two cars, Beulah Scott's and the Mayor's, and the *Spider* volunteered to make the hike to the more remote car with Nita van Sloan.

"You see," the *Spider* explained gravely to Mayor Grinnel, "there are some matters I must settle with Miss van Sloan before I leave. I'll drop her in town, and perhaps that fellow, Wentworth, will dare to come out of hiding now."

Nita said, sharply, "He's a better man than you are! He's faithful and true!"

The *Spider* lifted his brows, and they went off into the night together. Outside, Nita van Sloan walked stiffly apart, and the *Spider* watched her, with laughter in his eyes. She stumbled, and jerked away from his hand when he reached out to assist her.

Abruptly, the *Spider* caught her by the shoulders and pulled her about to face him. The moon peeped out of the clouds and he could see her face. Her lips were tight, and her eyes were angry.

"You didn't *have* to," she said, sharply. "That Mexican girl, and then Beulah Scott!"

The *Spider* grinned at her. "It must be my fatal charm," he said. "I can't help being fascinating!"

"You're insufferable!" Nita said.

"I know," he said humbly.

She pulled away from him, and he groaned. "My leg!"

Nita was back beside him in an instant. "Oh, I forgot your poor leg!" she gasped. "Does it hurt much? What can I do?"

He told her, and Nita slapped him, and then laughed. Her lips were not tight to his kiss.

"But you are insufferable," she sighed.

"The *Spider* is a cad," he agreed, happily. "When will you marry Richard Wentworth?"

THE END

BLOOD BOND by Grant Stockbridge

Many friends have asked me how Richard Wentworth first met that proud and doughty warrior, Ram Singh, and how a Sikh of the royal line (which in the Punjab means, actually, priestly line) could become a servant of a westerner. The Sikhs are a proud people, and Ram Singh was far from one of the least of them. Richard Wentworth discounts always the importance of that which he does, but the results speak for themselves. It was only after much persuasion that I elicited from him the events which I hereinafter describe...   **The Author**

IT WAS the season of the year which in the Northern hemisphere is known as Spring. In the Punjab, too, it was called Spring. In the high mountain passes that climbed toward the Himalayas, the snows were thawing. Richard Wentworth, climbing toward them, fought the blizzard stubbornly alone.

Before him was death in a thousand storm-built traps. There was death behind him also, in the rifles and the knives of the men who, officially, were his followers.

Breaking trail ahead of the meager yak and pony train, Wentworth knew a fierce joy. It did not matter that his back presented an excellent target for his men. It did not matter that the trail, skirting a six thousand foot gorge, was sheathed in ice and powdered over with a dancing wax of snow. There was strength within him that rose to meet the fury of this savage land. He loved it.

The gorge-funneled wind sliced like an assassin's dagger, shrieked with the voices of tormented souls in a particularly vicious Tibetan hell. Hail and snow alternated, first blinding and then slashing the skin of man and beasts. The wind seemed to possess a deliberate and evil intelligence that knew just when a man was off-balance and could be hammered over the precipice.

Behind Wentworth, a man shouted hoarsely and Wentworth peered back to find a vacant spot in the tight-lashed line of ponies and yaks. The man who had been in charge of the pony, muffled to the frosted eye-brows, pointed out over the abyss and lifted his shoulders heavily.

Wentworth was at the man's side in an instant. There was icy flame in his eyes. "If another pony goes over, you will carry a pony's load!" he rasped, and his harsh Hindustani had a bitter and commanding edge.

The man made no answer but, in the swollen belly of his coat, there was a slight movement and Wentworth knew he had gripped the butt of a revolver! There was hatred in the man's eyes, but Wentworth was accustomed to that—beyond the Sutlej river. The British Raj had refused him permission to enter the Sikh land, where terrorization and assassination were rife. They had tried to stop him at the rail-head in Simla. But Wentworth was here, in the heart of the land where the *jathas* of Babbar Akalis were using every pretext to slaughter native leaders who might be in any way connected with the government. For the authority of the British Raj extended exactly as far as its soldiers patrolled. And here there were no soldiers. Besides, Wentworth did not have the backing of the government!

His eyes flashed beyond the man who defied him. There were three other men in plain sight, and others beyond the veil of the flying snow. Each of those three had his rifle ready to his hand, instead of slung over his shoulder.

Wentworth faced them all with a stern curve to his lips that was close to smiling, and a flash of his icy stare. Outwardly, he was motionless, in one of those split-second pauses that decides the life and death of a man. Inwardly, his brain raced. He did not think they were ready for a showdown yet. This was still bandit country, where the *jathas* might strike. Why kill a man here, when he could defend and lead them for another three days until they were safely across the boarder in the "heavenly, blessed land" of Tibet? After that, it would be safe to kill him.

THIS, THEN, was a good time to force the issue, while the men were still undecided. He reached out his left hand, eyes never leaving the flat black gaze of the man before him. He lifted a bundle from the back of the pony beside him and flung it at the man's feet.

"Put that upon your back!"

He made no move to draw his own weapon. His

hands swung, gloved, at his sides. That was the only way he could win. If he took out a weapon, he would be instantly killed by any one of a half dozen guns! The man glared at him while stubbornness grew in his black eyes.

Wentworth lifted a slow hand and laid it beside his nose. He turned his head and spat downwind. Then he shut his eyes, tipped his head and began to chant. It was a barbarous sounding thing—it was in fact the German of Goethe's Faustus, intoned without music.

There was a whimpering moan from the Tibetan. "My putting on the pack," the man pleaded. "My being better than perfect. My being good. Your not putting spell on my!"

Wentworth chanted two more verses, then looked at the man. He still held his finger beside his nose.

"It is too late to stop spell now," he said gravely. "But if my praying for you five times five days, your being only have boils, instead of losing all fingers and toes, then all feet and hands, then all legs and arms, then—"

"Aiie!" the man howled. "Your praying, Rikorth! Your praying!"

"My praying, your being all good!" The man stuck out his tongue in the Tibetan gesture of submission.

Wentworth swung about and surged once more to the head of the line, breaking trail. The joy lifted in him. He had laid a bond upon the Tibetan that would make the man his willing slave for twenty-five days, by the end of which time, Wentworth would have reached the lamasery of the manhant, Mar-lar-delan, where Wentworth proposed to spend some years in study.

Despite the incredible gullibility of the superstitious natives, there were in this mysterious land of the East many great masters of powers, psychic and spiritual, of which the materialistic West as a whole had no cognizance, and took no interest. Wentworth himself did not care to meddle with these powers. When a man reached the proper stage of development, these things came to him. Before that time, it was folly to peer too far beyond the barrier that separated the material from the matrix. But, here, in the East, they were masters of another art that Wentworth coveted. It was the art of self-control; of the complete subjection of the physical self to the commands of the will! And that absolute control was necessary for a man who had set his foot upon the trail of selfless service to the ideal of justice for all humanity!

Lost in that prospect, Wentworth was surprised by the opening of trail into a rock-strewn plateau; and more surprised by the sudden ghostlike rising of many forms among the rocks! Even as he saw them, rifles crashed out... faint in the shriek of the wind! His train was attacked by one of the marauding "holy" *jathas* of cutthroat Sikhs!

Wentworth flung himself prone and whipped out with gloved hands the twin revolvers he carried for protection. In these high cold altitudes, the automatics he preferred were out of the question. Their oil would freeze them.

Five times, the revolvers spoke, and five men kicked out their life in the freezing blizzard. In that brief while, Wentworth swore between locked teeth. He braced his hands against a rock, lifted his feet... and sent himself tobogganing backward toward the verge of the six-thousand foot gorge!

A HARSH cry burst from the lips of the attackers. One of them sprang to his feet and, with waving knife, raced after Wentworth! He had his rifle across his back. As the leader of the expedition, he would carry the best arms and the money. They did not want his body to plummet over the edge!

Then, when the man was almost upon him, Wentworth dug his spike-studded boot toes into the ice. He stopped abruptly and the charging knifeman somersaulted out into space! His scream was swallowed in the swoop and bellow of the wind... and Wentworth ducked out of sight among the rocks.

Once there, he calmly reloaded his revolvers, laid his rifle beside him... and waited. He was sheltered from the storm in the cranny. His men—

Abruptly, Wentworth twisted about, revolver ready. "No, Rikorth!" a man wailed. "No, do not shoot! Wah! I came to rescue thee, Rikorth!"

It was the man on whom Wentworth had cast a "spell."

"Thy name?" Wentworth snapped, though he knew it well.

"Ras Dong!" the man wailed. "Thou knowest me, Rikorth!"

Wentworth smiled thinly. "Five times five days must I pray for thee," he said, carelessly. "Yet death is here."

The man wailed, "Nay, nay, Rikorth! Here is no death for thee!"

Wentworth made no answer, but waited for wait be done around the bend of the trail. He could retreat along the trail. He could retreat along the trail and now, with the help of Ras Dong, he might hope to make the last village they had left where Govid Singh was the chieftain priest. But he could expect short shrift at the hands of the Sikhs there. Before, he had had ten armed men with him.

Wentworth smiled faintly. "Ras Dong," he said. "You are going back to the village of Govid Singh, alone!"

Ras Dong shook his head violently.

"You are telling Govind Singh that a *jatha* of lion Akalis is on its way to kill him and loot his village."

Ras Dong looked at Wentworth with waiting sly eyes.

"You are telling your master, Rikorth, is holding back the *jatha* in a pass. You are reminding Govind Singh of my eating his salt. My being pukkah sahib; my remembering my eating his salt. My hearing *jatha*-men saying they will kill him, carry off his wives, his gold, his guns. Tell him I am holding *jatha* in pass while he comes with his men."

Ras Dong spat down the wind. "Govind Singh is not a fool," he said sagely.

Wentworth laughed. "You remind Govind Singh how his son, Ram Singh, wanted to fight me. How he did not fight because I ate his salt."

Ras Dong pushed out his chin, pointing toward the gap. Wentworth threw a glance and a bullet that way, and a man screamed out his life.

"You will tell Ram Singh," Wentworth resumed, "that I will forget about salt if so be he still wants to fight me."

Ras Dong's eyes slyly considered Wentworth for a long moment. Then he stuck out his tongue in submission. "Rikorth almost being wise as men of heavenly blessed land," he conceded. "My going. Ram Singh being fool liking fight. His coming. When fighting, my shooting him in back. Your praying five times five days."

Wentworth laughed, and made no answer, and

the Tibetan faded backward into the spit of the storm. Crouched against the face of the wall, Wentworth began to know the biting cold of the "Spring". He had to battle the assassins around the bend, of whom there were still a score or more; but more than that he had to fight the cold. On the plateau, in the shelter of the rocks, the men built fires of yak chips. Wentworth kept warm by beating his arms about his body, by running down the trail and scrambling back. But one thing he had guessed correctly, as snatches of words about the fires told him: the *jatha* was on the way to attack and slay Govind Singh!

The long night wore its way out with a shot now and again from the sentries of the *jatha,* but most of them slept. It was a cold and screaming dawn of wind and icy blue skies when at last Wentworth caught far below him the flash of sunlight upon weapons. His message to Govind Singh had won support! The *jatha* was astir now and, presently, they began to sneak to points of vantage where they could snipe at Wentworth. He was forced to crowd his body more deeply into the rock niches and get out his rifle. He had shot four snipers, and the day was half-gone—the ice was icy water now—when the first of the approaching Sikhs came in sight behind him.

WENTWORTH threw a quick look toward the oncoming men. The old Sikh, Govind Singh, walked in the lead in full fighting regalia. Wentworth's eyes warmed briefly at sight of the chieftain. He was a true *Pahul* of the *Khalsa,* an initiate of the strict "purity" religious sect from which he took his name of "lion." He wore the five "k's" the kes, or unshorn hair; the *kachh,* drawers reaching only to the knee; the *kara,* the iron bangles which symbolized obedience; the *kirpan*, or sword; and the *khanga,* or hair comb, which symbolized purity of mind.

Behind him stalked his eldest son, whose every item of dress and manner simulated his father. His teeth flashed white as he recognized Wentworth and his hand went to the hilt of the *khanda,* the two-edged dagger at his waist. Wentworth lifted a hand in answer and slid toward them, close to the ground.

"There is a defile a quarter mile back," he said briefly. "I explored it during the night. We can go by that route, half of us, and take them from behind."

"Wah!" grunted Ram Singh. "Art thou the man I came forty miles to fight? Dost thou have to take enemies from behind? These are rats, not men! They will flee at the sound of my voice!"

Govind Singh turned his head and his fierce dark eyes smiled on his son. "I will lead the attack, my son," he said. He sounded the Sikh war-cry and, sword flashing over his head, he led the Sikhs in a leaping charge up the trail!

Wentworth swore softly and, instead of following, he scrambled up the wall where, with his rifle, he could command the plateau. He began firing at once, dropped four men who were ready to ambush the old Sikh. In another instant, the *jatha* had risen from hiding and was charging upon the spearhead of the Sikhs. Another small wedge cut across the head of the trail, which they commanded with ready rifles, and began to mow down the followers of Govind Singh and his son who, alone, still battled on the plateau!

Wentworth pumped out all but the last bullet from his rifle, then he flung himself to the trail and, revolvers in his fists, he charged toward the men who blocked the trail. When he shot down the last of the killers there, only three of the Sikh fighters were left on the feet. At their head, then, Wentworth charged out upon the plateau. Govind Singh was down. Over him, whirling the long keen-edged sword, was his son! There were five men about him and, as Wentworth raced forward, a bullet forced Ram Singh to his knees!

In an instant, Wentworth was beside him. His last bullet smashed down a ready rifleman. Then, Wentworth snatched up the old Sikh's sword and leaped to the attack!

Wentworth flung a glance to right and left. Two of the Sikhs were on his right hand. On his left were one Sikh and Ras Dong. The Tibetan hung back, revolver and knife in his fists.

"Your not being hurt, Rikorth," he wined. "My needing those prayers very much!"

Wentworth laughed again and faced the ten men who, spread in a thin semi-circle behind their glittering steel, came on warily. For a moment, before the charge, they hesitated. In that moment, Wentworth shouted the war-cry of the Sikhs and leaped forward!

FOUR swords leaped out to meet him, slashed at head and body and legs! Wentworth swung his own sword in a defensive circle that hammered all those blades ringingly aside and, at the end of the parry, he thrust with a strong forward lunge of his whole body! His blade point slipped out of sight in the throat of the leader of the *jatha* and, on the recovery, Wentworth slashed sideways and caught another of the swordsmen.

The man stumbled backward. His arms dropped

impotently and his sword point, striking rock, rang a clear bell-note in the screaming wind. But Wentworth did not pause. As he delivered that stroke, he was leaping forward again. In that single swift exchange, he was leaping forward again. In that single swift exchange, he had sliced through the middle of the enemy line... and was behind them!

The two halves of the line wheeled in confusion to attack him, and the Sikh swordsmen fell upon the killers from behind. Wentworth leaped in and out, slashed, parried, chopped and lunged.

In a few split seconds, the battle was over. The entire *jatha* lay dead or dying upon the snow.

Ram Singh was on his feet again—he had been only stunned by a bullet—and he supported his wounded father with a brawny arm. There was a heavy scowl on Ram Singh's face.

"Thou hast put shame upon me and upon my father," he said, fiercely, "for thou hast led our men and uttered our war-cry, and cut down the enemy whose life was forfeit to me for the injury they inflicted upon my father. Nevertheless, thou hast also put an obligation upon me, for thou hast saved my aged father's life and kept the killers from my own worthless throat!"

Wentworth waved a hand airily. "Let us call the score even," he said. "Thou hast equally saved my life."

Ram Singh ripped out a rolling oath. "Dost thou consider thy life equal to that of a Singh?"

The old Singh lifted his head heavily. "Nay, my son," he said slowly, "he has eaten our salt, and he has remembered as few sahibs do. You put shame upon thy *khanda* by such talk." He lifted a hand in blessing. "Wentworth sahib, in my village, so long as I or my sons live, it shall be remembered that you, a sahib, were true to the salt. If you will return to the village—"

Wentworth shook his head. "I am in haste, Singh badsha," he said. "I am eager to see the high pinnacle of Aling Kangri, and the lamasery of the mahant whose council I seek. I will go on!"

Ram Singh growled in his beard. "I like not this obligation. Wentworth sahib, thou hast promised to forget the salt; to fight me!"

WENTWORTH smiled upon the man and there was love behind his eyes. He liked Ram Singh for the doughty fighter that he was, in spite of his belligerence. Once bend this man to discipline and he would make a companion second to none!

Wentworth looked to the old Sikh and there was a wisdom in the eyes of the younger that matched the tired knowledge in the gaze of the silver-haired Punjabi.

"Father," Wentworth said, "I must keep my promise to your son. Is it possible that your man can return you to your village, if I kill your son?"

"It is possible," Govind Singh said, "for more of my men are coming."

Wentworth stepped back from Ram Singh, laid his hand upon his girdle as if for a knife, and then started as he glanced toward Ras Dong.

"Ras Dong," Wentworth cried, "release me from my vow to you!"

The Tibetan wailed. "Nay, nay, Rikorth, it may not be!"

Wentworth argued with Ras Dong, but the man was obdurate. Wentworth faced Ram Singh with a scowl. "I have it in my heart to kill you," he said harshly, "but for five times five days I may not risk my life since I have made this vow. Yet I would free thee from thy obligation by allowing you to try to kill me."

Ram Singh turned toward his father and held out a beseeching hand.

Govind Singh lifted his hand in blessing. "So that you may fulfill your desire and fight this man when his vow has expired," said the old Sikh, "I give thee, my son, permission to follow him, even to the ends of the Earth!"

Ram Singh uttered a cry of joy and confronted Wentworth. He was taller and broader than Wentworth and his great shoulders swelled beneath his tunic. "I shall kill thee!" he roared.

Wentworth nodded to him gravely. "I will read you the future, Oh warrior lion," he said. "You will not kill me, but save my life many times, and it shall be my happy privilege to do the same for you. I see that we shall fight side by side against many enemies, and they shall not stand against us."

"In five times five days?" Ram Singh jeered.

Wentworth laughed, and the sound of it was bright with challenge. He turned and stalked off up the road without farther parley and shouted his orders to Ras Dong, who began to chivy yaks and ponies ahead of him toward the rising trail. The fading gleams of the sinking sun struck across the glistening white crown of Nanda Devi to westward and touched it with blood.

Wentworth laughed and led. Ram Singh scowled… and followed.

Wentworth did not know it, but it was in that hour that he first learned that he might become... the Master of Men!

THE END

THE MAN BEHIND THE SPIDER

Norvell W. Page was born in Richmond, Virginia in 1904, the son of one of the Old Dominion's first families. He had young aspirations to become the next Edgar Allan Poe. Estranged from his family for eloping from William and Mary College to marry fellow classmate Audrey Rohr circa 1924 at the age of 18, Norvell—contrary to family wishes that he make more of his life—became a newspaperman, working for *The Cincinatti Post* and the *Norfolk Virginia-Pilot*. Later, he joined the Great Depression migration of newspapermen to Manhattan. While working as a crime reporter for the *New York Herald-Tribune*, he moonlighted as a prolific pulpster.

Norvell W. Page

Page first broke into print—accounts vary—either in *Western Trails* or *Detective-Dragnet*, both Magazine Publishers' titles. It was the early Depression. His father, an executive with the Wurlitzer Music Company, had been wiped out in the Stock Market Crash of 1929.

At first, he wrote as "N. Wooten Poge"—a nod to his interest in Poe, one imagines—as well as a shield from family concerns. But before long he was himself, Norwell W. Page, a rising star in the pulp firmament, who penned the popular Ken Carter series in *Ten Detective Aces* and cracked the prestigious *Black Mask* in 1933.

His big break came that same year, when he jumped on an opportunity to write the lead novel in the revamped *Dime Mystery Magazine*, making Page a pioneer in the emerging Weird Menace field. This led to him taking over *The Spider* series from the departing R. T. M. Scott, quickly making it his own.

Over the next ten years, Page was feverishly prolific as "Grant Stockbridge," the nominal *Spider* author, a tenure during which he transformed Richard Wentworth from a 1920s style hero into a hardboiled 1930s pulp icon. He also pounded out yarns for Popular's *Terror Tales*, *Horror Stories* and *Ace G-Man*. Occasionally he moonlighted by ghosting a *Phantom Detective* novel like *Death Glow*,

or the odd spiderized Black Bat tale. He revived the "N. Wooten Poge" byline for the salacious Bill Carter stories in *Spicy Detective Stories*. Whenever Popular Publications launched an important new title like *Detective Tales* or *Strange Detective Mysteries*, they tapped Page to help kick off the first issue.

As the 1930s shaded into the 1940s, the fevered *Spider* novels cooled somewhat. Reader tastes were shifting, and the old "bang-bang" wild action was growing dated. Page retooled as best he could and branched out to writing classic fantasy novels for *Unknown* that are still remembered today.

The Spider began winding down in 1943. Ten years is a long time in the pulp game. Everything had changed. The Depression was a fading ache. The nation faced another World War. Paper shortages were punching away at the pulps. The *Spider*'s days were numbered. Page may or may not have cared. His first wife died of tetanus that October. Page fled *The Spider*, and forever abandoned the familiar pulp jungle of Manhattan for a government position in Washington, writing for the Office of War Information. After the war, he wrote speeches for Congressman Lyndon Johnson and reports for the Atomic Energy Commission.

He never returned to *Black Mask*, never became the next Edgar Allan Poe—and never looked back. He died in 1961. He is remembered today as the soul of the *Spider*.

Near the end of his *Spider* career, Norvell Page wrote one fan: "Think of me as Wentworth, if you will. The line between us is not too distinct...."

Perhaps that might be as true an epitaph as any.

—Will Murray

Thrill to the adventures of the greatest superheroes from the Golden Age of Pulp Fiction in double-novel trade paperbacks, available from SANCTUM BOOKS; P.O. Box 761474; San Antonio, TX 78245.

CAP FURY by Wallace Brooker
C-1: The Red Heart Pearls & Black Daylight

DOC SAVAGE by Kenneth Robeson
D-14: The Man of Bronze & The Land of Terror*
D-15: The Red Spider & Cold War Stories
D-16: Secret in the Sky & The Giggling Ghosts
D-17: The Czar of Fear & World's Fair Goblin*
D-18: The Monsters & The Whisker of Hercules*
D-19: The King Maker & The Freckled Shark
D-20: The Thousand-Headed Man & Gold Ogre
D-21: Hex & The Running Skeletons
D-22: Mystery Under the Sea & The Red Terrors*
D-23: The Fantastic Island & Danger Lies East
D-24: The Black, Black Witch & WWII stories
D-25: The Red Skull & The Awful Egg
D-26: The Annihilist & Cargo Unknown*
D-27: Murder Mirage & The Other World*
D-28: The Metal Master & The Vanisher*
D-29: The Mental Wizard & The Secret of the Su
D-30: Quest of the Spider & Mountain Monster
D-31: Devil on the Moon & I Died Yesterday*
D-32: The Feathered Octopus & The Goblins
D-33: Quest of Qui & The Devil's Playground*
D-34: Man Who Shook the Earth & Three Devils
D-35: Meteor Menace & The Ten Ton Snakes
D-36: The Phantom City & No Light to Die By*
D-37: Mystery on the Snow & Peril in the North
D-38: Murder Melody & Birds of Death
D-39: Poison Island & They Died Twice
D-40: Mystery on Happy Bones & WWII stories
D-41: Seven Agate Devils & The Flying Goblin
D-42: Men Who Smiled No More & Pink Lady*
D-43: Spook Legion & Three Times a Corpse
D-44: Roar Devil & Satan Black
D-45: Merchants of Disaster & Measures for a Coffin*
D-46: The Mystic Mullah & Terror Takes 7
D-47: Weird Valley, Let's Kill Ames & The Green Master
D-48: Red Snow & Death Had Yellow Eyes*
D-49: The Terror in the Navy & Waves of Death
D-50: The Pirate's Ghost & The Green Eagle*
D-51: The Land of Fear & The Fiery Menace
D-52: Violent Night, Strange Fish & Screaming Man
D-53: Ost & According to Plan of a One-Eyed Mystic
D-54: The Yellow Cloud & Men of Fear
D-55: The Time Terror & The Talking Devil
D-56: The Black Spot & The Terrible Stork
D-57: Dagger in the Sky, Death Lady & Monkey Suit
D-58: The Derrick Devil & The Spotted Men
D-59: Pirate Isle & The Speaking Stone
D-60: He Could Stop the World & The Laugh of Death*
D-61: The Man Who Fell Up & The Three Wild Men
D-62: The Flaming Falcons & The Too-Wise Owl*
D-63: Awful Dynasty, Angry Canary & Swooning Lady
D-64: The Headless Men & King Joe Cay
D-65: Mystery Island & Trouble on Parade
D-66: The Midas Man & The Derelict of Skull Shoal*
D-67: The Invisible-Box Murders & Target for Death
D-68: The Crimson Serpent & The Exploding Lake
D-69: The Munitions Master & King of Terror
D-70: The All-White Elf & The Wee Ones
D-71: The Angry Ghost & The Disappearing Lady
D-72: The Purple Dragon & Colors for Murder
D-73: Land of Long Juju & Se-Pah-Poo
D-74: The Motion Menace & Fire & Ice

*Also available in James Bama variant cover editions

THE SHADOW by Maxwell Grant
S-22: Tower of Death & The Hooded Circle
S-23: Smugglers of Death & The Blackmail King
S-24: Washington Crime & Quetzal
S-25: The Gray Ghost & The White Skulls
S-26: Vengeance Is Mine! & Battle of Greed
S-27: The Python & The Hawk and The Skull
S-28: Master of Death & The Rackets King
S-29: The Shadow's Rival & The Devil Master
S-30: The Sealed Box & Racket Town
S-31: The Dark Death & House of Shadows
S-32: The Silver Scourge & The Book of Death
S-33: Strange Disappearance of Cardona & The Hand
S-34: The Blackmail Ring & Murder for Sale
S-35: The Condor & Chicago Crime
S-36: Crime Rides the Sea & River of Death
S-37: The Third Skull & Realm of Doom
S-38: Dead Men Live & Dictator of Crime
S-39: Face of Doom & The Crime Ray
S-40: The Crime Clinic & Cards of Death
S-41: Chain of Death & Death's Premium
S-42: Bells of Doom & The Murdering Ghost
S-43: The Key & Case of Congressman Coyd
S-44: Atoms of Death & Buried Evidence
S-45: Terror Island & City of Ghosts
S-46: House That Vanished & Wizard of Crime
S-47: The Living Shadow & The Black Hush
S-48: The Eyes of The Shadow & The Money Master
S-49: The Shadow Laughs! & Voice of Death
S-50: The Man from Shanghai & Golden Dog Murders
S-51: The Living Joss & Judge Lawless
S-52: The Crime Master & The Fifth Napoleon
S-53: Garden of Death & The Vampire Murders
S-54: The Golden Quest & The Masked Headsman
S-55: The Green Hoods & Silver Skull
S-56: The Embassy Murders & Hills of Death
S-57: The Five Chameleons & The Wasp
S-58: Castle of Crime & Dead Man's Chest
S-59: The Green Box & The Getaway Ring
S-60: Prince of Evil, Messenger of Death & Room 1313
S-61: The Triple Trail & Murder Genius
S-62: Cyro & The Man Who Died Twice
S-63: The Devil's Paymaster & The Wasp Returns
S-64: The Ribbon Clues & Death Rides the Skyway
S-65: Gypsy Vengeance & The Veiled Prophet
S-66: Ghost of the Manor & Foxhound
S-67: Death Clue & Xitli, God of Fire
S-68: The Thunder King & The Star of Delhi
S-69: The Garaucan Scandal & The Death Sleep
S-70: The Man from Scotland Yard & Zemba
S-71: Spoils of The Shadow & House of Silence
S-72: Intimidation, Inc. & Wizard of Crime
S-73: Seven Drops of Blood & Death from Nowhere
S-74: The Crystal Buddha & The Vindicator
S-75: The Golden Master & Death's Bright Finger
S-76: Death Ship & The Black Dragon
S-77: Temple of Crime & The Curse of Thoth
S-78: Circle of Death & The Sledge-Hammer Crimes
S-79: Crime Circus & Noose of Death
S-80: Shiwan Khan Returns & Invincible Shiwan Khan
S-81: Murder Every Hour & The Time Master
S-82: The Spy Ring & The White Column
S-83: Crime Over Boston & Crime Over Miami

THE SPIDER by Grant Stockbridge
SP-1: Citadel of Hell & The Spider and the Sons of Satan
SP-2: Devil's Paymaster & Benevolent Order of Death

www.shadowsanctum.com/pulps.html